COWBOY CAVALRY

BY
ALICE SHARPE

MILLS & BOON

First Published in Great Britain 2016
By Mills & Boon, an imprint of HarperCollins*Publishers*
1 London Bridge Street, London, SE1 9GF

© 2016 Alice Sharpe

ISBN: 978-0-263-91920-2

46-1016

Our policy is to use papers that are natural, renewable and recyclable products and made from wood grown in sustainable forests. The logging and manufacturing processes conform to the legal environmental regulations of the country of origin.

Printed and bound in Spain
by CPI, Barcelona

Alice Sharpe met her husband-to-be on a cold, foggy beach in Northern California. Their union has survived the rearing of two children, a handful of earthquakes, numerous cats and a few special dogs. Alice and her husband now live near Portland, Oregon, where she devotes the majority of her time to pursuing her second love, writing. Please visit her at www.alicesharpe.com for information about upcoming titles.

This book is dedicated to my family, who make everything worth doing. I love you all.

Chapter One

Kate took a seat at an outdoor waterfront table and settled back to wait. She was purposefully early, wanting time to catch her breath, to go over what she would say and how. Normal life as of late afforded few opportunities for introspection and as she closed her eyes and turned her face to the sun, she realized she was a little rusty when it came to intrigue.

No matter. She may have grown up here in Seattle, but she'd spent the last eight years in Arizona and appreciated the rare May warmth currently caressing her skin. When was the last time she'd been free to just sit for a few moments without distraction? She couldn't remember, and even now, the urge to get back prevented her from fully living in this moment.

"Kate West?" a male voice inquired and she opened her eyes with a start. She glanced up to find a man of about thirty staring down at her. Sun-streaked brown hair combed away from his forehead framed bluish gray eyes that echoed the water sparkling behind him.

"Yes, I'm Kate," she said.

"I knew it." His smile was dazzling as he offered his hand. "Gary Dodge told me to look for a stunning blonde."

"You must be Frank Hastings," she said, suppressing laughter and an eye roll. She was well aware she looked dog-tired, worn-out and frazzled.

"Please, call me Frankie," he said as he released her fingers. "May I sit down?"

She nodded and watched as he took a seat across from her. She'd seen his picture so she'd known he was attractive, but the photograph hadn't caught the energy pulsing through his body. It also hadn't caught the lively curiosity behind his eyes. Her confidence in her ability to stay one step ahead of him took a nosedive as he returned her gaze with open appraisal.

She knew that along with his father and brothers he ran a huge ranch in Central Idaho. Assumedly, he had picked up the golden tan of his skin the honest way, by being outside but there was also something decidedly uncowboylike about him, too, and that was interesting.

He smiled again as though aware she was sizing him up. The whites of his eyes and teeth almost glowed in his face and she found herself comparing him to her ex. She looked down at her hands immediately. Thinking about an ex-boyfriend wasn't going to get her anywhere. She warned herself to concentrate on her grandmother.

"Is something wrong?" he asked.

She ran fingers across her brow and shook her head. "No."

"Thank you for agreeing to meet me," he added as a waiter showed up. He ordered crab cakes and a salad, without glancing at the menu. She ordered iced tea and nothing else. "I've heard about your...issue with our project," he added after the waiter left. "I'm anxious to set your mind at ease."

"Are you?"

"Yes, of course. Why do you say it like that?"

"It seems kind of hopeless," she said. "Gary, your producer, has already tried to convince me how wrong I am. I'm afraid you drove all the way here from Idaho for nothing."

His eyes narrowed a hair. "Just give me a chance," he said as her tea and a basket of bread appeared on their table.

"Listen," she said, tearing off a hunk of sourdough, hoping it would settle her stomach. Darn nerves. "I understand that my eleventh-hour objections to this movie—"

"Not a movie," he said. "A documentary."

"What's the difference?"

He shrugged. "Pretty vast. A movie can be pure fiction or a takeoff on known facts. Either way, liberties are taken. A documentary sticks to the truth, not conjectures."

"Truth as interpreted through a human lens," she said.

"You mean the angle the director decides to emphasize?"

"Yes."

"That's true, but this is all pretty cut-and-dried stuff. One hundred years ago, four men robbed the bank in what was once known as Green Ridge, Idaho. That's a fact. Two days later, three of them were caught by a posse—Samuel and Earl Bates and a guy called William Adler. They were taken back to the big oak tree two miles outside town and hung. That's a sad fact, but a fact nonetheless. The fourth man got away. It's generally assumed he took all the gold with him.

"The robbery more or less killed Green Ridge, though in all truth, the mine was close to playing out. A few years after the town emptied, a new generation of gold diggers found a small vein, but nothing more. All that remains now is a dead mine and a ghost town both of which are on our land, practically in our backyard. And the hanging tree, of course. Our historian has found two descendants of men who might be the elusive fourth man. I spoke to one of them last week and he said he had something pretty special to show me. It's an exciting time."

She'd chewed on her chunk of bread while he spoke. It wasn't helping her nerves at all. She already knew everything he'd told her and she was certain he knew what she was about to say, too. Gary Dodge would have told him. She said it anyway.

"What you have to remember," she began, "is that my great-great-great-grandfather Earl Bates and his brother, Samuel, were two of the men killed by that vigilante posse. It's well-known they received no trial and there was no hard evidence against them. They may have been innocent—they certainly deserved better justice than hysterical murderers taking the law into their own hands. I couldn't live with myself if I didn't try to keep you guys from glorifying their killers."

"We have no desire to glorify anyone or anything," Frankie said, and for the first time, his voice reflected irritation. She knew that both Frankie and Gary Dodge had worked on this project for over a year. It was important to them. Seeing Frankie's less polished side made dealing with him both easier and more difficult for her: easier because his feelings were involved and who better than she knew how that could warp a person's judgment? Harder, because she could feel his enthusiasm and that made him a little irresistible.

"Maybe not," she protested, "but it's not too difficult

to imagine that's exactly what will happen. I'm the last of my family. For decades, Samuel and Earl have just been footnotes no one really cared about. Your project has the potential to change that."

"And perhaps give meaning to their deaths," Frankie said suddenly as though he'd just thought of this angle. They were both silent as his meal was delivered. It looked delicious, but Kate didn't think she could have eaten it even if she could afford to buy it.

Frankie ignored his plate. He sat forward. "You've brought up some interesting facts. I'll make sure they're addressed."

Now you're just being glib, she thought as she shook her head. "No," she said. "The truth is I have an appointment to meet with your backers very soon. If they don't walk away, I'll keep talking until somebody listens."

Frankie stared at her for a minute. It was obvious his mind was racing. She could almost picture him running along a hall, throwing open door after door, looking for the right response that would get her to change her mind. She'd expected this from him—she'd been warned that he was formidable when thwarted.

"Okay, here's the thing, Kate," he said at last. "You're young and smart and articulate and maybe worse, from our point of view, you're very pretty. Social media will love you. You may not have a lot of legal ground to stand on when it comes to stopping us, but you could do damage with negative publicity. More than that, though, our backers are a cautious lot. They're going to come to the same conclusions I have when they meet you and I'm afraid they'll get cold feet. This matters too much to me to risk that. What can I do or say to change your mind?"

"Nothing," she insisted.

"There has to be something."

"No," she said. "There doesn't. I tried to warn you."

He took a breath. "Please, can't you just be reasonable?"

"You're calling me unreasonable?"

His jaw tightened. "You've brought up interesting points, I admit that, but they can be dealt with fairly. We work with a dedicated researcher, a historian, who checks all our facts. We aren't interested in rewriting history. Can you say the same?"

She put down her fork. This guy was conceited or was that her guilty conscience making excuses for her own motivation? She picked up her tea glass and took a sip, giving herself a chance to calm down, check her watch and take a deep breath. "I understand that making this documentary is important to you," she said. "You grew up with this story, you live close to where it all happened—it's intimate to you in a way it isn't for me. This is all I can do to honor the memories of the men who died without the opportunity to defend themselves."

"Believe it or not, I have empathy for the men who were hung. It was a gruesome way to die. Can't you find it in your heart to trust me with their story?"

"I sense you mean well," she said carefully, "but I don't know what the rest of your family is like and according to Mr. Dodge, they play a big part in this thing."

He steepled his fingers and gazed at her. "I have an idea," he said at last.

"What is it?"

"Come to Idaho. Meet my father and brothers, and Grace, my stepmother. You'll love her, everyone does."

"Your father," she said slowly. "What kind of man is he?"

Frankie appeared surprised by her question. Maybe she shouldn't have asked it.

"A decent man," he said. "A man who puts his family first."

"Family first," she mumbled. "Over everything?"

"What do you mean?"

"Over his land, for instance? Over money?"

Frankie's brow wrinkled. "I'm sorry, Kate. I'm not sure what you're getting at."

"It doesn't matter," she said, and straightened her shoulders, figuratively if not literally. "How many brothers do you have?"

"Three. All older." He sat back. "None of us have a secret agenda of any kind. We just want the past recorded in a fair and honest way. This story has always fascinated me. Come meet everyone. Come get to know the countryside where this happened, walk the dead streets of a once vibrant town, get a feel for the folks who lived and loved there, understand their struggles and that includes your own relatives. In other words, come back to Idaho with me."

"Now?" she said. "Just like that?"

"Yes."

She stared at him. Would this be easier if he wasn't so good-looking? Maybe.

"As a matter of fact," he added, as though sweetening the deal, "on my way home I'm stopping to meet with one of the descendants I told you about. You're welcome to come along and meet him, too."

"Why would I want to do that?"

"Just to get a feel for our approach. The man I'm talking to is the great-great-grandson of a guy named Matthew Dalton. Dalton was a lawyer in Green Ridge.

He married a woman named Mary two days after the robbery and they left town the day after that. Accounts hint it was all very sudden. Maybe he was the fourth man, who knows? Hopefully we'll learn something that can help us piece together the truth. Will you give me a chance, say a week or so to try to awaken a little curiosity in you?"

"I don't know," she said softly.

"If it's your job—"

"I...I work at home," she said quickly. "There are arrangements that would have to be made, of course, but it's not that. My car is kind of on its last legs..."

"You can ride with me."

"It's not the getting there that worries me," she said. "I just don't know how comfortable I'd feel on your turf."

"Well, you can leave whenever you want, of course." He shook his head and added, "I didn't even think. Is there someone you'd like to have come with you? A family member, a friend?"

"No," she said and quickly averted her gaze. Luke had once told her he could read her mind just by staring into her eyes.

When still she hesitated, he lowered his voice. "Just so you know, one of my brothers is married and expecting a baby any second, another is getting married this summer and Pike's girlfriend is due for a visit at the end of the week. She's a private investigator in New York. In other words, there are lots of women around so if you're worried about being stuck with a bunch of guys, don't be."

"I'm not worried about being with men," she said.

He flashed her a devil-may-care smile. "Really? Now that's...interesting."

In that moment, Luke's memory pierced her heart

like a poison dart. He'd had this same throw-caution-to-the-wind-and-say-whatever-he-was-thinking quality.

"Sorry, I was just joking around," he added quickly. "Thought I'd lighten things up."

"I know. It's okay."

"Please say you'll give my suggestion some thought."

She glanced at his uneaten food as her mind raced, then she glanced at her watch. She'd been away almost two hours!

"If you'd rather travel on your own," he said, "that's fine, too. We'll pay for you to rent a car or buy you a ticket. Just promise you'll keep an open mind."

"No matter what you think of me, I am capable of being fair," she said.

"Good."

She nodded once. "Okay, I'll come. I'll meet everyone and look around, all of that. But you and Mr. Dodge have to understand that none of it may change my mind and I expect both of you to respect that I have a right to my opinion."

"I get it," he said. "And I appreciate your honesty."

"Under the circumstances, I'll take the rented car."

"Fine. If you trust me to do it for you, I'll make the arrangements and have it delivered to your house later today. Let me jot down directions to our ranch," he added. "Or give me your email address and I'll send them to you."

"That won't be necessary. Let's say we meet at the Hertz car rental place at the airport tomorrow morning at nine. I'll follow you to your interview and then on to your ranch."

"That sounds great," he said. "And, Kate, thank you for giving us this chance."

"Just remember that's all it is," she said softly, meeting his gaze straight on, bracing herself for the intensity in his eyes. "A chance."

Chapter Two

Frankie was almost positive there was more to Kate West than met the eye, although there was nothing at all wrong with what met the eye. Midtwenties, long spun-gold hair, forget-me-not blue eyes, skin like polished seashells.

But there was something else, too. How many times had she looked at her watch for instance? Gary hadn't said a word about her being distracted when he met her. Did that mean she normally wasn't or had Gary been too engrossed in preproduction dilemmas to notice?

She'd contacted Gary first. He'd immediately called their historian, Patrick Lowell, to make sure she was legitimate. Pat was a fuddy-duddy of a man, a former junior college teacher turned freelance researcher, hired by Gary for several projects through the years and thorough with dates and facts. He'd confirmed Kate's claims. Gary called Frankie who left the ranch in Falls Bluff and drove all night to meet with Gary and Pat.

Pat had admitted he didn't know much about Kate's current situation, just that she'd once been a grammar schoolteacher in Arizona. He'd suggested Frankie invite her to the ranch so she could meet the family. Gary had seconded that idea. Obviously, they both thought

Frankie's family would be more successful at winning her over than Frankie would.

But Frankie had settled on lunch instead and he'd gone to the restaurant dead set against inviting her anywhere. Once she'd met everyone, then what? What in the world would he do with a stranger intent on causing him problems? It was a busy time of year and taking care of her would fall on his shoulders. He really didn't like babysitting people. Left to his own devices, he would have invited her to do her best to convince the world the documentary didn't deserve to be made and he'd do his best to prove her wrong by making sure it turned out so damn good, there could be no doubt.

But he wasn't in this by himself; Gary was involved, too, and so when Kate unconsciously laid the groundwork for an invitation, he went ahead and made it. The truth was that getting to know her was not an unpleasant idea. Who didn't like a little mystery in a woman? He was even a bit disappointed that she wanted to drive separately.

But first he wanted to know what she was hiding and that's why he'd paid for lunch and left the restaurant before her, which wasn't easy as she was obviously champing at the bit to be gone herself.

Why? Had she privately arranged to talk to the backers earlier than she'd claimed? Had she agreed to the ranch trip just to mislead him? He intended to find out, even if it meant he had to sneak around a little.

From the restaurant exit, he glanced back at their table to see the waiter boxing his untouched lunch. Waste not, want not, huh? Maybe she had a dog. He hurried to his car and had just ducked inside when she stepped onto the sidewalk. She turned a fair number of heads as she walked down the block, blond hair floating out behind her in the gentle breeze, skirt swirling around excellent legs, small white paper bag dangling from one hand.

Babysitting her wasn't going to be that difficult, he admitted to himself. He just had to remember to treat her like a loaded keg of dynamite and not the living, breathing, sexy beauty that she was.

As she came to a halt at a nearby bus stop, her gaze darted between her wristwatch and the street until a bus passed Frankie's parked car and pulled to a stop in front of her. She boarded. He wasn't sure where it was bound because he'd been too busy admiring Kate's willowy form to notice the destination. He followed along behind as it made its way through traffic, expecting a downtown route. Instead it slowly made its way toward the suburbs and one of the many small communities surrounding Seattle proper. He continued following its stop-and-go route, watching as Kate made a couple of transfers, curious now despite the increasingly remote possibility her destination had anything to do with him. She finally got off the bus and began walking.

At first, the streets and sidewalks were crowded and all he had to do was drive slow and stay behind her. She kept making turns that led her away from the artsy-craftsy streets toward a row of ordinary houses, circa 1950. He stayed as far back as he could, her gold hair a beacon up ahead until she turned another corner and he sped up to find her again.

Many of the houses on this street were in the process of renovation but a few looked as though they hadn't been tinkered with for decades. He stopped as she opened the gate to one such house and walked across the barren yard. It appeared to him she knocked before unlocking the door with a key she took from her shoulder bag.

So, what had he learned? Not much. She apparently lived on a street showing signs of promise in a house whose property value undoubtedly superseded the worth of the structure.

As he sat there undecided about what to do next, the door opened again and a small older woman emerged wearing nothing but a baggy sleeveless dress. The door swung closed behind her as she walked across the yard and out through the gate, right into the middle of the street. She stopped suddenly and stared down at her bare feet, clutching her thin arms with her hands, her gaze traveling the block as though trying to place herself.

Frankie looked toward the door. No sign of Kate.

He pulled the car forward and got out. He stood there a second, kind of lurking behind a bush, willing Kate to come out and take care of this woman before he had to blow his cover and do it himself. The door stayed closed. A car came around the corner and started down the street and he knew it was time to act. He took off his jacket as he crossed to the woman and draped it over her shoulders. The car sped by them and Frankie suppressed a wave of anger lest the old woman thought it was directed at her.

"Can I help you?" he asked gently.

She didn't respond. He applied soft pressure to her arm to urge her to come with him back to the curb. She looked up at him as though just aware of his presence. "Do you know where Dennis is?"

"No, ma'am, I'm sorry, I don't," he said.

She looked down the street but didn't move.

Another car had pulled to a stop a few feet away

and the impatient driver tapped the horn. The old lady jumped.

Frankie cast the driver a look that would have sent a pack of coyotes off at a run. "Ma'am, please," he said. "Come with me."

She peered at his face and blinked. "Do you know where Dennis is?"

"Gram!" Kate yelled from the yard. She tore open the gate and ran out into the street, glancing up at Frankie as she ground to a halt in front of him. To say she looked surprised to see him was an understatement. Shocked was more like it. The old woman gazed at Kate without changing expression. Kate's arm wrapped protectively around her shoulders. "Your dinner is almost ready, Gram," she said softly. "Let's go back inside. It's chilly out here."

"I can't find Dennis," the old lady mumbled.

"We'll look for him in the house," Kate promised as she led her grandmother back to the yard where Frankie now saw another woman waiting on the porch. Kate took Frankie's jacket from around her grandmother's shoulders, hooked it on the gate and glanced back at him, anger blazing in her eyes.

"Kate," he said but she shook her head and held up a hand as if to silence him. Without another word, she took her grandmother's arm and ushered her quickly inside the house, the other woman following behind. The door closed with a resounding thud.

Frankie, still in the middle of the street walked toward the car that had honked. The driver's window rolled open.

"You proud of yourself?" he asked the driver.

A narrow-faced man about his own age responded. "Just get off the damn street before I run you down!"

There had been a period in Frankie's life where he would have pulled this bozo out of his car and punched him square in the nose. The desire to do just that was still there but time had tempered him. He stepped toward the curb and the car sped by.

Frankie retrieved his jacket from the fence and stood there awhile, sure Kate would come back outside and demand an explanation although he wasn't sure what he could offer. The door stayed resolutely shut. She'd really meant that final shake of her head. He finally got back in his car and drove off toward the airport where he rented a room for the night.

Would Kate show up tomorrow? Doubtful bordering on hell, no. He didn't have her phone number. Of course, he could call Gary and get it, but then Gary would sense there was a problem…no thanks, he didn't want to start fielding questions, not yet anyway. Besides, part of him admitted he'd already intruded enough.

The older woman was obviously Kate's grandmother but who was Dennis? Did these people have something to do with Kate's desire to stop the filming of the documentary?

Why hadn't he quit following her when it was obvious she wasn't going to a business meeting? What had compelled him to know about her? Was he treating her like an adversary? That was fine if that was the case because she was an adversary, she'd chosen that role when she announced her intentions.

As he lay in bed that night, he knew that he had probably just sabotaged his own project and he swore under his breath. If Kate refused to talk to any of them again and went instead to the backers fueled by her anger with him, he didn't think he'd have the stomach to try to stop her.

"IS THERE ANYTHING I can get you before I leave?" Rose McFadden whispered from the doorway.

Kate glanced from her slumbering grandmother to the retired nurse and shook her head. Her voice equally soft, she responded. "No thanks."

"I'm going home to pack a bag but I'll be back tomorrow morning bright and early, okay?"

"I don't know," Kate said. "I'm not sure—"

"Now, please, child, listen to me," Rose said, stepping into the room. "I'd hate to see you cancel your trip because of what happened today. Anyone can make a mistake and forget to lock the door after themselves."

"I never have before," Kate said. She'd been preoccupied when she got home, her mind processing the lunch with Frankie Hastings, reliving the conversation, wondering if she'd slipped up anywhere. And as a result, she hadn't relocked the door and her grandmother had walked outside into the middle of the street. If Frankie hadn't been there who knows what would have happened?

"I'll be here like we arranged," Rose said. "I promised Mr. Abernathy I'd help you and your grandmother and I intend to keep my word. Try to get some sleep."

Kate sat in the darkened room for what seemed like hours, the sound of her grandmother's breathing the only noise in the whole world. Today was the longest she'd been gone in a year. How could she leave again? What had she been thinking to agree to this?

List your choices, her subconscious demanded. Easy: zero.

She glanced from the stack of bills on the corner of the desk visible through the open doorway to the unframed window she was in the process of replacing here in the bedroom. The house needed new plumbing, the roof was forty years old and she suspected termites had had their way with the foundation. She was going under, not slowly, but fast.

When Kate's grandfather had died, Kate had cried for days. That was the last time she'd allowed herself tears. She didn't even cry for Luke because she was afraid if she started she'd never quit. But now she felt them swell in her eyes and roll down her cheeks and she seemed unable to stop them.

"Dennis?"

Kate's head jerked toward the bed where she found her grandmother staring up at her. "No, Gram, Grandpa isn't here right now. It's just me, Kate."

Gram blinked a couple of times as though trying to process Kate's words. She'd once had dark blue eyes like Kate's but as the fire inside her soul slowly fizzled away, it seemed her eye color followed suit. Kate hastily wiped at her cheeks, but her grandmother caught a tear on her finger and touched it to her own lips.

"Oh, Gram," Kate said. It had been two decades since Gram had done the exact same thing when Kate ran her bike into a mailbox and gave herself a black eye.

Kate scooted down on her chair until she could rest her head on Gram's pillow. The old woman grasped her hand and Kate started talking in a soft, unhurried voice. "A week ago, I met an old friend of yours named Greg Abernathy," she began. "He's been abroad for years but he recently moved back to Seattle and came to see you.

He was so sad that Grandpa had...well, he got all choked up. And then he told me something.

"He and Grandpa were coworkers a long time ago. He remembered Grandpa telling him about a long distant uncle who was a diamond merchant. When this guy stopped during his travels, he would put his diamonds in the bank of whatever town he was staying in. Well, it turns out that this one time, the bank was robbed and the diamonds were taken along with the gold. He never made a claim on what he'd lost because he didn't want anyone to know what he did for a living.

"Now this is where fate takes a hand," she continued. "Mr. Abernathy and Grandpa shared an office at the college. When Mr. Abernathy left to teach overseas, he stored a whole lot of boxes of books and papers. When he got back to Seattle recently, he decided to clean out the storage and it was while he was doing this that he found a file of Grandpa's in with his things and in the file was a copy of a paper detailing where the diamonds had been hidden after the robbery. He came here to give the file to Grandpa and to ask if Grandpa had ever tried to recover them."

Kate lowered her voice. "Mr. Abernathy could see that we're...struggling. Those diamonds are yours now, and they could make all the difference in the world. It's not a fortune, but it's probably enough to get the house up to code so we can remortgage and get some of the bills paid. The trouble is, they're on the land of a greedy, possessive man. If he were to claim the diamonds as his own and take us to court—well, how could we pay for that and, anyway, by the time it was settled it would be too late for you...for us. I have to find them, Gram. Mr. Abernathy said he would go but he's old now and, besides, this is my obligation, not his. It's an opportunity and I can't think of anything else to do. Only thing is, it means I have to leave for a couple of days…"

Gram's hand had grown slack. Kate turned her head to find the older woman's eyes closed. Kate had a very strong premonition that if she left her grandmother's side it would be for the last time. Of course, she felt that way every time she left the house, every time she kissed her good-night. It was always goodbye.

"I don't know what to do," she whispered into the night.

Frankie arrived at the car rental place early armed with coffee and a sheaf of papers Gary had given him to look over. He'd give Kate an hour to stand him up and then he'd hit the road.

A female shape pushed off from where she'd been leaning against a fence and he recognized Kate's lovely face despite the huge sunglasses resting on her nose. As she approached, he reminded himself to close his mouth instead of gaping in shock. She'd come?

Why?

As he grabbed the door handle to get out of the vehicle and start the process of renting her a car, she opened the back door, shrugged off a backpack and set it on the seat where it clanked as it landed. A second later she slipped into the passenger seat.

Today she wore jeans and a black windbreaker. Her long, blond hair had been woven into a thick, loose braid that trailed down her back. She took off the sunglasses as she turned to face him. Dark smudges under her eyes were more pronounced than they'd been the day before.

"I can't believe you came," he heard himself say.

"Neither can I but I said I would so I did. Let's get something straight, though. My grandmother is none of your business."

"I—"

"You went behind my back. You asked me to trust you and then you—"

"Sneaked around," he interrupted. "I know. I'm sorry. I wish I could take it back—" The scowl on her face cut his words short. "Okay, I get it. Well, let's rent you a car and get on our way."

"There's no need now," she said. "I just didn't want you to know where I lived. I like my privacy."

"I sort of figured that," he said dryly.

"Let's just go."

"Sounds good to me," he said, and started the engine before she could change her mind.

Chapter Three

As the luxury car ate up the miles, Kate didn't have the slightest idea what to say to the man behind the wheel. He'd offered her his untouched coffee but she'd declined—she didn't drink coffee anymore. The nerves that had taken up residence when this situation began made almost everything taste like dirty dishwater and sit uncomfortably in her stomach.

He seemed as willing to let the miles pass in silence as she was but probably not for the same reasons. Yesterday, sitting outside with the breeze ruffling their hair and the sound of seagulls mingling with the chatter of other diners, Frankie's energy and charisma had been hard enough to handle but not as over-the-top scary as now.

She took a deep breath that didn't help as the subtle scent of his aftershave wafted into her nose. She was aware of his hands on the wheel, his long fingers almost graceful. Her hands looked more like work hands than his did and she squashed the urge to sit on them.

"You're very quiet," he said, glancing at her. His dark lashes coupled with his grayish eyes made his gaze so intense her cheeks felt hot. That's what a guilty conscience could do to a person.

"Just tired," she said and that was the truth. After deciding to scrap this adventure, she'd tackled that stack of bills and reality had settled once again on her shoulders. She needed money and quite a bit of it if she was to keep Gram safe. She couldn't afford to allow fear to rule her decisions. Premonitions were notoriously overrated. She'd be back in two days, tops.

She'd had to leave so early this morning to catch the bus to the airport that she hadn't been able to say goodbye to Gram. Rose would take care of her and goodbyes never lasted in Gram's memory for more than a few seconds anyway, but it added to the unease churning Kate's gut. She turned her face toward the window where her pal, Mr. Sun, warmed the glass. Her eyes drifted closed.

She woke with a start, heart racing. Where was Gram? Had she gotten through the door again? Full consciousness returned with a sucker punch and she took a deep breath as she scanned her surroundings. Frankie Hastings stared at her. He'd pulled up in front of a diner and Kate's stomach growled.

"We've been on the road for four hours," he said. "We're almost at Dave Dalton's place. He's the guy I told you about who's descended from the lawyer who left town after the robbery. I'm kind of hungry and it looks like we could get a sandwich here if that's okay with you. It isn't fancy, but it's convenient."

She sat up straight. Her mouth felt like it was stuffed with old socks. She blinked a couple of times. Her wallet held about forty dollars and that had to get her back home. What she needed most and could actually afford was a free glass of water.

"I meant to remind you," he added. "LOGO, that's the name of Gary Dodge's production company, intends to cover your expenses for this trip. That included the rental car that you didn't use but is still an option when you want to return to Seattle." He smiled at her and added, "And no, we're not trying to buy you. I don't imagine you come cheap."

She raised her eyebrows.

"I didn't mean it that way," he said, and for once, he looked ill at ease, which strangely made her feel better.

"I am thirsty," she said.

"Good. Let's give this place a try."

The diner turned out to be a far cry from the waterfront bistro of the day before. Kate ordered a grilled cheese sandwich and it actually seemed to sit okay in her stomach for once. Toward the end of the meal, Frankie took out his cell phone and studied it. "I'm reminding myself how to get to Dave Dalton's place," he explained.

"Do you know what it is he wants to show you?"

"Not a clue. I'm curious, of course,"

"Is he expecting me to be there, too? If it's awkward, I can sit outside in the sun or something."

"I doubt your being there will be an issue but no, he's not expecting you. I arranged this meeting about a week ago, before I knew you'd be…with me."

"Before I made trouble," she said.

"Yeah. Listen, as long as I have my phone out, why don't you give me your email and cell number? Phones don't always work out at the ranch, but—"

"I don't have email or a cell phone," she said.

He stared at her a second as though he couldn't believe what he'd just heard her say.

"I moved here from Arizona over a year ago," she added. She had to give him some explanation so she went with the truth. "My grandparents didn't have internet or the…inclination…to install it. When my tablet died, I just, well, people lived for generations without computers, right?"

"You sound like my father's kind of girl," he said. "He's not big into them, either."

She did not want to be compared to his father. "I loved my computer. I mean, you can't get through college nowadays without...well, those days are long over. Now there are other things to keep me busy."

"Like what?" he said.

She looked down at her hands and shrugged. "You know, work."

"What kind of work do you do?"

She should have anticipated these questions. They were the kind almost everyone asked, she was just woefully out of practice fielding idle curiosity. Not sure why she felt the need to take the sting out of her words, she smiled. "Remember that whole I like my privacy thing?"

"Yes," he said. "Sorry."

She pushed herself away from the table and they both stood up. "Thank you for the sandwich and the tea," she added. "I'm going to the ladies' room. I'll be right back, I know you're anxious to get going."

"I'll wait for you in the car," he said as he stood. As she watched him walk to the cash register, the strangest pang of longing came over her.

Now what was that all about?

DAVE DALTON LIVED down a tree-lined lane a mile or so outside Spokane, Washington. The road was rutted with parallel tracks. Kate had gripped the edges of her seat as Frankie did his best to stay in the ruts, but inevitably the tires found all the uneven spots. Dalton needed to grade his long, bumpy driveway.

Frankie's gut feeling that Kate was hiding something just wouldn't go away. Sure, she was touchy, but it had to be more than that. Touchy was understandable. She'd accepted an invitation from a virtual stranger who openly questioned her convictions. He was a little wary of her, too. But it was something more, like the way she avoided direct answers to simple questions, hiding behind the privacy thing. Still every once in a while, he caught an unguarded comment or look and it made him smile inside.

When had he last been serious about a woman? Almost a year, he realized with a start. She'd been a nurse at the urgent care center, pretty and fun-loving, full of hopes and dreams. He'd broken it off with her when she got too clingy and talk of her dreams became talk of "their" dreams, dreams he didn't share.

Right after that, he'd started building himself a very private home even his family didn't know about. Years before, his father had given each of his sons their choice of land on which to construct houses when and if they wanted. Frankie's oldest brother, Gerard, had chosen a river view parcel not far upstream from the main house. He and Kinsey lived in it and would soon be joined by their baby who was due momentarily.

Next in age came Chance. He'd built himself an A-frame. His fiancée's name was Lily and she and her small son lived on the ranch, too. Pike came next. He'd renovated a barn into a really cool house. His girlfriend, Sierra, split her time between the ranch and New York City.

Frankie knew he didn't quite fit into his family of overachievers. It was difficult being the youngest of four brothers, all with different mothers, all very capable ranchers and businessmen. His designated title as a kid had been the screwup. And now, between one thing and another, he just liked to keep part of his life to himself, hence his secret hideaway. Half the time when his family thought he was in town carousing or causing mischief, he was actually working on his place.

So, in short, he knew a thing or two about privacy and keeping secrets, but there was only one that made him break into a cold sweat every time he thought about it. With Kate, that seemed to happen constantly. She acted like she was under a lot of stress from a lot of directions and despite how prickly she could be, he felt for her.

But right now she was hanging on to her seat and staring straight ahead as a small house finally appeared in a clearing at the end of the private road. He pulled to a stop and heard her expel a long breath.

"You okay?"

"Just glad to have that road behind me."

"Don't forget we still have to get back to the highway."

"Let me enjoy walking around for a minute." They got out of the car and she took several breaths. Some of the color started to return to her cheeks as she gazed around them.

"It's quiet here," she said. "And warm." She unzipped her windbreaker and started to pull it over her head. As she raised her arms, her blouse rode up with the jacket and three inches of creamy, smooth, velvety skin appeared at the delicious curve of her waist. By the time she got the windbreaker off and tugged her clothes into place, he had looked away, alarmed at how enticing he found that tiny peek of her flesh.

The house had a small concrete slab for a front porch and a steeply pitched roof, probably because it snowed here in the winter. A trio of moldy, faded garden gnomes sat by the bushes in front of the window. Frankie knocked against the wooden door and they stood there waiting as insects droned in the tall grass.

"Are you sure he's expecting you?" Kate asked.

"I should have texted him to confirm things. Let's check and see if his car is here."

The detached garage shared the same shabby, spare construction as the house. A door that slid across a wide opening was slightly cracked. Frankie rolled it open enough that he could see a sleek white car so new it still had the dealer's advertisement where the license plate would eventually go.

"Wow," Kate said as she looked under his raised arm.

"Funny what people spend their money on, isn't it?" Frankie said. "The house looks like it's about to fall down while there's a seventy-five-thousand-dollar car sitting in the garage."

"Seventy-five thousand dollars," Kate said, whistling. "I repeat, wow."

"Well, he's probably here. Let's go knock again."

No one came to the door this time, either. Kate walked out onto the grass opposite the front window, approached the glass cautiously and peered inside.

"See anything?" Frankie called.

"Yeah. It looks like a…" She stopped talking as her hands flew to cover her mouth and she quickly backed away from the window almost stumbling over her own feet.

"Kate! What's wrong?" Frankie asked as he started to walk toward her.

"No, open the door. Hurry," she cried, casting him a wild-eyed look. "Open the door."

He turned back around and tried to twist the knob, then he rammed his shoulder against the door.

"Hurry!" Kate said.

Raising his leg, he kicked at the thing and this time the old wood creaked but it still didn't budge. He ran to Kate's side. "What is it?"

Her skin had drained of color. "A man," she said. He glanced at the windows but from that distance, all he saw were their reflections. "I think he's…he's dead," she mumbled.

Frankie grabbed one of the plaster garden gnomes and smashed it against the window. As glass shattered to the ground the foul odor of rotting flesh all but slammed him in the face. Kate turned her back to him, braced her hands on her knees and retched as he peered into the heavily shadowed room.

A small-framed man with sandy white hair hung from a rope attached to a rafter while an overturned stool occupied the floor under his dangling feet. From the smell and the appearance of his face, it was obvious he'd been there for quite a while.

Frankie moved to grasp Kate's shoulders as she heaved. He tried patting her back but he didn't say anything. What was there to say? When she had finished, she looked even more pallid than before. She accepted the clean handkerchief he offered her. "Thanks," she whispered. "I saw a faucet by the garage. I'm going to go wash out my mouth."

He took out his cell phone and dialed 911. What had Dave Dalton wanted to show him? It now seemed unlikely he'd ever know.

THEY SAT IN the car and waited for the sheriff's department and an ambulance to arrive. Kate breathed through her mouth. Even with the windows rolled up, she was almost positive she could still smell the rotting corpse of that poor man. Her empty stomach clenched.

The ambulance and the sheriff's cars came with sirens. Frankie and Kate answered a dozen questions that added almost no information that mattered one way or another. The deputy who entered the house came out looking almost as washed-out as Kate felt. He was about her age and she got the feeling this might be his first dead body.

"I can't believe old Dave killed himself like that. Sara is going to be real broken up by this."

"Sara?"

"His daughter."

"Then it is Dave Dalton in there," Frankie said.

"Yeah, though his own mother wouldn't recognize him now. No note or nothing, either. Shame you folks had to find him."

"Did he live alone?" Kate asked.

"Yeah. Has since Polly died 'bout five years back."

"I'd never really met the man," Frankie said. "In fact, I only talked to him one time and exchanged a couple of emails." He explained about the documentary and added, "He seemed interested in showing me something. It just seems odd that he'd kill himself before he could do it."

"What did he want to show you?"

"I have no idea."

"You never can tell what's going on in someone's head," the deputy said.

Two EMTs came out of the house rolling a body bag between them and loaded it into the ambulance. The deputy, Frankie and Kate watched with somber expressions.

"That's a nice car in the garage," Frankie said as the

ambulance left the yard. He'd already retraced the actions they'd taken since arriving at the Dalton house.

"He's got himself a hell of an entertainment system and a kitchen that looks like one of them that's on a cooking show," the deputy said. "I had no idea he had that kind of loot." The deputy took off his hat, scratched his head and pulled it back on. "Dave's dad died a few years back," he added. "Dave retired about then. Maybe he inherited some money. He wasn't exactly the chatty type."

"I guess it's true," Frankie said softly. "It takes more than money to make a person happy."

The remark hit close to home for Kate who glanced down the twisting road as the ambulance's taillights disappeared from view.

Chapter Four

Several hours later when they stopped for gas, Frankie asked Kate if she was hungry and she shook her head. "I don't think I could eat. You go ahead, though."

"I don't have an appetite either," he said. "Listen, Kate, I'm very sorry that you were with me today and had to see all that. I wish I'd known what we were getting ourselves in for.

"How could you possibly have known?"

"If I'd called or texted him and he hadn't responded we wouldn't have stopped…"

"Don't beat yourself up on my account," she said. "The deputy mentioned Mr. Dalton had a daughter. It's better that we found his body than she did, right?"

"I guess so," he said.

"Anyway, I was with my grandfather when he died." Now why had she told him that? When she'd signed on for this venture, she'd sworn she wouldn't talk about herself, invite confidences or reveal personal information. She had never lied to anyone before in her life and Frankie was making doing so now very hard because… well, she didn't know why exactly, she just found herself wanting to tell him things. She muttered, "Death happens."

"But not usually like that," he said.

"No, you're right. Poor man."

Once back on the road, the fatigue Kate couldn't seem to shake came back and once again she fell asleep. When she woke up, it was dark outside and the dashboard clock said it was half past eleven.

She'd been dreaming about people. Luke had been in one of them but she wasn't sure in what way. The most vivid had been of her grandmother who had been baking. She'd offered Kate a taste of cookie batter from a long spoon. Kate had stared at her, tears running down her cheeks, mumbling over and over again, *Gram, you're like you used to be! You're okay.* And her grandmother had laughed. *Of course I'm okay.*

Kate swallowed a knot. "Where are we?" she asked as she glanced at Frankie.

"We just ran over the cattle guard that is the ranch's unofficial welcome mat. Did you have a nice snooze?"

"I think so," she said. "I'm sorry I keep falling asleep."

"It's no problem," he said. "When you live out this far, you get used to time alone behind a wheel."

She looked out the window. The waxing moon illuminated nothing but fields. Maybe there wasn't a whole lot else to see. They traveled a couple of miles down a dirt-and-gravel road before cresting a hill. Below, Kate saw a large house and a scattering of dark buildings, but her gaze went to the winding path of the river. Her heart jumped into her throat. The Bowline River…the real reason she was here. She tore her attention from that tantalizing U-bend and concentrated on the house instead lest Frankie sense the direction of her thoughts.

"That's my family's house," he said.

"Does everyone live there?"

"No. Gerard, Chance and Pike all built homes scattered about on ranch land."

"But not you?"

He shrugged. "The only people who live full-time in this house are my father and his wife, my brother Chance's fiancée, Lily, and her little boy, Charlie. They'll move out after the wedding. I've talked to Grace and she says you're welcome to stay with them."

"What about you?"

"I have a room at the house for when I'm here or once in a while I stay with Pike."

"Then you don't live on the ranch?"

He cast her a quick glance. Dashboard lights illuminated part of his face and the dazzling white of his eyes. "I like my privacy, too," he said.

"Touché," she muttered.

Three dogs greeted them when they got out of the car. They all had dark fur though two also sported patches of white. Though difficult to tell in the semidark of the night, one looked like a Labrador retriever and the others like some kind of shepherd mix. Kate hadn't had a dog since she was fifteen and she knelt to pat them and accept welcoming licks across the cheek. Frankie handed her the backpack. "What did you pack, rocks? This thing weighs a ton."

She'd meant to grab the pack herself and gotten distracted by the dogs. She didn't respond to his remark, just took the pack and moved off while he retrieved a small suitcase from his trunk.

As she approached the house, she heard the sound of moving water and unable to resist, walked along the path to a point where she could glimpse the moonlit river below. Its banks could be her salvation if she kept her mind on her priorities and goals.

"Kate?" Frankie said.

At the sound of his voice, she jumped about two inches into the air.

"It's beautiful, isn't it?" he asked, his voice soft.

"Huh? Oh, yes. It is," she said and hoped he couldn't hear her heart hammering in her chest.

"Do you like rivers?

"Why do you ask?" she said, startled.

She sensed as much as saw the rise and fall of his shoulders. "Oh, you know. Some people are into mountains and forests, others crave the desert sun, some like the water."

She thought of Luke and the icy Bering Sea. "I guess I appreciate different things in all of them," she said, looking up at his face. There was just enough light to see the curiosity at play in his eyes, curiosity she had no desire to arouse.

Or did she? When was the last time she'd felt as alive as right that moment? All day she'd been fighting a bone-weary fatigue except for the few hours spent in numb shock after discovering Dave Dalton's body. Now, however, she was wide awake and most of that was because of what this river signified if she accomplished what she'd agreed to try. But she also knew that some of the way she felt was because of Frankie's shoulder grazing her own.

Was she unconsciously soliciting his attention? Was this part of that urge she had to level with him? Why had this plan been so much easier in theory than it was turning out to be in reality? She stepped away from him, her backpack held in front of her chest like a shield. If he'd had X-ray vision what would he make of its contents?

"It's getting late," he said, touching her arm and sending a shiver straight to her spine. "Let's see if anyone is still awake."

She turned away from the river and from Frankie.

Tomorrow she'd get started. With any luck, she'd be gone by the day after.

And Frankie? He was an obstacle, yes, but he was also an illusion. There was no room for fantasy when a pack of hungry wolves howled at the door.

"YOU TWO MUST be exhausted," Harry Hastings said. His gaze traveled from Frankie to Kate. "Young lady, how are you holding up?" This demand was made in his usual take-no-prisoners style.

Beside him, Kate kind of bristled. Frankie had called his family after he spoke to the police to report the hanging death of Dave Dalton so they could alert Gary Dodge and Pat Lowell, but he hadn't told them that Kate required kid glove treatment.

"What do you mean?" she said.

"That horrible suicide, of course," he replied, reaching for her backpack. "Hell of a thing for a young woman to come across."

He was dressed in his pajamas and robe and explained that Grace was spending the night over at Kinsey and Gerard's place. The baby was technically overdue and Grace spent as much time over there as she did here.

Kate tightened her grip on her backpack. "I'm fine," she said. "Mr. Dalton's…death…was tragic, of course. I feel bad for his family."

"I've never understood suicide," he replied. "Anyway, let me take that pack for you. Grace fixed up the downstairs room…"

"No, thank you," she said firmly, her grip on her pack growing tighter. "I've got this."

He held up both hands and laughed.

"Sorry," she said and smothered a yawn. "It's been a long day."

"Of course," his father said. "Frankie, get our guest settled. I'm off to bed. I know you have your hands full," he added, "but I was hoping you'd have time to help me tomorrow morning. Pike and Chance rode out yesterday to the high pastures to check things out and they called to report seeing one of the mares with a brand-new foal. Not sure how she slipped by us, but I'd appreciate your bringing her and the baby closer to the ranch. They're out near Bywater, somewhere around Ten Cent Creek."

"No problem," Frankie said. He turned his attention to Kate and added, "Would you like to come along?"

"No thanks," she said quickly.

"Saving your riding legs for the ghost town and the… hanging tree?"

"It'll give me a chance to sleep in," she said after a moment.

He gave her a double take. All this woman did was sleep. Was she ill?

Harry Hastings wandered out of the kitchen and Frankie, careful not to even glance at Kate's backpack, led her down the hall to the open door of a modest room with twin beds.

"Is there anything else I can get you?" he asked.

"No, everything looks very nice."

He nodded as he gazed down in her eyes. He could

not shake the feeling something was wrong or deny his desire to try to get her to open up.

"See you tomorrow," she said, still holding on to her pack.

"It shouldn't take me long," he said. "I'll be back before noon."

"Noon," she repeated as though committing it to memory.

"Yes. Well, good night," he said, and damn if he didn't feel a pull toward touching her lips with his and double damn if she didn't seem to broadcast the hope he would do just that.

They both stepped back at the same time. As he walked down the short hallway back to the kitchen, he heard the door close and the lock click behind him.

He'd never been around a woman who sent so many mixed messages. In her unguarded moments, he liked her—she was amusing and interesting and so beautiful it was hard not to stare at her. That hair! Like gold, smooth and long and framing a perfect oval face. But when she got tense, whoa, back off. She'd all but bitten his father's head off. Why?

Was it just nerves at finding herself in what she considered the enemy camp? His dad could be formidable. Maybe that's all it was.

Or maybe it was something else….

AFTER A RESTLESS NIGHT, Kate found that her window looked out over the ranch yard affording a decent view of Frankie leaving the house and crossing to a picture-perfect barn. It was the first time she'd really had a chance to watch him from a distance.

He wasn't nearly as burly as Luke but easily twice as

striking. Luke had had a gentle nature to go along with his brute strength. She put him out of her mind, determined to stay strong.

Frankie came out of the barn a little later leading a saddled horse. He walked it over to a horse trailer attached to a big white truck. Once the horse was tucked safely inside, he drove the rig out of the yard. She knew little of how ranches operated, but she had to assume he was driving to a certain point and then riding the rest of the way on horseback.

A pang of desire hit her hard. How desperately did she want to be in that truck with Frankie, free to go looking for a horse and her baby? Who didn't love a baby horse? Free to do ordinary things, free to just be herself. The pang was immediately followed by shame. She spent the next fifteen minutes braiding her shower-damp hair and dressing, then strapped on her backpack and left her room.

A pleasant-looking woman of about fifty turned as Kate walked into the kitchen. Kate had assumed no one else was awake and so she was caught off guard and stumbled to a halting stop. But this was good. She'd been worried about taking a horse without asking and this way she wouldn't have to do that.

"Harry had to leave. Some trouble with the dang water pump. I'm Grace, Harry's wife. I assume you're Kate?"

"Yes," Kate said, shaking the woman's hand.

"Sorry I wasn't here when you arrived," Grace continued. "My daughter had a few twinges."

"I thought it was Frankie's brother having the baby," she said.

"That's right, but Gerard is married to my daughter." She laughed. "It's a long story. Get Frankie to tell it to you." She poured a mug from the coffeepot and set it on the counter in front of Kate. "I heard you were going to sleep in today. Frankie left a bit ago. I'm afraid you missed him."

"I just couldn't sleep anymore," Kate said, which was the truth. She looked at the cup of coffee, debating whether to be polite and take a sip or admit she didn't drink the stuff. Politeness won, but one taste later, she put down the cup. Her face must have reflected what she'd tasted because Grace winced.

"I brew it strong for this crew. I'll make a new pot—"

"No, that's okay. It's such a lovely morning. Would you mind if I borrowed a horse? I spent my teenage summers working at a dude ranch so I'm comfortable with animals."

"That's a grand idea. There's a red mare out in the barn that Pike's girlfriend, Sierra, adores."

"That sounds great. Thanks."

"You're welcome." She paused for a second before adding, "If you're riding out to the ghost town, you'll need directions or you'll get lost. And listen, dear, don't feel embarrassed about wanting to come here and get a feel for things. I think your concern for your forefathers' reputations is admirable."

"Thank you," Kate said, uncomfortable with the un-warranted praise this kind woman gave so generously. "For now, I'll just stay by the river. That way I can't get lost."

As if she wasn't already...

Chapter Five

Kate strapped her backpack on the back of the saddle and rode down the small lane that ran parallel to the river. The morning sun beating down on her shoulders helped ease some of the tension of the morning.

She wished she'd had the means to buy a cell phone. She'd given Rose the Hastingses' phone number in case of an emergency, but she could imagine all sorts of things going wrong that Rose might not think of as an emergency. Kate wasn't sure if Gram recognized Kate as her granddaughter or not, but it did seem pretty clear that Kate's presence and the home she'd lived in for fifty years were the very foundation of what little stability she still had.

Kate had promised her dying grandfather she would keep that house as long as her grandmother lived. Trouble was, his illness had eaten up every available penny. The Hastingses didn't seem quite as ruthless as they'd been portrayed, but she'd also been assured they hadn't the slightest idea what she was looking for even existed. Since her subterfuge actually hurt no one, why did it feel so bad?

She rode past a smaller house set on the hillside with a view of the river. This must be Grace's daughter's house and just as that thought surfaced, a very pregnant woman about her own age, opened the door and stepped outside carrying a basket and heading for a fenced garden. She was small in stature with light brown hair and a smiling, warm face. She waved. "Are you Kate West?" she called. "Where's Frankie?"

Kate stifled a sigh. How was she supposed to conduct a covert search when everyone was so dang friendly! "Out looking for a mare and her foal. Are you Grace's daughter?"

"Yes. Are you going for a ride by the river?"

Grateful she'd been up-front about her plans, Kate nodded. "It's too nice to stay indoors."

"I know." She cradled her baby bulge and added, "I miss riding. I also miss my waist and my feet and being able to bend over. Well, I won't keep you, have fun."

"Thanks," Kate called and rode off down the road until it ended and only a trail meandered closer to the water. As the horse made her way along the trail, Kate thought about the details she'd been given that would hopefully help her locate what she was after.

Number one: a bend in this river, the Bowline, and somewhere within a mile or two of this exact spot. There was just such a bend right smack in front of the main ranch house but hopefully, there were others. She didn't even want to think about the possibility of conducting a search out in the open like that.

Two: there had once been a small well to supply water to a cabin that had burned down several years before the information was recorded. Three: a snagged tree. Four: a view of an unnamed mountaintop. Five: a rock that had been described as looking like a bonnet.

The trouble was pretty obvious: rivers change course

and while maps certainly existed a hundred years before, the kinds of details she'd been given were flexible. Trees rotted, rock foundations disappeared under vegetation, fires swept the landscape, large boulders eroded or were now underwater, mountains visible once were now camouflaged by a forest. The most reliable source of information on all these things was the Hastings family but, of course, she couldn't ask them.

Greg Abernathy had tried to prepare her for what she might find, but being out along uninhabited, overgrown riverfront turned out to be daunting. She glimpsed a small rise ahead and aimed for that, hoping it would provide an overview of the area. Once she'd reached that higher elevation, she looked in all directions, then got off the mare and walked to the edge of the small bluff. A bend in the river lay directly beneath her position. There was even a rock although it didn't look much like a bonnet from this vantage point, but she was hopeful. If this was the spot, she could leave the next day after pretending to rethink her stand on the documentary.

She took the horse's reins in her hand and began the search for the way down to the riverbank below. The sun had already risen high in the sky and it was hot in with the overgrown berry vines and weeds. It didn't take long until perspiration dotted her forehead. The vines were young and vigorous, their thorns like little sabers tearing at her clothes. Behind her, the horse skittered along on the uneven ground. It took about twenty minutes before they stepped onto a narrow rocky shore. She untied the backpack, set it on the ground and opened it. Behind her, the forest crowded the shoreline.

Time to get to work.

FRANKIE KNEW THERE were some days on a ranch—or anywhere else—that nothing seemed to go right. A simple job could take three times as long as expected when equipment broke or helpers didn't show up on time. But nothing slapped a wild card down on the table like dealing with animals.

Today was not one of those days. He arrived out at the Bywater pasture, unloaded the previously saddled gelding, tightened the cinch and rode thirty minutes down the gully toward Ten Cent Creek. He ran into the bay mare and her foal standing apart from the rest of the ranch horses who spent their off time in this pasture. The colt was a long-legged, spindly-looking little guy with white socks and a blaze down his nose. While the mare was dusty and had stickers caught in her mane and tail, the newborn practically sparkled. Frankie dismounted and checked them out—both appeared well. He fed the mare an apple he'd stuffed in his saddlebag, slid a halter around her head and mounted his own horse. Leading the mare, the colt frolicking behind her, they made their way uphill to the transport. He loaded all three animals and got back in the truck.

The whole thing had taken just a little over two hours, and by the time he drove back into the yard, it was well before noon. There would be plenty of time to take Kate out to the ghost town and show her the hanging tree although he needed to come up with a more sensitive name for the thing first.

He tied his mount to the railing of the fence as he released the mare and colt into a stall inside the barn. He made sure they had fresh feed and water, then crossed the yard to the house. Grace sat at the table hand-sewing the hem of a yellow sleeper. Kinsey and Gerard had

elected not to know the sex of their first child, prefer-
ring the old-fashioned wait-and-see approach. Grace,
who treated Lily's son like her grandson, was excited
about having a baby around the house.

She looked up as he entered. "You're back early,"
she said.

"Things just fell into place," he explained. He looked
down the hall. "Where is everybody?"

"Today is Lily's turn to help at Charlie's school. Your
dad spent part of the morning fooling with that antique
water pump, then he went to sign some papers at the
bank. Your brothers are out with a couple of summer
hires windrowing the hay in the south fields."

"What about Kate? Is she still asleep?"

"Heavens no. She left soon after you did."

He'd been headed toward the refrigerator to grab a
bottle of juice but stopped short. "She didn't sleep in?"

"No."

"Did she ride out to the ghost town?"

"She said she was going to stay close to the river. I
saw her riding toward Kinsey's house."

"The river? Did she say why?"

"Not really. She didn't say a whole lot."

"Did she ask you any awkward questions?"

"Awkward?"

"She's trying to get a feel for us and find out about
the film, so she's bound to want to know about things."

"I can't say she asked anything except to borrow a
horse. Truthfully, she seemed a little preoccupied. But
finding Mr. Dalton yesterday—maybe that upset her. It
would have gotten to me."

"Yeah," he said. He turned toward the door. "I think
I'll see if I can intercept her."

"Good luck," Grace said. "Oh, and tell her someone named Rose called. She didn't want to leave a message except to ask that Kate call her back."

"I'll tell her if I find her." He left the kitchen without the juice and got back on his horse, directing it down the road toward Gerard's house. By now he was used to the nagging feeling that he was playing catch-up with Kate. He had to figure her out. Something was weird.

She had limited time, or so she claimed, so why was she out sightseeing? The passionate, determined woman in the Seattle restaurant had had one goal—stop the documentary. Now she was here, now she could investigate what it was she so opposed but instead...something didn't add up.

"Stop being so suspicious," he told himself as he passed his brother's house and kept going. There were fresh tracks leading beside the river. Curious, he followed. They disappeared up the rocky slope of a small knoll that he rode to the top. He'd been up and down this river many times over the course of his life and he knew from there he could see several hundred feet of both sides of the river before another bend hid it from view. He got off the horse and stood there with wildflowers brushing against his legs until a sound drew him toward the edge.

He saw Ginger tied to a tree on the beach below. Kate's big bulky backpack sat on the rocks near the horse but there was no sign of Kate. Thinking he would climb down to make sure everything was okay, he began to turn but movement off in the forest caught his eye and he stopped. Not sure why he did so, he stepped back a little and watched as Kate emerged from the shadows under the trees.

She walked out into the sunshine, holding what appeared to be a short machete in her hand.

A machete? Where had that come from? What in the world was she doing?

Her hair had come loose from her braid and sported all sorts of leaves and debris while her windbreaker had a three-inch gash down one arm. She folded the machete into a towel and put it in her pack and then she raised her arms to pull off her jacket. This time, both the light windbreaker and the T-shirt beneath it slid over her head.

He told himself to look away but he didn't budge. For one thing, he didn't want movement from him to make her look up and catch him watching her. For another, he couldn't bear not to look.

She dumped her clothes on the top of the pack and walked to the water's edge, her gold hair trailing down her mostly bare back catching every ray of sunshine, her surprisingly lush bosom bouncing gently as she moved. She knelt at the water's edge, cupped her hands and splashed water up onto her face and chest, washing drops of blood off her arms and pushing back her hair from her face before standing and staring back into the forest.

Half-naked, damp splotches on her sky blue bra, skin glistening with water, she was nothing short of breathtaking. He knew she would never forgive him if she caught him watching her and willed her to turn away so he could get out of there. It had been a stroke of luck that he was upwind from Ginger so she hadn't caught scent of his horse and given him away. How long could he depend on luck?

Finally, Kate leaned over, separated her T-shirt from her jacket and pulled it over her head. Any second now and she would remount Ginger and retreat up this hill—

it was the quickest way to the ranch. He waited until her back was to him and, hoping the water breaking over the rocks in the river a few feet away from her would disguise any noise he made from above, led the horse to the other side of the knoll, mounted and rode downhill. He kept going until he was almost back on the road to Gerard's place, and then he turned around and started back the direction he'd just come.

With any luck, it would appear he'd only now ridden out to find her and she would never know he'd seen her on the beach.

The unintentional display of partial nudity aside, however, the basic question still existed. What had she been doing in the forest with a machete?

KATE FOUGHT THE urge to continue her search. She knew she couldn't get discouraged after one failure but the thought had begun to cross her mind that it was unlikely this venture would be completed within one day.

It was closing in on noon as she left the rise, and as soon as she headed back, thoughts of her grandmother flooded her head. After over a year of being responsible for the woman's care every second of every day, being away felt wrong. She knew total control was an illusion, but it was her current life's main motivator—if she was present, she could fix things, anticipate trouble, keep all the little plates spinning on their poles.

The red mare whinnied and Kate's mind focused back on the here and now. She glanced ahead to find Frankie riding toward her. She smoothed her hair off her forehead and tugged her T-shirt away from her damp skin.

"Hi," he called as they met on the path. The horses

sniffed each other as Frankie looked directly into her eyes. "Have a nice ride?"

"Very nice," she said.

"Where'd you go?"

"I found a rock close to the water and read for a while," she said, biting her lip and hoping he didn't ask what she was reading because her mind was a sudden and complete blank.

"Did you do anything else?"

"Like what?" she said, suddenly nervous.

"Oh, I don't know. Take a walk, maybe? There's a lot of pretty forest around the river."

"It looks pretty dense," she said.

"Hmm. By the way, you got a call from someone named Rose."

"Rose called! What—"

"Grace said she didn't leave a message except for you to call her back." He dug in his pocket and extracted his cell phone, which he handed to her. "I'm going to ride ahead and make sandwiches. Take your time."

As she accepted his phone, their fingers brushed and the next thing she knew, he'd gripped her wrist and gently turned her arm. He was staring at the scratch she'd acquired in the woods that was once again bloody. "What happened?" he asked.

"I...tripped into some blackberry vines. I can be such a klutz."

He stared at her an additional few seconds, then gently dropped her hand. "See you in a while," he said, kicked his horse and rode away, his figure tall and straight in his saddle. He left her with the distinct feeling that he suspected something. There was no way, though, none at all. She turned around to make sure her backpack wasn't hanging open revealing a bunch of tools, but it was buckled tight.

Unable to fight the urge to check on Gram another moment, she pulled the mare to the side of the path and punched in Rose's cell number.

"Is something wrong?" Kate asked the minute Rose responded.

"It's been quite a night," Rose said.

"Is Gram—"

"She's just fine, honey. I don't even think her toes got wet."

"What? What happened?"

"The hot water heater broke," Rose said. "I had to call the plumber in the middle of the night because I didn't know how to fix it. He said it's been leaking through a corroded pipe for a long time. It's in that closet near the utility room and it managed to do some significant damage. Anyway, the plumber advised us to get out of the house until it can be dried out and checked for mold spores on account of how long it's been leaking. I'm afraid you lost the carpet…anyway, we're okay and your grandmother has already forgotten anything happened."

"Where is she?"

"I wanted to bring her to my house but I have three cats, two big dogs and a grandson living in my basement. I finally checked her into a care facility for dementia patients. They had an empty room and agreed to a week-long stay upon her doctor's recommendation. He gave it and I settled her in there this morning."

The very thing Kate had been killing herself to prevent had happened the minute she left Seattle. Her grandmother was in a home. "I don't know what to do," she heard herself say.

"There's nothing you can do," Rose said. "Your grandmother is safe. Mr. Abernathy contacted your insurance company. You're covered for a lot of what needs to be done. There will be a deductible, of course, and they ask that you call to give authorization. I'll visit your grandmother every day."

"Is she terribly upset? Maybe I should come home."

"Suit yourself," Rose said. "But the truth is she almost looked happy to see other people. Of course she's asking them all if they know where Dennis is, but there are a lot more people to ask now." She paused a moment before adding, "I'm sorry to say this, but she'll forget you're in Seattle two minutes after you've left her side whether it's now or a week from now."

In her heart, Kate was already on a plane landing in Seattle. She could picture walking into Gram's room. But the smile of relief and welcome she tried to visualize on Gram's face just wouldn't come. Those expressions and the reasoning to create them had disappeared a while back.

"You're right," she said at last. "I have to see this through. Where exactly is she?"

"Pine Hill. Here's their number and the one for the insurance people."

Kate dug a pen out of the backpack and wrote the numbers on her arm. Then she clicked off the phone and immediately dialed the facility. She talked to the manager of the home and was assured Gram was wandering the circular hallways and had eaten lunch with the others.

She hung up from that call still riddled with indecision, torn between staying and leaving, angry at herself for going away in the first place. She put her hands over her face as guilt and remorse flooded through her body, gripping handfuls of Ginger's russet mane to keep from sliding off the saddle.

Where was the woman who had held back tears? Who was this blubbering waterworks of a human being? She sat up, mopped her face and squared her shoulders. Enough was enough.

Chapter Six

Kate was relieved when Kinsey didn't appear at her door. She knew she must look puffy and tear-streaked. In a perfect world, she could beam herself back to the bedroom without having to talk to anyone.

But that was not to be, for as she slid from the saddle and took the mare's reins to enter the barn, a good-looking guy with sun-browned skin exited. She tried averting her face, but there was no polite way to do that.

"Are you okay?" he said at once.

"Yes." Knowing her face told a different story, she added, "Darn allergies."

"I'm Pike," he added, offering a smile that evoked thoughts of Frankie. "You have to be Kate West. Welcome to Hastings Ridge."

"Thanks."

"Let me take care of Ginger for you."

"She's a sweetheart," Kate said, patting the horse's sleek shoulder.

"That she is. Sierra adores her."

"She's your girlfriend, right?"

"Yes, she's my girl. Well, her and Daisy, my dog. You might not mention that to anyone else, though."

"I won't say a word," she said, marveling at how comfortable this guy was in his skin. He looked a little like Frankie, but there was something more peaceful about him. He began unstrapping Kate's backpack from the saddle. She couldn't exactly demand he not touch it so she waited for the inevitable comment about its clumsy weight. The contents clanked and Pike's eyebrows furrowed, but he made no comment as he handed the pack to Kate and took the reins from her.

Kate thanked him and walked toward the house, the backpack an unwieldy burden thumping against her legs. Sure enough, a van with Washington state plates and the company's name, LOGO, had pulled in next to Frankie's car. She walked into the kitchen to find Frankie signing what appeared to be a stack of business papers while Gary Dodge, a lanky man of about fifty with graying sandy hair and wire-framed glasses, stood nearby. He looked at Kate and reached out for the backpack. "Let me relieve you of that—"

"No, that's okay," she said, hugging it against her chest.

"It's good to see you again," Gary said. "Frankie was just telling me about Dave Dalton. Man, that's terrible."

"Yes," she said.

"Have you heard anything more from the police?"

This last question was directed at Frankie who shook his head though his gaze was glued to Kate's face. "Not a word. Don't really expect to unless there's a problem of some kind."

Gary nodded and looked back at Kate. "Well, what do you think of this beautiful ranch and the fine family that owns it?"

"Everything is…amazing," Kate said.

"Nice and subtle, Gary," Frankie said.

Gary grinned. "Just want to make sure things are okay. Before Grace walked over to Kinsey and Gerard's house she mentioned you'd gone riding. I gather you already investigated the river this morning."

"Investigated?" Kate said, struggling to keep the alarm out of her voice. She glanced at Frankie who was watching her closely. "I don't know about that, exactly," she said. "It's very peaceful by the water and Frankie had ranch business so I had a little free time."

"Excellent."

"We're about to visit the ghost town," Frankie told Gary. "You're welcome to come along."

"I have to get back to Seattle for a meeting this evening. I just wanted you to sign this contract and I also wanted to tell you some fabulous news."

"We could use good news," Frankie said.

Gary fairly beamed. "I heard from Pat Lowell. He's spoken to the other man he had lined up. Turns out he isn't a descendant himself but his wife was directly related to a guy who claimed to know all about the robbery."

"What man?"

"Dare we hope the missing man?" Gary said with drama. "The fourth robber, the one who got away. If so, it looks like he was a drifter from out of town. This guy Pat talked to, his name is Jerry Stillwater, inherited his deceased wife's mother's estate when she died. He found a bundle of old letters that had been in their family for decades. Pat is pretty sure he'll eventually be able to pinpoint the exact location of the missing gold that was stolen from the bank. According to the letters, the gold never left this area. If he can do that and the gold is still buried here and we can find it, can you imagine what a great ending it would make for the documentary?"

"I can't believe this," Frankie said with an unmistakable edge of excitement to his voice. "Have you seen these letters yourself?"

"Not yet. I just got his call this morning. Pat's engaging an expert down in Boise to go over them—apparently there's fairly significant water damage to contend with. He says he saw nothing that mentioned the Bowline River but he did pick out Ten Cent Creek and the hills near the area called Bywater. There's also some mention of a cave. He's afraid to keep looking until the papers are stabilized but his expert says it should be done within a few days."

"Is he sure about the Bowline? It's the biggest river around here. I always thought that if the gold was still around, that's where it would be." He suddenly narrowed his eyes and glanced quickly at Kate and away again. She swallowed hard. A guilty conscience was a heavy, ponderous burden she wasn't used to managing and fancied every stray uncomfortable thought that popped into her head appeared on her face.

But what could he know? Nothing. She was being paranoid. "Who would the gold belong to?" she asked to diffuse the speculation in his eyes.

"The lawyers can figure that out later," Frankie said.

"Won't your father insist it's his?" Kate said. Everything Greg Abernathy had told her about the man suggested he would never let anything valuable leave his land no matter to whom it belonged.

Frankie cast her an annoyed frown but said nothing. She shouldn't have said anything.

"Ownership isn't the issue right now," Gary said. "The

discovery is what's important—well, that and the identity of that elusive fourth man. This could be the wow moment we've been missing."

Frankie apparently allowed his suspicions to subside as he broke into a wondrous, wistful smile. "Wouldn't that be something," he said softly. He glanced down at Kate yet again. "Maybe there will be something in those letters that will exonerate your great-great-great-grandfather and his brother."

"Or possibly reveal the extent of their involvement," Gary warned.

Kate nodded. Frankie's concern for her sensibilities despite his obvious misgivings touched her more than she could bear to admit and she wasn't positive how to respond. She'd always thought getting invited to the ranch would be the hard part of this situation—well, that and uncovering the treasure; she hadn't figured on the difficulty of maintaining her point of view in light of the fact that when it came to the documentary, she didn't have one. But what she did have were gigantic concerns for her grandmother's safety and that's what mattered, that's what she had to keep in mind at all times.

However, the historian they kept talking about puzzled her. Why hadn't this Pat Lowell researched her phony claims? Maybe he was too deeply involved in these letters to even think of it but it seemed odd.

"I'm not afraid of the truth," she said and wondered if anyone had ever told a bigger lie.

"Neither are we," Frankie said.

FRANKIE HELD HIS tongue as they approached the trail paralleling the stream that led from the back of the house up the hill and eventually to the plateau above. But thoughts and images churned in his head until he finally had to say something. "Tell me one thing," he said as they crossed the stream single file. "Are you really here because of your relatives or is there another reason?"

"Another reason?" she said, and her voice sounded so surprised he shot a look over his shoulder to glimpse her face. "Like what?"

"Just what I said. Are you here because of Earl and Samuel Bates, or is there something else you're not telling me?"

"Of course there are things I'm not telling you."

"That is a nonanswer," he protested and cast her another glance.

"I can assure you, however, that I would not be a guest of your family and work against you."

"Well, pardon me for saying so, but you seem to have a lot on your...mind."

She didn't respond as they ducked their heads to pass under some low-hanging branches. He stopped talking. Holding a conversation in that manner was pointless. So much of what Kate said showed on her face. Without being able to see her, he felt lost.

The path hadn't been used a lot since spring and for once wasn't muddy. It was a pleasant ride in the shade of the trees, but he waited until they erupted out of the heavy canopy of trees onto the plateau to restart their discussion. The ghost town was off a couple of miles to the right. He directed them left, toward the scattered oaks that dotted the rugged landscape.

"I have another question," he said as he reined in his horse to keep pace with hers.

She glanced at him. "Go ahead," she said.

He measured his words carefully. "Why are you so negative about my father?"

She looked away from his face but answered immediately. "He kind of reminds me of my own father, kind of full of himself. I shouldn't have judged him so quickly, though. I apologize."

He smiled as he shook his head. "That's not going to wash, Kate," he said. He corrected the course to avoid a gully and dug in his saddlebag for the sandwiches he'd tucked there. He handed one to her. "See, I remember you said something snarly about him the first time we met," he added as he unwrapped roast beef and cheddar on sourdough. "If you'd never met him, then why—"

"Someone told me he was...selfish," she said, her cheeks turning a delicate pink as she stared at the unwrapped sandwich in her hand.

"Who told you that?"

"I'd rather not say. Can we drop this? There's no excuse for my behavior, at least none I can offer. I'm sorry."

"Consider the subject dropped."

They rode in silence for a few more minutes, concentrating on the boulders and gullies, the big oak growing ever closer. Frankie ate his sandwich with relish—he could make a mean sandwich if he did say so himself—but he noticed Kate tuck hers away in that giant backpack that never left her side. Did the woman ever eat? At least she was awake, that was something, right?

"This is the tree," Frankie finally said when they rode into the shade underneath the long, sweeping branches. Roots like petrified snakes erupted from the earth and spread outward. "It was smaller back then but big enough for the posse's needs."

"Three people died here," she said softly as she slid

out of the saddle. Her hair was back in the long braid and he watched her stare through the limbs above for a moment or two as though getting a feeling for the tragedy the tree had helped commit. He shook his head to dispel a sudden memory of her bare, translucent skin and got off his horse, dropping the lead, knowing it wouldn't wander far away from the shade where a few blades of tender grass undoubtedly looked tasty.

He perched on a root that had reached near chair height. She looked down at him. "Why does your family call you Frankie instead of Frank?"

"Isn't that kind of personal?" he said. As a surprise question from out of the blue, she'd just won the gold medal.

She smiled. "Yes. Sorry."

"To answer your question, my mother is a little bit of a nomad. She's been traveling her whole life and seems totally incapable of stopping. The best thing she ever did for me was to give me a man for a father with three other sons and firm roots. Even then, it was rough growing up with her floating in and out of my life like a butterfly."

"Is she still alive?"

"Oh, yes. I don't hear from her often, but every once in a while, she shows up with a few fascinating stories and a breezy kiss and then she's off again."

"Did she grow up around here?"

"I'm not sure where she grew up. Dad says the first he was aware of her was when she appeared at the ranch one day lost. She said she was looking for someone but he can't remember who it was. He'd just had his fourth divorce, she was a real beauty, and one thing followed another. They were married soon after and then I was born."

Most people commented on the number of marriages his father had willingly entered. In fact, Grace was wife number seven, or lucky number seven as Harry Hastings affectionately called her. But this information didn't seem to lodge for a second in Kate's mind. "I wonder who your mother was looking for."

He shrugged. "Dad says she never mentioned anything about it again."

"Can't you just ask her?"

He smiled. "No one can answer a question and say as little as my mother," he said. "Except for you," he added under his breath as he met her blue-eyed gaze. "The past doesn't interest her much. Maybe she just wanted to meet my dad and used that as an excuse."

"And all this ties into your name because?"

"Oh, yeah. Because she named me in honor of her grandmother's father. In a way, my name is a small link to my shrouded maternal past."

"It seems kind of strange, doesn't it?"

"In a way, I suppose it is. Dad theorizes that Mom was wounded as a child in a way she couldn't bear to face and that she reinvented herself and resolved to move forward and not look back. He thinks I'm the only living relative she has. She didn't even tell me that tidbit about my name until I was eighteen and in a spot of...trouble. Okay, this is way more story than you bargained for." He stood up and gazed down at her. "Now it's your turn."

"What do you mean?"

He took a deep breath and hoped his unplanned object lesson in sharing had made an impression. "Forgive me for bringing this up. Your grandmother has Alzheimer's, doesn't she? And Dennis, who is he?"

For a second, he thought she wouldn't answer, but

then an almost imperceptible sigh escaped her lips. "Dennis was my grandfather. He died a little over a year ago. Gram had been getting bad before that but with him gone, she really went downhill."

"And you moved in to save her."

"Yes." Her eyes suddenly flooded and she bit her lip. He wondered how to comfort her without incurring her wrath, but when she covered her face with her hands and her shoulders shook, he threw caution to the wind and just put his arms around her.

As she leaned against him and allowed herself to cry unabashedly, the strangest sensation stole over him. Had he held her before? Not really, but this didn't feel like the first time their bodies had touched. In fact it felt like he'd held her in his arms a thousand times before and that it was destiny he hold her a thousand times again.

Okay, this was stupid. He told himself to release her, to step back, not to touch her. None of those things happened. It was as though he was frozen into place and he was suddenly afraid of breaking this connection with her, afraid it would hurt one or both of them and that made no sense at all.

He looked down at the top of her head and somehow his face drifted toward her and he felt his lips touch her hair. She immediately startled and looked up at him, her moist blue eyes deep and secretive.

Her delicate pink lips all but called his name.

Who was he to resist the siren call of destiny?

Chapter Seven

The kiss was almost over before it started, but for the instant it existed, Frankie's imagination seemed to shoot through the stars. Then Kate pulled away from him and stood staring into his eyes.

He swallowed a knot of alarm. He'd kissed any number of women in his lifetime and most with a far deeper sense of intimacy, but this was different, just as holding her was different. "Kate, I am…sorry, I…so sorry," he blubbered, unsure what to say, longing to reach for her again but shoving his hands in his pockets instead. What in the world had come over him?

"It's my fault," she said quickly, her voice trembling.

"How could it be your fault? No, I take full responsibility. My gosh, you're a guest here—"

"I know it's hard to believe, but I used to be the most self-confident woman you'd ever want to meet. I never, ever cried."

"That's not hard to believe," he said gently.

"I hardly remember that girl. Now, all I do is second-guess my decisions and regret…poor Luke—"

She stopped abruptly as though shocked she'd said too much and blinked back tears as she looked up into the boughs overhead.

Who the heck was Luke? "It's this tree," he offered. "Gerard says the aura of the tragedy that happened here still lingers. I don't know, maybe he's right."

"What do you mean?" she asked, sniffing back the last of her tears and wiping at her eyes.

For a second he debated telling her anything else that would upset her. But he didn't have long to convince her the documentary would be honest and truthful so he waded in feet first. "Do you know the history of what happened after the hangings?"

She shook her head.

"They left the bodies here to rot, both out of fury and to serve as a warning to the man who got away. Can you imagine how awful that must have been for every living creature around here? We knew this story as kids. It was exactly the ghoulish kind of information little boys love. When Gerard was pretty young, a group of older kids tied him to this tree. Dad didn't find him until way after dark and Gerard has never really gotten over it."

"That's terrible," she said, shuddering.

"It was. And what happened a hundred years ago was a million times worse, and I am extremely sorry that your family was involved. And yet, that's what happened. That's what history is, just the past, nothing more. It's what we do with it that matters. And as compelling as the tree's story became, I have to admit it's the town that's always fascinated me. I know you need to leave the ranch very soon, but I'd like you to see the town before you go, I'd like you to imagine it alive and teeming with people and hope."

He could see the wheels turning in her head though he didn't know why they would.

"As a matter of fact, I have a little extra time," she

said carefully. "My hot water heater exploded or leaked or something. The house has to be empty for a week. Gram is in a...home."

"I'm sorry," he said. His instinct was to reach out and touch her arm or squeeze her hand, but no way was he touching her again. "Don't you need to return to Seattle?"

"I can't leave here yet," she mumbled. "I need to see this through first."

"See what through? Whether or not you oppose the making of a documentary? This isn't more important than your grandmother."

"It's dreadfully important to me...and her," Kate insisted.

He shook his head. "How can you be concerned about the reputations of two men you never met while the grandmother you love and support—"

"Don't tell me how to support my grandmother," she interrupted, her eyes suddenly flashing.

"I wasn't," he said, but he knew she was right, that's exactly what he'd done.

"You don't know my whole story," she added. "You don't know about Grandpa or the bills or what the last year has been like."

His eyebrows tilted. "There's a reason for that," he said. "You haven't told me."

She shook her head. "Please, can't you just mind your own business?"

"Sure I can. Wait, this ranch is my business. This documentary is my business."

"Why are you so obsessed with making this film?"

He started to explain but caught himself short. "Oh,

no you don't. You're switching the attention away from yourself."

She rubbed her forehead as though it hurt. His head hurt, too. How had they gotten to this point? Was he crazy? His whole reason for having her here was to convince her to see things his way. *Not* to kiss her. *Not* to follow her around. *Not* to alienate her.

They couldn't go forward until the air was clear and his gut told him it had to start with her explaining what she'd been doing with that machete and why she'd lied about her morning activities. Was there some way she knew about the gold? How was that possible when Gary had only heard that morning? But why else was she clearing brush in the forest?

But he knew she wouldn't explain herself if he asked, she'd just get sneakier. And, too, there were those few minutes of not so gallant voyeurism he'd have to explain away and he really didn't want to go there, especially now. "This is getting us nowhere," he finally grumbled.

"I know."

"Just be honest with me. Am I spinning my wheels when you've already plotted a media blitz?"

"No," she said, for once meeting his gaze straight on. He heard no equivocation in her voice. "I'm taking this more seriously than you'll ever know."

"You understand this makes no sense."

"Not to you. It does to me."

"One more thing. I will not stand by and watch my family hurt in any way. I owe them more than you'll ever know and no one gets past me to threaten them."

"Are you accusing me of wanting to hurt your family?"

"Not entirely. But damn, something is going on with you. Right?"

"No," she said firmly.

Could he trust her? Hell, no. "It's getting late," he finally grumbled. "Let's ride out to the ghost town."

"I'd like to do it tomorrow," she said.

"What?"

"Unless you have previous plans—"

"I have no plans," he said, but even he heard the sarcasm running through his voice. "Summer on a ranch is just one big vacation," he added. He shook his head and kicked at a root. "Sorry. Okay, we'll do it your way. Tomorrow morning—"

"How about the afternoon instead?"

His eyes narrowed. "Would you rather one of my brothers take you?"

"No."

"You're sure?"

"Would you rather one of them—"

"No," he admitted. "No."

"We can behave ourselves, right?" she added.

He shook his head as a reluctant smile twitched his lips. "Yeah, I guess we can," he said but all he could think of was this guy Luke. Who was he?

AS THEY LEFT the cover of the path by the stream and emerged into the main yard of the ranch house, Kate decided not to tell Frankie her real plans to go to the river. It was obvious he knew something about her didn't ring true and that heartfelt speech he'd made about protecting his family hadn't fallen on deaf ears.

If he felt she represented a threat, she'd be gone in a New York second.

"I've got some work to do before dinner," Frankie announced as they led the horses into the barn.

"I guess I'll go take a nap," she said doing her best to take the pack off the horse without struggling with its weight.

"Wait just a second," he said.

She waited as he stared at her, his mind obviously racing. He finally sighed and hitched his hands on his waist. "I pride myself on a couple of things," he said. "One of them is my ability to read people. But you fly off my radar. I'm constantly trying to figure you out. I know I messed things up this afternoon. In some ways it's really clear how I got off track but in other ways… I don't know."

How did she respond to this? He was absolutely right about her. A wave of shame washed through her stomach making her glad she hadn't eaten.

"I feel like all we do is apologize to each other," he added.

"I know," she said at last. "Listen. Tomorrow afternoon you're going to show me the ghost town and I promise to do my best to see it through your eyes. I'm going to think about what you've said about history. Maybe I overreacted about all this. At any rate, the day after tomorrow, I'll be gone and your life will go back to normal."

"You'll be gone," he repeated but his voice didn't sound as happy about that prospect as she assumed it would. "I know you don't eat a lot, but Grace plans dinner for around seven."

"I'm looking forward to it. I want to get to know your family."

His expression clearly said he was once again confused by her comment and she couldn't blame him. She fought the urge to just tell him the truth.

A few minutes later, he drove the big truck out of the yard and across the bridge. She watched it climb the road on the other side of the river until it disappeared, then she saddled a fresh horse, tied the backpack to the saddle and took off down the road toward Kinsey's house and the river beyond.

Kinsey was outside again, and if anything, she looked bigger than she had that morning. As she was cutting roses near the road, Kate slowed the horse and stopped to say hello.

"Do you know what you're having?" Kate asked.

Kinsey shook her head. "Gerard didn't want to know. I kind of hope it's a girl because of Heidi."

"Heidi?"

"Oh, I'm sorry. Heidi was Gerard's daughter with his first wife, Ann. Both of them died in an accident before Gerard and I met. I don't know, maybe it would be better to have a boy. I guess it's all academic anyway, I mean, the baby will be whatever the baby will be."

"It's very exciting," Kate said.

"I think so, too. Babies are great, aren't they?"

Kate nodded. She hadn't really thought much about babies in her life but there was no way she was going to rain on the maternal joy glowing in Kinsey's eyes. "You bet. I can hardly wait." Wanting to change the subject, she added, "I haven't met your husband yet, but everyone seems to love him."

"They have to, they're all related to him," Kinsey said with a smile. She took a sudden deep breath and put a hand on her belly.

"Are you okay?" Kate asked, immediately sliding

from the saddle and reaching out a hand. The second her feet hit the ground, her head began to spin and she stumbled. Kinsey was the one who did the steadying and they both chuckled.

"Lot of help I am," Kate said.

"You all right?"

"I haven't been eating a whole lot for the last couple of months," she explained. "My stomach...well, nerves, you know how it is."

"Come inside and let me make you something."

"Thank you, but I have a sandwich that Frankie gave me. I'll eat that. But what about you? Are you okay?"

"I've been having these contractions all day," Kinsey said. "I guess they're a warm-up for the big event. Gerard came home for lunch a while ago and I had to force him to go mow hay. Between him and my mother sharing the duties of a 24/7 baby watch, I'm going a little nuts."

"Grace said something this morning about how you're her daughter and Gerard is her stepson?"

"That's right. She's actually the reason we met. She asked Gerard to do a favor for her, he was injured while doing it, I helped him find his way home. And that's how I met Grace, Harry's new wife and the mother I never knew I had." Kinsey's eyes filled with tears and she flicked them away with her finger. "I cry at the drop of a hat."

"So do I lately," Kate admitted. "Between crying and sleeping, that's how I spend most of my free time. Frankly, it sucks."

"But it's worth it," Kinsey said.

Kate wasn't sure what she meant unless she was alluding to caring for her grandmother. Of course she was. Everyone here knew everything about everyone else.

Coming from a small family, this kind of networking seemed daunting.

"Are you off on another ride?"

"I'm going to read by the river," Kate said. "I guess I better get going."

"Have a nice time," Kinsey said and waved as Kate rode off.

These people were too nice. It made all the deception worse and Kate felt her eyes sting.

"Oh stop sniveling for heaven's sake," she lectured herself and took a deep breath. Maybe this time would be the charm—she sure hoped so.

Chapter Eight

Frankie backed his truck against a cluster of poplar trees that grew on the south side of the river, aiming to conceal it as best he could. He took the binoculars out of their case and left the cab, positioning himself where he had a clear view of the north shore, the side of the river Kate had been exploring this morning. It was the easiest way he could figure out how to see what she was up to without alerting her.

This was another place where the Bowline made a turn, much like the one he'd found her near earlier that day. Here, too, a big boulder stood close to the water's edge. He eventually picked out a trail of whacked vegetation leading back into the trees. Adjusting the glasses, he found she'd cleared a sizeable rock. Snowball, their white gelding, was tied to a nearby branch.

He turned the glasses toward the sparse woods and glimpsed Kate tangled in underbrush. It looked as though she was trying to free herself by attacking the stems low to the ground with the machete.

She finally yanked her leg free and took a deep breath. From this angle, he could see she'd created a kind of makeshift sling and wore it over her shoulder. There, resting against her back, hung a small folding shovel.

The weight and clunking sounds coming from her backpack began to make sense.

The plot thickened.

She moved off to the right and untied the horse, then leading him along the shore, disappeared around the bend. Another truck pulled up as Frankie walked back to his own.

"Car trouble?" Gerard asked through the open window.

Frankie leaned against the truck. "Nope, just birdwatching. How's Kinsey doing?"

"Still holding on." He glanced across the river and back at Frankie. "I believe your bird is leading Snowball down the beach," he said with a grin.

Frankie resisted the urge to throw himself to the ground as he turned his head to see Kate retracing her route. He could tell she hadn't seen them. Gerard picked up on his unease and both men stayed silent and still until Kate walked around another bend.

"What's going on with you?" Gerard asked.

"She's up to something."

"What?"

"I don't know. Have you heard about Pat Lowell's belief that he's on the threshold of figuring out if the stolen gold might be still buried around these parts?"

"Yeah. Word gets around. Pete Richards was helping us mow. You remember Pete?"

"Sure. He used to work summers."

"Yeah. He's helping with the mowing. You should have seen his eyes light up when Dad told us what Gary said. There's something about buried treasure, isn't there?"

"Yeah, there is." Frankie paused for a second, then went ahead and added, "Kate's searching for something."

"Are you suggesting she has advance word of the gold and thinks she knows where it is?"

"I don't know what I'm suggesting. I asked Pat to double-check her claim to be related to Earl and Samuel Bates. I'm getting some really weird vibes from her."

"From what I just saw, the girl is a knockout. You sure those vibes aren't sexual?"

"Pretty sure."

"Talk to her."

"I don't know. She's slippery. Pretty, sexy, sweet but slippery. If you ask me it's a guilty conscience. I know something about that. I recognize the symptoms."

"Frankie, take some advice from your oldest brother," Gerard said. "Just tell her exactly what you've seen and heard that alarms you." He glanced at his watch. "I need to get home to stare at Kinsey. She loves it when I do that."

This last line was delivered with a smile and a slap on Frankie's shoulder. As he drove away, Frankie's phone rang and he took it from his pocket. Pat Lowell's name glowed on the screen. Good.

It was a smaller than average group that gathered around the table for dinner. Grace talked about her pending grandchild, Harry talked about rebuilding a mile of fence over by the Bywater pasture, Kate asked seemingly disjointed questions about the changes in the Bowline River and Frankie surreptitiously watched Kate.

Why was she asking about the river? Pat Lowell's call should have been reassuring. He'd assured Frankie she was exactly who she said she was. Frankie had asked Pat if it was possible she knew something about the missing gold. Pat had laughed. "Absolutely not. That girl hasn't done anything but try to keep her grandmother from having to enter a state-run home for the past thirteen months. Before that she taught kids. I can see where her hacking around the forest seems odd, but if she's not hurting anything, I'd give her a break. She minored in science, maybe she's just curious. At any rate, I didn't find anything negative."

Frankie's thoughts returned to those around him when he caught his father's next comment. "Oh, the Bowline has changed course a lot even in my lifetime," he said, apparently in response to one of Kate's questions. "But before that, there was the flood of 1926. That washed out the riverfront part of Green Ridge—that's what the ghost town was called back in its day—and the old bridge. By then, the town was all but abandoned because of the robbery. The river itself shifted course. Rocks that had been submerged were suddenly on the beach. You know how it is. There was also a fire that took out a couple of houses, but that was before the town was even established."

Grace's phone rang halfway through the meal, and she answered it at once and listened intently before hanging up. "Kinsey and Gerard are on their way to the urgent care facility," she reported with a smile. "Oh, Frankie. I spoke to your mother today."

"Mom?" Frankie said, surprised. "Where did you see her? I didn't even know she was back in Idaho."

"I didn't see her and she's not back though she will be tomorrow evening. She lost your phone number so she called Harry and he was in the shower so I answered. She was in a rush but said you can expect her tomorrow night for a couple of hours. She wants to talk to you."

"Sure," Frankie said, meeting Kate's gaze. Man, when it rained, it poured. He wasn't sure he was up to handling the fickleness of his mother on top of the perplexity of Kate.

Grace insisted on cleaning up the table, saying she was too nervous to sit. Harry grumbled about driving down to see if the pump was working yet. Frankie asked Kate to take a walk with him.

She tried to squirm out of it but he persisted. "I'll wait for you out on the bench by the back door." He said it with enough finality that he could see her bristle. "Take a damn walk with me, will you, please?"

THERE WAS JUST about nothing on earth Kate wanted to do less than be alone with Frankie Hastings.

Well, that wasn't entirely true. Part of her craved his company. She knew very little about him but what she did know she liked. Another time, another place and she would have pulled out all the stops. Right now she knew she'd lost too many pounds except for her breasts and they seemed as full as they'd always been. Her hair needed trimming, she'd given up even minimal makeup and she desperately needed a manicure. But what was worse than her appearance was what Frankie thought of her character—she could hear it in his voice and see it in his eyes—and that was something she couldn't afford to repair.

"How is your grandmother?" he asked when she joined him on the porch.

"Seemingly content," Kate said, momentarily reliving the moment when she'd asked how much a week in that privately run home cost and been told a staggering amount. She tried not to reveal how devastating this news was. She was working hard to keep her grandmother from entering the state's care—which would require becoming a ward of the state and would mean her house would be lost. Juggling concern about her grandmother's state of mind, her health and money, too, was tricky. It required a positive outlook and that was a fight to maintain. Kate gripped the rail and faced the ever-present river running through the valley.

"Kate," Frankie said softly. "I want you to know that you're welcome to stay on this ranch as long as you like. There's plenty of room and you cost next to nothing to feed."

She smiled. "I used to eat like a horse."

"Hard to believe. Anyway, while your grandmother is being cared for, maybe you could use this time to, I don't know, relax maybe."

"I thought summer was a busy time of year for you," she said.

"It is. But you don't need me to entertain you. You're an excellent horsewoman and knowing that your long-lost relatives came from this area, it might be fun to poke around. I mean once you make a decision about what you want to do about the documentary."

"So, if I support it, I can stay—"

"No," he said, shaking his head and smiling at her. "Don't go putting words in my mouth, that's not what I meant. No matter what you decide, you're welcome to stay here. That's all I'm trying to say."

"Are you people really as kind as you seem?" she asked.

"That's a strange question. The answer, I guess, is yes, in at least as much as we're pretty much exactly what you see."

She bit her lip. He was unwittingly offering her enough time to complete her search. "I do love the Bowline River." She sighed. "Well, thank you for the offer. Let's see what happens."

They walked toward the river, pausing at a bench Frankie told her Pike built a couple of years before. "Please, sit down," he said.

She did as he asked and he took a seat next to her. The bench was relatively small so this meant he was close enough to send a wave of warmth from his body to hers and she could not deny how good it felt.

By now it was twilight. The bench overlooked the river and the bridge below. Harry Hastings had said a previous bridge washed out a few years after the robbery. Where had the original been? As there was very little on this side of the river, it must have connected to a road that led up the opposing hill.

Was it possible she was looking too far upstream and on the wrong side of the river? She almost laughed—of course it was possible. The directions had been vague, at best. She found her gaze straying toward the far shore. Though it was more or less barren directly across from the house, she could see signs of heavy vegetation in the distance. A surge of hope made her breath catch.

At last Frankie spoke. "Who was Luke?" he asked. She snapped back into the moment. He immediately backpedaled. "I'm sorry. I didn't mean to ask that. It's none of my business."

"No, it isn't," she said. "But I'd like to tell you anyway."

Chapter Nine

"Luke Beckworth was a very nice guy who rented the house across the fence from my grandparents' place."

That's where she knew she should stop talking. Right there, not a word more. But she found she couldn't stop, partly because she was so relieved he hadn't asked about something she'd have to lie about but mostly because she wanted him to know.

"After Grandpa died, like I told you, Gram just lost it. It was a...well, an overwhelming time for me, too. I'd been this happy-go-lucky woman who did well in school, got my degree and a job teaching all in the same week. I loved Arizona. I had friends, hobbies, an apartment...you know, all the usual stuff people starting off have. And then the world just all changed, not just for my poor grandmother, but for me, too. She just started to disappear."

"It sounds lonely," Frankie said.

She nodded. "It was. And that's why when Luke started talking to me, I was so glad. After a while, I knew he cared more about me than I did him, so I told him we had to slow down. I didn't want to use him. He said he knew that I didn't love him the same way he loved me, but that I might someday if I just gave it time. I knew that was wishful thinking on his part. Love can grow, sure, but there has to be a spark and I just didn't feel it.

"He knew I was struggling, that Gram's house was falling apart and that I was doing my best to get it up to code. Anyway, he knew about the bills and the promises I'd made. He knew because I told him. I should never have done that. It was selfish of me..." Her voice trailed off. She couldn't stop now, though she knew in her heart that whatever misgivings Frankie had about her were going to get a lot worse.

"And then he came up with a plan he believed would ease my immediate worries," she continued. "He left Seattle and moved to Alaska to fish the snow crab season. He didn't tell me his plan face-to-face. Instead, he left me a note. He'd said he was going to make a lot of money and save every dime and give it to me. I knew he'd fished up there before, and I knew it was really dangerous work. I called him and told him to come back, that I wouldn't take his money, but he refused. He said if I wasn't so stressed-out, I could learn to love him. I tried to make him understand stress had nothing to do with my feelings, but he couldn't or wouldn't listen to me. In the end it didn't matter because within three weeks of starting that job, he was swept off the deck of the trawler and lost in the freezing sea. I as good as killed him."

She managed to get through this story dry-eyed for the simple reason she was too exhausted to shed another tear.

Frankie took her hands. "He was a grown man, Kate. He made his own decisions. Maybe his motives were misguided, but he sounds like a decent guy. Wouldn't he hate knowing his death weighs on your conscience?"

"Probably," she whispered.

"Come here," he said and pulled her against his side, his arm around her shoulders. "Maybe he was right," he said against her hair. "Maybe without all the worries, you would have been able to love him."

"No," she murmured as she inhaled the good, clean smell of his skin. She looked up at his shadowed face. The strong jaw, the hint of a beard, the tawny brown of his tanned skin, the contrasting whites of his eyes. She knew stress didn't stop attraction—indeed, she'd seldom been more stressed than right that moment, but Frankie still managed to draw her into his orbit. His lips were very close to hers. She recalled their earlier kiss with a haunting rush of desire and maybe that memory telegraphed on her face. The next thing she knew, he had lowered his lips to hers and this time she didn't hold back.

The last man she'd kissed with passion had been Luke, and it hadn't felt like this, not ever, not even when they made love. And she knew in her head it wasn't a matter of method or body parts or anything like that—it was feelings and passion that pulsed through her veins, that sparked the fire.

Because that's what it was: fire. Her whole body seemed to burst into flames and, as the kiss evolved, she grew increasingly heated until she had to break away to take a breath, to fall back to the scorched earth.

His phone rang at that moment and as it was still in Kate's pocket, she jumped in surprise. Frankie chuckled.

"Maybe it's about Gram," she said, fumbling in her pocket. She looked at the screen but it was the wrong area code. Fear had done a good job of dousing the inferno in which she'd been engulfed, but Frankie's arm still around her shoulders felt wonderful.

"I don't recognize this number," he said as he took the phone from her hand. "I'd better answer it."

After a quick greeting, he talked for a few seconds and Kate tried not to listen, but he was too close for that.

"I see," he said. "Okay." He glanced at his watch. "I can meet you tonight. The Three Aces? Yeah, I know the joint. Say thirty minutes? Fine. See you then."

He clicked off the phone, pocketed it and kissed her forehead. "I have to go," he said. "There's someone I need to meet."

"Oh," she replied, intensely disappointed.

"Come with me."

She meant to decline. It was pretty clear to her that learning about Luke wasn't really the reason he'd asked her to take a walk, that he had another agenda and by going with him, she'd increase the opportunity he'd remember what it was. Better to refuse the invitation and go hide out in her room.

There was also another, equally compelling reason to stay behind. What in the world was the point of continuing this flirtation? But she heard herself agree to his request, and on some level understood that the point was being alive, the point was being Kate West, twenty-six-year-old woman for one more day, able to kiss a great-looking guy who made her insides flutter. There could be no other point.

She just needed to figure out why she couldn't stop spilling her guts to him!

As they drove up the main ranch road toward the highway he shot her a quick look. "You haven't even asked where we're going."

"I don't really care," she said.

"That somehow seems out of character."

"After going on and on about my sorry life—"

"Don't do that," he said gently. "Don't put yourself down. I think you're remarkable. But you have to know—we're meeting Sara, Dave Dalton's daughter."

"Oh, good," Kate said. Her heart went out to the poor woman; had she been in her place she, too, would have wanted to speak to the people who found her father's body. "Do you know what, exactly, she wants?"

"Not really," Frankie said, casting her a swift glance. "But I'm hoping she might know what it was her father was going to show me. I should warn you. The Three Aces can be a little on the raunchy side."

"It's been ages since I went into a raunchy bar," she said with a strange jolt of anticipation. "Bring it on."

THE TAVERN WAS CROWDED, noisy and dark. The air-conditioning barely functioned. Several men standing or sitting near the long, black bar greeted Frankie with slaps on the back and semiribald comments while eyeing Kate. Their gazes inevitably lingered on her breasts thanks to the snug T-shirt she'd changed into before dinner. It clung to every sumptuous curve; indeed, he'd been distracted by it all evening. He wanted to tell them to stop ogling her but that would just egg them on so he quietly led her away instead.

"Come here often?" Kate asked.

"Not anymore," Frankie said, omitting the fact that years before he'd called this place a second home and those guys at the bar his buddies. When he'd straightened out his life, he'd let destructive friendships lapse. Jay Thurman, the man he most dreaded seeing, wasn't here tonight; hopefully he was still serving time.

A solitary woman in her forties sat at a small table

nursing a glass of red wine. "Sara?" Frankie asked as they paused in front of her.

"You must be Frank Hastings," she said with a tense smile. Her eyes were red-rimmed. "Please, sit down."

Frankie introduced Kate, as the waitress showed up at their table. He turned to Kate. "What would you like?"

"Iced tea would be fine," Kate said. Frankie ordered a draft beer, and the waitress left.

"You were there, too, weren't you?" Sara asked, gazing into Kate's eyes.

"Yes. I'm so sorry for your loss."

Sara tucked a strand of short black hair behind her ear as she ran a finger around the base of her glass. There was a hard edge to her appearance and a tendency to fall short of making eye contact. Frankie could not associate her with the man he'd seen swinging from the rafters.

"I had to see you," she began, "I have to know if you've remembered anything since yesterday that might help me understand what happened to Dad."

The waitress returned with their drinks and Frankie paid her. "I can't think of anything off the top of my head," he said. He was glad she'd shown up after the ambulance left. No child should have to see a parent in her father's ultimate condition. "Can you, Kate?"

"No," she said, lifting the tall glass to her lips.

"He had so much to live for," Sara added with a slight catch to her voice and a darted look that flicked away. "He loved retirement…he loved life."

"I had a good friend in college who committed suicide," Kate said gently. "It left everyone who knew her absolutely stunned, especially her family."

"You don't understand what I'm trying to say," Sara protested. "I think someone killed my father."

Frankie had just taken a drink of frothy ale and it almost shot out of his mouth. He choked it down. "Have the police found some kind of evidence—"

"The police have insinuated I'm too upset to think clearly."

"What about the coroner?" Kate asked.

"His report says everything is consistent with a suicide."

"I take it they never found a note?" Frankie said.

"No. And that's because he didn't write one."

"I was under the impression he'd been dead for several days," Frankie said carefully. "When was the last time you spoke with him?"

"A week before the day you found him. He got off the phone when there was a knock on his door."

"Do you think that was his killer?" Kate asked, her blue eyes wide.

"I have no idea. We know what time the visitor knocked because the time and date of our call was still in his phone's memory, but we don't know who came to the door. You've been to his place, you've seen how remote the house is and how few neighbors he has...I can't find anyone who saw anything and neither can the sheriff's office. We're not positive exactly when he died."

"Can't forensics determine the time of death pretty accurately?" Kate asked.

"It was warm, the house was closed up, things...deteriorate faster. But you're right, they can get close. There just hasn't been time yet to finish all the tests."

"Did he have any enemies?" Frankie asked. "Anyone with a grudge?"

"No," she responded quickly. "I mean, he was a private guy but well respected. He drove a crane at a metal recycling plant for thirty-five years. Everyone liked him."

"So," Frankie said, striving to understand, "your conclusion that he didn't kill himself is based on a gut feeling?"

Again a direct look. "You say that like it's a bad thing, but it isn't. But that's not all. My dad was a methodical guy and he let something very important die with him. That's not like him."

"Something important? Like what?"

She paused and took another shallow breath. "I can't talk about it."

"Okay," Frankie said.

She stared at him for a second and sighed. "Oh, who am I kidding? You're not a policeman or anything, right?"

"Right," Frankie said and wondered what in the world Sara was struggling to say.

"I have to tell someone," she said. "There's no one else... My dad had something his father gave him. It should be mine now."

"What kind of thing?" Frankie asked.

She looked uncertain as she took a hasty sip of her wine.

"That's okay," Frankie said. "You don't have to tell us."

"Gold coins," she said so softly it was hard to hear her.

Frankie caught Kate's startled gaze.

"Every year or so, Dad would take some of these coins to this guy he knows in Boise who deals with things like that and he'd sell them," Sara continued. "He'd share the proceeds with me."

"Do you know where the coins came from?" Frankie asked.

"Not really, just that they'd been in the family. Dad hid them just like his father had. They came with the warning not to tell anyone about them and not to spend too many too fast because that would call unwanted attention. And then he just clammed up. I begged him to tell me where he'd stashed them in case he died or something, but he just wouldn't. Still, he wouldn't have killed himself without telling me where he put them."

"What about a safe-deposit box or—"

"He didn't have one. He didn't trust banks."

"He was going to show me something," Frankie said quietly, looking around the tavern, trying to see if any of his former pals were paying any attention to this conversation. They didn't seem to be. "That's why I went to his house yesterday. I'm doing a documentary about stolen coins from a bank robbery a hundred years ago. Your father's name came up as a descendent of a man who used to live in this town, a man named Matthew Dalton."

"He was a long-distant relative of mine, right?"

"Yeah. He moved out of Green Ridge soon after the robbery back in 1915."

"That's right, now I remember. I've forgotten a lot of the details. He was Dad's great-grandfather. I think that's what it was, anyway. I seem to recall he married a local girl. I can't remember her name. Mary, maybe. Dad could have told you more."

"We have an historian working with us," Frankie said, "so we know Matthew Dalton died five years after he left these parts. His widow was a younger woman named Mary and they had two children, a little boy named George who was born to Matthew's first wife, and a girl named Amelia who Mary gave birth to. I was hoping your dad would have additional information. See, one of the robbers got away with a bag of gold."

"Gold? In what form?"

"Coins."

She opened her mouth and closed it quickly. After a minute or so, she leaned across the table. "Are you saying that Matthew Dalton robbed a bank? That Dad's gold is from that robbery? Wasn't Matthew Dalton an attorney? That doesn't sound like a bank robber to me."

"I agree. We know his first wife died when he overturned their carriage and that was a good year before he left Green Ridge with his second wife and his infant son, George. His left leg was crushed in the accident and he lost part of it. I guess he lived in constant pain."

"He doesn't sound like a prime suspect, does he?" Kate asked.

"No," Frankie said.

"And he died impoverished," Sara added. "That's what I always heard. If he had access to gold, why wouldn't he have used it to support his family?"

Frankie shrugged. "Still, the coincidence of his great-grandson inheriting a stash of secret gold coins is pretty startling. I'd sure like to see one."

"So would I," Sara said. "I have no idea where they are. Or the letter."

"There was a letter?"

"Yeah. Written by a woman. Dad didn't tell me who she was."

"Maybe he was going to show me the letter," Frankie mused. He thought for a second before adding, "Who inherits his estate?"

"Me," Sara said.

"But why have you told us all this?" Kate said softly.

"I can't find the coins. I thought maybe you would remember something that would help me figure out who wanted him dead. I have to find out if his killer stole them."

"I'm sorry, but I can't think of anything," Frankie said.

"I figured it was a long shot," Sara said, as she looked around the room then back at him. "I had to try something."

They sat in silence for a moment before Frankie cleared his throat. "Sara, would you be willing to tell me the name of the coin dealer? He was the only other person who knew about your father's treasure, wasn't he?"

"He knew about the coins, but Dad wouldn't have shared details," she said suddenly. "Maybe he guessed, though."

"Can you tell the police what you've told us?"

"No," she said firmly. "I promised my father I wouldn't tell anyone and I'm not going to break that promise. Except I already did. I told you two."

"We're not going to blab about it," Frankie said. "If those coins are from the robbery, there's no saying who really owns them now. What if I go see this coin dealer? Maybe he still has one of the coins and I could at least examine it and maybe sound him out about your dad."

"I guess that would be okay," Sara said.

"To ease your mind a little, we've recently had news that there's a good chance the stolen gold is still buried near the old town. In that case, your coins came from somewhere else. And one more thing," he added, "If you ever find the letter, would you let me read it?"

"Yes, of course. The coin dealer's name is Ed Hoskins. That's all I know about him." She drained her glass and rose. "I have to get back. I have a funeral to plan."

Chapter Ten

"This is your night for eliciting confidences, isn't it?" Kate said as they drove over the cattle grate onto Hastings land. "First me, then Sara."

"It's been quite an evening," he said.

"What did you make of Sara's story?"

"I think she believes her father was murdered," he said, "but that doesn't mean it's true. And I have to wonder why she was willing to tell us about the gold but won't tell the police."

"Well, we have no way to take it from her," Kate said. "They could."

"We could bop her over the head or talk about it to others and one of them could go after it. Trust me, there's no lack of people in this world anxious to line their pockets with another person's treasure."

He finished that statement with a strange undertone in his voice that she was momentarily too distracted to investigate. The comment had hit a little close to home. "Fear can push people in strange directions," she finally said.

"Or guilt," he said. "Or greed. Or just plain stupidity. The list goes on."

They drove a half mile or so before Kate gestured at

a road leading off at a right angle toward the hillside. "Where do all these roads go?"

"That one goes to Pike's house," he said.

"And all the others?"

"Chance's place, equipment barns, hay storage, distant pastures, a water tank, old sheep pens, pump houses, loading gates…here and there."

Kate studied his profile as he spoke. The evening seemed to have brought them closer and that was a double-edged sword if there ever was one. "You might be an uncle by now," she said, suddenly remembering Kinsey and wondering how she was doing.

"I hope so," he said. "I adored Gerard's first daughter. Do you know about her and her mom?"

"Yes. Kinsey mentioned them this morning."

"What a tragedy. But look what he managed to rebuild for himself. You never know about life, do you?"

"I guess not," Kate said. "But sometimes it seems like nothing is ever going to change, even though in your head you know that's not true. Everything changes."

"That's why you can't give up," Frankie said and there was an odd tone to his voice.

"You sound as if you have some experience with that," she mused.

He flashed her a quick smile. "Thanks to my misspent youth. Anyway, did you know Grace is Dad's seventh wife?"

"Seven!"

"All my brothers and I have different mothers. Dad started early and until Grace came along, his love life was a revolving door. I think all four of his sons have vowed not to recreate his pattern. We've all been very careful about choosing the right people—well, they have at least, but that's my plan, as well. I'd like my kids to all have the same parents."

As an only child, Kate had never really given this much thought. From where she stood now, which was pretty much alone, having siblings looked like a wonderful thing no matter who their parents were. She suspected Frankie was very lucky that he and all his brothers had had the option to stay with their dad so they grew up in the same house.

They passed a spur off to their left with a keep-off sign dangling from a chain across the road. He drove on about twenty feet, stopped the truck and looked across the gear shift console and straight into her eyes. "You in any rush?"

A little voice in her head chanted at her not to extend her time alone with him. Like every other warning her conscious mind tried offering when it came to Frankie, she ignored it. "No," she said.

He backed up. Then he got out of the truck without saying a word, took down the chain, drove the truck through and got out to replace the chain.

Still with no explanation, they rambled along a dirt road for a while, the headlights picking up increasing signs of forestation. Kate wondered what was going on but as she was pretty sure this road paralleled the river and might actually be taking her where she planned to sneak off to by herself tomorrow, she stayed quiet and tried to decipher landmarks in the dark. When through a gap in the trees she noticed a light flashing high above the river on the opposite shore and at some distance, she gestured at it. "What's that?"

"Radio tower on top of Mt. Jinx. Mt. Jinx is the location of the old gold mine located in Green Ridge."

"Is that its real name?"

"No. People just started calling it that when two miners died in separate accidents a week apart. On the survey maps, it's referred to as Green Peak."

As he turned a curve, Kate caught a glimpse of moonlight on water flowing down below. After that, all she could discern in the headlamps was an ever thickening grove of fir trees. And when he turned off the ignition, even they disappeared.

"Let's get out," he said and she saw the whites of his teeth as he smiled.

"Okay, you've got me curious," she said as they stood together in a small clearing. Moonlight had a hard time penetrating the trees. "Why are we here? What is this place?"

He took her hand. "Follow me," he said and led her deeper into the trees along a wide trail he was obviously so familiar with he could walk it in the dark. Debris crunched under their feet. The air smelled woodsy and clean and she inhaled deeply as the cool air bathed her face. She liked the feel of Frankie's strong hand holding hers, the warmth that spread through her fingers. He finally stopped and put an arm around her.

She all but vibrated with the anticipation of the touch of his lips against hers, the desire to be in his arms, to feel his body pressed against her, his hands on her skin.

"Look up," he whispered against her forehead. In the same instant she heard a soft click, a hundred tiny lights flashed on in the trees above.

"Oh, my gosh," Kate gasped. "What's up there?"

"I'll show you," he said as he pocketed a small remote. Thanks to the lights now twinkling above, she could see a spiral ramp encircling one of the tall fir trees, leading up into the branches. Still clutching Kate's hand, Frankie started climbing and she followed.

Around and around the tree they climbed until they stepped onto a railed deck that surrounded the small building constructed using the tree as its anchor. Frankie opened a door and flicked another switch on his remote. Two hanging lantern type lamps immediately sprang to life, revealing a circular room with a roof made of varnished boards rising to a peak. The small building was set up with an efficient kitchen including a gas stove and a table with two chairs, a bed, a small chest and shelves of books. Pictures hung on the walls and a built-in desk occupied a small alcove.

"I can't believe this," Kate said looking around in wonder. "It's absolutely beautiful. Did you build it yourself?"

"Yeah," he said.

"So this is your retreat?"

"That's right. I've been working on it for years. There's a generator located downstairs but I don't use it unless I plan to spend a good amount of time here. The damn thing makes a racket and I like the peace and quiet of the forest."

As he spoke, he walked around the room and pulled on dangling cords that raised bamboo blinds over windows allowing the outside lights to shine indoors. Kate walked over to peer outside. One window turned out to be a door with a glass panel leading to a walkway covered with more lights. It traveled nine or ten feet to the trunk of another tree where it connected to the beginnings of another platform. "I'm starting stage two of the house later this summer when things slow down around here."

"How many stages do you plan on?"

"Three. Eventually, this will be the living room, the next tree over will be the kitchen, and the last will be a bedroom."

"What about the family you mentioned wanting?"

He smiled. "That's a long time away."

She looked around again. "I can't believe this place. I have a little experience pounding nails, but this is something else."

"I like construction. My brothers built their houses, as well. We all pitched in to help each other."

"Did they take part in creating this masterpiece?"

"No, this one I wanted to do alone. I'm not sure if anyone knows it's back here. I've tried to keep it private, but knowing my family, who knows? I suspect some of them might figure I'm not always off causing trouble when I disappear for a few days at a time. I haven't announced it, though. It's a little fanciful for most cowboys' taste."

"I love it," she said, looking up at the high ceiling. Between the gold of the wood and the oranges and yellows of the materials covering the floor-bound mattress, it had an *Arabian Nights* kind of feeling. Warm, she thought, like its builder. She sat down on the mattress, her arms around her bent legs.

"You look beautiful in this soft light," he said as he sat down beside her.

She smiled. "Frankie, why did you bring me here if it's your private space?"

He raised a hand and touched her hair. "I'm not sure," he said.

"Is it because I told you about Luke? Did you want to share something with me because I shared something with you?"

He studied her face for a moment. "Maybe."

She leaned toward him and touched her lips to his. "I had to do that," she said a moment later. "I've been wishing you'd kiss me since the minute we got out of your truck."

"I've wanted to," he said, "but it seemed kind of presumptuous for me to show you my house with this nice big mattress and then make a pass."

"Good point."

"There's something else I've wanted to do all night," he added.

"And what is that?"

He clicked off the lamps and the room turned into the interior of a magical, woodsy globe, the smell of fir and nature vying with his own masculine scent to drive her crazy. He raised his hands and reached around her head. The next thing she knew, he'd loosened the band that held her braid in place, releasing her heavy blond mane. He ran his fingers through the waves, bringing her hair around to fall beside her face where he smoothed it with his hands. At last he cupped her cheeks.

Staring into her eyes, he whispered, "You have the most exquisite face I've ever seen." And then he kissed her, and if she'd thought the kiss up by the house had created a firestorm, it was nothing compared to what happened this time.

She had a few seconds to think how far she was willing to let this go. She'd not had a whole bunch of lovers in her life and while she'd been fond of every one of them, none had touched her as deeply, affected her as completely. His hot breath fanned her neck as he rained kisses on her throat, and physical sensations soon overwhelmed the emotions she'd been dealing with since the moment he first said her name.

"Tell me when to stop," he whispered against her ear, and with that drew her down to lie on the bed beside him.

She'd known him only three days but his body stretched beside hers felt familiar and good. Three days though…and three miserable lying days they'd been. He thought she was one kind of woman and she knew she was another. Making love to him was not only premature but likely to lead to hurt and pain for both of them.

It took her several minutes of battling desire with willpower before she found the strength to take his hands from her breasts and hold them in hers. By then, she was half-undressed and shaking with desire. So was he. Climbing down off the tower of passion they'd built proved as treacherous as descending a mountain during avalanche season. But he seemed to understand her unspoken message and gradually their kisses grew less intense until he held her in his arms and they both lay staring up at the twinkling lights dancing across the floor and walls as the breeze outside stirred the wires that held them.

"I'm glad you're staying here longer," he whispered. "I couldn't stand it if you left tomorrow."

She peered into his eyes but didn't say a word. The truth was she felt exactly the same way.

The potential for disaster loomed like an angry grizzly, baring its teeth and growling a warning she knew she'd probably ignore.

Chapter Eleven

Frankie drove Kate back to the ranch and kissed her in the moonlight as the three ranch dogs milled about their legs. He hadn't asked her about her exploits on the river and he no longer wanted to. He didn't want to spy on her, either. If Pat Lowell said she was okay then she was okay and the thought he might distance her before he knew her well enough to establish a bond was too much to bear, especially after the last hour.

She felt like she belonged in his arms and, face it, he could not wait to consummate their relationship. After hearing about her involvement with Luke, however, he could see where he would need to be patient.

Patience had never really been one of his virtues; on the other hand, he had learned a little restraint and he'd also learned that acting rashly could have dire consequences. And when exactly was he going to share his past with her?

Later, he decided. Not tonight. Tonight was his to tuck away. It was a beginning, he could feel it in his bones. There was something unique and special about Kate.

He said good-night to her at the door and that felt weird. "You're not coming in?" she asked.

"No. I'm going back to the tree."

"Why?"

"I'll dream better there," he said and laughed at how silly it sounded. "Truth is I don't trust myself to sleep in the same house with you."

KATE FOUND LILY standing in front of the stove dressed in a robe and slippers. Lily gestured at the small saucepan on the burner. "My mom swore warm milk helped her sleep. Time to put it to the test."

"You're having trouble sleeping?" Kate asked.

"Yeah. Kinsey is still at the hospital. I haven't heard anything for an hour or two."

"I've heard labor can last a long time," Kate said.

"I know. I just have a special place in my heart for Kinsey and Gerard and I want everything to be perfect for them."

"Frankie said you and Chance are engaged."

"Yes," Lily said with a smile as she poured the steaming milk into a mug. "Have you met him yet?"

"No. I haven't met him or Gerard. Are they a lot like Frankie?"

"Not really. For four men raised in the same house, they all have their differences. Frankie and Chance were the hellions when they were younger. But they turned out really well. You never know."

Kate laughed. "I guess so."

Lily's voice grew soft. "Charlie is just crazy about Chance. And Chance is fabulous with Charlie. We're getting married in September and neither one of us can wait to have another child. When I look at where my life was a year ago and where it is now—well, I owe it all to Chance and the Hastings family."

"You're happy," Kate said.

"Yes." Lily tasted her cup of milk and made a face. "Bleech!"

"My grandmother likes warm milk, too," Kate said. "It never did much for me."

"I know how to fix it," Lily said, and took a bottle of chocolate syrup out of the fridge. She squeezed in a dollop and stirred. "Better," she said after a sip. "Okay, I'll try again. 'Night."

"Good night," Kate said but she stood there in the darkened room for a few moments. Why was she suddenly so anxious? Had some of Lily's concerns about Kinsey rubbed off?

Maybe her tightly stretched nerves had more to do with concerns about her own tumultuous life and talk about grandmothers than it did any real fear for Kinsey. Kate picked the phone off the counter and called Seattle. Pine Hill assured her Gram was asleep.

Kate walked back to the little bedroom and sat on the bed. Her backpack was in the closet, out of sight, but she could feel it calling, reminding her tomorrow was a new day, and she had another stretch of river to search.

She wanted the comfort of Frankie's arms and cursed herself for running away from him tonight. She wanted to be beside him in his bed. She wanted his warmth and strength to push everything else away.

Was that using him? Was she falling into the same trap she'd fallen into with Luke? Was she comforting herself at someone else's expense?

The questions had no direct answers but she suspected comparing her feelings for these two men was as useless as comparing the men. They were different people with different qualities. Luke had offered uncomplicated comfort, at least at first. Frankie did not. He was as stim-

ulating as he was relaxing, just as scary as compassion-
ate. And so sexy that even thinking about him made her
steaming hot.

Would he welcome her back?

There was one way to find out.

She left the house and walked toward the barn. The
dogs kept her company as she saddled a horse, the red
one again, and took off. She rode over the moonlit bridge
and down the main road until she reached the chain and
the Keep Out sign. Leaving it in place, she maneuvered
the mare around the post that supported one end of the
chain and trotted down the road.

She found the clearing and got off the horse, leading
her down the path a few steps but stopping short when
she smelled cigarette smoke.

Did Frankie smoke? She'd inhaled his scent many
times that evening and without exception had found it
as clean and refreshing as running water. He must have
a visitor, but it surprised her he would allow someone to
smoke that close to the tree that held his home.

She stayed where she was, unsure what to do, listening for voices. Meeting someone out here was totally unexpected but how could she say that? She was
the stranger around these parts. This could be one of
Frankie's brothers or his father. Did she want them knowing she had come to pay a midnight visit?

Nope.

But how did they get here? There'd been no vehicle
where Frankie parked. More to the point, how did she
get away without them hearing her and the horse move?
A minute later, she heard a deep cough and she peered
through the underbrush to glimpse the dark shape of
a man twice as bulky as Frankie. He coughed into his

hand again—a smoker's cough—then swore. The shape lumbered toward her, heavy steps breaking twigs on the forest floor. Her heart lodged in her throat and she willed the horse to stay silent. A car door opened, which shocked the shoes off her—she hadn't anticipated anyone would drive on the path.

The interior lights illuminated the pale, jowly face of a man in his midthirties. He heaved his bulk into the car and closed the door.

She immediately moved off the path.

The only Hastings brothers she hadn't met were Chance and Gerard and if that man was either one of them, she'd eat her saddle. All the Hastings men she'd seen were tall and fit, bronzed and honed by hard work. They all bore more than passing similarities. But this guy, so briefly glimpsed, had left a lasting impression of pasty skin and a shifty tilt to his eyes. It appeared he hadn't shaved in days.

She heard the car start but the headlights did not go on. The path must be a lot wider than she'd thought when she walked it in the dark with Frankie. For a second, she wondered why he hadn't driven all the way in to the tree, but then she thought she knew. Approaching it on foot, holding hands…it had enhanced the magic and the thrill of discovery. It had been a gift and she smiled with the warmth of the memory.

Lights still off, the car moved closer to Frankie's tree until she heard the creak of brakes. A flash of illumination announced the driver had once again gotten out. A moment later, headlights and engine noises came from behind her. Someone else was coming. She pulled the horse off the path and a second later, Frankie's truck passed her by—he was home and the mere fact he'd arrived calmed her.

But why in the world was Frankie meeting someone in this way? He'd made it sound like his home was a sanctuary, a secret even, and yet here was this man, waiting for him in the dark. The only thing that made sense to her was that Frankie didn't know what was coming and that made her anxious.

Good sense demanded she turn around right that moment and head back to the barn. But good sense couldn't battle the powerful pull of curiosity or her growing unease. When she heard Frankie's engine turn off, she tied the horse to a branch and sneaked forward on her own.

"About time you got back," a low, gruff voice boomed.

"Who's there?" Frankie demanded. The small lights in the tree flashed on and she heard Frankie's sharp intake of breath. "Jay? Jay Thurman?"

"In the flesh, buddy."

"Are you smoking?"

"So what if I am."

Kate had adjusted herself to see through the branches. "This is a damn forest, you idiot," Frankie said as he grabbed the cigarette from Jay's mouth and stubbed it out with his boot. "I thought you were still doing time," he added.

Jay's laugh held no mirth. "What would you know about doing time? You're the golden boy with the rich father and the Get Out of Jail Free card. You sold me right smack down the river. I got out a week ago and, funny thing, all I could think about was renewing our… friendship."

"We were never friends," Frankie scoffed. "You used me."

"We used each other. But I paid the whole bill and you got off scot-free."

"I didn't get off scot-free," Frankie said, his voice low now. She could hear the anger boiling underneath the words.

"I figure you owe me," Jay continued.

"How did you find this place?" Frankie demanded.

"I've been hanging out at The Three Aces every night. I knew you'd show up eventually and tonight was the night. I followed you back here. You were so struck on that little gal, you didn't even notice. You two looked mighty cozy up there on that nice, soft bed. It's been a while since I had a woman. Maybe I could borrow her."

"Get out of here," Frankie said. "And don't talk about her again."

"Touchy, touchy. But I ain't going nowhere."

"Get on with it, Jay. What do you want?"

There was a long pause before Jay spoke again. "I wonder how your old man would feel about you if he knew the truth."

"If that's all you've got to say—"

"No, that's not all. I've got a proposition."

"What kind of proposition?"

"Not here, not now," Jay said after a minute.

"Then when and where?"

"Tomorrow night at The Three Aces. Ten o'clock. That'll give you time to imagine the fallout if I'm... forced...to speak my mind. I'd show up if I were you."

"Just get out of here."

Jay laughed. "Sure, boss. Anything you say."

Kate heard the car door again, then the engine gunned and the car lurched backward. She kneeled down in the bushes and hoped the man didn't look forward until her horse was out of sight. She didn't take a deep breath until she heard the car screech and groan and eventually speed away.

She lifted a foot, every instinct in her body urging her to run to Frankie, to offer support to ask what all this meant.

He'd disappeared from view, but seconds later she heard a muffled oath and then footfalls as he climbed the ramp.

How could she ask for an explanation? Couldn't he demand the same thing from her? She waited until the slam of the door in the tree high above her rang in the night air, then she turned and trotted back to the mare.

Who was Jay Thurman and what truth did Frankie fear him exposing?

Chapter Twelve

To Frankie's surprise, Grace was back in the kitchen when he arrived at five in the morning. His dad was at the table tucking into bacon and eggs.

"Can I make you a plate?" Grace asked him.

"No thanks," he said and realized at once how impatient he sounded. He showed her the thermos. "I came to bum some coffee to take out to the combine."

"Of course," she said.

"Where'd you spend the night?" Harry asked.

"I've asked you not to ask me that," Frankie said.

His father laughed. "It's okay, I was young once, too."

Frankie knew what his father assumed and he ignored the wink that went with the comment. Instead he addressed Grace. "Do we have a baby yet?"

"No," she replied as she handed him the full thermos. "Kinsey came home in the wee hours of the morning. No baby. They said it was false labor. Surely it can't go on much longer, can it? She was due over a week ago."

"You were a nurse," Frankie said. "I daresay you know a lot more about this than I do." His gaze traveled down the hall toward the back of the house.

"She's not up yet," Grace said.

He was on the verge of asking Grace what she meant,

but he stopped himself from acting the idiot. "Will you tell her I'll be back at noon so we can ride out to see the ghost town?"

"You still haven't made it there? Isn't she leaving early tomorrow morning?"

"I don't think so. Her house flooded and her grandmother is in a home for a week so she has a little extra time here. I assume that's okay?"

"Of course it is," Grace said. "The girl is no problem at all."

"Kind of a loner, isn't she?" Frankie's father said.

Frankie shrugged. "Kind of. Thanks for the coffee," he told them and left the house, disappointed not to have even glimpsed Kate and yet relieved, too.

The conversation—if that's what last night's discussion with Jay Thurman could be called—had peppered his sleep with random dreams. And when he'd woken up, as he had off and on all night, every noise became Jay coming back to taunt him...or worse. The fact he'd seen Kate with Frankie was worrisome, as well. He didn't want that animal anywhere near her.

How ironic that the one man in the world he least wanted to know his exact location now knew it. How had he driven home without noticing he was being tailed? The main road was easy to explain...there had been traffic last night and he'd been full of thoughts about Sara's conviction her father was killed and the information about those mysterious gold coins. A tail was the last thing on his mind. You would have thought he would have spotted Jay's car once they got to the ranch, though, but by then he and Kate were talking and Jay must have switched off his headlights. Somehow he'd seen Frankie use the turn-off and from what he said, he'd even looked through a window.

That was a sobering thought.

Jay was a loose cannon, a wild, impetuous man with a violent temper and a mean streak a mile wide. Tonight had vanquished any hope he might have changed.

Frankie had been a fool to get involved with him ten years before. As it was, the experience had taught him some hard life lessons, but those had come with his father's loss of respect, which Frankie had worked years to reestablish. He felt he finally had it—the thought Jay could ruin this made his gut twist. And it wouldn't be just his father, either—his brothers, the women who lived on the ranch and now, Kate, too.

Secrets could start out innocent or self-serving, but so many of them grew exponentially in the dark recesses of their habitats, exacting a high price in the end. Jay's silence was also going to cost—Frankie didn't know how much, but he knew money would be involved. He hoped he had enough to satisfy the guy. No way was he borrowing from family or friends. And how did you take a loan from a bank to cover blackmail?

KATE MET FRANKIE at noon. He seemed distracted but maybe that was just the spin she put on his curt manner since she knew what had happened the night before. She looked deep into his gray eyes and for the first time since she'd met him, he broke the connection.

It wasn't her imagination.

They rode in silence, which was okay with Kate as she'd spent the morning searching the shoreline of the river on the southwestern side of the current bridge and had a lot to think about. She'd been told that the site she sought existed within a mile of that bridge. She'd pretty much exhausted possibilities northeast of there, but then she groaned. She hadn't looked on the southeast side of the river because she'd had things turned around in her head. It suddenly seemed a daunting task. Everything would need to be repeated on the opposite shore and farther west. She wished she could confide in Frankie and ask for help.

A dozen times that afternoon, the words almost left her lips but she always swallowed them whole.

The ghost town turned out to be fascinating in its own way and she wished they'd come before Frankie's mood took a nosedive. She could see why it fascinated him. He told her why some of the buildings were burned—the fire that had killed Lily's husband was responsible for that. He also pointed out the collapsed roof of another building—that's where Gerard's first wife and daughter died.

"This place really is filled with ghosts," she said as they walked down the street.

"That's the bank," he said, pointing at a faded building on the corner whose top floor seemed to have fallen in on itself.

"Are all the original buildings here?"

"No. Some were private homes that disappeared a long time ago."

She looked around. The structures on the main street seemed to huddle together to support each other like a very old, very feeble family who had fallen on hard times.

"The place is too decrepit and too structurally damaged to repair," he continued. "After we shoot this documentary, we're going to raze it. It presents too much of a hazard and probably should have been done decades ago."

"I'm beginning to see why it captures your imagination," she told him as they wound up at the old mine. A new-looking barrier appeared to be bolted over the entrance.

"I can see people walking these streets," he said. "I can imagine them going to the mercantile and the bank. The saloon must have been hopping on paydays. People lived and died, loved and laughed, cried and longed for better days, all right here on these streets, inside these buildings."

She loved it when he talked this way and looked up at him. They'd shared a special hour together the night before but it was over. She couldn't help feeling a piercing stab of regret.

"So what do you think?" he asked as they walked back down the street.

She longed to assure him she wouldn't stand in the way of the documentary. Eventually, he would probably discover their historian had been wrong about her claims and wow, would he detest her then. As if to protect herself a little longer, she wanted his approval now, she wanted to see him smile, to be happy.

But in his current state, might not the news that he needn't worry about her trying to stop the film cause him to hasten her on her way? She had a gut feeling that despite earlier blunders, she would find the spot she sought and uncover the treasure that would help her fulfill her promise to her grandfather. She couldn't take that risk.

"I'll have an answer for you by tomorrow night," she said.

He stopped dead in his tracks and stared down at her.

She could tell his bad mood was pushing him over the top. "Frankie—"

"You just like keeping me on the hook, don't you?"

"No, I—"

"After last night, I'd think you'd care more about… this."

"Last night?" she said. "Is that why you took me to your tree house? Is that why you kissed me?"

"You kissed me first," he said.

"No, you kissed me when we sat on the bench."

"Yeah," he said. "That's right, when we sat by the river. The river you can't take your eyes off. The river that fascinates you to the point—" He bit off his own words and stared at her, then he grabbed her upper arms and pulled her to him. His kiss was provoking in a way that pushed blood through her body like a fire hose. After an all-encompassing second or two, she pulled herself together, broke their connection and raised her hand to slap him.

He caught her wrist. "Come off it," he said.

"I never would have thought this of you," she whispered.

"That's because you don't know me."

"I thought I did."

"In three days? That's enough time to know you're hot for someone, not enough to…"

"To what?"

"To…care."

"Man, you are all over the map, aren't you? What's going on?"

"Nothing," he said. "Maybe you'd like to tell me what's going on with you. Why you lug that backpack around and why—"

His ringing phone cut him off midsentence.

"Yeah," he barked into the phone, listened a minute and shook his head. When he spoke again, he'd modified his voice. "Thanks for calling me back, Mr. Hoskins. I'd like to talk to you about gold coins. May I make an appointment to visit your store?"

That had to be Dave Dalton's coin-dealing contact. At least Frankie could talk civil to a stranger. The thought seemed to telegraph to his head from hers and he turned his back on her and stepped away.

"Your place is in Boise, right?

"Oh, I see. May I ask where?" He paused as if listening to another question.

"It's important," he said as though Hoskins was dragging his feet. "No, sir, today would be better." Silence continued and then Frankie took a deep breath. "That's great. No, actually, that's closer than Boise. In about two hours? Thanks." He switched off the phone. When he turned around to face Kate, he all but winced.

"Kate—"

"I gather Mr. Hoskins will talk to you?"

"Thank goodness he called."

"That coin is really important to you, isn't it?"

"Yes, but that's not why I'm thankful. It stopped me from making more of a jerk of myself. I need to apologize for my behavior."

"Let's just forget it, okay?" she said. He'd been getting awfully close to uncomfortable territory when the call came. She was not anxious to resume their conversation.

He stepped closer to her. "I don't have any excuses to offer," he said. "I wouldn't blame you if you left right now and started the biggest internet campaign the world has ever seen. All I can tell you is that I have another issue that's making me nuts and I took everything out on you."

"I understand," she said, wishing with all her heart they could just speak the things that needed to be said. He leaned down and kissed her forehead. "I did not take you home last night to seduce you in order to get your cooperation with the documentary. I don't expect you to believe me—"

"But I do believe you," she said. "Or at least I want to."

"I don't need a reason to try to seduce you," he said as his fingers brushed against her face. "The fact is I'm crazy about you. I know it sounds nuts."

She didn't trust herself to speak. Her throat had closed off for a second and her heart drummed against her ribs. He was crazy about her—the feeling was mutual.

"I wish we'd met under different circumstances," he continued. "At a different time in both of our lives."

"I do, too," she said and stepped into his arms. He kissed her gently as though in apology for his earlier effort and she closed her eyes. For several moments, they stood together in the middle of the old town. If the ghosts lurked nearby, they at least had the decency to remain hidden.

"Let's just get through the next day," she said. "Then we'll go back to our regular lives and maybe someday—"

"Someday?"

"When things are better, when we're, well, free. Or at least when I'm free. I know you are now except for the documentary…" She stopped talking because his eyebrows had arched and she realized she was rambling.

"Do you want to come with me to see Hoskins?"

Of course she did. "No," she finally muttered. "I really am exhausted."

He cupped her face, stared into her eyes and smiled. "Maybe a walk by the river would help you relax."

"Maybe so," she said, doing her best not to read too much into his words, but that smile…no, he didn't know exactly what she was up to but he wasn't an idiot and she hadn't exactly been subtle. The day after tomorrow, she'd be gone. This would all be over, and he would be a fond memory and nothing more and what he thought of her wouldn't matter. The important thing was that no one would ever know what she found—if she found it.

Although they chatted a little on the way back to the ranch, it was almost a relief when Frankie drove off the ranch and she could return to the river. This afternoon she would rule out the south side across from the area where she'd searched the day before. The shore there wasn't wooded, but so much time had passed, nothing could be taken for granted. And then tomorrow, she'd start in on the riverfront down the hill from Frankie's tree.

Time was running out.

Chapter Thirteen

Ed Hoskins lived almost as much in the middle of nowhere as Frankie did. His property was heavily fenced— actually more like barricaded. An electronic gate was accompanied with an intercom while two security cameras focused on the driveway. Frankie flipped a button on the intercom and a moment later, the voice he recognized from the phone came on the line.

"Is that you, Mr. Hastings?" the man said.

"It is."

"Are you armed?"

"No, sir, I'm not. Should I be?"

Hoskins chuckled. "I'll buzz you through."

For all the security, the house itself was a modest brick structure with a steep tin roof and iron grills over all the windows. Hoskins opened the door before Frankie could turn off the engine. He scanned the yard as though checking to make sure no one had come through the gate on Frankie's heels.

"May I see identification?" Hoskins asked when Frankie reached the door.

Frankie took out his wallet and handed it to Hoskins who made a point of studying Frankie's picture. As he did that, Frankie perused Hoskins. He found a short, plump guy with a flamboyant black mustache several shades darker than the gray ringing his head. Bushy eyebrows settled on top of wire-framed glasses. A pair of jaunty red suspenders kept his slacks from slipping down under his round belly.

"Come inside," Hoskins said and made a last hasty search of the fenced yard before closing the door and sliding home the dead bolt.

All this security remained a mystery to Frankie as he noted the details of the sparsely outfitted room: two chairs flanking a gas fireplace, television, area rug, stereo and a bookcase. Through an open arch he could see a small utility kitchen. A narrow door opened off the opposite wall but it was closed.

"You've got this place set up like Fort Knox," Frankie commented.

Hoskins chuckled again. "I like feeling safe."

"Is your store in Boise equally secure?"

"Of course," he said. He gestured at a set of wing back chairs. "Have a seat," he said and settled into one himself. Frankie sat down, as well. "Now tell me, what kind of gold coin are you looking for?"

Frankie took a deep breath, sat forward a little and planted his hands on his bent knees. He hadn't mentioned Dalton's name on the phone lest he scare Hoskins off but there was no reason to pussyfoot around it now. "I'm looking for a coin like those Dave Dalton sold you."

"Dave Dalton?" Hoskins mused as though trying to place the name.

"Dave is dead," Frankie added.

The bushy eyebrows bunched together. "How unfortunate for the poor man. Might I ask how he died?"

"The police are calling it suicide. His daughter thinks

he was murdered and we're both wondering if his stash of gold coins is the reason."

Hoskins stared at him for a moment before saying, "Why aren't the police talking to me?"

"Because his daughter doesn't want to reveal the existence of the coins to authorities."

"Why are you here, then?"

Frankie explained about the 1915 robbery and his determination to record the events on film before what remained of the ghost town disappeared forever.

"I know about the robbery, of course," Hoskins said. "To my knowledge, the gold was never recovered. I didn't know about the documentary. Fascinating."

"There's reason to believe most or all of the robbery loot is still buried on or near our family's ranch. We'll know soon."

"Then why do you wish to discuss this coin?"

Frankie explained about Dalton's connection to the town. "It strikes me as awfully coincidental. All I really need to know is what kind of coin it is and when and where it was minted. I can't prove a thing about who it belongs to. That's not my interest. But if we find the rest of the coins and this one is similar it raises additional questions. Dalton's daughter should be aware of that possibility. If the coins Dalton sold you were minted after the robbery, then this avenue of speculation could be closed."

Hoskins still hadn't admitted any involvement and Frankie was beginning to think he never would. Was it possible Dalton had misled his daughter to protect the true identity of his real contact?

"You had a run-in with the law," Hoskins said with one raised eyebrow.

Frankie was snapped from his thoughts. "A long time ago," he said.

"Thanks to the information age nothing is a long time ago anymore. It's still a matter of public record and information about it appears when your name is entered into a search engine."

"I did community service," Frankie said quietly. For years he hadn't dwelled on the idiocy of his youth and no one had mentioned it. Now, twice within a twenty-four-hour period, it was back. Maybe he needed to work on his karma. "I didn't actually go to jail," he added.

"Hmm." Hoskins steepled his fingers and held them against his lips as he stared into Frankie's eyes. "It would seem you've mended your ways," he said.

"I have sincerely attempted to do just that," Frankie said. "Why are you bringing this up? What's it to you? If you didn't know Dalton, it doesn't matter. If you did, I am merely asking you to tell me about the coin."

Hoskins narrowed his eyes, then dropped his hands to clasp the armrests of his chair. "You know what, young man? I like you."

This guy was just full of surprises. Frankie nodded. He could feel a *"but"* coming.

"Yep. You remind me of my little brother, Johnny. He was the youngest of four kids, just as you are."

"The internet mentioned that, too?"

"Isn't that thing great? But my point is Johnny started out a little rough around the edges just as you did, and now he's a tenured professor at Berkeley. Sometimes the youngest in a household of boys has to work hard to stand out. Sometimes, the way they stand out becomes... problematic. But he turned himself around and I believe you have, as well."

Frankie, damn near speechless, mumbled his thanks. What the heck?

"Come with me," Hoskins added.

He sprang to his feet and walked nimbly across the room to unlock and throw open the small door Frankie had noticed upon arriving.

They entered an unexpectedly opulent office with plush carpets, rich wood furniture, beautiful paintings, sleek computers and even a floor-to-ceiling antique wooden wine rack set into a far wall. Hoskins walked past the desk to the wine rack. Frankie expected the older man to pop out a bottle for them to celebrate... well, what? The fact that Johnny Hoskins had straightened out his life?

Instead, Hoskins dug in his pocket and withdrew a medallion shaped like a bunch of grapes with a couple of leaves. It matched an embossed decoration on the shelves. He inserted the ornament in the bookcase, pushed it with one finger and the whole unit pivoted on its axis.

Hoskins repocketed the medallion, reached inside and flipped on a light illuminating a flight of descending stairs. "Come along," he called to Frankie who sidled past him into the steep stairwell. When he glanced over his shoulder, he saw that Hoskins had silently closed the wine rack/door behind them and followed.

The stairs led to a cellar now ablaze with lights. There were no windows, nothing to advertise its existence aboveground. The brick walls were lined with charts, degrees, framed newspaper articles, some yellowed and old. What looked like a digital magnifier occupied a table while box upon box of presentation cases had been inserted into slots built into shelves made specifically for this purpose. All appeared to be carefully labeled.

"Of course I knew Dave," Hoskins said, sitting in a swivel chair behind a pile of other equipment including ultraviolet lamps, mint sheet albums and a coin scale. He motioned for Frankie to take a seat. "I can't help you when it comes to his death except to say the man seemed very content and happy. But one never knows. Money can't buy peace."

His words, spoken in one context, struck Frankie in another. He was banking on the fact Jay Thurman could be bought off, but for how long? It wasn't a permanent fix. What was? Maybe a nice big truck running over the oaf? Hey, a man could dream.

"This is quite a setup," Frankie commented.

"It's the heart of my business," Hoskins said. "The Boise address is my public face." He steepled his fingers again and peered at Frankie. "I knew Dave had a bunch of these coins and I was only too happy to get my hands on them," he finally said. "He kept his fortune private out of concern about theft, but mostly because he couldn't explain where he got them or how, and didn't want the government getting involved and demanding their share. That's about the extent of what he confided to me. I, too, am cautious or have been until now. You know the truth about me. What you choose to do with it I suppose is up to you."

"I'm not interested in trying to solve the mystery of Dalton's coins unless they somehow tie in to the robbery and I just don't see how they do. Will you tell me about the coins now?"

"I'll do better than that," Hoskins said and, taking a key from around his neck, unlocked a file drawer from

which he withdrew a ring of keys. He selected one of
these and inserted it in his desk drawer. A second later,
he produced a small display case that held a single gold
coin.

"This is the only one I have left," Hoskins said. "It's a
1904 Liberty, US Mint Gold Double Eagle, worth twenty
dollars at the time. This one is uncirculated although
some of his coins showed modest signs of wear."

"What did you pay for it?"

"I gave him fifteen hundred for this one. I have a
buyer interested for twice that. And as you know, the
coins stolen from the Green Ridge Bank were exactly
this mint."

"Did he ever give any indication how many there
were?"

"Dave could be cagey. I might not have been the only
one he dealt with. I got the feeling there were a lot of
coins, maybe hundreds. If they did come from the Green
Ridge bank robbery, they must have been hidden away.
It seems unlikely there would be any left if they'd been
dipped into over all the intervening years—to me, it
seems they must have been recovered within the last
few years."

"One more thing," Frankie said. "Did Dalton ever
mention the existence of a letter that came along with
the coins?"

"A letter? No, not a word. What kind of letter?"

"I don't think anyone knows," Frankie said.

Hoskins handed the small display case to Frankie
who studied the tiny embossed stars encircling Lady
Liberty's head. The coin didn't answer any questions;
in fact, it posed others. He handed the display case back
to Hoskins and thanked him.

Hoskins locked the coin back in his drawer. Ten minutes later, Frankie was back in his truck where he placed a call to Sara.

"I don't think Ed Hoskins had a thing to do with your dad's death," he said once she'd answered. "He admits he bought the coins. As I was leaving, he made a point of telling me to tell you that he would be delighted to discuss buying any you'd care to liquidate."

"Is he a trustworthy guy?"

"Within reason," Frankie said thinking neither Sara nor Hoskins were going to win any awards for honesty when it came to the disposition of those coins.

As soon as he hit the open highway, his thoughts leaped past the impending visit with his mother to the ten o'clock appointment with Jay Thurman.

KATE WAS BACK on the bench in front of the river when Frankie drove into the area between the house and barn. She couldn't deny her heart lifted at the sight of his truck and she got to her feet, wincing as her knee throbbed. She'd taken a tumble late in the afternoon as she attempted to climb a promising rock in her seemingly endless search.

Between the unsuccessful morning riverside excursion and the two later in the day—to say nothing of the ride to the ghost town—it had been a full day. Back in Seattle, she spent her time tending her grandmother and trying to fix up the house. Those chores took physical as well as mental strength, but the muscles engaged were not the ones required to walk and climb and descend rocky cliffs or ride horses. The end result was that she was acquiring a broadening collection of aches and pains.

And that didn't even begin to address the newest wrinkle: worry about Frankie. She didn't know what he was hiding but it sounded serious. Jay Thurman was dangerous, hence, Frankie was in trouble. It didn't sound as though he was going to allow anyone to watch his back and that scared her.

She needed to wangle an invitation to go with him.

Frankie smiled and paused when he noticed Kate coming toward him and some of the awkwardness with which they'd parted earlier dissipated. "Are you limping?" he asked, eyebrows furled.

"Just a little. Did you learn anything from Mr. Hoskins?"

"Yes and no," he said, peering down at her face. His gray eyes were as beautiful as ever, but she could see worry lurking in their depths. "Hoskins bought Dalton's coins," Frankie continued. "He even showed me one. Beautiful thing. He said most he saw were uncirculated. That fits in with what we know of the payroll shipment that was stolen. But as for any leads on Dalton's death—he doesn't know any more than you and I do. I think if Sara is convinced her father was murdered she's going to have to tell the police and chance losing the treasure. They can't investigate if they don't have a reason to suspect anything."

"But she promised her father," Kate said softly.

"A promise to a dead man? Does that take precedence over everything else?"

And that was a good—if uncomfortable—question. Kate had no intention of thinking about it right now, however, let alone trying to answer.

"What did you do this afternoon?" he asked. He glanced down at the tear in her jeans and then back at her face, using a finger to gently turn her head so her cheek was toward him. "You have scratches. Are you okay?"

"I fell."

"By the river?"

"Yes, as a matter of fact, by the river."

"Are you sure you're all right? Grace used to be a nurse."

"I don't need a nurse," she said breezily. "Besides, Grace and your dad are back at the hospital with Gerard and Kinsey. She's in labor again."

"Man, I hope it works out this time. All these stops and starts make me nervous," Frankie said.

She touched his hand. "What are you doing later? Could we get together?"

"Mom should be here any minute. I'd better figure out something for dinner."

He'd completely ignored her question. "I forgot to tell you that Grace left some kind of chicken dish in the slow cooker."

"That was nice of her," he said, but his attention had been drawn to a car now crossing the bridge. "That'll be my mother," he said, and they walked to the parking area, arriving about the same time as the car. The driver turned out to be a wispy blonde wearing jeans and a white shirt. As soon as she got out of the car, she took Frankie's hands and beamed up at him.

Kate stared at her in a little bit of disbelief. It was obvious she was Frankie's mother but at first glance, she appeared more like his sister. They shared the same gray eyes and high cheekbones. Features that looked masculine on him somehow looked ultra-feminine on her.

After a brief hug, she stretched her arms above her

head. "I am so stiff from driving. I can't believe I have to turn around and leave in an hour."

"Just an hour?" Frankie said.

"Yes. I'm meeting a friend in Boise at ten o'clock for a séance."

Ten o'clock. The time hung there for a second and then Frankie spoke. "Mom, this is Kate," he said. "Kate, my mother, Vivian."

"How nice to meet you," Vivian said, shaking Kate's hand. Vivian had to be close to fifty, but time had treated her well. Her skin showed no trace of makeup and was relatively unlined.

"Frankie, dear, what's wrong?" Vivian said as she studied him.

"Nothing," Frankie said uneasily.

"Your shoulders are full of tension," she said. "And your eyes…"

"It's been a long day, that's all," Frankie said, glancing down at Kate. How many times since she'd arrived on this ranch had she found herself in his exact position, caught between an unspoken truth and a reluctant lie of omission? Part of her knew she should be relieved it was him under scrutiny instead of her, but all she felt was sorry that she couldn't share his burden.

Vivian looked unconvinced. "I met a mystic in India this winter. He guided me on a spiritual journey inside my subconscious. I'm very sensitive to everything now, especially my one and only son."

"Let's go inside and have a bite to eat," he said.

"Oh, no, no thank you," she said. "I've gone vegan and I try to never impose my eating preferences on others. That's why I had a fruit smoothie in Falls Bluff. You two go ahead…"

Both Frankie and Kate said the same thing at the same moment. "I'm not really hungry," they broke off and smiled at each other.

"I only have a little while and there's something I want to talk to you about."

"I should leave you two alone," Kate mumbled.

"That isn't necessary," Vivian said with a smile. "I'm sure Frankie won't want to keep things from his girl-friend."

Both Frankie and Kate jumped in with denials that Vivian more or less ignored. "Is the old arbor still standing?" she asked.

"Yeah," Frankie said. "Let's go sit down." He led them to the front of the house to an area Kate hadn't noticed as it was shielded by the house itself and a lot of trees. The patio sported a brick floor and a wrought-iron table and chairs covered with a slatted roof. It reminded Kate at once of Frankie's tree house. A wall of climbing roses perfumed the evening air.

"I've always loved this spot," Vivian said as she took a chair and looked around. "It hasn't changed much in thirty years, has it? The roses are a nice touch, though."

As soon as the others were seated, she leaned forward. "Frankie, dear, do you remember how you were always asking me about my side of the family?"

"Yes, of course I do," he said. "You never had much to tell me."

"I know. My mother didn't talk much."

"Then you don't remember any more?"

"We'll get to that. First of all, I heard from a man who says he works with you and someone named Gary."

"Gary Dodge. Yeah, he's the producer of the documentary I wrote you about. Who contacted you?"

"He said his name was Pat."

"Pat Lowell," Frankie said.

"That's right. He said he's doing some background type work."

"Yeah, on the old ghost town."

"Well, he told me that he's uncovered proof that my grandmother lived in Green Ridge until 1915 when she moved away."

"The year the town started to die," Frankie said. "Wait a second... Dad told me you were looking for someone back when you guys met. Did you suspect you might be related to someone from the ghost town?"

"Yes. Well, kind of. My great-aunt had mentioned my grandmother just once or twice. Her name was Mamie. I was told she'd lived in Green Ridge way back when and at first I thought I'd see if I could find out anything about her. Great Aunt said Mamie was a hellion of sorts, a real spitfire in her youth. The fact she had spirit attracted me.

"But she's not the main reason I came here. See, my father came from around these parts, too. He was a... troubled...man. I knew he had another family before he married my mother and I wanted to find them and see if he'd done to his first daughter what he did to me."

She swallowed hard. "My father was an accountant for the county, but he was also a sexual predator. When I finally got up the nerve to tell my mother about his middle-of-the-night visits to my room, she called me a liar and kicked me out of the house. Keep in mind I was thirteen years old. I went to live with my father's elderly aunt who told me about his first family, a wife and a daughter, who lived outside Falls Bluff, Idaho. She hadn't heard from them in years but I knew that meant

I had an older sister and I started wondering what she was...like."

"Did you ever find her?" Kate asked.

"She and her mother died in a house fire about two weeks before I got here. My estranged parents are dead now, too. Everyone's gone." She glanced at Frankie and added, "I never told Harry about any of this. What was the point? And once he and I got engaged, I stopped thinking about Mamie and the past. I put it all behind me." Vivian had grown somber during this difficult conversation and now turned her palms upward, closed her eyes, took a deep cleansing breath and exhaled.

"The past is the past," she whispered like a chant. "The future is what's important." She patted the back of Frankie's hand. "However, I know you're curious. My father's past is a dead end now, but maybe you can find out something about Mamie."

"No last name?"

"None that I know of. I don't know what happened to her."

Frankie was quiet for a moment. "Mamie can be a nickname for Mary," he finally said. "A woman named Mary Dalton left with her husband and his son soon after the robbery. Dalton seems to have been a semi-invalid but it's possible he's connected to the stolen coins." He studied his mother's face for a second. "You might be related to Mary Dalton, Mom. That would mean I am, too."

She glanced at her watch and stood up. "Okay, I've done what I came to do, I've told you things you always wanted to know. Forgive me, but I have to go. I'll be back in the States around Christmas." She narrowed her eyes as she studied him and then added, "I still sense something is bothering you. My advice is to search inward. Nice to meet you, Kate."

They moved around to the parking area again and Vivian hugged her son one last time before driving away with a wave.

"She's pretty amazing," Kate said in her wake.

Frankie put his arm around her shoulders. "I had no idea her father had done that to her," he said. "I always wished I could have met him—now I'm glad I never did."

"I don't blame you."

"No wonder she's been running away from her past her whole life. I'm kind of glad to understand that it—"

"That it what?" she promoted when he paused.

"That it wasn't me she was running from," he finally said. He watched the dust trail for a few moments, then looked back at Kate. "But you know what I keep wondering? Why did Pat contact her about this link to her great-grandmother instead of me?"

"Odd, isn't it?" Kate said.

"Very."

Chapter Fourteen

Frankie drove up to The Three Aces and parked off to the side. The clock on his dashboard showed he was thirty minutes early but that's what he wanted. It was risky to let Jay call all the shots. The guy was the give-me-an-inch-and-I'll-take-a-mile type.

For a second he paused and looked down the steep slope to the tiny ribbon of the Bowline River flowing below. Forevermore he would think of it as Kate's river and long after she'd disappeared from his life, her beautiful face would come back to haunt him whenever he glimpsed its shores. As the river ran through the ranch, that promised to happen several times a day.

It had been a little awkward between them after his mother left, as though both of them were waiting for something to happen. Well, that's exactly what he was doing—waiting to come here, to hear Jay out. He had no idea what had been on her mind only that he'd found himself evading her suggestions they take a drive or go for a walk. The intimacy he'd struggled to create now worked against him. He wanted to tell her what was going on but didn't dare. His only hope was that he could buy off Jay for a little while so he could establish more of a relationship with Kate. Then when the time came to tell her the truth about himself, she'd know him well enough to see that he'd changed. He also needed time to figure out how to reveal to his dad the lies he'd told to get himself out of trouble.

An hour before he had to leave, Kate had finally given up and said good-night. With tremendous regret, he watched her walk down the hall to her bedroom, knowing he'd hurt her feelings but was powerless to fix it. In a super funk, he'd driven back to the tree house to get ready for this meeting but for the first time, the frivolous nature of the structure seemed to mock him. A tree house demanded a light heart.

As he passed by the usual crowd at the bar, he recognized Pete Richards, the kid who had worked summers on the ranch during high school. They greeted each other but Frankie kept moving. He was on edge about the coming meeting and wanted to find an out-of-the-way table.

After choosing a relatively dark corner with a clear view of the door, he ordered ice tea served in a whiskey glass, hold the ice. No need to advertise the fact he wasn't drinking. He glanced around to see if he knew anyone else. Neighbors a mile or two up the road were celebrating something at one table, a couple of the guys who worked at the hardware store in Falls Bluff sat talking over cold beers. No one else stood out though many sat with their backs to him and he wondered if Jay was biding his time among them.

That question was answered when the front door opened and Jay stepped into the room. A sort of hush descended, then some of their mutual cronies greeted him. He punched a couple on the arm, but he'd obviously seen Frankie sitting in the back and without hesitation made his way to the table, a cigarette dangling from his thick lips.

"So, you came," he said with a smug smile. He ground out the cigarette and sat down heavily in his chair. He needed a shave and a change of clothes. Stale cigarette smoke clung to him like dust mites.

"How much is it going to cost me to keep you quiet?" Frankie said, in no mood for small talk.

Jay sat down and signaled the waitress. "Double whiskey," he ordered and waited until she walked out of earshot. "It's going to cost you gold," he said.

"I don't have gold," Frankie said, but his heart kind of dropped. Why would he ask for gold? "Give me a cash number and I'll see what I can do."

"I heard via the grapevine that the old bank robbery loot is on your land and that you're figuring on digging it up for a movie."

Frankie shook his head. "Where did you hear a tall tale like that?"

"Around. People talk."

"Well, someone is pulling your leg," Frankie said, leaning back in his chair in an effort to strike a relaxed, unthreatened pose. As he did this, he caught sight of Pete Richards turning to stare at their table. Pete had overheard his family discussing the gold coins. He must have told Jay. That had to be it. The younger man turned quickly away and Frankie bit back a groan.

"Remember that guy on TV who opened Al Capone's vault?" Jay said. "All the cameras were rolling and the thing was empty." Laughter shot from his mouth. "Man, can you imagine how humiliating that must have been?"

"That was a live show," Frankie said as Jay lit up another cigarette. "Even if we could figure out where to look for the 'loot', we wouldn't be in that position. But you've got your facts—"

"Don't even try it," Jay said, eyes narrowing. "I know you're lying." He sat up straight and smiled as the server delivered his drink. He spoke a couple of lewd comments to her that Frankie suddenly realized were attempts at flirting. The woman rolled her eyes and left. Jay turned his attention back to Frankie. "You've got twenty-four hours to tell me where it is."

"I can't because I don't know. And even if I did, I wouldn't. The gold doesn't belong to either one of us."

"You're talking pretty tough for a guy with so much to lose."

"It's all immaterial," Frankie insisted, "because I don't even have a hint where it is."

"Says you. Stop stalling. We'll get to it first and take what we want. When the others go after it, they'll just think it was restolen years before. No one will know we took it now."

"I'll know," Frankie said, his jaw clenched.

"And you'll live with it." He took the cigarette from his lips and tossed back the drink. "This is serious money and I intend to have it. Help me and we share. Stand in my way and you'll lose a whole lot more than your family's respect."

"What are you talking about?" Frankie demanded.

"That cute little blonde, for instance…"

HE DROVE AROUND after leaving the bar. He'd done the same thing night after night when he was a late teen when he'd been too restless to stay inside the house. Since his father didn't approve of this behavior, he'd had to climb out on the roof and jump down to the top of the arbor, then leap to the ground, ride a bike to the hay barn and "borrow" the truck. Getting back inside was trickier. The year his dad installed a trellis for the roses fixed that problem, though.

He was restless again.

There was no running from the current impossible situation but the fact could not be ignored that he didn't know where the gold was or if it was still around and even if he did, he wasn't about to tell Jay of all people, let alone be part of stealing it. There was nothing to do but come clean and tell his father the truth. Not tonight—it was too late to wade into all that tonight. Tomorrow morning would have to do.

Back home, he cast a regretful look toward the ranch house and detoured onto his own little road. The drive to his tree house that usually filled him with anticipation and contentment did neither tonight. He parked close to the tree, got out of the truck and stopped dead when he heard a noise approaching him from the dark. He fumbled in his pocket for the remote that controlled the lights and clicked them on, thinking he was going to start carrying a sidearm until this was over.

Kate stood holding Ginger's reins. She blinked at the light, then covered her mouth with her hands as her eyes grew huge. Dropping the reins, she ran to Frankie who caught her.

"What's wrong?" he asked as she trembled in his arms. "Are you okay?" He leaned back to study her face. "Did someone hurt you?" Had Jay come here?

"Where have you been?" she cried, gazing up at him and he was alarmed to see fear on her face.

"Driving around," he said. "Kate, what's wrong?"

For several seconds she couldn't seem to answer and

his head raced through scenarios, each one more terrible than the one before. He looked her over from head to toe. "Kate, talk to me. What happened?"

"Nothing!" she finally blurted. "I thought...I thought something happened to you. I didn't know if I should ask for help or..." She gripped his arms and looked up at him. "Oh, Frankie, Frankie..."

He pulled her close and claimed her lips. The urgent rush of need that flooded his body coupled with the shock of finding her here and in this state made his head reel. He kissed her until they were both limp, then he stared into her eyes. "Come upstairs," he whispered.

"Yes."

"Hang on a second," he added and quickly slipped off Ginger's bridle and saddle and laid them on the ground. The horse wandered off. He knew she was safe—this was home territory and she'd find a nice patch of juicy grass to amuse herself before wandering back to the barn.

All this was done in virtual silence. At last he led Kate up the ramp. He'd locked the door before leaving but he still checked the place over before pulling her inside where he immediately folded her in his arms and held her like the very real, warm, soft lifeline she was. The few minutes between kissing her on the ground and kissing her in the boughs of the tree had done nothing to dampen the desire that sparked between them like a high-voltage wire.

Clenched together, they moved toward the bed, shedding clothes along the way. It was relatively dark inside the house as he hadn't opened the blinds—no Peeping Toms tonight, not now, not with her. Instead just the passion-driven energy that guided their hands and bodies.

"I can't believe you're here," he whispered at one point and she laughed very softly.

He knew it was crazy, he knew it made no sense but he also knew that she was the one, there would never be another. He wanted to make everything perfect for her—champagne, roses, music, candles—but that wasn't going to happen, not this first time. This time they would hurl through space, whizzing past stars and planets, two bodies rocketing together...next time would be romance. This time discovery fueled the flames.

There were a million words hovering on his lips, words he wouldn't say, words that weren't needed anyway. She was soft and yet demanding, her passion an equal match for his own, her body ripe and succulent, yielding. Every touch, every kiss, every moan amplified and quadrupled until they reached the peak of ecstasy and fell back to earth—together...

For a second or two he rested his weight on her. When he kissed her lips, he found them salty.

"Are you crying?" he whispered.

"No," she said, but obviously she was.

"Did I hurt you?"

She shook her head and he moved aside, propping his head on his hand to look down at her face. With his free hand, he touched her cheek and she closed her hand around his.

"Nothing's wrong," she said softly.

"But the tears—"

"—are ones of relief, of happiness, that's all," she said.

He leaned over and kissed her lips again. "You look beautiful," he said. "Like an angel."

She smiled. "So do you. Oh, Frankie, don't ever scare me like that again."

"I'll try not to," he said softly, his fingers grazing her petal-soft skin. His heart was as full as it had ever been, practically bursting. "You're incredible," he whispered into her hair. "You're perfect."

"No," she protested.

He lowered his head to kiss the succulent nipple of each breast. "Yes, you are," he said.

"Oh, those things," she said dismissively. "They just seem to get bigger and bigger."

"I'm not complaining," he said, inching his way up to kiss her lips again.

For a while they just lay in each other's arms, too comfortable to think about moving. But Frankie kept seeing her face when he drove into the clearing. "Why were you in such a panic?" he whispered at last.

She didn't respond immediately. He drew back and waited. She finally swallowed. "Frankie, I know where you went tonight," she muttered.

Her words could not have shocked him more than if she'd announced she was an alien. All the cozy, hopeful thoughts that had chased fear and worry away a second before now trembled in a corner. He sat up abruptly. "What do you know?" he asked looking back down at her.

She, too, sat. With one hand, she smoothed her hair behind her ear, with the other, she held the comforter against her breasts. "I know about Jay," she said.

"Oh, no," he groaned. "How in the world—"

"I came back last night after you took me home. I missed you and…well, you weren't here but someone else was. Before I could figure out how to sneak away without him hearing me, you showed up and by then I was curious and a little nervous for some reason."

"For good reason," he said softly.

"Frankie, I know he threatened you. I've wanted to ask if you'd need my help all day but it's been...awkward."

"I know," he admitted.

"I just never found the courage. I thought I would at least go up to The Three Aces and be there in case he caused trouble, but everyone around here is gone and I couldn't just take a car. When you didn't come home, I became so worried. I wondered if I should try to find one of your brothers and get them to go look for you. I didn't know if that would just make things worse so I rode back here one last time to see if you'd come home without my knowing, and when I was about to give up, you arrived. Only I didn't know at first it was you. I was just so relieved you were okay."

He leaned his head against hers for a moment. "You heard Jay tell me I had a Get Out of Jail Free card because of my father, didn't you?"

"Yes, I did hear that. But he doesn't strike me as the kind of man to see things as they really are."

"You're right about him, but what he said about my dad was the truth. I should have gone to jail. I would have gone to jail if Dad hadn't moved heaven and earth to get me the best lawyer in Idaho. And he did that because I swore I didn't know what Jay was capable of, that I'd had no part in the violence. Some of that was true, but some wasn't. I've been living with my duplicity ever since."

"So, what happened ten years ago was serious enough for involvement with the law," she said.

"Yes." He considered letting the details drop, but it was crunch time. He'd just made love to her and it hadn't been casual and it hadn't been...unimportant.

"You might as well hear it from me. Jay is a few years older than I am. At the time, I was still a minor but he wasn't. One night we drank a few beers and planned a robbery. Not like a bank or anything, just a convenience store a few miles outside town. It was more like playing a fantasy game than plotting reality. By the next morning, we'd sobered up and laughed the idea off. That was it until three days later when Jay showed up at the ranch. He said he was restless and wanted to go for a drive but his car was giving him trouble. I offered to drive and off we went. After a while, he told me to pull in to the store we were passing because he wanted to buy cigarettes. It wasn't until I'd stopped the truck that I realized where we were—the same place we'd talked about a few nights before. He said he'd be back in a minute and disappeared inside.

"Fast forward a few minutes. All of a sudden, I hear a gunshot and a woman scream. Next thing I know, Jay is running out of the store. Laughing like a maniac, he dived into the passenger seat and told me to get the hell out of there. I glanced in the rearview mirror as I started the truck. Two people came running out of the store. I panicked. We tore out of there like nobody's business.

"I found out later he took fifty dollars out of the cash register. The store owner ended up with a bullet in his head for fifty lousy bucks. The guy didn't die but he was in the hospital for months. When he got out, he sold his store and moved away."

"But you didn't know Jay had a gun, did you?"

"No! Still, I knew he was a loose cannon. I let him go alone into a store we'd joked about robbing. Worse, I drove him away from the scene of the crime instead of running inside to do what I could to help because, face it, I was terrified. He was waving that gun around. He wanted to go hit another store..."

"What did you do?"

"I ditched him and thought about running away... eventually I did the one bright thing I'd done since meeting him and that's turn myself in to the sheriff's department."

"That showed responsibility," she said.

"Well, better late than never maybe, but before you start thinking I had shaped up, let me finish. I told my father I was completely innocent, that I hadn't known what Jay had planned, that he'd merely said he was going to buy cigarettes, that he'd forced me to drive away. Jay disagreed with this version of the story, of course, but he was a perpetual liar with a record and a history of violence and I was a screwed-up rich kid that every parent hopes they don't get but kind of understands if they do. The fact I had never really hurt anyone was my saving grace. But Kate, man, I didn't want you to know what I'd done until you knew me better, until you trusted me."

She cupped his cheeks and touched his lips with hers. "I do trust you, Frankie. That's why I'm here."

He buried his face in the crook of her neck. How could she offer him such acceptance on the cusp of hearing what he'd done? The fact that she did warmed his heart more than he could say and he knew he would work to make sure he never disappointed her or hurt her.

But a nagging feeling tugged at him—Jay's last threat about the pretty blonde. Was Kate safe here? What if Jay targeted her to get to him?

He would not let that happen.

"I spent my college years doing community service," he added because it was important she know he tried to repair what he'd done. "And I worked my butt off for a lot longer than that to pay retribution to the store owner. I apologized to him, but why should he have given a damn? Nothing that happened to me compared to Jay's ten years of hard time."

She looked deep into his eyes. "Try to remember your crimes were different in magnitude."

He nestled his face in the crook of her neck. "Have you ever in your life done anything that shamed you down to the essence of your soul?" he whispered but she didn't answer. There was a chance she hadn't heard him but he thought it far more likely she chose not to answer because she didn't want to have to admit that of course she hadn't, that most people never did.

Whatever her reasons, he appreciated her effort but he knew what he'd done and how it had affected people. For now it was enough to put his arms around her, to bury himself in her lovely flesh and for them both to pass what remained of the night in each other's arms.

LONG AFTER FRANKIE'S even breathing announced he'd fallen asleep on his stomach with his arm draped over her abdomen, Kate lay awake listening to the sounds of the night. She heard an owl hooting nearby and the tiny footsteps of squirrels scampering across the roof. As the night wore on, a breeze stirred the boughs. The house didn't exactly rock, but the creaking and rattling sounds of wooden boughs made her feel as though she was aboard a boat anchored in a moorage as opposed to a house anchored in a tree.

She still felt warmed by the afterglow of Frankie's decision to entrust her with information he'd let fester in his heart for years. In a good world, she would now share with him the network of lies and half-truths she'd used to come to this ranch. In an even better world, he would help her figure this out and she would help him with Jay Thurman. But Jay wanted money; that was clear from what he'd said the night she overheard him talking to Frankie. If there was one thing she couldn't offer, that was it.

Frankie made a soft sound in his sleep, startled perhaps by a dream. His arm tightened across her abdomen and he turned his head so that his warm breath bathed her shoulder.

In a perfect world, this night would never end.

Chapter Fifteen

Kate wasn't sure how she would be greeted the next morning when she arrived back at the ranch with Frankie instead of wandering down the hall from her bedroom alone. As they drove up to the ranch, they could see several cars in the drive and Ginger standing outside the corral looking in at the other horses. They took care of her needs first before entering the main house.

"It's a boy!" Grace said the minute they walked into the room. She was drinking coffee at the counter. "You should see him, Frankie. He's just beautiful. I have a new grandson! Charlie will be so excited there's another child on the ranch to play with."

"That's great news," Frankie said.

"How is Kinsey?" Kate asked.

"Tired but beaming."

"Grace," Frankie said, "where's Dad?"

"He got an early morning call from Soda Springs. They have the one and only existing part to fix that blasted pump."

"You're kidding me," Frankie said.

"I know. It's some little esoteric thingamajig on a machine he's been nursing for years. I told him to get a new one. I normally would have gone for him, but with Kinsey coming home this morning—"

"She's home already?" Kate interrupted.

"Yes. As a matter of fact, she said to send you over as soon as you want to come." She looked back at Frankie. "Is something the matter, honey?"

"No," Frankie said immediately. "But I need to talk to Dad as soon as he gets home. It's important."

"He won't be back until dark," Grace said. "Soda Springs is a long ways away."

Kate wasn't positive what Jay had threatened Frankie with but now she guessed it had to do with spreading the truth about Frankie's participation in that robbery. If Frankie was asking about his father, it might mean he intended to bypass Jay's blackmail. She was nervous for him but also relieved. If he'd given in to whatever demands Jay made, it would be like handing the man a loaded gun to use whenever he wanted.

"How is Gerard?" Frankie asked.

Grace ginned. "On cloud nine."

"Want to go over and see the baby right now?" Frankie asked Kate.

"Maybe we should wait and let them settle in."

"I'll be busy later, but if you want to go alone—"

"They're not sleeping, trust me," Grace said. "Tell Kinsey I'll be up to help her after I finish things here but she can call if she needs me sooner."

"We will," Frankie said.

They decided to walk up the road and Kate was pleased beyond reason that Frankie took hold of her hand. "I didn't ask you last night," she said. "How much does Jay want to keep quiet?"

"A lot."

"More than you have?"

"More than I have. More than I'm willing to give even if I did have it."

"What are you going to do?" she asked. As always, the river drew her attention, the glimmering water taunting her. Somewhere along its bending curves a treasure lay hidden…a treasure that belonged to her grandmother and that her grandmother needed. Had she lost sight of this goal in her elation over finding Frankie? Perhaps, but it was back now in the cold light of day. That didn't mean she didn't have to fight the urge to tell Frankie everything, to ask for advice, maybe even help.

This was weakness on her part, she knew that, but it was something else, too…

"I'm going to tell Dad just like I should have years before."

"That's what I thought. Good for you."

He shook his head. "I have to admit I dread it. It's taken me so long to earn back his respect. It kills me to ruin it, but there isn't another choice."

She stopped walking and he turned around to face her. "Is something wrong?" he asked.

She stepped up close to him and raised her face to his. His lips were cool from the morning air, but there was also an undercurrent of thrilling heat and suddenly she wished they were back at the tree house. "I'm here for you," she said. "I don't know what I can do, but just ask and I'll try."

He smiled as he touched her face. "Thank you. The same goes for me in regards to you, you know that, right? You can tell me anything. But the only thing I want you to do concerning Jay Thurman is stay away from him."

"Okay," she said slowly.

"Which brings me to asking how your grandmother is doing," he added. "I know you called her while I was showering this morning."

"They say she's fine. She can't talk on the phone, you know. It's kind of like she's disappeared inside that building."

"You'll see her soon, I promise," he said, and kissed her forehead. "Let's go meet the newest Hastings."

Kate was startled by the inside of Kinsey and Gerard's house. Paintings adorned every wall and most of them used the Hastings Ridge Ranch and its inhabitants, both human and otherwise, as models. Everyone Kate had met was shown doing something or caught in a portrait. She'd heard about Kinsey's artistic talent, of course, and even seen examples of it in Frankie's place and around the ranch house, but she was stunned by the detail and quality, to say nothing of the sheer volume that resided in this two-story house.

"What did you name your baby?" she asked Gerard after Frankie introduced him. He was older than Frankie, very handsome and steady-looking with the bluest eyes she'd ever seen.

"Andrew," he said and for the first time she knew what people meant when they said a voice could caress a name.

"Is it a family name?"

"No, although his middle one is Harrison, like my father."

"Andrew Harrison Hastings," Frankie said. "That's a good name. May we see him?"

"Of course. Come on, I'll take you upstairs."

He ushered them into a pretty bedroom filled with baby stuff. But what drew Kate's attention was the woman propped up by pillows in a large overstuffed rocking chair, a bundle of yellow blankets cradled in her arms. Kinsey's smile was a tad on the weary side, but you could tell it came straight from the heart. As Frankie and Kate moved closer, she lowered the baby to rest on her knees and pulled aside the blankets.

"Oh, he's precious," Kate gushed. She hadn't been around too many newborns in her life, the last one a good three years before when a fellow teacher gave birth to a baby girl. This little guy had a dark fuzz and slate eyes. He looked round and pretty and so tiny.

"Isn't he huge?" Kinsey said.

Kate wasn't sure how to respond to that remark.

"Eight pounds two ounces," Kinsey added.

"He's perfect," Gerard said. "But when you're as vertically challenged as my beautiful wife, that's a lot of baby."

They all chuckled and stood around admiring tiny fingers and itsy-bitsy toes until Gerard and Frankie went off to discuss ranch business and Kinsey and Kate were left alone.

"Do you want to hold him?" Kinsey asked.

"Okay," Kate said and sat down on the ottoman beside the rocker. With utmost tenderness, Kinsey transferred her baby to Kate.

"You're a natural," Kinsey said as she looked at Kate cuddling her son. "Look, he's staring at you."

It did seem the little guy was peering upward at Kate who smiled back. His features were so small and sweet, his little mouth like a rosebud. "He's wonderful," she said. "He smells so good."

"I wanted you to have a chance to see what it's like. I know when I was pregnant and a lady in town let me hold her newborn it made it real for me in a way it hadn't been until then. When is yours due?"

Kate's brow wrinkled. "My what?"

"Your baby."

"My what?" she repeated so sharply it startled the baby in her arms. She instantly rocked him and apologized to Kinsey. "I'm so sorry, I didn't mean to scare him."

"It's okay."

"You better take him back," Kate said.

Kinsey took her son and held him up against her chest. The baby fussed for thirty seconds, then appeared to fall asleep.

"I'm not pregnant," Kate said, staring at Kinsey.

"I thought—"

"Why would you think such a thing?"

"Well, you were saying that for the last two months you've been dizzy and weepy and tired and nauseated…it sounded exactly like my first trimester. Plus my breasts did just what yours have done. And there's a kind of, oh, a look about you, a kind of inner glow—oh, God, I am so sorry. Listen to me rambling. Can you forgive me?"

Kate heard every word Kinsey said but even as she listened, her mind raced backward in time. When had she last slept with Luke? Not for a long time…

But no, that wasn't true. She knew she'd tried to erase the fact it had happened from her mind but one night three or four months ago, she'd let her guard down and slept with him. When she found out the next day that he'd left for Alaska, she'd been mortified. Had he assumed they were back together, was that what had propelled him into making the decision to risk his life?

"Kate, are you all right?"

Kate swallowed a lump of air and nodded.

"Blink," Kinsey said.

She blinked.

"Take a deep breath," Kinsey added. "Go on."

Kinsey took a deep breath. She finally met Kinsey's gaze.

"You look like you've seen a ghost," Kinsey whispered.

Kate licked her lips. "In a way, I have."

FRANKIE LEFT KATE at the house. He knew darn well that she would be back at the river before he got as far as the field where they were mowing that day. It was always right on the tip of his tongue to coax an explanation out of her and then he would hear Pat Lowell's voice urging Frankie to give her a chance, she'd been overwhelmed for months, she'd taken science classes... None of that explained what she was doing poking around the Bowline, but he let it pass anyway because he agreed with everything Pat said.

But it went deeper than that. He didn't want to challenge her. He didn't want her to think he thought she was up to no good when she'd been over-the-top understanding of him. And now there was an additional reason: Jay. She was vulnerable as long as she was here and the primary goal had to be to get her away. Maybe on the ride home tomorrow she would be forthright about things.

He'd almost forgotten the original reason she had come to the ranch—the documentary. How could he have forgotten that? And why did it seem she had, as well? He let all this go as he caught up with Chance and Pike both running combines out in the middle of a sun-blazed field. Chance was the closest and Frankie drove his truck over the rutted, mowed field to reach him. Off in the distance, he saw the second combine head their direction.

While they waited for Pike to arrive, Chance produced a cooler and poured glasses of cold water.

Pike's machine finally came to a halt, casting the field into silence. "Hey, Frankie, where have you been?" he asked, wiping the sweat from his brow as he accepted a cold glass from Chance.

"We went to see Gerard's new son," Frankie responded. "Have you seen him yet?"

"No. Lily went over first thing," Chance said, "but I was with Dad out in the equipment barn until he left for Soda Springs. You heard about the part?"

"Yeah. He should have replaced the pump this winter. It's not like everyone didn't warn him," Frankie said.

"What'd they name the baby?" Pike asked.

"Andrew Harrison."

"Big name for the little guy," Chance said. "Did Kate go see him with you?"

"She did." He thought for a moment and added, "She was kind of quiet when we left. I'm not sure—maybe a baby seems so far away for her it kind of makes her sad."

Chance chuckled. "I heard you were suspicious of her."

"Who told you that?"

Pike wiggled an embarrassed finger. "Gerard might have mentioned it," he said.

"I'm getting to know her," Frankie said. "She's hard not to like."

"I hate to change the subject," Pike said, "but I talked to Pete Richards this morning when he came by to pick up his paycheck. He mentioned he saw you at The Three Aces last night with Jay Thurman."

Frankie returned his brother's level-eyed appraisal. "Jay got out of jail a week or so ago." Sometimes being the youngest brother sucked...they all thought they had to police him.

"That guy is trouble," Chance said. "I told you that ten years ago and I'll bet my bottom dollar prison didn't improve him."

"You'd be safe making that bet," Frankie admitted. "He's still the same old Jay."

"You don't owe him anything," Pike said.

"I know that."

"He's the kind to think you do. Frankie—"

"Listen, I'll take care of this myself," Frankie said, anger warming his face.

"I just don't want you—"

"To get in trouble again, to shame the family. I know, I got it, I don't want that, either."

"What I was going to say," Pike said carefully, "is that I just don't want you to think you have to deal with this guy alone. We're brothers. One of us gets punched, we all get punched."

"Oh," he said, suddenly contrite.

"Pete said you looked angry but he also said you looked a little worried. What we're tiptoeing around saying, Frankie, is that Pete got the feeling there was a problem."

"Pete Richards probably helped create it," Frankie said. "Him and his big mouth."

"What does that mean?"

"He told Jay Thurman about the gold supposedly being on our land."

"He did not."

"He had to. How else would Jay have known about it?"

"I don't know, but if Pete told Jay anything I'd eat my hat. You're forgetting about his sister."

"Pete's sister? Paty at the feed store?"

"No, his older one. Kara."

Kara. Frankie thought hard for a second before he conjured up a pretty girl a year or two ahead of him in school.

"Don't you know what he did to her?" Chance said.

"No."

"It was right before you and he...well, before the convenience store thing. He slipped something into Kara's soda and forced himself on her. She refused to press charges so he got away with it. Pete knew about it— he's the one who told us. In other words, Pete hates Jay with a passion."

"I didn't know," Frankie said, his mind racing. It seemed impossible Jay hadn't bragged about a sick act like that. Why hadn't he? Frankie hoped it was because he'd sense Frankie would have drawn the line at such barbarous behavior. The bigger question was this: If Pete didn't say anything about the gold, who did? The answer was impossible to know. He might have told someone who told someone else.

"Maybe you'd better tell us why Jay is talking about gold all of a sudden," Pike said.

Frankie took a deep breath. "I can handle it," he said.

"Frankie, listen to me," Chance pleaded, his eyes intense. "For almost ten years you've been the Hastingses' version of a lone wolf, so tied up in knots about what choices you made that you wouldn't let anyone get too close. Let it go, man. Talk to us."

"He's right," Pike said quietly.

Frankie started to dismiss them, then looked each in the eye.

"Okay," he said, nodding his head.

He paused, uncertain how to start. "Jay seems to know about the possibility of the gold being on this land and he figures I'm a conniving rat like he is so I'll be willing to steal it out from under my family and the documentary and whoever legally owns it to split with him. That's why I thought Pete must have told him about Gary's visit."

"Man, if he didn't, who did?" Chance said.

"Exactly."

"What did you tell him?"

"I told him I didn't know where it was but that even if I did, what he wanted was out of the question."

"So that's the end of it," Pike said.

Frankie shook his head. "I wish. Unfortunately, there's more. He has something he thinks he can hold over my head."

Pike's jaw tightened. "He's blackmailing you?"

"He's trying to. When I didn't back down, he made veiled threats about Kate. He's…seen…us together and he knows I like her."

"So what happens next?" Pike asked.

"By ten o'clock tonight, I'm supposed to have examined my options and decided everyone's feelings about me are more important than things like honesty and honor. He said he'd contact me. He expects me to take him to the gold stash. He simply will not accept that I have no idea where it is or even if it exists. He seems positive it's here and I know about it."

"Brother," Pike said.

"I know."

"What's he using as leverage?" Pike asked.

Frankie met his gaze. "A truth I've kept from Dad. I'll tell you about it after I have an opportunity to talk to him."

Chance laughed, which earned him Pike's and Frankie's attention. "And what's so funny?" Pike asked.

"Us," Chance said. "Remember the old days? Especially me and you, Frankie. Nothing got in our way."

"Well, that throw-caution-to-the-wind attitude didn't work out so hot for me," Frankie said.

"Maybe not, but it made you who you are today. You can only live your own life journey, you know. Few people get close to their thirtieth birthday without making a few mistakes along the way."

Frankie narrowed his eyes, unsure where Chance was taking all this. Sure, both he and Chance had seldom walked away from confrontation, but Frankie had taken it further than that when he'd broken the law. And Chance? He was one of those guys who had flitted from one woman to the next—until he met Lily and then the world, for him, changed.

"But that's not what I was thinking," Chance added as Frankie stared at him. "I was thinking that Jay has opened himself wide up. In the old days we would have messed with him, all stops ahead, damn the torpedoes."

"What the heck are you talking about?" Pike asked.

"I'm talking about coming up with a plan to make him think he's got this all wrong."

"Oh, brother," Pike said, shaking his head.

Frankie folded his legs and sat down in the freshly mowed grass. "What do you have in mind?" he asked.

Chapter Sixteen

"Remember those old money bags from the Green Ridge Bank?" Chance said as he perched on his haunches. Even Pike had condescended to lean against the combine and listen.

"The ones Dad took when he was a kid?" Frankie asked.

"Yeah. Back when you could still get inside the old bank, before the cave-in. He took a whole stack of them."

"I remember him telling us about that," Frankie said.

"Yeah, he also took the iron grate off the door leading to the vault," Pike said.

"Which is now supporting the climbing rose in the arbor. Anyway, I know where those bags are."

"Where?" Pike asked.

"In the attic above the old cattle barn. They looked like they'd been there for decades and that was fifteen years ago. I came across them when I was showing a young lady the infinite opportunities for privacy on a ranch."

Pike almost smiled. "Really, a loft? Isn't that a cliché even for you?"

"Never underestimate the value of an oldie but goodie. Anyway, Dad must have thrown them there and forgotten about them. They're a little moth-eaten and dirty, but they've got the bank's name printed on them and a big black dollar sign just for the heck of it. Very picturesque, like in an old Western."

"What do we do with the bags?" Pike asked.

"We stage finding them," Chance said, clearly excited, "only to discover they're empty and the real loot is gone, taken a long time ago."

"What do you mean stage finding them?" Frankie persisted.

"Just what I said. We hide them and then lead Jay right to the spot! But the bags are empty, see, and that means the treasure is long gone, stolen again after it was hidden. We could use that cave on Mt. Jinx."

"You mean the old gold mine?"

"No, the cave on the other side of the mountain. We used to play in it when we were kids."

"I remember," Frankie said. "I always thought bears lived in that thing."

"I did, too," Chance said.

They smiled at each other until Pike cleared his throat. "And exactly why would we do all this?" he asked.

Chance opened his mouth as if to explain, and then grinned. "I'm not sure."

Frankie had to laugh. He clapped Chance on the back. "It would be fun, you're right, but don't underestimate Jay Thurman. He can be a real beast when he's thwarted. I'm concerned he's going to take out his aggression on Kate when he finds out I've told Dad the whole sorry truth of the robbery."

"You didn't shoot anyone, did you?" Pike asked.

"No. Of course not."

"Good."

"So, for now I just want to make sure Kate is safe tonight when I go meet Jay."

"She can come to the A-frame with Lily and Charlie," Chance said. "This is Lily's big shopping day and pizza is on the menu."

"You wouldn't mind?"

"Of course not. Then you can take care of business and know she's safe."

"Could she spend the night there? In fact, could both of us?"

"Sure, the place is big." He paused and grinned before adding, "Don't you want her at your tree house?"

Frankie stared from one of them to the other and shook his head. He should have guessed they knew. "You guys know about the tree house?"

Chance nodded. "Pike told me. He found it one day when he was out riding."

"I noticed someone had built a new well by the old one down by the river," Pike explained. "I was curious why anyone would do that."

"Does Dad—"

"I don't think so," Pike said. "I only told Chance when he started worrying about you falling back into old habits. I wanted him to know you were okay."

"Sorry," Chance said.

"No problem," Frankie said. He'd always figured he'd feel kind of trespassed upon if anyone knew what he did on his own time, but to his surprise, no such feeling shadowed his heart. "I guess that's what family does—look out for each other."

"That's right," Pike said as he got to his feet. "That's what family does."

KATE DECIDED TO walk to the river that morning. Not only was it a beautiful day, but she had a whole lot on her mind and liked the feeling of moving one leg in front of the other. However, her pack was heavy and ungainly and she arrived at her destination with a sore back. She forged her way down the steep, eroded, overgrown path that led to the rocky shore, knowing that Frankie's tree house in the forest at her back was probably less than a half a mile away.

For a second, she stared at the rushing water without seeing it. Emotional, weepy, tired, nauseous. Kinsey was right, she'd felt all of these things recently and written them off to worry, grief, guilt—name it, everything had been so easy to explain away.

But a baby? Could it possibly be true? Her free hand drifted toward her abdomen—Gram and a newborn at the same time? How would she take care of two dependent people at such opposite ends of their lives?

If it came to that, she just would. That's all. Somehow, she'd make it work, but now it was hard to ignore the fact that the possibility of finding the diamonds had taken on an added dimension.

A renewed sense of urgency coursed through her veins and it was at that moment that she glimpsed a funny-looking rock on the western end of the beach. It wasn't in the water as the original letter reported, but if you squinted just right and used your imagination, you could almost see a bonnet perched on a head. And from this vantage point, Green Peak, or as Frankie called it, Mt. Jinx, peeked over the tops of the trees on the opposite bank. One hundred years ago the forest between here and there must have been shorter making the mountain look higher.

As she dropped the pack to the ground and continued on for a closer look, she had to marvel at her luck. Was it possible she'd made an eleventh hour discovery? According to the letter, she would need to line up the bonnet with the mountaintop. What about the well foundation, the pile of old rocks she'd been looking for on the other parts of the river? Maybe it had been demolished during the plowing of the road.

No snagged tree, but she hadn't really expected to find that. As she studied the rock, she had the queerest sensation that she'd finally found the spot. Maybe this would soon be over and she could concentrate on finding a way to tell Frankie the truth about herself. She wouldn't think about that now. Now it was all about Gram.

"Well, well," a deep voice drawled as she turned on her heels. "If this isn't a coincidence. What are you doing down here all by yourself?" He laughed. "I swear, you're the icing on the cake, that's what you are." Jay Thurman stood on the ledge above the shore looking down at her. She unconsciously backed toward the river.

He jumped down the four-foot bluff in one giant leap, landing with a reverberating thud seven feet away, more or less between her and her only escape route off the beach. He was dressed much as he had been two nights ago when she'd seen him in the car lights—jeans, a plaid shirt. His facial hair had grown even bushier and if anything, he looked more wired than he had before. Some kind of hot, jittery waves seemed to emanate from him.

"I'm sorry," she said, aware of the tremor in her voice. Her heart had sprung into her throat when he jumped and now stayed lodged there. "I'm sorry, but I really have to go," she said. "I'm late. If you'll excuse me…"

She took a step to the right and he followed suit. She

stepped backward and then left. He grinned like a maniac as he mirrored her movements as though they were dancing.

"Listen," she said in her schoolteacher's stern voice. "Please move—"

"Or you'll what?" he said.

Her backpack lay behind him. What wouldn't she give to feel the handle of her machete gripped tightly in her hand? But her hands, like her pockets, were empty and he outweighed her by a hundred pounds. He seemed to sense the direction of her thoughts for he flexed bulging triceps.

"Please," she said, striving for control. "Someone is expecting me—"

Still smiling, he came another step closer. "Guess that someone is going to be disappointed," he said.

The thought of him grabbing her sent fear crawling over her skin like snakes. She stepped back toward the river and he followed suit. Then she pretended to step forward but instead twisted around and ran to the water. Almost at once, her feet started slipping on the mossy rocks but she managed to stay upright. Deeper, deeper, she had to get to water deep enough to carry her away, hopefully to the other side. She heard him wallow in after her. A second later, she thought she'd made it, but first one foot and then the other went out from under her and she landed with a splash, her butt hitting the rocks on the bottom, her hands scrambling to find something to grab on to, something to help pull herself into deeper water. Just as she finally felt the current lift her legs, Jay grabbed her hair and yanked her back. She screamed in both pain and outrage as he used her wet braid to drag her toward him and away from escape. Finally, with a heaving grunt, he hefted her weight up over his shoulder.

"You're going to pay for this," he growled, breathing hard as he lugged her out of the water and climbed the path with her still dangling over his shoulder. He smelled worse than a wet dog. She shifted her weight and kicked her legs in an effort to unbalance him. If he fell, she would have another chance to get away. But despite her efforts, he didn't falter. It was as though his shoes had spikes embedded in the soles.

"What do you want from me?" she demanded as he finally climbed onto the verge beside the dirt road and threw her to the rocky ground next to the old car she remembered from two nights before. She struggled into a sitting position as he stared at her.

He picked up a rock and weighed it in his hand, his gaze glued to her face, then he knelt on the ground beside her. Terrified, dripping wet, she faced him without flinching and repeated her question. "What do you want from me?"

"I want what's mine," he said and quick as lightning, slammed the rock down on her head.

FRANKIE TOOK OVER the combine for Chance who had promised to help Lily get supplies to the A-frame. He assured Frankie it would only take an hour or so and he'd tell Kate their plans for dinner if he saw her.

It was one of the longest hours Frankie had ever spent and he anticipated each moment of this day would drag in the same way as he waited for his father to return, spilled his guts and then went to face Jay.

How would Jay take the news that as far as Frankie was concerned, he could shout his threats from the rooftop?

Not well. If he couldn't get what he seemed so positive Frankie had and refused to share, then he would use violence. Frankie didn't doubt for a moment that Jay had tried blackmail first because it was easier, but violence would follow. All of a sudden, he wished he'd taken Kate home that morning.

But how did he run out on his family? There were currently three other women and now two children on this ranch. All of them were vulnerable, the men included. The ranch wasn't a fortress. That fact had been proven several times in the last year or so. Jay had to be stopped for good.

All these thoughts swirled in Frankie's head as he sat in the air-conditioned cab of the combine and mowed broad stretches of hay, row after row, with acres still to go. The tension inside his head began to build as Chance's predicted hour came and went. Finally, Frankie had had enough. He stopped the machine close to his truck and climbed down from the cab. Pike pulled up alongside him and got out, too. "Something wrong?" he called.

"I need to go find Kate," he said. "I can't explain why—"

"You don't have to," Pike said. "I know just how you feel. Last winter when Sierra was in danger, I about went out of my mind. Go find Kate."

Frankie's cell phone rang before he could climb in his truck.

"Howdy," Jay said.

Frankie's face must have revealed how unhappy hearing this voice made him because he saw Pike straighten his shoulders and narrow his eyes.

"Jay," he said so Pike would know to whom he spoke.

"Time's up," Jay said.

"No, you gave me until ten—"

"I changed my mind. Oh, heck, where are my manners? Someone wants to talk to you."

The phone was dead for a second and then he heard Kate's voice. Weak and indistinct, she muttered, "Hello? Gram?"

All the air rushed out of his lungs. "Kate? Where are you? Are you okay?"

"I don't…know," she mumbled.

Jay came back on the line. "Poor little gal. Listen, pal, one of you is going to pay for the ten years I sat in a cell while you lived like a king. It's up to you to decide which one of you it is. Throw her under the bus like you did me or stand up for once?"

"Let her go. I'll do what you want," Frankie said immediately.

"There now, you're finally catching on. I'll call you back in fifteen minutes. You'd better have a plan for getting that gold today." The phone clicked off.

Frankie looked at Pike. "He's got Kate. He knew I wasn't going to fold so he took her."

"Do you know where?"

"No. He's calling back in fifteen minutes…" It wasn't enough time to call for help or try to trace a phone and no doubt it was a burner anyway. There wasn't enough time to do anything. He took off his hat and slammed it down on the ground. All he could think about was what he'd heard that afternoon about Jay raping Kara Richards years before. What depravity was he into now? His heart thundered and bellowed in his chest as he picked up his hat and shook the grass from its brim. His mind jumped around in his head like a steel sphere in a pin-ball machine.

"What are you going to do?" Pike asked.

"Get her back," Frankie muttered.

"How are you going to give him gold coins you don't have?"

Memories of Christmases long past popped into his head. "You have some, don't you? Remember, Grandma Hastings gave each of us gold coins every holiday for ten or twelve years. I sold mine to help make restitution to the man Jay shot during the robbery. But you still have a dozen or so, right?"

"Yeah. So do Gerard and Chance. They're yours, but—"

"Call Chance, better yet, go to his place. Go get the bank bags, get as many coins as you can, set up the cave to look like the bags have been sitting there for years but someone dragged off the gold, just like Chance said. Sprinkle some of the coins around, hide them in the dirt under footprints—whatever, just make it look like someone missed a few coins."

"Will thirty coins satisfy him?"

"Not forever, but maybe long enough to save Kate. I'll take Jay the long way around, tell him about another site, anything to stall. You and Chance go the shorter way, up the stream and across the plateau. Hurry, Pike, just do it, please."

Pike opened his truck, took a shotgun off the rack built in the back and shoved it at Frankie along with a box of ammo. Then he got in his truck and drove off across the field toward the road, the truck springs squeaking in protest on the uneven ground.

Frankie's phone rang. It had been less than five minutes.

"Well?" Jay said.

Obviously, Jay was trying to keep him off balance. It was working.

"You win," he said. "I'll trade gold for Kate."

"Good decision."

"Where do you want to make the handoff?"

"Handoff? I'm not crazy, you know." All traces of the folksy, phony humor gone now, replaced with a tone of superiority. "You get what you want when I get what I want."

Frankie had expected this. "At least tell me where she is."

"Not going to happen," Jay said. "For now she's safe. She'll be fine until I decide otherwise. You'll come with me so I can keep an eye on you." He paused for a second, his breathing heavy as though he was exerting himself. "I'll meet you in thirty minutes by the road to your little hideaway in the trees. Bring what equipment we'll need. I don't need to tell you to come alone and not to go whining to the cops, do I?"

"No," Frankie said right before the line went dead.

Did Jay still have Kate? Could she have gotten away from him—or was it possible his heavy breathing meant he'd been on the move when he called?

His mind created a dozen scenarios, each one worse than the last. Thoughts like these got him nowhere. He jumped in his truck and took off, punching in Pike's number as he drove. He didn't trust Jay as far as he could throw him. Thirty minutes could mean ten.

"Did you find Chance?" he asked when Pike answered.

"Yeah. He's getting those bank bags and the coins he still has. I'm at Gerard's house. He's offered his gold, too. I'll stop and get mine and we'll bypass the ghost town and go straight to the old cave. Try not to worry."

"Remind Gerard someone needs to make sure Lily and Grace and Kinsey and the rest are safe in case Jay goes off the deep end."

"Do you know where Jay lives? I could call the cops and get them searching."

"I don't have the slightest idea where he's taken her."

"Well, keep your cell on Vibrate. If by some miracle we find her or she wanders back on her own, I'll text you."

"I will."

Pike paused a second and added, "I've got to go, Frankie. Gerard's here with his coins. Hang in there, kid."

Chapter Seventeen

Kate drifted in and out of consciousness. When awake, she tried to figure out where she was, but with something tied over her head and her arms and legs bound to a chair, she couldn't place herself. That said, there was something in the back of her mind that told her she'd been here before.

It was hard to hold a thought, however, for along with consciousness also came waves of nausea and foreboding. She knew a strong man with rough hands had slapped her conscious and tied her up, but that's all she knew for sure. She thought she might have talked to someone else, but that could have been in a dream. Maybe it was Gram.

Panic rose in her throat like bile. Where was Gram? Who was looking after her? Was the front door locked?

And she remembered thinking she understood why she'd not been acting or feeling herself lately, but even that was fuzzy and tangled in with other thoughts and impressions. Maybe it had something to do with the fact that she was wet—her clothes, her hair…how did she get so wet?

FRANKIE RACED BACK to the main ranch house. He parked inside the barn and began piling equipment into the back of the truck.

As plans for recovering a supposedly long-buried treasure went, this seemed too far-fetched to convince even Jay, but he didn't know what else to do. He felt his only hope was to act with conviction. A moment later he was back in the truck and driving toward the road that led to his place, expecting to find Jay's old Pontiac parked beside the chain blocking off his road.

He had arrived first. He got out of the truck, too anxious to sit still, listening for the sound of an approaching motor. The only sounds he heard were the droning of insects and the distant sound of the river. As always, the river brought immediate gut-wrenching thoughts of Kate.

Kate. It always came back to her. Kate poking around the river, Kate asking questions but never answering any; beautiful, enigmatic, loving, secretive Kate. Kate, whom he had decided to trust with a lot more than a little beachfront property—he'd given her a chunk of his heart.

She couldn't be part of Jay's scheme, could she?

His head all but exploded at the thought. But the timing…no. No! He refused to believe it—this was desperation talking, this was fear.

"You're alone," Jay said and spooked Frankie so much he actually jumped. He spun around to face Jay who stood just a few feet away holding a tiny silver gun. The weapon looked way too small for Jay's beefy hand, which probably meant he'd stolen it. He would have had to, given his prison record.

Even more curious was how he had arrived so soundlessly.

"I'm alone," Frankie said.

"Got a gun?"

"In the back. An unloaded shotgun."

"Throw it out," Jay said.

"It might come in handy."

"Throw it out."

With Jay still pointing the gun right at his heart—it might be small, but he knew it would get the job done—Frankie set the unloaded shotgun well off the road. Jay did a quick pat down and, convinced Frankie was unarmed, directed him behind the wheel.

For a second, they sat side by side in the front seat of the truck. The last time they'd done that the night had ended in disaster.

Frankie cleared his throat. "I'll try my best to help you," he said, "but tell me where Kate is."

Jay reached into his pocket and withdrew a small electronic device about the size of Frankie's cell phone. "This is a transmitter," he said. He turned it over so Frankie could see a tiny green light glowing in one corner. "As long as that light is green and steady, your girlfriend is alive and well. But if I push this button right here, it sends a signal, the light starts blinking, then it turns red and she's history."

"What have you done to her?" Frankie demanded.

Jay produced a creepy, leering smile. "For a time, I shared a cell with a guy they called the mad bomber. His motto was Retribution by Explosion. Your girl will never know what hit her but one minute she'll be a pretty little thing and the next she'll be a million pieces of bone and tissue." He put the device back in his pocket. "Okay, where's my gold?" He still held the gun pointed at Frankie.

Waves of anger had no place to go. Frankie had to shake them off, concentrate on the moment. "How did you know about the gold?" he asked. "And who convinced you I knew where it was?"

"I'm not answering any more questions."

"I'm asking because the truth is I'm not positive. If I knew who you spoke to—"

"Take it from me, buddy. You don't always get what you want. Get over it."

"Then we'll start with the Bowline River—"

"I warned you not to mess with me," Jay barked. One hand still clutched the tiny gun, but he'd buried the other deep in his pocket with the transmitter.

Relieved Jay wasn't interested in the river—surely that meant that Kate's agenda, whatever it was, did not tie in with Jay's—some of the tension leeched from his shoulders. "I was also told it might be in a cave up near the mine or it might be hidden in the ghost town itself," he said evenly. "In fact, damn near inside the actual bank from which it was stolen." He was betting Jay would prefer the ghost town. The Jay of a decade before had hated small, enclosed spaces.

"Might be?" Jay grumbled. "Come off it. I know you were told exactly where to search."

"I think your informant might have misled you. The truth is we were given three options," Frankie replied, meeting Jay's gaze straight on. He was making this up as he went along and knew he couldn't reveal even a trace of hesitation. "The river, the bank, the cave. If you'd waited, we would have narrowed things down. As it is… where do you want to look first?"

"Drive to the ghost town," Jay grumbled.

Frankie took off. To travel by vehicle meant crossing the river up near the main road and circling back across the southwest side of the plateau. The road wasn't used much except for fire equipment. The last time had been when Lily's estranged husband tried to torch what remained of Green Ridge several months before and Frankie's dad had driven a water truck up to stop the inferno.

Conversation in the truck was nonexistent. Jay was wired...nerves made his big body reek like sour milk. Frankie was afraid he'd say something that would reveal too much so he just kept his mouth closed.

Thirty minutes later, they pulled up outside the town limits of the ghost town. Each of them took an armload of tools out of the back and walked through a side street to access the bank.

Frankie hadn't been inside any of these buildings for a couple of years. The bank was especially unstable although it hadn't suffered any fire damage. He knew Gary Dodge wanted to film a portion of the documentary inside the building; in fact, Gary had discussed using a camera drone to make sure no human was hurt if the place came crashing down.

The second floor of the Green Ridge Bank, according to historians, had been used as offices and for storage but most of that floor had collapsed onto the first. Frankie hadn't realized the damage was so devastating and he approached the debris cautiously. They needed hard hats and bulldozers to excavate the building. The fiction Frankie had created about the gold being in this building was flimsy, at best.

However, in for a penny, in for a pound. He tapped this and that with a hammer, wrinkled his brow and shook his head. Finally, he announced they could move a few beams and some bricks and at least clear a section of floor.

As he worked, the mystery of this town and this bank seeped through his fear for Kate. The story of the robbery had always intrigued him—he'd read enough about the American West to know that men riding horses into town and stealing at gunpoint was more fiction than fact. In truth, there were few bank robberies, and by 1915, many areas of the country had switched payroll procedures. But that's how it had occurred in this little corner of nowhere and the story had always made his young heart beat faster. He supposed he always thought himself not so much as a member of the intrepid posse but of the thieves. His early foray into antisocial behavior had been as much imagination as reality.

Eventually, they found themselves looking down at dusty old floorboards. "Records say it could be hidden beneath these," Frankie said as he tackled cutting the boards to create an opening. A dark chasm loomed underneath. He knew what Jay didn't—there was no basement in this building, just a crawl space. He also knew Jay wouldn't trust Frankie to report what he found and despite his misgivings of tight, underground spaces, would force himself to accompany Frankie. If the bank chose the next fifteen minutes in which to collapse, they'd both be flatter than cow pies.

The good news was that all this hot, sweaty work had taken most of an hour and that would have given Chance and Pike an opportunity to prepare the cave. The bad news was the disturbing stillness of his phone. Kate must still be unaccounted for.

"You first," Jay said, motioning at the hole with his gun.

Frankie set the saw aside, rolled his shoulders, then picked up one of the lanterns he'd brought from the ranch. He let himself down into the crawl space. He wanted to corner Jay and overpower him in the worst possible way—what stopped him was the threat of that remote.

The crawl space turned out to be about two and a half feet high. Frankie doubted Jay would believe for a moment that someone had actually dug up the dirt to bury something down here. "Move out of the way," Jay said, now standing in the hole. Frankie moved. It was impossible not to feel the weight of the damaged building towering a few inches above his head. Jay's knees creaked as he lowered himself into a kneeling position. "Shine the light," he demanded.

Frankie did as directed but the light didn't go much farther than ten or twelve feet before running up against the rubble caused when the bank floor collapsed into the crawl space. Jay muttered a string of obscenities. Both men pulled themselves out of the hole.

"This is hopeless," Jay said, wiping his brow with the back of his arm.

"Yeah."

Jay's eyes narrowed and his jaw clenched as he apparently reviewed his options. The process looked painful. "We'll go check out that cave," he said. "There better be so much gold it burns my eyeballs or your little girlfriend is going to be sorry."

"No one hopes the damn gold is there more than me," Frankie said. Concern for Kate's safety gnawed at his gut—he'd never worried about anyone else like this. It was a terrible feeling made all the worse because this was his fault. Not only ten years ago when he didn't act responsibly, but ten hours ago when he made the decision to delay taking Kate to safety.

They dragged all the tools back down the alley and deposited them in the truck bed. Frankie got behind the wheel again and because he knew he was a lot more familiar with this area than Jay was, felt safe taking the long way around to the other side of Green Peak to eat up a little more time.

He and his brothers had found this cave twenty-five years earlier although it had probably been discovered by others in the years preceding that. As Frankie recalled, it started out very narrow, more like a slit in the rocks than a hole. After four or five feet of that, it opened up a bit and eventually erupted through a tunnel of sorts into a cavern beyond. This was where he and Chance always expected to find a hibernating bear, something Frankie now found terribly naive. How could a bear have made it through the first narrow gap?

It was midafternoon by the time they approached the cave. Frankie saw no sign of his brothers; indeed, it didn't look like anyone had been here in years and for a heart-stopping moment, he wondered if something had gone wrong and they hadn't come.

"How would someone get bags of gold in there?" Jay grumbled.

"One at a time," Frankie said. "Makes it a perfect hiding spot, though."

"There's probably bats or spiders," Jay said.

"And maybe gold."

"You go first but I want to see at least part of you." He jiggled his pocket before adding, "And remember. One little push and poof, the girl is toast."

"I'm not likely to forget," Frankie said and immediately sidled through the vertical crevice created by the rocks, keeping his shoulders back and his head turned to the side. A shovel and lantern dangled down by his legs. Jay had the pickax and another lantern. As Frankie investigated the cramped area leading to the tunnel up ahead through which they'd have to crawl, he heard Jay puffing and swearing. What if he got stuck? Would he panic and hit the remote? Frankie grabbed his arm and pulled on it until, like a cork from a bottle, Jay all but popped out of the crevice.

More swearing.

"Come on," Frankie said after a few seconds. "It's got to be close now. And remember, we're splitting fifty-fifty. You can take your half with you, but mine stays here until the documentary."

"Sure," Jay said.

Clearly, he had no intention of honoring that part of his deal. It was academic, of course, because there was no gold but it underscored the man's ruthlessness. He wouldn't leave Frankie—or Kate—to report him. Frankie had to make sure he not only got out of this cave but he somehow got that transmitter. "Looks like it's hands and knees up ahead," he said.

"Go first," Jay demanded, once again making a big deal of fidgeting with his pocket.

Frankie crawled through the tunnel, pushing the light ahead of him, trailing the shovel behind. It was roomier than the crevice and didn't last long before it turned into a space about the size of an empty train car.

It was much as Frankie remembered it from childhood: dark, claustrophobic. There was a second when he could have brought the shovel down on Jay's emerging head. Only fear of that damn button stilled his hands.

As Jay finished heaving himself through the tunnel, the light from Frankie's lantern caught the dingy, yellowing white of the ancient bank bags Chance and Pike had staged in a far corner. This was it.

"I see something," he said, once again pulling on Jay's arm and doing his best to sound excited.

Jay needed no further encouragement. He got to his feet, his eyes growing big as he registered a heap of bulging bank bags.

Bulging?

For a second, Frankie wondered if they'd actually found the lost coins and he worked at wrapping his head around the coincidence of it all. But as he moved closer he saw that the bags—and there were only a dozen or so—were really full of rocks. Other bags were empty and half-buried in the dry, sandy floor of the cave. Everything looked like it had been there for decades.

Jay played his light over what he'd hoped would be a fortune. "What happened to my gold?" he shouted.

Frankie shook his head. The desperation of the plan now struck him full in the face. One moment of anger and Kate could die. The little silver gun, which Frankie hadn't seen in a while, suddenly made a return appearance. *Shoot me*, he urged silently. *Just don't push the button.*

"Empty those bags," Jay demanded, and Frankie overturned the nearest one onto the ground. For the life of him, he could see no coins. Had Chance and Pike been here? Had they misunderstood when and where to go but if so, where did these bags come from?

A bunch of rocks—exactly like those that lay scattered on the ground, tumbled out of the old bank bag.

"I don't get it," Jay whispered. "What happened?"

Frankie didn't have to work hard to look scared, dumbstruck, anxious…no acting skills required. "I think it must have been stolen after it was hidden," he said slowly. "A long time ago, I mean. Maybe the fourth man, the one who got away, maybe he came back for it when his friends had been killed and the heat was off. Look," he added, running the light along the cave floor. "It appears someone dragged a heavy load across here through the tunnel."

"But why put rocks in the bags?"

Good question. "I don't know," Frankie said.

"Maybe whoever took the coins was planning on fooling someone," Jay said. "Maybe this happened years later, maybe a couple of guys, guys like you and me made a deal like the one we made and one tried to cheat the other." He turned his attention to Frankie and studied his face in the indirect light.

"I guess we'll never know," Frankie said, his mouth dry. For a moment, he thought the game was over. Jay's fingers tightened on the pistol grip, his mouth turned down at the corners, his eyes narrowed to slits. He looked over Frankie's shoulder at what he'd imagined would be a ton of gold to plunder but turned out to be a bunch of nothing and Frankie could feel the other man's blood pressure getting ready to explode like a geyser. And then Jay made a small whooping noise.

"What's that?" he said, and dropped to his knees. He scratched at the dirt for a second before holding up a small gold coin. An almost imperceptible gasp of relief escaped Frankie's lips as Jay held it up to admire. Pike and Chance must have been here—there was still a possibility this could work.

"I guess whoever did this missed one," Jay said. He got to his feet and once again pointed the gun at Frankie. "Empty every bag, search the floor. I want every coin the bastard left behind."

Frankie upended all the bags, almost certain Chance

had filled them. He could almost see his brother's grin as he imagined Jay's greedy gaze lingering over what appeared to be bulging bags of loot.

One coin tumbled out of the last bag. Jay grabbed for it as Frankie began searching the rest of the floor. He soon wished his brothers hadn't been quite so thorough at hiding the coins. He wasn't positive exactly how many they'd left here, but he eventually found thirty-six. He hoped to high heaven that their mint dates were old enough to make them believable although he really didn't care once Kate was safe. Jay could threaten and rage all he wanted once he had no hostage. He'd broken parole by carrying a weapon to say nothing of attempted blackmail and kidnapping. Jay was on his way back to jail whether or not he killed Frankie and Kate. Chance and Pike would see to that.

"Let's get out of here," Jay said.

"Give me the remote," Frankie countered.

"Not yet."

"I brought you to the coins like I said I would."

"Thirty-six lousy dollar coins, worth what, a couple thousand bucks? Big deal."

"That's not my fault," Frankie said. "And it's not Kate's. Keep your part of the bargain—give her back safe and sound."

"You're going to drive me to my car," Jay insisted. "Once I'm on my way, I'll tell you where she is."

"At least disable the remote."

"No. I don't trust you. This all seems like a setup to me. You haven't heard the last of me."

"Jay, I don't know what more I can do. I don't know where there's any more gold. If I did, you'd be welcome to it. All I want is Kate. You took a chance, it didn't pay off. Like you said, you don't always get what you want."

Jay reached into his pocket and withdrew the remote transmitter. His thumb quivered above the button…

"I'll find some way to pay you, just not in gold," Frankie said quickly. "My dad's rich, you said so yourself. I just want you to go away, that's all. Leave Kate and me alone and go far, far away."

He didn't like the gleam in Jay's eyes.

Jay's thumb stopped hovering. "You go first," he said, motioning toward the tunnel.

Frankie got down on his hands and knees, and much as he'd entered, left the bigger part of the cave, Jay on his heels. They both got to their feet as soon as possible. Jay held the remote in one hand and the tiny gun in his other. The time to act would be when they emerged from the cave. Frankie had to be ready. He started to go first again, but Jay put out an arm to stop him. "Stay here 'til I yell for you to come. I'm going first this time." He entered with the remote hand giving Frankie no opportunity to grab it.

Eventually, he heard Jay yell and he made his way through the crevice, wincing as the sun hit his face.

As he shaded his eyes against the brilliance, Jay shoved the gun against his forehead. "You double-crossed me," he said as though he'd had time to think about the past two hours more carefully.

"If there was a double cross, don't look any farther than the person who told you I was positive where to find the gold," Frankie said.

Jay dropped the gun and produced the remote. "I think it's time you suffered like I suffered. Time for you to lose for a change."

At that exact moment, the unmistakable sound of gunfire rent the air. Startled, Frankie dived to the ground. He looked at Jay in time to see the big man clutch the remote to his chest and then collapse onto the ground.

"No!" Frankie yelled, the word yanked from his chest as though it was his heart. "Stop firing," he yelled toward the trees as he scrambled to Jay's side. He could see no one about but in truth, he wasn't looking, his attention was focused solely on Jay Thurman's unmoving body. The bullet had obviously exited through his back; his shirt was soaked in bright red blood that had splattered all over the rock behind him.

Frankie tugged him over.

"Is he dead?" someone yelled as Frankie delicately uncurled Jay's bloody fingers from around the remote. "Is it safe now?"

Frankie couldn't respond. His mouth felt like a clay oven, his heart raced. The blinking red light on Jay's remote penetrated his brain.

It was too late. He'd failed. The bomb had been detonated.

Chapter Eighteen

Pat Lowell came to a halt a few feet in front of Frankie and stared down at the man he'd just killed with the scoped rifle he held in his hands. "What made him think there was gold here?" he demanded. "Thank goodness I came along in time."

Frankie didn't trust himself to talk. He couldn't make sense of anything. What was their historian doing here? Why had he shot Jay? He ignored Pat and got to his feet as Pike and Chance appeared, both out of breath like they'd been running. "What happened?" demanded Pike.

"I had no choice," Pat said. "The brute raised that black thing in his hand and I thought it was a gun. He was going to kill Frankie."

"That thing is a remote connected to a bomb set to explode to kill Kate," Frankie said, his voice as dead as his heart. "He activated it when you shot him."

"What?" Pat turned to Chance and Pike. "I didn't know. No one told me…"

"No one knew," Chance said. He knelt by Jay's body and dug in his pocket, extracting a set of car keys. A few of the gold coins recovered in the cave fell unheeded to the ground. Frankie hated the sight of them and turned his back.

His mind raced. How had Jay approached him near the Keep Out sign without being heard? He'd parked close by and walked, that's how. It was the only answer. And the only place to park out of sight was near Frankie's own tree house and that meant he'd been there the whole time, waiting for Frankie. And that could be where he'd stashed Kate. There might be a chance the bomb misfired or that there never was a bomb in the first place.

"Come on," he yelled, grabbing the car keys from Chance's hand. Such was the desperation in his voice that Pat and Chance piled into the back of Frankie's truck without asking why. Frankie got behind the wheel and Pike jumped in beside him right as Frankie shifted the truck into Reverse, backed around and took off toward the ranch.

He was way too preoccupied to talk. There was no point in talking anyway. If Jay had stashed Kate in his car and then blown it up, she was dead. She didn't feel dead to him. He wouldn't believe it until he had no other option. He could not fail her, he just couldn't.

He stopped the truck while Chance jumped out and undid the chain, then jumped back onto the rear bumper as Frankie tore off down his road.

Even before he saw Jay's old Pontiac still in one piece and squatting in the clearing, Frankie smelled smoke. He slammed on the brakes and jumped out of the truck, immediately breaking into a run. The tree house was on fire.

Pike thundered on his heels. "The bathhouse," Frankie yelled. He kept a few fire extinguishers down there. Pike would find them. He took off up the ramp. The smoke grew increasingly dense as flames licked through the roof and had started in on the branches above. He tore off his shirt and used it to grab the door handle, almost wrenching it out of the frame.

"Kate!" he yelled but heard nothing. He could see open flames licking at the walls near the kitchen area and knew time was short before the whole place went up like a tinderbox. His mind took in a dozen other details he didn't register. For now he was struck with the urgency of finding Kate. He heard a noise near the floor and dropped to his knees where vision was marginally better and the air more breathable. That's where he found Kate although he couldn't swear it was her as there was a sack of some kind tied over her head. She was tied to a chair. His knife was out of his pocket in one second and slicing through the bonds in another. He lifted her over his shoulder and carried her toward the door as Pike showed up with a fire extinguisher. Frankie hurried down the ramp with Kate, moving far enough along the road to get her out of the worst of the smoke.

He noticed that Chance and Pat Lowell had taken the truck, probably to get additional equipment. For now, he contented himself with removing the bag that covered Kate's head. Her face was very pink and dotted with sweat. Her eyes rolled open and she stared at him without really seeing him. He touched her throat and felt her heartbeat. It was fast, but it was also steady. He didn't know he was crying until he felt cool tears slide down his charred cheeks.

Pike showed up a minute later. "It's too big to put out with an extinguisher. I've called the fire department. Where's your water supply?

"Behind the bathhouse. There's a hose back there and the water feeds directly from the river. I'm staying with Kate."

Pike took a step back toward the tree house and then paused. "There's something you need to know. Gerard told me that Kinsey said Kate might be pregnant. She wanted us to know in case Kate was hurt. An ambulance is on its way."

Frankie nodded. Kate? Pregnant? They'd deal with that later. He picked her up and carried her farther away from the fire before putting her down again. Glancing over his shoulder, he saw the fire had spread to other trees. He brought her hand up to his face and kissed her fingers. His reward was that she opened her eyes again, and this time her focus seemed steadier.

"Gram?" she whispered. "Where's my grandmother? What have you done with her?"

Then she fainted.

"THURMAN RIGGED A pretty simple bomb and left it in your house," Officer Rob Hendricks told Frankie that evening. "We gather he brought Ms. West back when he came across her on the beach. Anyway, the fire marshal says the bomb shorted out when the signal was sent. The milk carton he'd assembled it in caught fire and then the fire spread. The house is gone. You lost several trees along a path down toward the river, as well. We're lucky it stopped when it got to your road." He looked down at Kate and added, "That was smart of you to tip your chair over so you'd be down on the floor where the air was better," he said.

"I'm not sure when the chair fell over," Kate said. "It might have been an accident. When it comes to the fire, everything before Frankie uncovering my face is kind of a blur."

"Is it all still a blur?" Frankie asked.

"No. It's coming back now."

Rob started writing down Kate's story of the abduction and waking up when Jay slapped her. If Jay hadn't already been dead, Frankie would have left the room to hunt him down.

But she was also kind of evasive when it came to saying what part of the river she'd been on when Jay found her. And she said he'd acted surprised to see her and taunted her about being the icing on the cake. Hendricks let most of this slip—Jay was dead, there wasn't a doubt in anyone's mind that he'd set himself up for disaster or that Kate had nothing to do with it so perhaps all the questions were more or less a formality.

Rob was a longtime friend of the family and his interview style was professional. He'd been Gerard's best man at his first wedding, but he'd also been on duty the night Frankie turned himself in after the convenience store robbery and this had created an awkwardness between them through the years. When Kate had finished, Rob shook Frankie's hand. "I'm really glad this ended well for both of you," he said before he left.

"Alone at last," Frankie quipped as he sat on a chair pulled up beside her bed and took Kate's hand. "How does your head feel? You have a charming bump."

She smiled. "I'm okay," she said.

He leaned over her face and kissed her cheek. Her long hair lay on the pillow around her head and smelled of smoke, but she looked beautiful.

"I need to call my grandmother," she said. "It seems like I haven't heard from her in weeks."

"You talked to Pine Hill this morning, but while I was waiting for the doctor to finish examining you, I went ahead and called them again. You'd used my phone so it was in the record."

"Thank you for doing that. What did they say?"

"They were real positive. Said she was eating a little better and had actually hummed along with a tune some-one played on the piano."

"Wow. That's great, isn't it?"

"Yes it is. They were alarmed to hear you'd been in a fire and urged me to tell you your grandmother is fine, just take care of yourself."

Her smile faded a bit. "Frankie, there are things I need to tell you."

"Like the fact you may be pregnant?"

"That and—wait, how did you know?"

"Kinsey warned Gerard in case you were injured. Gerard told Pike. Pike told me."

"I wasn't sure but they did a test when I got here."

"And?"

Tears filled her eyes as she nodded. "They're not sure if the smoke and everything hurt the baby. I could lose him or her."

"How do you feel about that?"

"I guess a lot of people would feel relieved, but today when Jay was tossing me around, I realized I want this child. The timing is terrible, but—"

"I understand. Is it Luke's baby?"

She nodded.

"This will be his legacy," Frankie said.

"But Luke has family," she added. "Parents and a brother who will want to know his son or daughter."

"Of course they will."

"So if you and I...if we...well, I guess I'm trying to say that I know you dreamed of your children all having the same parents. That can't happen if I have this baby. I understand if you—"

"Wait just a second," he said. "That wasn't a dream, Kate. That was a plan. Plans are flexible. The only real dream I have at this moment is that we continue what we've started. I don't want to lose you."

"Like you lost your beautiful tree house."

"The next tree house I build will be for a child," he said, touching her belly gently.

The nurse found them several minutes later, Frankie sitting on the edge of the bed, Kate in his arms, their lips locked together.

"Now, now, you two," she said with a laugh. "Take it on home, okay?"

Frankie smiled at her. As he helped Kate with her shoes, he looked up at her face. "Was there something else you wanted to talk to me about?" he asked.

She met his gaze, then shook her head. "It can wait," she said.

"WHAT DO YOU mean Pat's gone?" Frankie asked Pike after they returned to the ranch house.

"He drove in to Falls Bluff to be interviewed by the police. He'll be back tomorrow," Pike said.

"I don't get what he was doing here in the first place," Frankie said. "And how in the world did he end up at the cave?"

"He was on his way to Boise. The expert he had looking at those letters wants a face-to-face talk with him to discuss the results. When he didn't find anyone at the main house, he drove up to Gerard's. Gerard told him what was going on. He said he wanted to help and took off. Gerard called Chance to tell him to expect Pat. But

Pat didn't show up. We were waiting down the hill when we saw him drive past us toward the cave. By the time we caught up to head him off, he had disappeared into the trees and then I guess he saw you and Jay and decided to be a hero."

"And almost got Kate killed," Frankie said, his hand closing protectively on her shoulder. He was standing behind her chair and she tilted her head back to look up at him.

"Lucky for me I had a hero of my own," she said.

The door opened and Harry Hastings, looking tired from a full day of driving, entered from the mudroom.

"Did you get the part?" Pike asked.

"No. They read the damn serial number wrong over the phone and I went all that way for nothing. What did you guys get done today?"

Frankie and Pike looked at each other, then at their father. "I need to talk to you about that," he said. "Let's go into the office for a little while."

"If there's a glass of scotch waiting for me when I get there, I'm all ears," Harry said, and sighed.

Frankie leaned down and kissed the top of Kate's head. "I'll see you later."

KATE KNEW SHE had to retrieve her backpack from the river before someone else found it. Frankie was busy with his dad. She could be back here within an hour. All she needed to do was get her hands on a flashlight and wait for Pike to leave the house.

"I have good news," Pike said as he got up from his chair. He walked to the sink and rinsed out the glass from which he'd been drinking. "My fiancée, Sierra, is arriving tomorrow for a weeklong stay."

"That's great," Kate said.

"You'll still be here, right?"

"In all honesty, I'm anxious to get back to my grandmother but I'll be here through tomorrow."

"Good. Sierra's looking forward to meeting you."

They smiled at each other. Kate was surprised Sierra even knew she existed. Pike had probably told his fiancée that a woman determined to fight the documentary was visiting—just another example of the shame she would have to face when the truth came out.

"You okay?" Pike asked.

"Tired. I think I'll take a shower and call it a night."

"Sounds good," he said. "I was just hanging around in case you wanted company."

She touched his arm. "Thank you, Pike—for everything. I'll see you tomorrow." A moment later, the outside door closed behind him. Kate waited until she heard his vehicle climb the hill outside, then she grabbed a flashlight from the barn and headed toward the bridge.

Jay was dead—there was nothing to be afraid of. The dark was just night, nothing more. No boogeymen, no fire, no fear. Get the backpack, get back to her room, take a shower and figure out what to do tomorrow, her last day on the ranch.

It was either farther than she remembered or she was a lot more tired and soon she began to wish she'd taken a horse. The real reason she hadn't was that she didn't want to get caught out here by Frankie or another Hastings and have to explain what she was doing with the pack. She figured that on foot she'd have time to ditch it if she saw lights or heard voices and could claim a restless walk.

Boy, was she sick of all this pretending.

The smell of burned wood assaulted her nose and, with regret, she thought of the beautiful house Frankie had lost. He'd shrugged that loss off, but it had to hurt.

The backpack was right where she'd dropped it. She shrugged it on and turned to leave, but instead swiveled to face west. The rock, bathed in moonlight, looked more like a woman wearing a hat than it had in the bright light of day. Her heartbeat doubled. If she got out here early enough, she could find the jewels and then talk to Frankie. Perhaps if she showed her find to him instead of slinking away with it, he'd understand.

Shivers overtook her as she stood there and she twirled around, sure she was going to find Jay standing above her. Nothing there, of course, just memories. Time to go. She hadn't even cleared Frankie's road when she spotted lights approaching and quickly tossed the pack beneath the bushes as she kept walking.

The lights blinded her and she stopped to shade her face. Frankie got out of his truck. "I thought I might find you out here. Everything okay?"

"Fine," she said. "I'm just restless."

"Tomorrow is the big day," he said and for a second she wasn't sure what he meant. Had he figured her out? "Gary and Pat are both going to be here early in the morning. The expert came through with a location out by Ten Cent Creek. By tomorrow afternoon, we should know if we have a great end for the documentary or not."

"The irony of all that gold being hidden in a place called Ten Cent Creek is pretty sweet," she said.

He chuckled.

"I take it the talk with your father went okay?"

"He knew all about it, Kate. He's been waiting years

for me to get it off my chest, said he'd just about given up hope I ever would. The old man surprised me."

"Do you feel better?"

"What's the saying? The truth will set you free? So, yes, I do feel better."

The truth will set you free. She stared into his eyes, eyes that glittered in the ambient light of the headlamps off to their side, eyes that shone with affection—affection for her. All she wanted in the world at that moment was to fall into his arms, his bed, his future. "I have something I have to tell you," she said softly, gripping his hands and holding them tightly.

"Is it about your interest in the Bowline River?" he asked.

"Yes. But it's also about the lies I've told you—"

"Lies?" he interrupted. "What are you talking about?"

She swallowed hard. This was it. "I came here under false pretenses, Frankie. I've been lying to you since the day we met. I let you think you invited me here—"

He shook his head, his expression confused. "You've been lying to me?"

"Yes. I'm so sorry. I needed to come here for my grandmother's sake. See—"

"What does your grandmother have to do with you coming here?"

"Everything."

"The whole thing about the documentary—"

"A lie," she whispered.

He stared at her like he'd never seen her before. "Are you really even Kate West?"

"Of course. And Gram is my grandmother. Almost all the personal things I told you are true."

"Almost?" he said, and pulling his hands from hers, took a step back. "I don't understand."

"I know. I'm trying to tell you. The things that have passed between us are real. Just calm down and listen."

"Don't tell me to calm down," he said raising his voice. Jaw set, he hitched his hands on his waist and studied the ground for a moment, then he looked back at her. "Were you in cahoots with Jay Thurman?"

"How could you ask me such a thing?"

"You were down here when he 'found' you, weren't you?"

"It was a fluke. I had nothing to do with Jay. I'm trying to find something—"

"Gold?"

"No, diamonds."

"Diamonds!"

"They were stolen back when the bank was robbed."

"What are you talking about? There were no diamonds—"

"Yes, there were. The man who lost them decided to keep it quiet. The bank wasn't anxious to admit personal property had disappeared either, so—"

"This is gibberish," Frankie said, taking another step away.

"—so it never came out. Those diamonds actually belong to my grandmother now, Frankie. My grandfather was related to the man who lost them."

The seconds ticked by as he stared at her. "Is this the truth or another lie?"

She took a shaky breath. "It's the truth."

"So, you're here to what? Steal diamonds?"

"No, not steal them."

"Right," he said with sarcasm. "That's why you've

been so up-front with everyone. That's why you've been sneaking around. You had no intention of ever telling me any of this, did you?"

"No," she admitted, no longer looking in his eyes. They were mere slits now and whatever she'd seen sparkling in them five minutes before had gone away.

"I should have known it was all too good to be true," he said in a voice that broke her heart.

"What do you mean?" she asked.

"Us. You. All too fast...all too perfect."

"Frankie," she pleaded. "Please, I know you're angry—"

"Stop," he said and she raised her gaze at the tone of his voice. "Yeah, I'm angry. I feel used and I've only really felt that way once before when Jay—but, I'm also disappointed. I would hope by now that you'd recognize my priorities. What's important to me on this ranch are the people. If you'd only confided in me."

"I wanted to," she almost whispered.

"Then why didn't you?"

"I need these diamonds for my grandmother's safety. How could I possibly risk that based on the trust I began to feel for a man I was falling in love with? What if I was mistaken?"

He shook his head. "We all make mistakes," he said as though he'd almost made a huge one by believing in her. He looked toward the river then back at her. "I can't talk about this anymore tonight. I don't want to say things I'll regret. I need time to process what you've told me. Let me get through tomorrow morning and then we'll figure this out. Get in the truck and I'll give you a ride back to the ranch."

"I can walk—"

"I'm not leaving you alone out here," he said. She wasn't sure how he meant that and she didn't ask. She agreed with him: they'd both already said enough. She got in the truck.

Chapter Nineteen

Frankie loitered in the kitchen the next morning, waiting for Kate to appear. Gary Dodge, Pat Lowell, his dad and brothers were all out loading ATVs onto trailers they could use when they got to Ten Cent Creek. Gary had brought a bunch of cameras and digging equipment so they'd ruled out horses as transport. Grace had walked up to spend the morning with Kinsey. Lily and Charlie were both sleeping in since today was an in-service day at his school and there were no classes.

Kate finally appeared. He darted her a quick glance but it was long enough to tell she'd rested about as good as he had, which wasn't saying much.

"I waited for you," he said.

She nodded.

Was he still angry and hurt? Yes. Did he still yearn to see her smile, to wipe the worry out of her eyes? Yes to that, too. It was like being caught in a whirlpool, emotions spinning him around. "Kate, I don't want to go off worrying about whether you'll be here when I get back," he said and meant it.

"I wouldn't leave like that," she said.

"I hope not. Please, wait until this is over to do anything."

"I have to continue looking, Frankie. Nothing has changed about the diamonds except I'll have to prove they belong to Gram."

"You're a one note song on that matter," he said.

"I know. I have to be."

"Then let's compromise. I'll help you find them when I get back."

Tears gathered in her eyes and she flicked them away with her fingertips.

He gripped her shoulders. "Don't cry," he said with a swift glance.

"I'm just so ashamed," she whispered. "Are you ever going to be able to look directly at me again?"

"I hope so," he said with more honesty than either of them could bear. He leaned forward and kissed her forehead. "Just wait for me," he added. A horn honked outside and he tore himself away from her. It was time to shift gears and try to concentrate on buried treasure.

KATE SADDLED GINGER and rode her across the bridge, her goal to reclaim the backpack she'd ditched last night. This was the first morning in her life that she'd awoken knowing she carried a new life and the weight of that tiny responsibility had actually made everything clear.

A baby meant the future and though parts of hers were troubling, parts were sad and parts were devastating with their potential for loss, it was that future that mattered.

Seeing Frankie this morning had reminded her of the flip side of the saying he'd used the night before. The truth may set you free, but it doesn't always set everybody else free. She'd caused him a lot of self-doubt and pain and for that she was truly sorry. If he gave her a chance, she would try to make it up to him—it depended on him now.

Eventually, she found the ungainly pack where she'd thrown it in the underbrush and strapped it to Ginger's back. The beach was right up ahead, and curious to see the rock in the light of day, she rode on. Once there, she looped Ginger's reins over a branch and made her way down the trail. The sun had burned away Jay's ghost and she felt no foreboding, just rampant curiosity. On a whim, she trotted back up to Ginger and took her pack off the back of the saddle. Frankie had asked her to wait for him, but here she was and she found she couldn't. It wouldn't hurt to look around a little…

Down on the beach again, she reviewed what Greg Abernathy had told her as she unpacked her tools. She approached the rock slowly and circled it.

How did you bury something in a rock? You didn't, not without tools or explosives. It had been done on the run so presumably whoever hid the diamonds hadn't had climbing equipment and, besides, the rock had been in the water at the time. It must be that the mountain-top lining up with the boulder and the snagged tree that had existed at the time created a landmark. She turned to look behind her and almost fell over.

The fire had cleared a clear path back to where Frankie's house had once hovered in the boughs. And now visible through that gap was the top of an old, charred, snagged tree.

She moved to align herself and walked toward the verge, swinging her machete, climbing the rise of the bank carefully as she fought the inevitable vines. She did this for several moments until the ground evened out. Yesterday's fire had come within fifty feet and the vines here had shriveled from the heat. She swung the machete at the largest clump. It stopped abruptly as it hit rock, the impact vibrating up her arm.

Quickly, she cleared as much undergrowth as possible until she revealed the unmistakable circular shape of a crumbling old well. Once, there had been a house nearby, but that had burned to the ground before the robbery. The well had been abandoned for well over a century. Was it the hiding spot? She shone a light in the middle of the formation and discovered rocks had been piled inside the three-foot circle to within a foot of its rim. They may have been part of a collapse or they may have been put there. She glanced back at the river—this close to water, a well wouldn't have to be deep. The diamonds could be closer than she dared to dream.

There was only one way to find out.

"I WANT YOU to know how grateful I am that my rash actions yesterday didn't result in a tragedy for Kate West," Pat Lowell told Frankie as they unpacked gear from the back of a trailer.

"I appreciate that," Frankie said.

Pat was dressed as he always was, in a button-down shirt, this one bright blue, and tweed pants. He looked about as out of place in a field of livestock as was possible. He had used the notes the expert made to direct them to a small grove of trees close to the creek that would be three times as wide come winter. Horses and cattle watched the goings-on from a distance as Pike, Chance and Gary began digging in the rocky earth.

"I guess it wouldn't have happened at all if she'd only been here the day or two she originally planned," Pat added.

"I guess not," Frankie said. He set a stack of shoring lumber aside and narrowed his eyes. "Let me ask you a question. In all your investigations did you ever come up with any data or rumor about diamonds being stolen along with the gold?"

Pat's forehead furrowed. "Diamonds? What do you mean?"

"Loose diamonds, I guess. I'm not sure."

"There was zero mention of diamonds," Pat said firmly. "Why do you ask?"

Frankie shook his head. "Maybe she's still lying," he muttered.

"What? Who?"

"Nothing," Frankie said quickly. "Excuse me, I think I better go help Pike and Gary dig." He stalked off, wanting desperately to believe Kate and yet wondering if he was a fool to do so. He'd bet his left arm she was down at the river right that moment despite him having asked her to wait for him.

For two hours, he worked out his mixed-up feelings by attacking the ground with a shovel, widening the hole until it began to fill with water. "This is impossible," Gary finally said as mud oozed over his boots. "Let's take a break. We need to ask Pat if there's any indication in the expert's notes that will help us narrow the search."

They all paused to wash off in the creek. Frankie took off his shirt, dipped it in the water and wrung it out before putting it back on. It felt great against his overheated skin.

"Where's Pat?" he asked when he caught up with the other guys grabbing sodas from an ice chest.

"Dad said he felt a migraine coming on," Pike said. "It appears he took the notes with him so now we're playing a waiting game while he drives back to the house to get his medicine."

"I didn't know Pat had migraines," Frankie said. He looked at Gary. "Did you?"

"First time I've heard anything about it," Gary said.

As they sat on the edge of the trailers discussing their options, Frankie's mind wandered immediately to Kate—no surprise there.

Twenty-four hours ago, he would have moved heaven and earth to save her from Jay. He'd known exactly how he felt about her. And now?

What had she said last night? Something about not trusting him with the truth because she'd been falling in love with him. But last night she had spilled her guts— did that mean what he thought it meant? Did that mean she knew she was in love now?

And how did he feel about that?

"I'm going to go check on Pat," Frankie said because he didn't want to announce he wanted—he needed—to see Kate. This was 90 percent his project and walking out in the middle of it went against every instinct except one and that's the one Frankie couldn't ignore.

He was in love with Kate West. Upset with her, yes, that too, but in love. He'd been in love with her since first glance. He'd known it, too, he'd *felt* it.

Who was he to condemn her for being scared and telling a lie when to her, at first, he was a complete stranger? He'd done the same thing to his own father. He'd bet the ranch she didn't have a shred of evidence to prove the diamonds—if there were diamonds—were legally hers. She'd probably caught some rambling of her grandmother's or gossip passed from one relative to another and been desperate enough to move heaven and earth to try to find a way to save her grandmother's house. The bottom line was everything important about her rang true in the deepest recesses of his heart.

Now that he'd turned this corner in his head, he was anxious to share the news with Kate. He drove past the road that had once led to his tree house but as he passed it by, he slowed down. There had been a dust trail hanging in the still air and that made him curious. Had the fire restarted? Was Kate down at the part of the river where he'd come across her last night? He backed up and started down his road until he saw the back end of a red SUV pulled behind some trees. That was Pat's car—what was he doing out here? He parked next to it and looked inside in case the man had passed out or something. The car was empty.

He stood there a second until he heard the unmistakable sound of a horse approaching and turned quickly. Ginger wandered up to him, her saddle empty, reins dragging on the ground. There was no way to tell who'd been riding her but it was obvious whoever they were had been left behind and he couldn't imagine the horse had a thing to do with it. Chances were good this horse had been with Kate—so where was Kate?

He slipped off the saddle and bridle, dumped them in the back of his truck and sent Ginger on her way. Then he walked down the road. Reason said Kate might have fallen so he kept his eyes peeled. There was nothing to suggest she was in trouble. The sound of rock hitting rock finally reached his ears and it actually relaxed him a little as he vividly recalled the way she'd hacked at the rocks on the other side of the river. He'd known her curiosity would drive her down here!

But what did Pat have to do with anything?

That question turned more important when Frankie rounded the curve in the road and caught sight of a blue shirt and tweed pants. Pat stood very still up ahead, his back to Frankie, peering through the branches of the remaining stand of trees that had escaped the wrath of the fire.

He was about to call out to Pat and ask what was going on when Pat moved into the trees. The way he did it was so stealthy it couldn't help but arouse suspicion. A sudden whoop up ahead sounded excited. Pat paused midstep at the sound and Frankie drew back toward the shadows. He knew it was Kate's voice. Was it possible there really were diamonds and she'd just found them?

Pat was on the move again. A few seconds later he called out. "Kate? I've been looking for you!"

Frankie crept up to where Pat had stood a few moments before and found an unobstructed view of Kate standing in a clearing, up to her waist inside a circular depression. Dozens of toaster-sized rocks lay on the ground outside the perimeter and that explained what he'd been hearing. She'd been lifting rocks out of the old well.

Was that a good thing for a pregnant woman to do? Why hadn't she waited for him?

"Mr. Abernathy!" Kate said. "What are you doing here? Is it Gram?"

"No, no," Pat said as he walked into view. "I checked on her a couple of days ago—she's fine. I just got to thinking of you out here all by yourself. Thought I'd help." He paused before adding, "What's that you're holding? Did you find the diamonds?"

"I'm not sure. There's some rotting clothes in here

and boots, too. No bones but I just found this saddlebag and my hopes are high," she added.

"Let's get you out of that hole," he said, extending a hand. "I'll take that old thing."

She handed him the saddlebag before climbing out of the well. Holding it gingerly, Pat walked toward the river. "This thing is disgusting," he called over his shoulder as they both made their way down the incline.

"I sure hope this is it," Kate said as they reached the shore.

Frankie had been cautiously following along in their wake. He wasn't sure what was going on or what to do about it. Why did Pat answer to the name Abernathy? It sounded like he knew Kate far better than he'd let on. Some part of Frankie needed to see how this played out.

Pat swished the saddlebag in the river, then struggled with the leather ties, finally producing a knife to cut them. They both knelt on the shore as he withdrew a bag that looked exactly like those Frankie's father had taken from the bank decades before. Laying that on the ground between them, Pat sliced it open and they both gasped.

Even from where Frankie stood, the sparkle and glitter of gems flashed brilliantly in the sun. Pat laughed as he reached into a pocket and withdrew something he unobtrusively moved to hold behind his back. Frankie immediately froze in place. Pat clutched a small gun and to Frankie it looked exactly like the one Jay Thurman had wielded the day before.

It no longer mattered if any of this made sense. He had to get that gun.

Kate lifted an extravagant emerald necklace laced with sapphires and diamonds. She set it against her throat as though wearing it and, despite her flushed face, straggling hair and the smears of dirt on her cheeks, turned into a princess out of an old book. "It's beautiful," she gushed. "There's a bracelet and earrings, too, and a matching tiara." Her brow wrinkled. "But these aren't mine. My grandfather's great-uncle was a diamond merchant, you told me so yourself. What would he be doing with these precious old pieces? They must be worth a king's ransom."

"You're right," Pat said. "They're not yours. They're mine." The gun was in front of him now, pointed at Kate. She dropped the necklace and they both stood up.

Frankie was still close to the bank where overgrowth concealed him. He couldn't see how he could rush Pat without risking Kate's safety. Would he really shoot her?

"I don't understand," Kate repeated. "What about my grandfather's file and the diamond merchant—"

"There was no file. For that matter, there was no diamond merchant, either. I did know your grandfather but he wouldn't have shared an office with me if I were the last man on earth. We hated each other," Pat said. "But I knew he had a wife and I knew she was in trouble. I found out about you and your determination to save her... so I called myself Greg Abernathy and made you an offer I knew you couldn't refuse. I needed someone to look around and figured if I gave you a good cover story, the blasted Hastings wouldn't suspect you."

"But why?"

"Simple. I'm sick of barely scraping by. I lost my pension in a divorce...it doesn't matter. While researching this documentary, I came across a letter written by a woman a long, long time ago. It revealed the theft of priceless jewels that had never been disclosed. A man with ties to the Dalton family had it. I, ah, took it."

"You killed Dave Dalton," she said, horrified.

"It had to be done. Just like this has to be done."

"They'll figure out—"

"That I killed you, too? That I killed Jay Thurman before he could shoot his ugly mouth off about who hired him, who gave him a gun, who told him to make as big a distraction as possible just like I've got those clowns doing up at Ten Cent Creek right this minute? The truth is no one knows where the gold went. It was probably discovered and moved decades ago." He'd worked himself up a little as he talked, and now he lowered his voice. "Possibly someone will figure out what I've done, but by then I'll be in Mexico living off an empress's jewels."

"But—"

"Show-and-tell is over," he said jabbing the gun against her ribs. "I'll make it fast—"

Frankie knew it was now or never. He grabbed his key ring out of his pocket and threw it at the rocks on the bank to his left. As both Kate and Pat looked toward the sound, he took off at a dead run, Pat his target, seeing him through a haze of anger and hate, desperate to stop the man who had manipulated them all in order to line his own pockets. He saw Kate grab Pat's arm and heard gunfire. He registered the fact Kate was on the ground a millisecond before he barreled into Pat.

The impact knocked Pat into the water. Frankie went after him. Pat fired the gun again. Frankie ducked the shot as the older man plowed farther out in the river. Frankie followed. Both of them slipped, but Pat recovered and flung himself away. Frankie grabbed him around the waist and that propelled them both into deeper water. As they struggled, the current caught them and before Frankie could prevent it, they were both swept downstream.

He hung on to Pat, fighting to get the gun as the shore whizzed past. Within a minute, they passed under the bridge. So busy trying not to get shot, Frankie couldn't swim to calmer water. Pat threw his gun hand at Frankie's face and the cold metal hit his cheekbone. He grabbed at the gun right as Pat pulled the trigger. The gun fired and Pat's eyes grew round. Blood spurted into the water from a wound in his throat. Frankie supported his head to keep his face out of the water and began paddling toward shore. By the time he got to a point where his feet touched bottom, he was pretty sure Pat was dead but he dragged him out of the water anyway, dropped his shoulders onto the beach and made sure he wasn't breathing.

He wasn't positive one of Pat's earlier shots hadn't hit Kate. He took a deep breath and began the climb to the road where he'd parked his truck to spy on Kate a lifetime ago. As he stepped onto the road, he found his own truck hurtling toward him.

Kate sat behind the wheel and for a second, their gazes connected through the dusty windshield. She jumped out of the truck and ran to him. "You're hurt," she cried.

"I'm not hurt," he said looking down at himself. His wet shirt was streaked with red. "It's Pat's blood." He put his arms around her. "Are you okay?"

"Shaky, but yes, I'm okay."

"And the baby?"

"Still here," she said.

"Incredible," he whispered.

"What made you come looking for me?" she asked, staring into his eyes. This time he didn't look away.

"I needed to see you," he said, unable to take his arms from around her waist. "I needed to ask you to forgive me."

"For what? For being offended I lied to you? For making you feel used?" Her lips trembled and tears rolled down her cheeks. "For hurting you?"

"For judging you," he said. "For forgetting that I love you and that means I trust you and believe in you without reservation."

"You love me?" she whispered.

"More than life itself," he responded and without further delay pulled her into an embrace that would last a lifetime.

Epilogue

The letter was old and faded but legible, the writing feminine. It was found with Pat Lowell's things and was dated 1965.

"'If you are reading this letter, then you have found the coins I have been hiding for fifty years,'" it began. "'My legal name is Mary Dalton, but I will always think of myself as Mamie Covey. I have loved only one man in my life and his name was William Adler.

The time for excuses is long over. When I was nineteen, my father, who ran the Green Peak Mine in Falls Bluff, promised my hand to an emotionless, widowed attorney named Matthew Dalton. Father ignored my tears; he did not care that my heart and the baby I secretly carried belonged to William.

We wanted to run away but William was young and poor. The answer to our problem came when my father foolishly revealed that a sizeable gold shipment was coming to the bank. I talked my William into robbing it. He enlisted the help of the Bates brothers. I dressed up as a man. William cracked the safe within minutes. He and I went into the vault. Earl and Sammy stood guard. When we'd given them as much as they could carry, they left the bank. William and I went back inside. That's when I opened a drawer and gulped.

There was a woman staying at the hotel where I worked. I'd met her once or twice and she struck me with her low manner. I had heard she was once the mistress of an emperor and that when he grew tired of her, she stole his wife's priceless jewels before fleeing the country.

Those jewels were in the vault! I stuffed them into a bank bag. William cautioned me to not tell Sammy or Earl. When we left town, we each had two bags. The men's carried just gold. One of mine also carried the jewels. We split up when we got outside town. William and I went to the spot beside the river where a house had burned down a dozen years before. There is a bend in the river where a large boulder we call the bonnet rock divides the water's flow. We have named it snag hollow because of a tree…it is our spot. William hid the jewels along with my male clothing.

I dressed as a woman again. William left to join the others taking the full bag of my gold with him to ease my load. I went back to my bed and hid what gold I still had. I waited for word from William until the news spread about what the posse had done. I rode out to see and there was William and the others… I cannot say any more about this; it is too painful.

My father was suspicious of me. He insisted I marry Matthew Dalton. I said I would on the condition we leave this town. Seven months later, I gave birth to William's daughter, Amelia, who Matthew thought was his own child. He was not as successful as he led my father to believe yet I was never tempted to use a single coin. Matthew died young.

The cursed gold remains untouched. If I knew how

to repay it, I would. I am old now, my daughter is gone, her daughter is with child. I live with my stepson George and his family in the same house we bought when coming here. He knows nothing of this gold. It is hidden and hopefully remains that way for eternity.

I yearn only to see my beloved again whether in heaven or in hell.

Mamie.'"

"The fourth man was a woman," Kate said when they'd finished reading the letter.

"My great-great-grandmother," Frankie said. "No wonder that town always spoke to me." He kissed Kate's forehead. "Dave Dalton's father was Mamie's stepson so Dave and I weren't related by blood. Dave's father found the coins late in his life and spent them sparingly, passing them on to Dave when he died five years ago. I've talked with Sara who still hasn't found them. My guess is they'll turn up with Pat's belongings. Dave signed his death warrant when he showed that letter to Pat."

"He signed a lot of death warrants that day," Kate said.

Three months later

"GRAM IS DOING GREAT," Kate said as she handed Sierra back her cell phone. She had to break down and get her own. Finding one that worked both in Seattle and here was tricky; in a few weeks, that wouldn't be an issue. "Every time I tell her about the ranch and Frankie, she just beams. She can't remember any of it thirty seconds later, but they're a good thirty seconds every single time."

"Frankie said you sold her house," Sierra said.

Kate nodded. "They're going to tear it down and build

a condo. In a way it's sad but Gram couldn't even remember the place when I took her there the last time. I'm
moving her to a really nice facility in Falls Bluff in a couple of weeks so I can help Frankie build our new house."

Sierra spontaneously hugged Kate. Pike had been
right. She and his auburn-haired girlfriend had formed
a fast friendship. Kate was so glad Sierra had taken on
a partner so she could spend more time on the ranch.

They were sitting outside on the porch bench and
tucked their feet out of the way as Gary, Frankie and
their cameraman, Oliver, came out of the house.

"Then all that's left is postproduction work," Gary
was saying but Oliver shook his head.

"No, there's one more thing. Frankie had an idea and
I think it's great. We're going to burn down the hanging tree."

Gary glanced at Frankie. "Why am I just hearing
about it?"

Frankie took Kate's hand and pulled her to her feet
where he put both arms around her and looked at Gary
from over her head. "Because we just thought of it," he
said.

It was nice of him to share the credit, Kate thought,
but unnecessary. Still she thoroughly agreed with him.
The ghost town would be razed in the fall—it was time
for the tree to go, too. Not only was it very old, but it
stood only for misery.

That's how it came to be that a week later, the entire
Hastings family gathered on the plateau. Grace held her
newest grandson and sat next to Kinsey and Gerard in a
beach chair located a safe distance from the tree. Charlie had dug marshmallows out of his backpack and now
pestered Chance to carve a stick so he could roast them

once the fire got going. Lily and Chance produced chilled cider and paper cups, announcing they were going to make today their combined prenuptial bachelor parties for their wedding next week. Sierra and Pike sat on the tail of his truck, holding hands, smiling at each other, Sierra's diamond sparkling at the base of her throat. She was going to make a fabulous bride come spring, which left just enough time for Kate and Frankie to sneak in a Christmas wedding and welcome a Valentine baby.

As soon as Harry showed up in the tank truck with water to control the blaze, they started the fire. It was an indication of the tree's advanced age and hidden rot that it burned with a vengeance. Kate looked up at Frankie and he smiled at her as he looped his arm around her shoulders.

"I love you," he said close to her ear, "but I swear, sometimes I forget Earl and Samuel Bates weren't your real relatives. I was standing here thinking that we're giving them a Viking send-off."

"Along with one for your great-great-grandfather, William Adler," Kate said. "May he and Mamie rest in peace."

"Well said."

The tree burned for hours and other than spraying the dry grass around its perimeter, needed no intervention. People began wandering off after a while, but not Frankie or the documentary film crew. Nor Kate. There was nowhere in the world she wanted to be but right where she was.

As it burned deep into the ground, something caught Oliver's eye through the camera lens and he called everyone over. They moved as close as they dared.

The truth hit them all at the same moment.

There, under the tree used to punish the thieves, deep down in the roots themselves, lay the plundered coins. They watched as the intense heat reduced them to a lake of molten gold.

"I'll be damned," Frankie whispered.

* * * * *

"The person behind this doesn't have respect for law enforcement. They think they're above the law. They've killed once, and they won't hesitate to do it again. If we get close, our lives might be in danger."

Blake shook her head. "Just because we made a mistake in there," she said, pointing to the office, "doesn't mean that you have to be dramatic. We're fine."

Her words made goose bumps rise on his arms. Anytime he'd ever gotten complacent in his job, or thought he was safe, was when he'd found himself in trouble.

"Think about it, Blake." Her name felt like velvet on his tongue; it even tasted sweet. He paused as he just looked at her for a moment.

"What?" she asked, locking eyes with him. And when she did, all he could think about was closing the distance between them.

DUST UP WITH THE DETECTIVE

BY
DANICA WINTERS

First Published in Great Britain 2016
By Mills & Boon, an imprint of HarperCollins*Publishers*
1 London Bridge Street, London, SE1 9GF

© 2016 Danica Winters

ISBN: 978-0-263-91920-2

46-1016

Our policy is to use papers that are natural, renewable and recyclable products and made from wood grown in sustainable forests. The logging and manufacturing processes conform to the legal environmental regulations of the country of origin.

Printed and bound in Spain
by CPI, Barcelona

Danica Winters is a multiple award-winning, bestselling author who writes books that grip readers with their ability to drive emotion through suspense and occasionally a touch of magic. When she's not working, she can be found in the wilds of Montana, testing her patience while she tries to hone her skills at various crafts—quilting, pottery and painting are not her areas of expertise. She believes the cup is neither half-full nor half-empty, but it better be filled with wine. Visit her website at www.danicawinters.net.

To Herb—
You make everything possible.
Always and forever.

Acknowledgements

This book wouldn't have been possible without the help
of my community. Major thanks to the Missoula
County Sheriff's Office and Brenda Bassett for their
time and patience in helping to answer
questions. Sergeant Prather, it was an honor to have had
the opportunity for a ride along and to pick your brain.
Your advice was invaluable. And to all those who serve
our communities, you and your family's sacrifice are
appreciated. You help to make the world a better place.

Chapter One

Everything in Montana was measured by time, not miles driven, not quality and not sacrifice. For example, the trip from Missoula to Butte took just under two hours. And her boyfriend? Nearly three months. At sixteen, the relationship had been too short to be called serious, yet long enough to leave her with a child. Then, in less than ten seconds, the relationship was over and she had been left with a beautiful daughter and fading dreams.

That was thirteen years ago. Thirteen terrifying, humbling and gratifying years. Nights spent soothing her daughter when she had ear infections, and days spent struggling to get where she was—a sheriff's officer with a steady job and a stable income. She was the only one strong enough to support her mother and her daughter. They needed her.

Dreams were for those who could afford them—and that would never be Blake West.

Her antiquated patrol unit's radio crackled to life as the 9-1-1 dispatcher's voice filled the car. "Blake, your mom called. Said there's some kind of issue up at your place."

She picked up the handset. "Dispatch, feel free to

remind my mother that nine-one-one is to be used for emergencies only."

"You tell your mother that," the woman said with a laugh.

Blake shook her head, as she thought about telling her throwback-to-another-era Irish mother that she wasn't to do something. Blake had a better chance of convincing the Pope to give up being Catholic.

"Really, though," the dispatcher continued, "she said your cell wasn't working. She sounded really upset."

Blake picked up her cell phone. Just like half of Silver Bow County, there was no service today where yesterday there had been—just another perk of living in a state where technology was an unreliable amenity.

"Is Megan okay?"

"She didn't say. Just said she needed you to come home."

Blake stepped on the gas as she turned the car down the set of roads that led to their house. "If she calls back, tell her I'm on my way."

She flicked on her lights and sped down the pothole-ravaged road that led to the house on the outskirts of the mining-centered city of Butte. At one time the historical city had been beautiful with its brick buildings and Old West charm. There had been an uptick in the mine's activities around the city in the 1990s, but now it was a decaying mass of run-down miner's row houses and the home of a pit full of water so toxic that it even killed the birds that dared to land on its surface.

Most of those left in town were small-time miners, those who hoped the large mine operations would open again someday, or those who had retired from the Pit.

It was the city of the strong, a city of survivors—just like Blake and her mother.

Gemma West could handle anything. If she was as upset as the dispatcher said, something had to be majorly wrong.

Had something happened to Megan? She was old enough to know the rules, but that didn't mean she hadn't done something to put herself in danger.

Blake took a series of long breaths as she forced herself to remain calm.

Megan was probably fine.

She pulled to a stop in front of their beige ranch-style home, which rested behind a mature, though chemically stunted, pine. Near its base was a scar from her father's car the day he'd left so many years ago. She'd always hated and loved that tree. It was a visible reminder of days and lives spent scratching and tearing away in the mines that were the fulcrum of the corrupt city and how that city and its vices had destroyed her family. No matter how many years went by, the tree would never grow, never change. Too much damage had been done.

"Mom! Megan?" she yelled, hoping they would step out the front door to meet her.

It was dead quiet. She made her way up the steps and opened the aluminum screen door with a rattle.

"Mom, you home? Megan?" she called, her voice nearing frantic tones only a dog could hear.

The smell of home cooking, the kind done by generations who didn't care about waistlines or cholesterol, wafted from the kitchen.

"Mom?" she asked, moving toward the scent of fried chicken.

Something was terribly wrong. Her mother could

hear a car coming from ten miles down the road, and she was notorious for meeting Blake at the front door, judgment in hand.

She moved to call for her daughter but stopped as the sound of the back door's rusty hinges screeched.

She wasn't alone.

Out of instinct, she reached down and put her hand on her Glock, unclicking the snap that held it safely in its holster. After slipping the gun out, she raised it, ready to meet whatever or whomever she would find in the kitchen.

The old wooden floor creaked as she tried to sneak down the hall. Pressing her back against the wall, she readied herself.

Had someone broken in? Was someone trying to take her daughter?

Her daughter.

She lowered her gun. Maybe it was just Megan. The girl loved to surprise her—to jump out from behind walls and make her scream. If it was, she couldn't let her law enforcement training come into play. She couldn't risk hurting someone she loved.

"Megan, is that you?" she asked, trying to sound playful instead of terrified. "Pumpkin, you need to answer me." She lowered her gun and hid it behind her hip as she eased around the corner and into the kitchen.

On the counter under the window, a fresh plate of fried chicken sat cooling, its oil oozing into the paper towel underneath. A can of beans was next to the plate, the can opener still resting on its lip, as if her mother had been opening it but had suddenly been called away.

A movement outside caught her eye as something

scuttled across the backyard and disappeared behind the shed.

The hair on her arms rose. *What is going on?*

She took a step toward the back door.

Megan's scream pierced the air. The sound resonated from the darkened shed.

Blake ran outside. Gun raised. Ready. If someone was hurting her daughter, they would die.

Through the thin particleboard door of the shed, she heard muffled voices. She stopped, trying to quiet her breathing as she listened. She could barely make out her mother's voice.

She moved to the door. "Get down! Get down on the ground!" she yelled, kicking open the door, smashing it against the wall.

Megan was sitting at the table, her back to her. A man stood in the shadows, his arm raised. He was holding something.

"Put down your weapon!" Blake ordered.

The man moved, and a thin light from the tiny, dirt-covered window reflected off the blade of a hacksaw.

"I said put down your weapon!" She aimed her gun at his center mass.

The man looked at her. In the shadows she could make out only the whites of his eyes and the slight movement of his lips as he started to speak.

"Mom, no!" Megan turned around. Her round face was covered in sweat, and her eyes were wide with fear.

She raised her hands. Her wrists were in shackles.

Blake's finger trembled on the trigger as the man slowly lowered his weapon to the floor. "What in the hell do you think you are doing to my daughter?"

Chapter Two

"Not every situation requires a gun," Gemma said as she walked up the steps to the back door. "You scared poor Megan. Didn't she, honey?" Her mother wrapped her arm around her daughter and gave her a reassuring squeeze.

"I'm fine, Grandma, really." Megan tried to wiggle out of her embrace.

Blake snorted lightly. If the girl was a bit older, she would have realized that, for good or bad, no matter how much she struggled, she would never be out of Gemma West's grip.

"I'm sorry about this mess, Jeremy. Having a gun pointed at you isn't much of a thank-you for your help in trying to get Megan out of those handcuffs," her mother continued.

Blake looked over at Jeremy Lawrence. She'd always thought of him as the gangly neighbor she had once had a crush on, but seeing the grown-up detective now, it was clear he was nothing like the boy she remembered. Now he stood tall with impossibly wide shoulders, a chiseled jaw and the piercing green eyes of a stranger. Everything from the way he walked, solid and firm, to the way he watched their every move, in control and ever vigilant, screamed alpha man.

"You're a tough one, Megan," Jeremy said as he held the door for them. "You remind me of my daughter. I think you'd like her. Once she got ahold of my handset and started playing Simon Says on the radio. It was funny, except for the fact that it was on a live channel. I thought the dispatchers were going to lose it." He turned to Blake and smiled like he understood what she was going through as a single mother.

She gave him a thankful nod, but he couldn't possibly know how hard it was. How each day she was plagued with Mom-guilt—the overwhelming fear that no matter what choices she made, she should be doing more for her daughter. As it was, she tried her best to be there for Megan, but because of the crazy nature of her job and her unconventional schedule, Megan was often left with her grandmother—who never missed an opportunity to remind Blake of all the things she could do better.

There was no way Jeremy could understand all the hats she had to wear to make it through the day.

"Were you mad when your daughter messed up, Mr. Lawrence?" Megan asked him as she made her way into the house.

Jeremy shook his head as he smiled at Blake. "It was my fault. It hadn't occurred to me she would play with my scanner."

"See, Mom, he wasn't mad when his daughter screwed up." Megan looked back at her as if gauging her residual anger.

"I'm not mad," Blake said as she followed her mother and daughter inside. "I just don't understand what possessed you to take my handcuffs out of my drawer and put them on. You had no business—"

Jeremy put his hand on her lower back as he followed her inside and let the door close behind them. His hot, familiar touch made her stop midsentence.

"I'm sure she didn't mean to upset you, Blake. Did you, Meg?" he asked, smiling as he gently moved his hand away, leaving behind the warmth of his touch.

Did he know what he was doing to her? The last man who had touched her, at least in that way, had been Megan's father. Sure, she and Jeremy had known each other as children, but he couldn't touch her so familiarly—not when their friendship had existed a lifetime ago.

"I'm sorry, Mom," Megan said.

"Jeremy's right. It's your mom's fault," Gemma said as she moved through the kitchen. "If she wouldn't have left the handcuffs where you could find them, none of this would have happened." She turned to face Blake. "And it would have been nice if you would have answered your phone."

She loved her mom, but the jab pierced deep, puncturing the little bubble of guilt that she tried to keep out of reach. Her mother was right; she had messed up. She shouldn't have left her cuffs where Megan could find them. But... "Mother, I have no control over where and when my phone works—you know this."

"Well, I don't think you have any business traipsing around the county without a phone that works. Do I need to call the sheriff to make sure you get a satellite phone?"

She looked to Jeremy. He didn't need to hear any of this. The last thing she needed was another officer thinking she was incompetent, or worse—that she needed her mother to fight her battles.

He gave her a Cheshire-cat grin, the same mischievous grin that he'd always used to get them out of trouble when they were kids.

"Mrs. West, is that your famous fried chicken?" He motioned toward the plate on the counter.

Her mother took the bait, brightening up at the chance to feed a man. "Oh, are you hungry? Why don't you have a bite?" True to her nature, the question was more an order than a request. "I'll throw the beans on, and it'll be ready in a jiff."

"That sounds great, but I need to get running home. I'm just up from Missoula for the night."

"Really? Is everything okay?" From the look on her face, it seemed like Gemma meant the question to come from a place of concern, but her voice made it clear that she was more curious than empathetic. As if she looked forward to some thread of gossip that she could share at the next bunco party.

"I'm sure everything's okay. Right, Jeremy?" Blake hinted, hoping that he would take this as his chance to get out before he and his family became the central focus of the Butte Red Hatters Bunco Club for the next six months.

He looked at her, his eyes shimmering with something she could have sworn resembled lust, but she shrugged it off. There was no way he would be interested in her. He was married.

She glanced down at his ring finger—his ring was missing. *That's right...* He'd gotten a divorce. When her mother had told her about it a few months past, she had pushed the news aside as irrelevant. Yet, with him standing in front of her, it seemed more relevant than ever. The knot in her gut tightened as she forced herself to look away from his naked hand.

Even if he wasn't married, he wouldn't want her. No man would want to take on a single mom who lived with her mother and was struggling to make it in a small-town sheriff's department—unless he was a glutton for punishment.

"Things are a little rough. You know…family drama."

Her mother perked up. "What's going on?"

"It's just my brother. He's going through a hard time."

"Is that right," her mother chimed. "Is there anything I can do?"

"Thanks, Mrs. W, but it'll be all right." Jeremy sent her a grateful but guarded smile. "Unfortunately, I'll have to pass on the chicken—but it smells great," he added, as her mother's face fell.

"Oh, okay," she said, her voice specked with disappointment, the kind that always moved Blake into doing whatever it was Gemma truly wanted.

Jeremy's body tensed, his biceps pressing hard against his cotton T-shirt. Apparently, Gemma West's shaming worked on someone besides her. Why did her mother have to put everyone under her spell?

Megan thumped down in the chair by the dining table. "Mom, I'm hungry."

"Thank you, Jeremy, for helping us out," Blake said, motioning toward her daughter.

He glanced at her and smiled again. The way he looked at her made her temperature rise. No one had looked at her like that, like she really existed as something more than a mother or a sheriff's deputy, in a long time.

She turned away as she scolded herself. He was just looking at her. It didn't mean anything. She was lonely. She needed to get a handle on her emotions. Crushes were for those who had a chance—which she didn't.

He needed to go. She simply could not be around a man like him.

"I need to get back to work. After you?" She walked to the door and opened it, motioning for him to leave.

He turned to walk out.

"I hope everything goes well with your brother. By the way, which brother is it?" her mother called behind him, throwing a speed bump into Blake's plans.

Jeremy looked back over his shoulder. "Robert."

"Where's Casper these days?" her mother continued.

Blake's sweaty hand slipped on the open door.

"He's working up north with Border Patrol."

"That's wonderful," her mom said, turning to her with a raise of the eyebrow. She flashed a glance back at Jeremy, like she was trying to coach Blake on how to get him to stay. "Isn't that nice, Blake?"

"Yes, that's great, Mother."

Jeremy chuckled. "If you need me again, Mrs. W, I'll be in town for a couple of days." He brushed against Blake as he made his way out the door. His touch magnified the need she was trying her best to ignore. "Hey, if you need a break, maybe we could meet up sometime," he whispered so low that only she could hear.

In a flash, she was back in high school, and they were planning to sneak out of the house. The thrill of being caught and the excitement that came with breaking the rules filled her. Just as quickly as the feelings rose, she stomped them out. She wasn't sixteen. She was a mother. And her daughter came first—no matter how badly she wanted to take Jeremy up on his offer.

"Thanks, but maybe next time you're in town."

He nodded, but there was a faint look of hurt deep in his eyes as he turned away. She couldn't help taking one last look as he walked away. His jeans were the kind with the fancy stitching on the back pockets, the kind that always drew a person's eye to them and, in this case, to his perfectly round behind.

Clearly the man worked out.

Dang it.

She forced herself to look away. What was wrong with her today?

She could feel her mother's eyes boring into her back. She needed to leave, to get to work, but she let the door close as she turned back to her family.

"That right there is why you don't have a man in your life," her mother said with a *tsk* as she flurried around the kitchen, getting the potato salad out of the fridge.

"Maybe I don't have a man in my life because I don't want one," Blake retorted. Instantly she wished she hadn't, because it would only allow her mother to continue on her soapbox.

"That Jeremy, he's got a good head on his shoulders. You need a man like him. You would get one, if you weren't so hard to please."

That was the pot calling the kettle black.

"Here you go, sweetie." Her mother set a plate of fried chicken and potato salad in front of Megan and went back to the can of beans.

"Thanks, Grandma."

Blake glanced down at her watch. "I need to go." She gave Megan a kiss on the top of the head while her daughter chomped away. "Please don't get into any more of my things."

"Wait," her mother said. "Why don't you eat first?"

There was a rumble in her stomach, but she had to escape the mess that was her personal life. Work was so much easier. "I'm good, Mom."

"Fine then." Her mother's disdain was palpable. "At least take the rest of this food over to Jeremy and his family as a thank-you. You know, he didn't have to come over here to help us. It was just lucky he was even around. We could have been all day if we had to wait for you."

The sharp edge of her mother's words deepened her wounds. It wasn't that she didn't want to be closer to her family, but she had to work. She had to support the people she loved most, even if they sometimes forgot how much pressure she was under.

Her mother covered the plate of chicken with plastic wrap, then shoved it into Blake's hands. "Now run along. And don't get lost with my chicken." Her mother pushed her out the door. "And make sure you let his mother know that I'd like my plate back."

It was like she was eight years old again, her mother moving her along in her pursuit toward her own means. She would never be exactly what Gemma wanted her to be, would always be a disappointment, constantly seeking her mother's approval and trying to make her proud. No matter how badly she wanted them to, some things would never change.

Chapter Three

Splitting the blanket. Trimming away the deadweight. Losing one's other half. Detective Jeremy Lawrence had heard them all, but they all meant one thing: he was divorced.

He thumbed the empty place on his ring finger where his wedding band used to be.

Genevieve had made such a big deal about the ring when they were first together. She hadn't wanted him to wear yellow gold, claiming it would clash with her engagement ring—a ring she'd also picked out—and he couldn't get silver as it would tarnish. He'd felt like an idiot standing there in the jewelry store getting told that tungsten was really the best option for him, but at twenty-two he'd been young and dumb and willing to put up with anything if it meant he got to marry her. Heck, he'd thought himself lucky. She'd been the cheerleader, the girl who could light up a room with a smile and, better yet, make him burn with want with the mere trailing of her fingertips.

Everything, all the way down to her name, had to be classy.

The marriage had been over the minute she had figured out he was just a regular guy, not the idealized version she must have had in her mind.

He reached in his pocket, pulled out the ring and let it drop on his dresser, the dresser he'd had since he was a child. It was funny how a piece of unloved furniture could last longer than a marriage. If nothing else, it proved that a dead oak was stronger than a life built on feelings. Maybe there really was something to being cold, lifeless…at least you could weather the storms.

None of it mattered. He'd gotten a daughter out of their screwed-up marriage. He could be thankful for that, even if Penny didn't live with him. At least he had something to hold on to.

His father's footsteps echoed down the hall toward his room; there was a knock on the door. "Jeremy, you in there?"

"Yeah, Dad. What do you need?"

"Your mother's wondering when you're going to run out to Robert's. It would be good if you could get out there before dark," his father said, as if he hadn't heard them fighting over Robert for the last ten minutes.

It was funny; he'd been home just a few hours, but when he had set foot in the door it was like he had stepped back in time—parents fighting, brother missing and him searching for a way to escape. Just like when he'd been a kid, he'd found refuge at the neighbors', but instead of being the one who needed to be saved, this time he'd paid them back for all the times Mrs. W was there for him. Finally things were coming full circle.

And just like the past, Blake had rushed him to the door while she made a point of being out-of-bounds.

He took one last look at the ring, now at home tucked

safely away in his past. "I was just about to head out," he told his father.

"Good," his father said, turning to leave. "Oh, and Blake is here. Brought over some supper as a thank-you."

He figured Mrs. W must have forced her to come over. It really was like all those years ago. He loved his family, but he needed to get the hell out of Butte and away from the ghosts that haunted this place—regardless of how beautiful one particular ghost was.

Blake stood in the living room, her hand on the doorknob. She was talking to his mother, who was sitting in her recliner. Blake's uniform top was stretched tight over her bulletproof vest. The buttons gaped slightly, revealing a T-shirt underneath. As she moved, he caught a quick glimpse of her black bra strap, and he felt his body shift in response. There was just something so *right* about a woman who wore a uniform and sexy lingerie underneath.

He wanted to rip open her shirt and her vest, kiss the lines of her lacy bra, slip what he figured would be matching black panties down her legs.

Jeremy forced himself to look away, focusing on the painting of a meadow that had hung on the living room wall so long that there was a faint brown smoke line around it.

"Blake was just telling me that she has seen Robert lately," his mother started. "Isn't that right, Blake?"

Blake nodded.

"Apparently she was out to his place a few weeks ago." His mother tapped her fingers on the armrests of her chair.

"It wasn't anything that major," Blake offered.

"There was just a minor dispute. It was in the *Montana Standard*. I thought you must have heard."

He hadn't read the local newspaper in years, but Blake was right. It was surprising his mother hadn't gotten a call from the phone tree. Her friends lived for nothing more than to read the obituaries and scan through the weekly police blotter.

"What happened?" Jeremy asked.

Blake chewed on her lower lip, and her gaze flickered to his mother, as if there was something that she didn't want to say in front of her. "You know, just the normal thing."

"Was it something to do with his wife?" His mother turned to him. "Tiffany has been threatening to leave him for months now. I told you that Robert needed your help. I wish you could've been here earlier, Jeremy."

"Well, Mom, you know how it is. Work's been busy," he said, but he was focused on Blake and how she shifted her weight from one foot to the other.

His mother said something under her breath that he was only too glad he couldn't hear.

He made his way to Blake and opened the door. "You busy this afternoon?"

Blake glanced down at her watch. "Why?"

He waited for her to step outside and let the door close behind him. "I'd appreciate it if you can fill me in on what's going on with my brother," he told Blake.

She waved goodbye to his mother through the glass storm door. "Look, I appreciate what you did with Megan, but I don't want to get involved with you or whatever it is you have going on."

"Whoa." He breathed out, unsure why she had been so abrupt. "I just thought—"

She raised her hand. "No, stop. I shouldn't have lost my temper. I'm not upset with you. It's just my mother." She motioned toward her house.

She had every right to be upset after what she had walked into. It would have taken more than a little fried chicken to talk him down if he'd walked into a scene with someone holding a hacksaw over his daughter's head. Unlike her, he didn't know if he could have held back from shooting.

His gaze drifted to the utility belt at her waist. "Lots of calls coming in?" he asked as they walked across the lawn toward her house.

She slipped out her cell phone and glanced down at it. "To be honest, no. But I should be on patrol."

"What time do you get off?"

"Not for a few more hours."

"Well, if you aren't busy, I would really appreciate you running to Robert's with me."

She looked up at him, her blue eyes reflecting the color of the sky.

"I would hate to be walking into a mess up there." He silently hoped she would say yes, and it wasn't just because he wanted her to tell him about Robert. It had to do with the desire that seemed to rise in him every time he caught a glimpse of her.

"You heading up there now?" she asked him.

He nodded.

She nibbled her lip again, making him wonder if he made her as uncomfortable as she made him. "I did want to talk to Robert, make sure everything had smoothed out. You could ride with me, but you know—"

"I'll follow you up there." He motioned toward his

truck. "I'd hate to get you in trouble. We have to follow protocol."

There was a hint of a smile as she looked at him.
"You say that, but we both know you've always been
the kind who likes to make his own rules."

ROBERT'S HOUSE SAT off a dirt road, shrouded by trees and
brush. On the neighboring property, old cars and trailers in varying stages of rust were parked in a haphaz-
ard pattern. Between the rusting carcasses were piles
of downed trees and garbage. A few of the detritus hills
were covered with tarps whose prime of life had passed
years ago and now were nothing more than weathered
strings broken up by little squares of blue.

He'd always hated this place, the world his brother
called home. The drive that led to Robert's house was
a steady climb, and Blake was taking it at a crawl in
her patrol unit, twisting and turning as she attempted
to miss the washed-out ruts in the dirt. This wasn't
the kind of place in which one wanted to find oneself
stranded. Everything about the deep woods spoke of
danger, from the road all the way down to the twisted
faces that peered out from the windows of the derelict
homes they passed.

Rising from the brush was a building, still covered
in Tyvek plastic wrap, as if any day the construction
company would come back and finish siding the house
they had built—only it had been years since they'd been
there. The roof sagged in the middle from too many
heavy snows and too little care.

His brother had always cared more about what was
in the earth than what was on top of it, and it had even
been that way with his wife, Tiffany. The poor woman

had more than her fair share to deal with when it came to Robert. Then again, Jeremy wasn't in a spot to judge anyone else's relationship. For years, everyone had told him how great his marriage was, yet behind closed doors it was a different story—late-night fights about his schedule, the stress that came with being in law enforcement and the money. In the end, there was never enough money, time or even love.

Blake pulled to a stop and got out, waiting for him.

He parked next to her and met her at her car. "So, fill me in. What kind of trouble has my brother been getting himself into now?"

Robert had always fallen in and out of the bottle and usually directly into the hands of the law, leaving Jeremy to clean up his mess. The last time he'd talked to Robert they'd had one hell of a beer-fueled fight, ending with Robert on the ground and him promising to never lift another finger to save his brother's lousy carcass. Yet here he was again.

"I was called here a few weeks ago, but it wasn't for Tiffany, as your mother assumed." Blake leaned against her patrol car, the round curve of her hips on full display. "This time, Robert was having an altercation with his neighbor, Todd O'Brien." She pointed in the direction of the property that was full of rusted-out shells of cars.

"This happen before?"

She nodded and gave a slight shrug. "You know how it is—most people out here live with a militia-like mentality. It's all about the guns, the freedom of speech and action. Out here the law is more of a recommendation than a reality. When something needs to be handled, vigilante justice reigns."

It was funny. No matter where you were in Montana—whether in the city of Missoula or the hillsides on the outskirts of Silver Bow County—some of the same problems arose. Usually they centered on two things: guns and liquor. Sometimes he couldn't help feeling like he lived in the Wild West.

Jeremy looked up at his brother's house. The lights were off, and the doors were closed. Leaves littered the front porch. "You think Robert said something, and it set this O'Brien off?"

"We couldn't make much of the situation. Neither wanted to press charges, but we left them both with a warning that they needed to bring the conflict down and keep it under control." She sighed. "Without one of them wanting to press charges, there wasn't much we could do. Your brother was pretty upset about the guns, though, wanted us to at least write O'Brien a ticket for a noise disturbance, but we hadn't heard any of it."

Jeremy nodded. "My brother has a way of pissing people off and getting in trouble. You out here often?" Somehow it felt like a poorly timed come-on.

She nodded, with a faint smile like she had heard it, too, but was letting it go. "Your brother has some issues...but I always said you can't judge someone by their family."

He raised an eyebrow. "You think?"

"I'm nothing like my mother—at least I hope not." She laughed. "And from what your mother's told me, I assume you're nothing like your brother."

There was something in her voice that made it clear she didn't necessarily like Robert. But did that mean she liked *him*? He shook the thought from his head. He couldn't read anything into this.

She made her way up the front porch and knocked on the door.

There was no answer.

"You think he's still working in the mine?" Blake asked.

"Probably. We can run down there and take a look. It's not too far," he said, motioning her to follow him as he led the way down the well-worn path that headed to the Foreman Mine.

Though he tried not to, he kept glancing back, making sure she was okay. Each time he checked on her, she looked away as if she was purposefully avoiding his gaze. The air between them filled with the crunch of dead pine needles as they hiked.

"He mine copper?" she asked, as if she was as uncomfortable with the silence between them as he was.

"Yep, but he finds gold and other heavy metals, as well. Makes a decent living, but you couldn't get me to do what he does."

"Mining is hard work."

"That's not it," he said. "I couldn't handle being underground all day, every day." Though, as he said it, it reminded him of his own job. There he was usually sitting behind his desk, exploring the dark corners of a crime, looking for any clue that would lead to the mother lode.

"You scared of the dark?" She looked at him with a teasing smirk. "It's good to know that even a tough guy like you has a weakness."

It wasn't the dark he was afraid of. No…it was the fear of the world collapsing in around him. He'd already had it happen once when his marriage ended. He wasn't about to open himself up to such a failure again.

He glanced over at her, catching her gaze. "We all have weaknesses."

She slipped slightly, catching herself with the help of the branch of a small pine.

He took her hand. Her sweaty fingers gripped his just long enough for her to get her feet under her, but she quickly let go to brush herself off.

"Ha!" she said, her cheeks turning a light shade of red. "I guess my weakness is walking."

Jeremy laughed, the sound out of place in the quiet, stunted forest. For a moment he considered holding her hand the rest of the way down to the mouth of the mine, but she didn't seem like the type who wanted help, and he couldn't just elbow his way into her life—she wasn't his wife. She wasn't anything but a former crush. In truth, he didn't know her anymore. All he really knew was that she had her daughter, her mother and a job that, when she spoke of it, made her entire body tense.

He motioned for her to take the lead, admittedly because he wanted to watch her butt but ostensibly so he could make sure she was safe as she steadily made her way down the hill. He wasn't disappointed as he watched her. She moved with a quiet grace, smooth and steady as she carefully picked her way between the granite boulders as they headed into the maw of the earth.

Blake took out her flashlight and clicked it on. "Is this it?" she asked, motioning toward the dark, cave-like entrance.

In truth, it had been years since he'd been to the mine. The last time he'd been there the opening had been easily identifiable. Yet as she flashed her light downward, all he could make out were mounds of peg-matite-rich, reddish dirt.

"It should be here. Right here." He frowned. Grabbing his phone, he clicked on the light and moved into the muddy hole. "There should be a way in here." He prodded around, but the ground that filled the entrance shaft was as solid and compact as cement.

"Are you sure this is the place?" Blake asked.

"I thought so."

There was something wrong. The dirt in the entrance was wet, but it hadn't rained in a month. And even though the dirt that filled the shaft's entrance was compact, the ground under their feet was loose, compressing as he shifted his weight. It had to have been freshly exposed.

He took a step forward. His toe caught on a loose rock, tripping him. He shone his light at the ground. Beneath the cobble that littered the area was a crushed lantern—the lantern Robert hung on the entrance of the mine any time he was underground.

"You don't think—" Blake started.

Jeremy stopped her with a raise of his hand. He couldn't stand hearing what he already knew—the mine had collapsed.

He prayed Robert wasn't inside, but the lamp told him all he needed to know. Robert was trapped, and there was only a slight chance he could still be alive.

Chapter Four

The insides of Jeremy's hands where covered in blisters. Dirt caked his nails, and his knuckles were bloody where he had torn them against the earth, but the job of freeing his brother had been too big for one man.

Blake watched the firefighters milling around outside the mine, taking a break from their attempts to break through the concrete-like blockade that filled its entrance. They had been at it for hours. They'd finally gotten an excavator on-site and received the go-ahead to start a full excavation. From the look on Jeremy's face, it had already taken too long.

Blake walked up the hill toward Robert's house and motioned for Jeremy to follow.

Jeremy walked beside her, his movement slow and numb. She had to do something, anything to help. For the second time that day, she felt powerless in her inability to control the events that swirled around them.

"Have you asked your parents if they've heard anything from Robert? Maybe he's tried to call?" As soon as the words left her lips, she knew they were in vain. Of course he couldn't call, but she had to say something to make the agonizing look on Jeremy's face disappear.

"There's no cell service in the mine—I can guarantee

it." His eyes darkened, and his face tightened, the sexy lines around his eyes deepening. "Besides, there's no use in getting them up in arms. If we call them, they'll ask too many questions."

He was right. There was no sense alerting his parents that something was amiss if this was some kind of wild-goose chase. She could just imagine her mother getting a similar call. In a matter of minutes, Gemma West would have been on the scene and attempting to tell the crew exactly how they should be doing their jobs. No, family could wait.

She stepped up onto the porch and pressed her face against the window in the door. Inside Robert's one-room cabin was an open sofa bed and a wood-burning fireplace. The walls were covered in pictures of elk and bear, and a mounted trout hung over the kitchen window. A gun rack hung over the bed, and a small-caliber rifle sat nestled in its grips. It was as if the place had been intentionally stripped of all things feminine.

"Do you think it's possible Tiffany left him?" she asked.

Jeremy shrugged, staring ahead as if he was lost deep in thought.

"Is this what the house looked like the last time you were here?"

"What do you mean?" Jeremy moved beside her and peered inside.

"I...uh...I just mean I don't see anything of Tiffany's. Wouldn't you think if she was still living here you'd at least see a stray hair tie or something? It's almost like there hasn't been a woman here in a long time."

"Robert and Tiffany..." Jeremy gave a tired sigh. "They have more issues than *National Geographic*.

They're constantly at each other's throats. If she left, good for her. It's the best for both of them."

Robert's personal life was in shambles. Could that have meant he would have wanted to end things? As a miner, he had everything he needed to cave in the mine's entrance. Maybe it had been his way of never being found.

On the table underneath the window was a ledger. She squinted through the glass as she tried to make out the penciled notes. She read the most recent one scrawled onto the time sheets.

September 23 Time in: 06:30 Time out:

The time out sat empty, echoing all the things it could possibly mean—or the one thing she feared most.

"Was your brother having any other issues? Anything going on as far as his mental health is concerned?"

Jeremy stepped around to the bay window and peered in through the glass. "My mother said he's been agitated lately. Thought it had something to do with Tiffany."

"Any signs of depression?" She instinctively looked toward the sofa bed, where the sheets sat in a rumpled mess at the end of the mattress.

"I don't know. It's hard to say. Robert has always been one who kept his cards close to his chest."

There was something in Jeremy's voice, almost as if there were pangs of guilt that rested just under the surface of his words.

"Do you think he would have ever tried to commit suicide?"

Jeremy jerked.

She shouldn't have just thrown it out there. He was

feeling something…some sort of guilt or perhaps vulnerability; she couldn't be sure. She should have been softer in her delivery, but the officer in her corrected her. She had to ask the questions that needed to be asked. She couldn't censor herself to spare his feelings.

"I would hope not," he finally answered. "I would hope he wouldn't do anything so stupid."

"Stupid?" She thought a lot of things about suicide, and what a mistake it was for anyone to take his or her own life, but rarely did she think it was stupid.

"That's not what I meant," Jeremy corrected himself. "I would just hope that he would ask for help before he made the choice to end things."

"You said he was tight-lipped."

"He is…but…" Jeremy's mouth puckered and his eye turned storm. "Look, he's probably fine. Let's not go there, okay?"

He'd shut her down. Not that she could blame him. Maybe he was right. Maybe an accident had caused the cave-in, and Robert was sitting in the mine, hoping someone would find him.

"I'm sorry, Jeremy."

He seemed to force a smile, the lines of his lips curled in harsh juxtaposition to the rest of his face. "No…you're fine. If I was in your position, I'd be asking the same thing."

She nodded, not sure of what exactly to say that would make things less tense between them, but there was no fixing what riddled the air.

A fireman walked up the hill after them, stopping before he reached the porch. His cheeks were spattered with dirt and sweat. "We've broken through. Looks like the mine shaft is intact."

"Great. That's great," Jeremy said. "Was there anything that could give us a clue as to why the mine entrance collapsed? Any evidence of explosives?"

The fireman shrugged, his sweaty shirt hugging his chest as he moved. "The excavator did the trick in getting us in, but it tore the hell out of everything. It's hard to say what you and your investigators will find."

Firefighters were like Wreck-It Ralph, always tearing and bulldozing away anything that stood in their way, but this was one of those times that Blake was happy to have their help.

They followed them down the hill, night trailing them. Ahead the fire crews had set up industrial-strength lights that burned away the darkness. All except for the oblong entrance of the mine, where the light disappeared like it was being sucked into a black hole.

"We haven't sent anyone in. We were waiting for you," the fireman said, stopping at the mouth of the cave.

"Robert!" Jeremy called, his voice echoing in the mine and cascading deep into the darkness.

There was no answer. Instead they were met with the excavator's treads rattling and clanging as a man drove it up the embankment and toward the waiting tractor trailer.

Jeremy moved forward, but Blake grabbed hold of his biceps, stopping him. "Wait."

"My brother's in there."

"I hear you, but we need to be careful."

Jeremy gazed into the mine.

Blake took out her notepad and turned to the firefighter who'd headed the excavation. "How deep was the cave-in?"

"It varied, but mostly everything was about ten to fifteen feet."

She made a note and, after sliding the camera from her pocket, took a picture of the scene. "But you didn't find evidence of an explosion?"

The fireman shook his head. "No, but look," he said, running his hand down a structural support beam they must have put into place to keep from having the mine fall back in on itself. "We found support beams like these every three feet. You'd have to check on the code, but with these four-by-fours like that, it seems like more than enough structural support to sustain the weight above. There's been no earthquakes, at least that I know of, and no major rainstorms or weather that would have caused the ground to give way. I'd bet my bottom dollar that someone did this on purpose. If it was imploded, it was with a low-grade explosive. Nothing big enough to cause major damage, just enough firepower to get the job done."

Blake nodded, taking note of his opinion. It wouldn't be admissible in court, but at least she had an idea of what could have happened and she could write it up when she filed her report.

"Is it stable deeper in?" she asked.

The firefighter shrugged. "It's hard to say what you'll find. Oftentimes, explosions can have a bit of a cascading effect. If you go in, you need to make sure you take your time and be safe. You want me or one of my team to go in with you?"

"I've got it," Jeremy said. "I'll go in. There's no sense

in you all going in and putting yourself in danger." He turned to look at her. "I don't want anyone to get hurt."

A faint heat rose in her cheeks, but she tried to staunch the fire. "Jeremy, you may be a detective, but this isn't your jurisdiction. You can't go in. It's my job."

"But this is my family."

If she were in his shoes, she wouldn't have taken no for an answer, either. She had to follow the rules, but it didn't feel right leaving him out. "Since you're the only person who's been in the mine, you can go in as a search volunteer. Nothing more. Don't touch anything. Got it?"

He nodded.

"Here," the fireman said, handing them each hard hats complete with headlamps. "You're going to need these."

They took them, and Jeremy put his on. In the night's shadows, he looked like a miner from an old tintype photograph, dirt smudging his cheeks and his eyelashes covered in dust.

"Let's go," Blake said, starting down the shaft.

The place smelled of dank, wet dirt and iron-rich minerals, the scent of deep earth—full and heady. The tunnel was wide enough for two to walk side by side with their shoulders rubbing against the walls. A tendril of claustrophobia wrapped around her, but she ignored the way it tightened around her chest and threatened to squeeze until panic oozed from every pore.

No. I'm strong. I can handle this.

She repeated the mantra over and over as she moved deeper, but it did little to quell her anxiety.

She walked, Jeremy close beside her, until the tunnel branched in a Y shape. She suddenly wished they had found a map, anything to help them avoid getting lost in the maze.

Jeremy took a large breath of air, like he was going to yell, but Blake shushed him. "Don't yell. If anything is unstable..." *We could be killed.* She resisted the urge to voice her fears. "Just don't."

He looked around them, like he could almost read her mind, and nodded.

A bead of earth slipped loose from the wall and cascaded down the side like an earthen waterfall.

"Right or left?" she asked, motioning toward the break in their path.

"Left. Robert never did anything right in his entire life." He gave a dry laugh.

She went left. The walls seemed to move in closer and the dark seemed even more ominous as they made their way deeper into the mountain. Each few hundred feet, the tunnel grew narrower, until she had to turn sideways to squeeze through. Her heart thrashed in her chest as her claustrophobia intensified.

She hated small spaces. What if she got stuck? What if the earth shifted around them and they were trapped? What would happen to Megan? What would happen to her mother?

The tunnel narrowed even more. Her chest brushed against the rock. And, as she exhaled, the warm air bounced off the rock in front of her and she could feel it on her cheek.

It was too close.

The walls were too close.

Jeremy was too close.

She couldn't do this.

Something ran over her shoe. She jumped with a squeal, slamming her hard hat into the top of the cave.

"I can't, Jeremy." She tried to control her breathing, but now it was coming in rapid, panicked heaves.

He took her hand, running his thumb over her skin. "Okay. It's okay," he soothed.

His heartbeat was so strong that she could feel it through his grip. Did he hate this as much as she did?

Jeremy led her back down the tunnel from where they'd come, until he reached a spot wide enough for them both to stand. "Let me take the lead."

She nodded, but his voice sounded like it was coming through a can. The world spun around her slightly, forcing her to lean back against the wall and close her eyes. "Just a minute," she whispered.

"Are you okay?"

"I'm fine," she lied as her head started to throb and a faint wave of light-headedness washed over her. She pulled her hand from his, afraid that it wasn't just the claustrophobia or the bump to the head that was making her feel adrift.

She braced herself against the walls of the cave. The earth was cool and damp under her touch, and the dirt had given way to hard rock. The jagged edges scraped her hands, but the pain made her come back to herself. Lifting her hand, she wiped a speckle of blood from her palm.

Jeremy took her face in his hands. "You're fine. Everything will be okay. You're safe with me."

In their little cocoon of warm yellow light, and wrapped in his hands, she believed him. She looked up into his face. She focused on the green depths of his eyes, blocking out everything else around her. After a while her breathing slowed as he caressed her face, moving a stray hair back from her neck.

"We won't have to be in here much longer," he whispered. "He has to be close."

Jeremy's warm fingertips brushed the skin right under her bottom lip, his touch making the cold rock beneath her feel that much cooler. Leaning in, he stole her lips, kissing her with a tenderness far deeper than the mine.

Everything around her disappeared. There was only him. His mouth on hers. The luscious texture of his tongue as it brushed over the curve of her lip, lightly caressing hers. He flicked his tongue, making her thighs tense, warmth rise from her core and her thoughts rush to the other places his mouth could explore.

His hands roamed down her neck, over her curves and down her hips. He pulled her against him, pressing her against his responding body. She didn't know what it was. The fever with which he touched her, her long drought from masculine contact. Whatever it was, she kissed him back with a ravenous hunger. It felt—

From somewhere deep behind them, near the entrance of the cave, came the sound of a crackling radio. The high-pitch static cut through the air and brought Blake back to reality.

Jeremy jerked with the sound. "I…I…shouldn't have done that," he stammered, wiping his lips with the back of his hand. "I just meant to make you feel better. I'm sorry."

"You're right. You shouldn't have." She stepped away from him and out of the light in an attempt to cover the hurt that must have shown on her face. He wasn't the only one who had made a mistake. She shouldn't have let him kiss her. Now everything was going to get confusing.

"Let's go back. I think this way is blocked—it's getting too narrow." *Entirely* too narrow, as far as she was concerned. She couldn't be this close to him.

He started to say something but stopped. "Okay."

She led the way back, and, as they neared the Y, a warm breeze blew in from the entrance, making her aware of how cold it was in the cave. Between their moving and the kiss, she hadn't noticed the icy chill. If Robert was hurt somewhere in there, was it possible that he could have become hypothermic? If he couldn't move, in the damp cold of the mountain's underbelly it wouldn't have taken long.

She walked a little faster down the right branch of the tunnel, moving ahead of Jeremy just enough that she was outside the range of his light. Her foot struck something, and it sent her tumbling. Her shoulder connected with the floor, mud kicking up into her face and splattering over her light, dimming its brilliance as her helmet rolled away.

"Dang it." Her wrist throbbed where she'd tried to catch herself as she fell. She sat up and tried to wipe the dirt off her face, but the slick mud only smeared over her skin.

She should have been more careful. She should have paid more attention, but all she could think about was Jeremy...his lips...the way his body felt as it pressed against hers.

Blake grabbed her hard hat and wiped the dirt from its lamp. As the light brightened, it caught on something metal, sending a reflection against the far wall of the cave. She turned to find the object. There, at her feet, were the legs of a man.

The body was slumped forward and slightly to the side, propped against a rock. All of his clothes were in place, and if his skin wasn't gray and mottled, it was almost as if he could have simply fallen asleep. His feet were crossed loosely at the ankles, indicating that at the time of death he had been standing—she'd once heard it was because the left side of the brain shut down first and it caused the person's legs to cross as they fell, but whether it was that or simply inertia, she couldn't be sure. Yet, only those who were standing at the time of death fell as Robert had.

"Jeremy, stop," she called down the tunnel, but it was too late. Jeremy stepped into the light.

"Oh, my God," he whispered, looking down at the body. He moved his light, shining it on the man's face.

His skin was pale, mottled to the point of gray— the color of death. His eyes were open, but they were opaque and unseeing.

"Robert..." Jeremy illuminated the side of his brother's head.

There was a streak of dried, congealed blood down the side of his face and neck. His jacket was stained red and brown, and a pool of blood had settled and dried in his lap.

A gun was on the ground by his left hand. Next to the gun was a single spent casing.

One shot, one kill.

Jeremy dropped down to his knees as he stared at the man.

"Jeremy, you should go," she said. "I can take it from here."

"My brother…" Jeremy started, stunned. "This is my brother."

"I know. And he's always going to be your brother, but right now this is a crime scene."

Chapter Five

Jeremy wouldn't let her leave him outside the mine; instead he watched as she and her team documented the crime scene, taking measurements, pictures of the body and close-ups of Robert's face and the wound at his temple. They were doing their jobs, but it made his stomach churn every time he looked up and saw his brother's face.

Robert had had his fair share of issues, but Jeremy had never expected them to land them here—his brother dead and him watching as Robert's body was poked and prodded.

Blake looked to him as one of the investigators took a close-up of the bullet wound. "You okay? Are you sure you want to stay down here? It's been a long day."

"I'm fine."

She frowned, like she didn't believe him, but she didn't say anything. She turned to the other officer and handed him her camera. "Did they get a video?" Blake asked.

"Yep," the investigator answered.

"Great. Make sure to get some more pictures. Especially of the spatter."

The officer nodded, taking the camera. The strobing flash made Jeremy flinch, as if each picture was the crack of a bullet that had come too close.

He had to pull his crap together. For the next hour or so, he couldn't see the body as his brother if he wanted to get through this. This couldn't be Robert—it had to be just another face, or he'd never be able to be right again. And for dang sure, he didn't need Blake worrying about him. She needed to focus on her investigation.

He took a deep breath.

Blake took a swab of the body's hands. She tried to move his arm, but he was at full rigor. Leaning down, she sniffed his hands and then wrapped them in paper bags.

"You smell anything?" he asked, glancing down to the place where the handgun rested.

"Hard to say," she said with a slight shrug. "His hands smell heavily of dirt. That can cover the scent of powder."

He nodded.

"You want to take a sniff?" she asked, motioning to the bagged hands.

If this was his scene, he would have done it, but he still couldn't let go of the fact it was Robert. No matter how badly he wanted to, he couldn't feel his brother's cold, lifeless flesh.

"I'm good, but make sure you're getting everything." He pointed at Robert's underarms. "Did you get a picture of his coat? How it's bunched up where someone would have put their hands if they were dragging him."

Blake frowned like she didn't agree, but she motioned to the officer taking pictures. "Make sure we get a picture of that."

The man nodded, his camera flashing.

"After the coroner's done, I want you to bag that gun and send it off to the crime lab. I want prints pulled and a ballistics test. Got it?"

"No problem," the officer said between pictures.

She turned to Jeremy. "You know I'm sorry about your brother and everything that's going on in your life right now, but that doesn't mean you can come in and tell me how to run a crime scene."

That's not what he had implied, but apparently he had hit a sore spot. "Right."

She pulled off her blue gloves with a snap and turned to the other investigator. "You done?"

The officer nodded, handing her camera to her. "I think we've got everything you'll need." He started down the tunnel, leaving Blake standing alone with Jeremy.

She stood up and brushed off her knees. "Don't worry, Jeremy. Even though it's just little ol' me in charge, we can figure out what happened."

OUTSIDE THE TUNNEL, Blake set the camera on the table at the makeshift command post and she tried to control her breathing. The vic may have been Jeremy's family, but that didn't mean that he could come in and try to tell her how to do her job. She never should have let him trail along. She should have trusted her gut and kept her distance.

The industrial lights made the night as bright as midday. Jeremy sat outside the mine's entrance as a few other officers milled through the grass and brush looking for any other evidence. The coroner walked down the trail from Robert's driveway, and she gave him an acknowledging wave.

She flipped through her camera, looking at the different photos of Robert's body, the gun and the walls in and around the scene. The last picture was of the blood spatters on the wall behind the body. The spray had moved far in the chasm, but the heaviest was just to the right of where Robert had slumped.

She made a note in her investigation report as the coroner stopped beside her.

"Have a dead one, eh? Lucky for you, the state's hotel is always open," he said, trying to make a joke. She didn't find it funny.

Blake nodded in Jeremy's direction. "That's the vic's brother, so be careful what you say."

The older man's flabby, jovial face turned placid. Most coroners were former police officers and more of the quiet type, but this one had come out of Wyoming and seemed to live for his job.

"Got it. So what do you think? Suicide?" He looked over her shoulder at the camera. "Oh, that's some nice spatter."

She put the camera down and out of sight of the death-happy coroner. "Right now I'm unsure. It's presenting like a suicide, no drag marks."

"Hmm…" The coroner made a note. "Anything else?"

"The vic had a bullet wound to the left side of his head."

"Was the vic left-handed?"

She hadn't thought to ask Jeremy. "I don't know."

The coroner nodded. "Well, I'll see what I can make of it."

"Sounds great, thanks. My investigator will take you

to the body." She pointed to the other officer, who motioned for the coroner to follow him.

The coroner talked constantly as he and the other man made their way into the mine.

She opened her computer and pulled up her investigation report. Based on the rate of algor mortis, rigor mortis and livor mortis, the man had been dead approximately twelve hours. She looked at her watch. That put time of death at a little before noon, but the family hadn't been able to contact him for several days. Was it possible that Robert had been trapped in the mine and, instead of waiting to asphyxiate, had chosen to take his own life? Or had there been others involved? Had someone collapsed the entrance of the mine in hopes of covering up a murder?

Robert was a recluse. If someone had wanted to murder him, hiding him in the mine was a hell of a way to take care of his body. If things had gone another way and his family hadn't reported him missing, he may never have been found.

She looked over at Jeremy. His head was in his hands and his shoulders were slumped; he looked broken. Guilt flooded her. She should have been more patient with him and his interference in her investigation—he'd only been trying to help. She walked over to him and put her hand on his shoulder. "I'm sorry."

He nodded but didn't look up.

"We're going to get to the bottom of this. Don't worry."

"I just don't understand it. Robert had problems, but...I never thought..."

She sat down next to him, their legs brushing. Though they barely touched, she hoped that her nearness brought him a small measure of comfort. "You and I both know that no one ever thinks this is going to happen. The only thing we can do for Robert now is to piece together how he ended up where he is."

Jeremy shifted slightly, like he was recoiling from the words…words he had no doubt said himself many times over.

"Do you know—was Robert left-handed?"

Jeremy nodded. "He could have done this to himself. But you know Robert…*knew* Robert," he said, correcting himself. "He wasn't the kind who'd do this. He was too angry. Too cynical. He lived to prove the world wrong."

They sat in silence as she watched the firemen pack up their gear and head out. Once in a while Jeremy would move like he was going to stand up, but he would quickly stop and sit back down.

Finally the coroner appeared at the mine's entrance and, spotting her, made his way over.

"What did you find?" she asked as they both stood up to greet him.

The coroner looked back as two men carried a black bag containing Robert's body out of the mine and toward the coroner's van. "You were right about the jacket, but I don't think he was moved. The lividity didn't point in that direction."

"You think it was a suicide?" Jeremy asked.

The coroner shook his head. "The stippling around the bullet's entrance wound was a little wider than what I normally see in cases of suicide, but it doesn't rule it out."

Blake moved to speak but Jeremy interrupted. "What about the spatter?"

"It's consistent with the body's presentation, but again, I think the gun was a little farther back at the time it was fired."

"So it's possible that he was murdered?" Jeremy asked, his voice filled with anger.

"Right now we know the cause of death is the gunshot wound, but until we get the medical examiner's findings, I'm ruling the manner of death as undetermined."

THERE WAS NOTHING worse than notifying the next of kin...especially when it was your own family. Jeremy had put it off as long as he could, waiting until the next afternoon, but his parents needed to find out before they heard the news from someone else in the small town.

He took a deep breath as he entered the pizza joint. It was full of families, and the roar of Skee-Ball from the game room in the back filled the air.

His family had been coming to this place since he was a kid. Everything from the red-and-white-checkered tablecloths to the hanging stained glass lights was the same. It even smelled the same—yeasty with a hint of garlic and overcooked dough. The place was nostalgic in all the wrong ways.

His parents were sitting at their regular booth, and he made his way over.

"Hiya, Jeremy," his mom said in an overly chipper voice.

He nodded and sat down next to her.

"Did you talk to Robert?" his father asked.

Maybe it had been an error to meet them in a public place to tell them about Robert's death, but at least this way they couldn't start fighting.

He picked up the napkin in front of him and started rolling the paper into little balls. "I saw him."

"Did you tell him that he needs to call his mother?" she asked, taking a dainty sip of her pop.

"Actually, I couldn't tell him anything." He laid the napkin to rest on the table. "Mom, Dad, I have some bad news."

"Is Robert in trouble again?" his father started. "I tell you, I'm going to have to sell our house to pay for his bail this time. He's got me about tapped out."

"He's not in jail." Jeremy ran his hands over his face and looked up, across the table at his father. "Robert's dead."

His father's mouth hung open, and his mother turned to stone next to him. He instantly wished he had taken Blake's offer of coming along to tell his family. Maybe she could have softened the blow. Maybe the news would have been better coming from a woman. Yet, after their kiss, it felt like the only thing she wanted to do was get away from him. No, there was only him to impart the news of his brother's death.

"We found Robert's body. It's on its way to the Missoula Crime Lab for an autopsy. Right now the cause of death is unclear, but we should know soon."

"You don't know how he died?" his mother asked in a stunned whisper.

He put his arm around her and pulled her close. "He died instantly from a gunshot wound. Other than that, there's not much I can say."

He envisioned Robert's body slumped over. The gunshot to his head. The blood trickling down his neck, staining his shirt. He tried to blink the images away but failed.

His mother looked across the table at his father. "I told you that you should have gone out there sooner, Glen," she spat. "If you would have just listened."

"Veronica, this is hardly the first time Robert hadn't called us back. If I ran out there every time you wanted to, we'd practically live with him."

"If we had, maybe he wouldn't be dead." His mother started to cry. She pulled away from Jeremy's hug and ran out of the restaurant.

The *beep, beep, beep* of some video game in the back room echoed through his thoughts. He had hoped things wouldn't have gone this way, but his parents would never change—they would forever live in a state of turmoil.

His father was staring at his hands. "Do you think he did it to himself?" he finally asked.

Jeremy shrugged. If he had to guess, the whole scene felt *off*. When most people committed suicide they left something to explain why, and normally there was some sort of indicator. Sure, Robert had been acting strange, but if he had been planning on suicide, he would have been getting rid of personal effects and saying his good-byes—but none of that had happened.

Then again, maybe it was impromptu. Things with Tiffany were going to hell, so maybe he thought he could make her pay by taking his own life. But that didn't account for the mine entrance's collapse. Either there had been some kind of accident that had led to the collapse or someone else had been involved.

If he listened to his gut, someone had murdered his brother. He thought of Blake. She must have been thinking the same as he was.

"I don't know, Dad."

"Robert and I have had our fair share of problems, but just like you, he's my son…I need to know what happened."

"Don't worry, Dad. Come hell or high water, I'll get to the bottom of this. And if someone had a hand in his death, I'll make them pay."

Chapter Six

The next afternoon, Blake found herself standing in front of Detective Engelman's desk. While he talked on the phone, she stared at a stray bit of fuzz that was stuck to the graying stubble on his chin. The minutes ticked by. From the sour look that appeared on his face when he looked at her, this meeting couldn't be good.

Finally he hung up and turned to her.

"Thanks for waiting," he said, tenting his fingers in front of him on the desk. "I looked over the report you filed after last night's call."

She sat forward in her chair, readying herself for anything. "I took copious notes and documented everything. Was there a problem?"

He glanced over at his blank computer screen like he was expecting to see the report pulled up. "Why didn't you call me? You are a deputy, aren't you?"

She nodded.

"Look right there," he said, pointing to the brass nameplate that adorned his door. "What does that say?"

"Clark Engelman, detective," she recited.

"Exactly. If there is the possibility that a case may be a felony, it is your job to call me. I'm the detective in this county, not you...and not some guy from Missoula." He leaned back in his chair and put his hands behind his head. "It is your job to bring me in on cases like these."

"I'm sorry, sir, but this case hasn't been ruled a felony."

His face contorted with rage, but then it quickly disappeared, replaced by an air of dismissal. "Look, I understand how it is. You get to a scene. You find a body. Your adrenaline starts pumping. But that doesn't mean you get to skirt our policies and procedures. It is your job to notify me."

Something was happening here, something she couldn't put her finger on. Did he know something about this case that she didn't?

"You and I both know that the moment this case became a death investigation, you should have called me."

He was right, but in the cases of suicides, it wasn't a requirement that a detective be called in. With everything that had been happening, and with Jeremy involved, the thought of notifying Detective Engelman had slipped her mind. Apparently now there would be hell to pay.

There was a knock on the door behind her. "Clark?" Investigative Captain Prather asked, opening the door without waiting to be invited in. He looked to Blake and gave her an acknowledging tip of the head, as if he had expected to find her sitting in the hot seat.

"What is it, Captain Prather?"

"I'm glad I caught you both." He took a seat on the edge of the detective's desk and looked down on him. "I heard you had a bone to pick with West here over last night's vic."

Engelman looked slightly shell-shocked, and his

hands balled into tight fists. "I—" he started to protest, but the captain cut him off with the wave of his hand.

He turned to her. "I just got done looking over your investigation findings. No drag marks, eh?"

She shook her head. What game had she just become a pawn in? Things between the investigative captain and Detective Engelman were always tense. Most thought Engelman had only gotten the position thanks to the fact his brother was the mayor, but usually the two men in front of her did their best at hiding their indifference toward each other.

"Look," Detective Engelman started, "I will not be pushed out. I'm the damned detective here, not some little pissant deputy. If you were smart, she would be behind some desk, not working this investigation."

Blake stood up and slammed her fist down on the desk as she leaned into Engelman's face. "How dare you? I didn't ask to investigate this case. If anything, I did you a favor—"

"Don't say something you'll regret, West," the captain said, stopping her before she flew deeper into a rage. He gave her a sharp glance.

She slid her fists from the wood of the desk, letting them drop down to her sides. "Captain, I request that I be made lead investigator on the Lawrence case," she said robotically as she forced her anger from her voice.

The captain glanced at Engelman and nodded. "You have a bucketful of cases, isn't that right, Detective?"

"You have no reason... This is my... You can't just throw your weight around—my brother and his wife will hear about this," the detective stammered in argument.

"I look forward to chatting with your brother," the

captain said. "Feel free to send him my way when you get the chance." Captain Prather stood up. "In the meantime, I want you to catch up on one of your many unsolved cases."

Blake muffled her laughter as Engelman glared at her.

"West, you come with me." The captain walked out into the hallway and she followed, closing the door behind them.

"West, you better do your best with this one," Prather said. "I'm sure it's clear how far I've stuck my neck out. Don't let the hatchet fall, or it will catch us both—got it?"

"Sir, how did you know that Engelman would be after me?" She motioned toward the detective's door.

"Let's just say I have an inkling that things aren't on the up-and-up with him. Let's leave it at that. Now, you get out there and do your job."

"I filed the search warrant to get into Robert's cabin this morning."

"Good. We need to get a handle on this case before the mayor has a chance to retaliate after he finds out that one of his boys won't be in the driver's seat."

BLAKE SAT IN her patrol car and stared at the search warrant that she'd been issued by the judge. She wasn't a detective. She hadn't meant to step on Detective Engelman's toes, and she damned sure didn't mean to start a war in the department. Yet here she was—stuck in the middle of a political battle and unsure of whom exactly she could trust.

Her mind went to Jeremy. He didn't have any real ties to her department. He couldn't be swayed by the politics that were going on just under the surface. Plus, he had a vested interest in the case. But that might cause more trouble than it was worth.

But somehow being around him calmed her. He was like a breath of fresh air after being stuck in the stuffy politics of a little town. If nothing else, he could be a consultant—Captain Prather had told her to do her best, and she could only do that with Jeremy's help. He could be a sounding board. With his help, she could handle this.

She thumbed the ridges on the steering wheel as she thought of the sexy detective and the way he always had a little bit of a five o'clock shadow.

If she asked him to be involved, he couldn't question her methods. This was her case. This was her chance to prove herself—and to show Engelman that she was just as good, if not better, than him at her job. If Jeremy was the man she thought he was, he would understand how important this case was to her.

Before she realized it, she was parked in front of Jeremy's parents' house. The historic brick home spoke to generations of miners past, of lives spent searching for something more. It stood in direct contrast to the stunted tree that formed a sort of fence between their property and her mother's.

She had leaned against that tree the first time she had been kissed. In the logic of a teenager, she had hoped that Jeremy would see, get jealous and finally make his move. But that had never happened. Instead, one kiss had led to another, and another, until suddenly she had fallen for Chuck Garnet, the boy from the wrong side of the tracks, and had been left pregnant and at her mother's mercy.

If only Jeremy had played by the rules she had set for him in her head.

She closed her eyes, and she was back in the Foreman Mine, panicking. Pressed against the wall. Jeremy's warm breath on her cheek. His lips caressing hers.

Life could have been just like that moment—with Jeremy there to help her through her times of panic. To make her see sense when everything else seemed to be falling in on her. They could have been each other's everything.

Could they still?

No. That kiss had been a fluke. A man's attempt to stop a woman from losing her cool. He was helping her in the only way he knew how. No doubt it meant nothing to him. He was far too guarded, too linear, to want to get involved in her life. He had his own in Missoula.

There was a tap on her window, and she opened her eyes. Jeremy stood on the other side of the glass, looking at her. "What's up?" he asked with a slight tip of the head. "Did you find out something?"

She shook her head as she rolled down the window. "Hey, get in. I need to run to your brother's place. Thought maybe you wanted to go with me," she said.

He got in the car.

She wasted no time. "How do you feel about working as a consultant on your brother's case?"

"I didn't think that was a question." Jeremy looked at her with a spark in his eye.

She wasn't sure if it was excitement or something else, so she quickly glanced away. If it was something else, it would only complicate things. As much as she wanted to kiss him again, it couldn't happen.

She clicked on the radio and let the country music

fill the tense air between them as they bumped down the road.

She darted a glance his way. Some of the color had returned to his face, and he looked better, less in shock than last night.

"You doing okay?"

He nodded and looked out the window and away from her. "How long you been a deputy?" he asked, changing the subject.

Although he looked okay, he must have been wrestling with what had happened, and she wasn't about to make him bring it back up.

"Just a few years. When were you promoted to detective?" Blake tried to ignore his cute half smile.

"I'm surprised that between my mother and your mother, you don't know all about me. Every time I call I get a full report on you."

He was right. Their mothers talked often and, until the last year or so, she had been given the details of his life…all the way down to how his daughter was doing in school. Yet, after a while, it hadn't seemed right to be a passive bystander to his life, and she had asked her mother to stop telling her things.

"You don't think our mothers would be crazy enough to try and set us up, do you?" he continued with a laugh.

The laugh chased away the little puff of excitement she was feeling. He wasn't interested. And if he wasn't, then neither was she—at least as far as he could know.

"My mother knows well enough that I'd never date another cop. And I'm not one for long-distance relationships. Tried that before."

"Crashed and burned, huh?" he asked, a line of tension running through his voice, almost like he wanted to ask more.

"I've never been good at relationships. Long distance or otherwise."

Not even next door.

"I get what you mean." He looked away like he was drawing on a memory. "You ever think of getting married?"

Was he really grilling her on her thoughts on relationships because he cared, or was this just his awkward way of filling the time as they drove?

She pushed down the accelerator a little harder, forcing the patrol unit well past its comfort zone on the little dirt road that led out to the Foreman.

"I…uh…" she stammered, unsure how to answer his question.

"I get it. You are probably enjoying your single life."

"Do you?" she asked.

He shrugged. "Some days. Some days I miss being married."

The little wiggle of jealousy in her grew. She wasn't sure if she wanted to know about how much he missed his ex-wife. He'd had so much. Even though he was divorced, he'd been given a real chance at a relationship. He hadn't been stuck in a nowhere town, without a spouse, and living with his mother.

She was thankful to see the cabin approaching as they turned up Robert's driveway.

"Thinking about marriage, how long were Robert and Tiffany together?" she asked, avoiding the conversation that Jeremy seemed adamant to have.

"They've been on and off now for the last few years. I can't tell you exactly how long they were together, though—they eloped in Vegas. Never told my mother. She was devastated when she found out."

"Where's Tiffany from?"

"I don't know…someplace in Southern California, I think. As far as I know, she's never been too stable. Moved around a lot."

She nibbled the inside of her cheek. If this woman was like Jeremy said, there was the possibility that they may never track her down. "The soul of a gypsy, huh?"

"I call it unstable."

So he was the kind who liked stability. Well, that she had in spades. She hadn't ever moved. Hadn't ever gone out and experienced the world. She was living the same life she'd always lived; she had just gotten older. Somehow her kind of stability didn't seem like what he was looking for.

"You try to find Tiffany yet?" he asked.

She nodded. "I've been trying her all morning. It's been going straight to voice mail. I couldn't find any numbers for her family."

Jeremy gave a light snort, as if he wasn't surprised. "They aren't much better than she is. From what I hear, they are the type that likes to live out of their car."

They'd need to find Robert's wife to notify him of his death, but there wasn't much more that she could do.

She pulled the car to a stop in front of the house and got out. Robert's cabin was cold as they posted the warrant and walked in. The place carried the scent of stale cooking, man and dryer sheets.

"You hear anything from the medical examiner?" Jeremy asked as she walked over toward the kitchen and stopped at the sink.

She shook her head.

"Don't you think you should have called them? Maybe we could get a better idea of what we need to be looking for."

"Look, Jeremy." She said his name as if it carried a pit. "I thought I made it clear to you when we were in the mine that I know what I'm doing. I don't need you, or anyone else, telling me how to do my job."

He stepped back as if her words were lashes. "Whoa. That's not what I meant," he said, putting his hands up like he was motioning for her to stop.

She wasn't a horse. She wouldn't be commanded.

"Then what did you mean? I'm tired of this. Just because I've only been a deputy for a couple of years, it doesn't mean I don't know how to function on a crime scene. It doesn't mean I don't know how to handle this investigation. When the medical examiner is done, he will call. He doesn't need me telling him how to do his job."

Jeremy stepped forward and moved like he was going to take her hand, but then he stopped and just stared at her as if he was afraid she would bite.

"Look, I know how it is—how it always feels like you have to prove yourself, but you don't have to prove yourself to me."

She relaxed slightly. Hopefully he meant what he said. She couldn't fight him, too. She had enough battles on her hands.

"Sorry," she said with a sigh. "It's been a long day."

"What happened?"

She told him about her meeting in Detective Engelman's office. As she spoke, his face tightened.

"I'm so sick of this crap," he said, pressing his hand hard against the countertop as though he were squishing a bug. "I just dealt with something like this in Missoula."

She'd heard about it and had followed the story of a series of arsons that had led to the death of the battalion chief in Missoula's fire department and whispers of unanswered corruption. In the end, Jeremy had been called to the stand and forced to testify about the incident.

"I don't think this is the same thing. It's just normal politics—with a touch of nepotism."

"Oh, nepotism…" he said, rolling the word over his lips. "That never complicates a situation."

She chuckled. "Regardless, I'm glad to have you around. Get a fresh perspective on all this." Her cheeks warmed as she thought about all the other reasons she liked having him around.

His sexy grin returned, as if he could read her mind.

She forced her thoughts back on the case. "As for what we're looking for, I filed the search warrant so we could locate your brother's financial and mining records. I thought that would be a strong place to start our work." She moved her weight from foot to foot as she tried to look at anything besides his smile. "Do you know where we could find them?"

He walked over to the pullout bed and lifted up the end. Packed underneath the metal frame were boxes overflowing with paperwork. "The last time I was here, he had some stuffed in the bathroom cabinets, as well," he said, pointing toward the only other room in the small space.

Blake grabbed one of the boxes from under the bed and slid it out to the middle of the floor. There, on the top of the papers, was a letter from the county.

"Hey, take a look at this," she said, picking it up and

reading its contents. "It looks like your brother has a tax lien." She handed him the certificate. "I think we have a clue as to why he may have wanted to commit suicide."

Chapter Seven

The word *suicide* left an ashy taste in Jeremy's mouth as he tried to swallow what Blake was saying. Robert wouldn't have committed suicide over some property tax lien. He wasn't the kind to roll over and just take a hit like that. He would have fought long and hard to protect what he had always called his "little corner of heaven."

He stared at the paper in his hand. According to the paperwork, the tax lien certificate was supposed to go to auction if his back taxes weren't paid. He looked at the date the letter had been issued. Three weeks ago. No doubt his brother had been worried about some company buying his lien and foreclosing on him.

It was just strange that his parents hadn't mentioned Robert's financial trouble. Robert must have been keeping it from them. Either he had the money and had intended on paying, or he had been trying to get it—without going to them. Maybe they were his last resort.

Jeremy shook his head. It didn't make sense. Something didn't feel right. "Let's keep looking. Maybe we can find more that will help us make sense of this."

Blake bent down. Her blond hair had started to wiggle loose from her tight ponytail, and a few stray locks fell into her face, making her look soft, touchable. For a moment he considered pushing the hair back from her face, but if he got that close again, it was hard to say what she would do. After what had happened between them in the mine, it was likely that she would get upset—and he couldn't risk his chance at having a hand in solving his brother's case.

Family came first, no matter how badly he wanted Blake...or how badly he had wanted her ever since they were in high school.

She pushed the hair out of her face, annoyed. "Your brother needed a better filing system," she said, pulling a stack of papers out of the box and setting them on the floor.

The hair fell loose again, and this time he turned away. He couldn't think of her like that...like anything other than a childhood friend or, better yet, a colleague.

He sat down on the floor next to her and started shuffling through the receipts, bills and pamphlets. They worked for at least an hour. No matter how badly he wanted to concentrate, all he could seem to focus on was the way her arm bumped against his as they each shuffled through the papers. Why couldn't his brother have lived in a house that was something a little bigger than a glorified garage?

"Have you found anything?" He leaned toward her, his arm grazing hers as he looked into the pile of papers she had sitting in her lap.

She flipped through the pages. "Not much, but your brother did seem to keep a constant record of his copper sales." She lifted up a receipt that had a four-figure number circled at the bottom. "Do you think that is his haul for a month or a year?"

Jeremy shrugged. "Hard to say. Let's make a pile though. See if we can track his income."

He picked up his stack of papers and scanned through them, pulling out any possible income sources that Robert had in the last year. As he worked, Blake's nearness became less uncomfortable.

The income stack grew and started to spill over. Jeremy picked it up and began to add the numbers in his head. "Just looking at these," he said, picking up the stack and straightening it, "Robert had to have pulled in more than a hundred thousand dollars last year. I'm sure he had some sizable expenses, but that seems more than enough to pay the taxes on his property."

Blake looked up at him. "I haven't seen much in the paperwork to indicate that he had any significant form of debts—but maybe his outgo was in another box."

Jeremy reached under the bed and grabbed the next box. He opened the lid and threw it to the floor.

"Oh…" he said, staring at the pile of women's panties and bras. On top was a folded purple lace thong. He grabbed the lid to hide the box's contents.

"What is it?" Blake asked, peeking over. "Oh…" She giggled, the sound that cute noise between embarrassed and amused.

The pink hue of her cheeks darkened into full red as she blushed. She looked young, vibrant, as the color moved through her features and all the way into her ears. She reached over and picked up the panties. They unfurled in her long fingers.

"Something tells me that these probably aren't in Robert's size." She laughed, dropping them back into the box. "He and Tiffany must have been having a good time…at least at some point."

For a moment, as he looked at her, he thought of her wearing those purple panties and a bra to match. In his daydream, she was sauntering toward him, her curves bouncing ever so slightly, teasing him as she moved.

"It's funny. I think I have the same pair in blue," she joked, winking at him. "In fact, I might be wearing them now." She reached down and unclipped her utility belt and carefully let it fall to the floor. Peeling back the waistband of her pants, she revealed the top of her panties. "No, they're cotton. But they are magenta," she said with a laugh. "So close to sexy, but so far."

"Hey, I think cotton can be sexy," he said, wishing he could have seen more. He suddenly felt a little more at ease than he had before.

Her giggle returned. "Then you would love my bra. I think it's even beige. You haven't seen sexy until you've seen me in a nude-colored cotton bra and mismatched panties."

"Oooohhh, baby." He fanned himself as he laughed.

He liked this side of her, the relaxed, playful and unlocked version of herself that he had never seen. He started to tell her. He stopped out of fear that if he said it, she would close up and the little spark he was seeing would fade away.

"You've seen mine," she teased, motioning to her panties. "It's only fair if I see yours."

He tried to stop the lust that rose in his core. Dang, Blake was sexy.

He stood up and walked over to the radio, then flicked it on. A Bob Seger CD clicked to life, and the song "Night Moves" filled the air.

"What are you doing?" Blake asked with a playful

frown. "Are we having a little Throwback Thursday thing here?"

"First, it's not Thursday. And, second, I happen to like Bob Seger. Or at least I did when I was a kid," he said with a chuckle.

"I bet you're a Billy Ray Cyrus fan, too, huh?"

He started to sing "Achy Breaky Heart."

"Oh, my God, please stop. Once that song gets in your head it never leaves," she said, moving her hands up like she was guarding herself from his singing.

"Come on. I'm not that bad of a singer, am I?"

She looked up at him with a twinkle of glee in her eye. "If I were you, I would stick to being a detective."

He lunged toward her like a teenager, unthinking as he pulled her into his arms and growled. "How dare you?" he teased as her breath caressed his cheek.

She put her arms around him. As her chest pushed into his, he could feel her heart hammering. Suddenly he realized how close they were, how she felt like she belonged in his arms—more, in his life. Everything just felt so good. So natural. So real.

He leaned in, kissing her lips. They were welcoming and firm, echoing his own needs and fears. She kissed him back, their tongues moving against each other, waking every nerve ending in his body.

She ventured closer, forcing him down to the hard floor as she moved atop him. Blake sat up, pressing her warmth against him, gently rocking as she teased his responding body. He reached down, taking hold of her hips, slipping his thumbs under the edge of her uniform top. As his cold fingers touched her hot flesh, she went still and just stared at him.

He wished he could know what she was thinking.

Then again, it probably wasn't too hard to guess. She was probably wondering if this was the right decision. If this was the right time. If it was a bad idea to take things down this road with him.

What they were doing was wrong for so many reasons. They were in his brother's house searching for clues about his death, but if Robert's death had taught him anything it was that he couldn't let moments like these pass him by. Life was too short to play by the rules. This moment—holding her in his hands and feeling the warmth of her breath against his skin—this was right.

He pushed his thoughts aside. Blake was the kind who took what she wanted. And he was eager to give it.

BLAKE LOOKED DOWN at him, the way his muscular chest pulled against his T-shirt, accentuating the lines of his pecs. How had they gotten here at a time like this?

She stopped herself. They were working, but it didn't matter. All that mattered was that her fantasy, the thing she'd wanted forever was happening.

His thumb caressed her skin, his touch reassuring but at the same time making her core warm and her belly stir. He wanted her. He looked at her with his piercing green eyes; in their depths she could see a gleam that spoke of carnal appetite.

Had he been without sex as long as she had? From the way she instinctively rolled her hips, her body hadn't forgotten how glorious it could be—and how good it could be with Jeremy.

Reaching down, she lifted the edge of his shirt and let her fingers trace the waistband of his jeans. There was a fine line of dark hair that trailed down, disappearing under his clothes. She wished she could follow that line, all the way down to—

He sat up, breaking her wandering thoughts. When she thought he would step back from her and end this sensual assault, he leaned in and kissed her again. This time his kiss was deeper, headier than the last. She could taste his flavor, salty, sweet and faintly minty. He tasted so good, and she sucked at his lips, pulling the bottom one into her mouth.

He moaned, the sound deep and throaty, hungry.

She pushed him back, gently but firmly, and slid her hands down and unbuttoned his pants.

"Boxers kind of guy?" she teased, pulling at the elastic band of his red flannel underwear.

"I'm just like you. I'm a cotton man."

"My favorite kind of guy." She laughed. "I don't know what I would have done if you were wearing a G-string."

He laughed, and as he moved his body shifted under her. He pressed hard against her, making her nearly forget what they had been laughing about. All she could focus on was the way he felt under her and all the things she could do with his reacting body.

She moved off him to between his legs. Ever so slowly, she edged down his pants, kissing his skin as she pulled them lower and lower down his thighs.

His pheromone-laced scent nearly made her mouth water as she kissed over the cloth at the intersection of his legs and groin. He tensed under her touch, and she felt him come to life beneath her lips. Much as she didn't want to, she stopped. He needed to want her more than he had ever wanted anyone before. She wanted him to beg her to let him have her. She would take her time in seducing him, pushing him to the edge and reeling him back in, again and again.

The pants thumped as they hit the floor. But that was not the sound that stopped her. It was her phone. Vibrating loudly, it started to ring.

"I better answer that," she said, a bit breathless.

He nodded, but his face fell with disappointment.

She stepped away from him and grabbed the phone. "This is West."

"I'm calling in reference to Robert Lawrence." It was the medical examiner, Les Taver. The man had always been short on frivolities, but maybe that was what happened when you worked with the dead all day.

"I'm glad to hear from you, Les. What's going on?"

"After performing a full autopsy, I've made a ruling in Robert's death. It's a homicide."

Chapter Eight

Falling into Jeremy's arms had been a mistake. One Blake couldn't repeat. He was off-limits for so many reasons. Not the least of which was his brother's murder. Now that she had a homicide on her hands, anything between them could be seen as a conflict of interest. She couldn't risk being pulled off the case because of her feelings toward him. She had promised the captain she would do her best to solve this case, and a relationship with Jeremy would only jeopardize everything.

She slid her belt back on and clipped it into place. "Put your pants back on, Jeremy," she said, her voice riddled with an air of forced indifference.

He opened his mouth to say something, but she shot a look at him. "That was the medical examiner. He's ruled your brother's death a homicide."

Jeremy stood up and threw his clothes back on, jumping around as he pushed his legs into his jeans. "I knew it."

She tried to stop herself from feeling the urge to watch as Jeremy zipped his pants.

He looked at her, measuring her in a glance. "What did the examiner find?"

"He said that there wasn't any gunpowder on Robert's hands. He couldn't have fired the gun."

She looked down at her phone. "He said he was going to email me his findings. It sounds like there was also some kind of note."

"A note?"

"Your brother had put it inside the waistband of his pants. Maybe it was his way of sending us a clue."

She nodded as her phone buzzed to life. She clicked on the email from the medical examiner. "It's here."

The handwritten note was slightly grainy, but she could easily make out the words as she read.

To whoever's gonna read this letter,

The moment before lightning strikes, electricity fills the air. Metal vibrates and rings. Hair stands on end. The only thing a miner can do is lie down and pray. Pray violently. Pray like you ain't never prayed before. Then you wait for the moment that a million volts strike...and you hope that death doesn't find you.

Until now, I always thought my biggest fear was lightning, that I would be struck down, a pickax in my pack and a shovel in my hand. I realize now what a fool I have been. It wasn't lightning I should have feared. I shouldn't have feared the earth. I should have feared my fellow man. If I had paid more attention, I would have known that the thing I love most would be the death of me.
Robert Lawrence

What did the letter mean?

Jeremy walked over and stood beside her, staring

at her phone. "The thing I love most," he read aloud. "What did he love the most?" he asked rhetorically, tapping his fingers against his bottom lip.

Sitting on the floor, beside the box, was the tax lien paperwork. "Do you think he meant the land? Maybe his mine?"

Jeremy nodded. "Absolutely, but why would someone want to kill him for it?"

She picked up the financial papers. "Look at this. He's been making money hand over fist. Maybe someone found out. Someone who wanted what he had. Money and love are the most common motivators in a murder."

He handed her back her phone, and she slipped it into her pocket. "Who issues a tax lien?"

"In this case, it was the county. I think the county treasurer holds it until it's paid or it goes to auction."

The blood drained from her face as she remembered the name of the treasurer.

"What's the matter?" Jeremy asked, taking her by the arm like he was afraid she would faint.

"I...I know him."

"Who? The treasurer?"

She nodded, her body stiff and numb with realization. "His name's Roger Davy."

"Okay." Jeremy frowned. "What does that mean?"

"Roger Davy is the mayor's brother-in-law. Detective Engelman is his brother..." She forced herself to take a breath. "What if the mayor has something to do with this?"

She had to have it all wrong. Just because her leads pointed toward the Engelman family didn't mean that a corrupt system was behind this murder. She had to be missing something.

But if she was right, she was in over her head.

Had this been what Captain Prather was hinting at? Why he'd wanted her to take the case—because he knew she didn't have a connection to that family? Was he setting her up to take a fall or to find the truth?

She had to sit down.

"It's possible...but why? What would the mayor want from my brother?" Jeremy's eyes turned dark, and she could have sworn she saw a shadow of hatred in them.

She shrugged. "I don't know. But maybe they filed the lien and then had to keep Robert from paying it. He must have had enough money, or at least access to enough. If he couldn't pay his tax lien, then anyone could buy his land. They could take the property for just a few thousand bucks."

"Does that give them the mineral rights, as well?"

"I don't know for sure," Blake said. "But probably, if it's all on the same deed."

"Just because these men are related doesn't mean that they're in it together. I mean, why would the mayor put himself into a compromising position?"

"Most of these tax liens are bought out by holding or investment companies."

"So?"

"The largest investment company in the county is Tartarus Environmental Investments. And who do you think the CEO is?"

Jeremy shook his head.

"The one and only Mayor John Engelman."

"This is still only circumstantial evidence. There's nothing that directly ties the mayor to Robert's death."

"Not yet, but I have a feeling if we just look hard enough, we'll find what we're looking for."

"Hold on." Jeremy leaned against the back of the couch. "We need to proceed slowly. Let's not jump to any conclusions."

Maybe Jeremy was right. She needed to slow down. If she had this wrong, there would be fallout.

"We need to get this evidence back to the unit," she said, staring at the papers strewn over the floor.

"First we need to make sure we have pictures of everything. If what you are saying is true, there's a good chance something could disappear."

She made sure to get a clear picture of every piece of paper she thought could be of any use in their investigation. Then they dropped the boxes of paperwork off with the evidence unit.

As they drove away from the office, Blake called the captain.

"West, how's it going?" Captain Prather asked.

She told him about the medical examiner's findings and the connection between Engelman and Davy. The captain was silent for several moments.

"Dang it," he said finally in a muted whisper. "Do you have any direct evidence?"

"No, sir."

"Then don't you dare utter a word of this to anyone else. If you're wrong, this could cost us both our jobs."

"I know, sir." She paused, then, "Sir, do you have the number for the mayor's PA? I was hoping that maybe I could talk to them and at least get a line on the mayor's whereabouts at the time of Robert's death."

He rattled off a number.

She tapped it into her phone.

"West," Captain Prather continued, "you better hope that you're wrong. This kind of thing could bring everything down on top of the entire county."

"What exactly do you mean, sir?" She wasn't sure, but she could have sworn from the tone of his voice that he was suddenly regretting ever putting her on this case.

"Nothing, West. Just tread softly."

The phone line went dead.

She looked to Jeremy, who was sitting in the passenger's seat, his head in his hands. He must have heard everything. "Heck of a way to spend your days off from your department, isn't it?"

"It looks like I may need to take a few more days off," he said, forcing a smile.

She started to reach over to take his hand but stopped. Something about touching him seemed wrong. They had already taken things too far. They couldn't do that again. It could compromise everything—their friendship, her investigation and even her job. And if the mayor was involved, as she assumed, it was hard to tell how far those political ties went. Montana was a large state, but when it came to connections and secrets, sometimes it was entirely too small. Both of them could be in danger.

She had to call the mayor's personal assistant. She had to eliminate the mayor and his cronies from her list of suspects. They couldn't possibly have been involved. They didn't get to where they were by being stupid and getting mixed up in homicides—at least ones that would point directly to them.

She dialed the number the captain had given to her, and the mayor's PA answered.

"This is Deputy Blake West. I was hoping to catch

up with the mayor today. Do you know where he is?" she asked, trying to avoid the question she most desperately wanted to ask.

"He's in Helena today with his wife. He should be back tomorrow morning. Can I let him know you called?"

"No," she said, maybe a bit too emphatically. "No," she repeated, this time a little softer. "It's fine. By chance, when did they leave for Helena?"

The PA was quiet for a moment. "Well, he had the finals for the Montana Shooting Sports Championship here in Butte this week, so he had to wait until this morning to leave, but his wife is set to arrive in Helena this evening."

A gun championship? If Engelman had been competing, then he may have an airtight alibi for his whereabouts at the time of Robert's death.

"Oh, I heard the about the championships," Blake lied as she tried to draw the PA into a conversation in which she could learn more. "How did Mayor Engelman do?"

The PA laughed. "Oh, he wasn't shooting. He was just making an appearance. Anything for a little publicity and a few bucks, you know."

The knot in her gut tightened. "I see."

"Is there something you wanted to talk to him about?" the PA asked.

An edge of panic cut through her. No one else could catch wind of her investigation or where it was pointing—especially not the mayor.

"No, but thanks."

"Are you sure?" the PA pressed, her voice flecked with suspicion.

"Yes. I'll try and get in touch with him later. Our department was just wondering if he would be available later this month. We're working on a public event," she lied, trying to cover her tracks.

"Oh, okay." The warmth returned to the PA's voice. "I'm sure he'd be interested."

"Great, just great," Blake said, the panic returning to her voice. "Talk to you soon." She hung up the phone.

Blake's feint had worked, but there would be no guarantees for how long. It had been a bad idea to call the PA. Now her name would be on the mayor's radar. And if he was responsible in any way, he would be alerted to the possibility that he was under investigation. She let out a ragged breath.

"What's the matter?" Jeremy asked, staring at her.

She tried to shake off the thoughts that plagued her. "Nothing. No worries."

"I know you. You can't lie to me."

Was that true? Did he really *know* her? She had been on her own for so long now that she balked at the thought that a man—no, not just some man, but Jeremy—really cared enough to think that he *knew* her. She looked at him for a moment, taking in the barely noticeable crow's feet that adorned his perfectly almond-shaped eyes. Eyes that seemed to look straight through her. Eyes that seemed to see her for who she really was, and not the hard-edged person she tried to show to the world.

She looked away. She couldn't fall for those eyes, or the man behind them. She couldn't let herself lose her focus or her edge.

"I think I got a lead," she said, skirting the issue.

"Mayor Engelman was at the Shooting Sports Championship."

"That's not much of a lead."

"No, but we have a solid place to start investigating our number one suspect."

Chapter Nine

At the gun range men and women were standing in the trapshooting fields, and the sharp echoes of shotgun blasts and the scent of spent gunpowder filled the air. In a strange way, the smell of the powder made Blake comfortable. She'd spent so many days on the range with her standard-issue Glock 22 .40 caliber pistol. Every officer in combined city and county sheriff's office, known as the Butte–Silver Bow County Sheriff's Department, had been issued the same gun, but over time hers had become special. It had become a part of her. She reached down and touched its familiar grip.

She and Jeremy made their way to the clubhouse. A man in his early twenties sat behind the counter reading a *Guns & Ammo* magazine. He looked up as they approached.

"How can I help you, Officer?" he asked, setting the magazine down on the counter and giving them his full attention.

She smiled. "I was just wondering about yesterday's competition. Was the mayor here?"

"Yeah," the clubhouse manager said with a sharp nod. "Mayor Engelman gave a great speech on the need for enforcing our Second Amendment rights."

"How long was the competition?"

"The prelims started last week. Yesterday was the finals." He rambled on about the winners and their shooting averages, while Blake pretended to listen.

"Was the mayor here the entire time?" Jeremy asked when the man took a break between statistics.

The manager nodded. "He was here on and off throughout the week, and yesterday he was here most of the day. Made a big thing out of it. You should have seen it—he even took a turn on the shooting stage. Missed just about all the clays, but you know how it is, not being his gun and all."

"He's not a good shot?" Jeremy asked, giving her a questioning look.

The manager passed them a grin. "Hey, I ain't saying he's bad. He just ain't a shotgun man."

If the mayor wasn't a good shot with a shotgun, it didn't mean that he wasn't necessarily a good shot with a handgun—particularly the one that had been used in Robert's murder. Heck, anyone could have been a good shot at such close range. Then again, would the mayor really have wanted to get his hands dirty? Would the glad-handing, speech-making, baby-kissing mayor really be capable of pulling a trigger to get something he wanted?

Jeremy laughed. "Hey, we can't all be good at everything. Am I right?" he asked, chumming up with the club's manager.

"Hey, I heard he's real good with a sidearm."

"Is that right?" Blake asked, perking up.

"That's the talk around the clubhouse. I had a guy in here yesterday. Said he was shooting with the mayor just last week. He said the guy could shoot a solid grouping at twenty-one feet."

"Who was the guy the mayor went shooting with?" Jeremy asked as he leaned against the counter in what she assumed was his attempt to look nonchalant and nonconfrontational—anything to put the manager at ease and make him talk a little more. It was enthralling to watch Detective Lawrence in action, the way he looked at the man like he was a friend rather than a source feeding them much-needed information.

"I think the guy's name was Todd. Maybe Todd O'Banyon or something."

"O'Banyon?" Blake asked. "Do you mean O'Brien? Todd O'Brien?" *Robert's neighbor.*

"That sounds about right. The mayor and Todd were in the bar," he said, motioning over to the door on the other side of the clubhouse, which must have led to the tavern. "Todd had a few beers after the mayor left, and then he finally stopped talking about what good friends they were. He was thinking himself some kind of big man. I think maybe the mayor even bought a gun off of him."

"Do you know what kind of gun?" Blake asked.

The man shrugged. "Some kind of Glock. I don't remember. Like I said, the guy had a few beers under his belt. From what I heard, it's possible that he was just making it all up."

"What do you mean?" Jeremy's body tensed, but the manager didn't seem to notice.

"I don't know. The guy was just talking all kinds of nonsense—about how he was going to be a millionaire if he played his cards right. You know. Crazy talk."

Had they gotten it all wrong? Was O'Brien the

man they were looking for? Or was he involved in the mayor's plot? Why would the mayor be buying a gun from someone—especially Robert's neighbor?

"Did he mention how he was going to be making these millions?" Jeremy asked, a cold edge to his voice.

The man shifted in his chair. "I dunno," he said with a shrug. "It was Greek to me. Something about buying investment properties or something."

She thought back to Todd O'Brien's property. It was covered with rusted-out car frames and filled with garbage. How could a man who couldn't afford the upkeep for his property afford to invest? Todd O'Brien had never had a job, as far as she knew.

"Is there something I should know about?" the clubhouse manager asked.

Jeremy shook his head. "Nah, it's no big thing. We're just looking into a few different things. If necessary, though, would you mind if we came back and asked you a few more questions?"

The manager smiled. "Not at all. I appreciate all that you guys do. You have the hardest job of anybody, protecting the streets. The least I can do is answer a few questions."

Sometimes she loved living in Montana, where law enforcement officers—for the most part—were treated with respect. It wasn't the same everywhere else. She read about it in the national headlines all the time, officers being shot or their homes vandalized simply because of the job they were drawn to do. And those in her profession were constantly struggling with the stigma of being crooked.

She thought of the mayor. Maybe he was part of the problem. There were always a few in public service who were corrupt. It was the political way. Unfortunately, across the country it was her brethren who had to pay.

Jeremy flipped through the saved pictures on Blake's camera as he waited. He scrolled past the images of Robert's body and stopped at the picture of the gun that sat next to his brother's hand. It was the standard police-issued Glock.

Every fiber of his being told him that this gun was the same one the manager had told them about. Instant hatred flooded his veins. The mayor was likely behind his brother's death. Now he and Blake would just have to prove it.

He looked over at Blake, who was having the club-house manager sign a statement. The man had taken the questioning remarkably well. In Missoula, things were a little tenser with the public—especially after the strings of arsons and his involvement in the investigation. He and his department were still trying to win back the public's trust.

It was hard to know who to trust anymore, and the public felt the same way. In a world full of lies and corruption, few stood above it; few wanted to live with honor.

He looked back at the photos on the camera and started scrolling through them. He came to the ones they'd taken earlier, at Robert's house. Some of the documents in the photos were ones that Blake had gone through, and he hadn't seen them. Now he took his time, scanning through them. He clicked again. On the screen was a picture Blake had taken of a photograph in Robert's files; it was of a car parked in Todd's driveway. The date marked on the photograph put it at having been taken a week ago.

Why would Robert have taken a picture of a random car and then slipped it into his files? He must have wanted to keep it as a record of something, but what?

The picture was dated one week prior to his brother's death.

He zoomed in on the license plate. It was the blue vanity plates that celebrated Glacier National Park. He made note of the number.

After picking up his phone, he called Dispatch. A woman answered, and he gave her his information. "I need to run a plate," he said, reciting the number.

There was a long pause as the dispatcher clicked away in the background. After a moment she came back. "The license plate is for a 2015 silver Land Rover registered to John Engelman. Is there anything else you'd like to know, sir?"

His breath wheezed from his lungs. "No, thanks," he said, forcing the words from his body.

His brother had left him a sign. He had left Jeremy the evidence he needed to bring the sucker to his knees.

Chapter Ten

The ride back to their houses was tense. How could she have missed the picture of the mayor's car? Jeremy's face was tight as he stared out the window. Whether he was angry or just preoccupied with the details of the case, Blake couldn't be sure.

Hopefully he didn't think she was incompetent. She was working this case as fast as she could, and sometimes things fell through the cracks, but that didn't mean she didn't care. If anything, she cared about this case more than she should. Most of the time, even when she knew the victims, she could gain emotional distance—but not this time, not when the vic was Jeremy's brother.

Maybe she was too close. It had certainly been a mistake to find herself on the floor with Jeremy. It had been so exciting, so euphoric to be wanted by him, to be in his arms and desired, but she shouldn't have let down her guard. It had added a degree of tension to everything they did, every expression he made—like now.

As soon as she parked he got out of the car and slammed the door.

"Wait," she called as she went after him. "What's your problem?"

He looked surprised as he turned back.

Had her insecurities made her jump to conclusions? Was he not really upset with her? She instantly regretted her tone.

"What?" he asked.

"What's going on with you, Jeremy?" she asked, trying in another way to see if she was crazy or not.

He frowned. "Nothing."

That was a cop-out. Everything about him, from the way his eyes had darkened to the way that even now his body turned from her like he was desperate to run away, said otherwise. "Don't lie to me, Jeremy."

He turned to face her. "There's nothing wrong," he said, his voice hard and his words abrupt.

Blake walked toward him so they were toe-to-toe. "You don't get to be angry with me. You missed that picture, too. If nothing else, it's just good that we found it. Now we have evidence—"

"That's not it," he said, looking toward her house.

She followed his gaze. The lights were off inside, but that didn't mean that her mother wasn't watching. She turned her back to the windows. "Then what is it, Jeremy? Are you mad about what happened at your brother's? If that's the case, it won't happen again. It was a mistake in the first place."

He took her by the arms and looked into her eyes. "Stop. I'm not upset with you."

"Then why are you so pissed? Why have you barely spoken to me since the range?"

He looked toward his parents' house. "I'm not pissed. I'm just…I'm just…I don't know. Look. Here's the deal. In a few minutes, I'm going to have to walk in there," he said as he motioned toward his parents' house. "And

I'll have to tell them that we don't have a suspect in Robert's case. They are going to want to know everything the medical examiner said and what we've done. It's going to be brutal."

"You don't have to tell them anything," she said, softening under his touch.

"You know that isn't realistic. If you think your mother's bad, imagine what she'd be like if something happened to you."

She shuddered at the thought. Her mother would be distraught. As much as they got under each other's skin, they were everything to each other.

"My mother is more upset than I've ever seen her." He rubbed his thumb over the fabric of her uniform. "The worst part of it all is that I don't know what to do. I've never been good at that sort of thing. I don't know the right words."

"Just listen to your heart and be honest." As the words fell from her lips, she couldn't help but feel like a hypocrite. Here she was telling him to be honest, to follow his heart, but that was the last thing she was going to do. She couldn't tell him how she felt...how she had always wanted him. It was too big of a risk, putting her trust in someone else.

"I—" He stopped.

"What were you going to say?" That little part of her heart that held all her desires sprang to life with the hope he would say what she wanted to hear—he wanted her and they could be together.

He let go of her arms and stepped back from her. The way he moved made it seem as though he wasn't putting just physical distance between them but emotional distance, as well.

"I appreciate what you're doing, Blake," he said, his hard-edged voice in direct opposition to the softness of his words. "I mean with the investigation and all. You're doing everything you can."

She waited for the "but."

"But," he continued as the single word made her heart sputter and her fingers go numb, "what we did at Robert's...you were right. What happened was a mistake. I have only been divorced for a little over a year. I know that seems like a long time, and I would be okay, but I have my daughter to think about."

She nodded, not sure if she could handle standing there and listening to what she knew was coming.

"I'm sure you feel the same way," he said.

He couldn't have understood the way she was feeling right now—the way she wanted to run away, to crawl under her sheets and hide. Still, another part of her wanted to stand up and tell him he was wrong—that they could have it all, that they could be together. That they could figure it out if they both loved each other enough.

Love. The word dropped like a stone in a bucket. It rippled through her, the weight of its meaning cascading all the way down to her toes. That was the problem. Neither of them could have love.

There was no room left in their hearts.

BLAKE SAT ON the edge of Megan's bed and stroked her daughter's damp blond hair. She smelled like lavender shampoo and innocence.

"Get some sleep, pumpkin." She leaned down and gave her a kiss on the forehead and then she turned and slipped the book back onto the shelf, next to her daughter's well-loved redheaded doll, one of the mementos she'd kept from her childhood.

"Mom, wait," Megan called just as she moved to stand up.

"What, honey?"

"Mom," Megan said, her voice smooth but laced with sleepiness. "Are you going to ever get married?"

The question came out of left field and forced Blake to slump back onto Megan's bed. "What do you mean? Where did that come from?"

"Well, Grandma was on the phone today and she was talking about Jeremy. She said that she hoped you'd get married to a man like him." Megan took her hand; her skin was warm and soft. "Do you love him?"

Why did her mother have to put ideas like this into Megan's head? There was no right answer. No matter what she said, Megan would riddle her with more questions—questions that a thirteen-year-old didn't need to ask. She just needed to enjoy being young and not worrying about her mother's romantic relationships—or lack thereof.

She thought of Jeremy and where they had left things with each other. Maybe he had been right in pushing her away with the excuse that they needed to think of their children first. If things were like this, confused and up in the air, the last thing she wanted to do was involve Megan. Above anything else, her daughter needed to be protected.

"Pumpkin, I love *you*." She pushed a hair off Megan's slightly sweaty neck.

"I know, Mom, but it would be kind of cool, you know…"

"What do you mean?"

"Well, I don't know," Megan said, skirting around what she wanted to say. "I guess it would be just kind of cool if I had a dad. I mean a dad I actually saw and stuff. Think about it. I could even have a sister if you married Jeremy. It would be so fun."

She didn't want to burst Megan's illusion by telling her that in real life, relationships weren't that simple. They were just another method through which you could get hurt.

"We don't need a man in our lives just to make us happy, pumpkin. Women are so strong. We can do anything," she said, flexing her arms as she tried to make light of the multiple layers of her daughter's innocent but pain-inducing words.

"Oh, I know you're strong, Mom." Megan waved her off. "But he makes you smile. I like it when you smile. You look beautiful."

"Not as beautiful as you." She wanted to take her daughter by the arms and tell her that she wanted a man, too, but instead she simply kissed her good-night and slipped out the door. She pressed her back to the wall and took a deep breath.

She wanted a whole family for Megan, but she couldn't tell her the truth—Jeremy didn't want to get involved.

This time, the truth was just too painful.

Chapter Eleven

The next morning, Jeremy was already waiting by her squad car when she made her way outside to go to work. He looked too handsome, wearing a snug pair of jeans that still had the crease of newly bought pants and a fresh plaid shirt that made him look like a logger in all the right ways.

He had a cup of Starbucks coffee in his hand and he extended it to her as she approached. "I hope you accept my peace offering."

She frowned, trying her best to be cute in an attempt to show him all that he was missing by not choosing her. "What kind is it?"

"Pumpkin spice latte. I even had them put the whipped cream on."

Most of the deputies she worked with loved their coffee unflavored and black—like it was some kind of symbolic gesture that they were tougher than the average person who needed added flavor, cream and sugar in their coffee. Unlike them, she loved pumpkin spice. Did he know, or was it just a lucky guess?

"Whole or skim?"

"Whole milk," he said with that trademark grin he

seemed to reserve especially for her. "Nothing but the best for you."

"Thanks." She took the coffee, careful to avoid touching his tanned hands. "Why the sudden about-face?" As she asked the question, she wished she could take it back. That was one conversation she didn't want to open. "Never mind. Don't answer that," she added, trying to put the cork back in the bottle.

"No, you're right. I shouldn't have said what I did."

She waited for "I'm sorry," but it didn't come. Did that mean he shouldn't have said it, but he still meant it?

She took a long drink of the hot coffee, not knowing what to say.

"I was hoping, if you're not upset, I could go with you again today to see the mayor."

So that was it. He wasn't sorry. He was worried about not getting the chance to work on the case. She considered telling him to get lost, but the truth was that she couldn't turn him away when everything centered on his brother... This was personal.

"Fine. Whatever. Get in the car."

He smiled and got in the car, but this time the cute smile didn't have the same stomach-clenching effect. This time she had to withstand the urge to punch him in the nose. Why did all men have to be pains in the behind? Why couldn't they be as simple as they always claimed they were?

She got in and accidentally squealed the tires as she backed out of the driveway. The ride was silent, but she noticed that Jeremy kept glancing over at her as if he was trying to gauge her anger. The third time she noticed him looking her way, she had to bite her tongue to keep from saying something she would regret.

"I talked to Penny this morning, before she went to practice," he said finally, almost like he'd been searching for and found a way to open a conversation that wouldn't bring up anything about last night. "She's playing soccer. Is Megan into sports?"

Did he really think that talking about their kids would make things easier for him?

"Nope."

"Play an instrument?"

"No," she answered, careful to stick to the safe, monosyllabic responses.

"That's too bad," he said, but from the way he peered over at her, it was clear that he wasn't really commenting on Megan's after-school activities, or lack thereof. "Penny loves soccer," he said, looking away, careful to maneuver around her anger. "She's been playing since first grade. She's pretty good, too."

"Oh, yeah?" Blake said as she turned down the main road that led to the mayor's office.

There was a silver Land Rover parked in front of the building. Apparently Engelman was in.

"Look," Jeremy said, pointing to the car as if she hadn't seen it.

"Yep."

He jerked in his seat, as though he'd had enough of her being short with him. "If we're going to go in there together, then we can't be at each other's throats. We need to show him that we're a united front or he's going to take advantage of our weakness."

She wasn't weak, and Jeremy was a fool if he thought she was.

"Then maybe you should stay in the car."

"Stop it, Blake," he said, with a pained expression on his face. "I said I'm sorry."

"No, actually you didn't. Instead you made it abundantly clear that all you care about is the investigation—and that's fine. I get it. Your family is important to you, and—"

I'm not. She stopped before she let the words fall from her lips. She didn't want to come off as self-pitying.

"You're important to me, too," he said, reaching for her hand, but she pulled it away.

How could he have known what she was thinking?

"That's why I said what I did." He left his hand open between their seats, as if he was waiting for her to place her hand in his. "I don't want either one of us to end up hurt here. We don't live in the same place. We both have lives that, when this is all figured out, are going to pull us in different directions. It would be naive to think we could have it all."

She understood his logic, but her heart screamed for her to be unreasonable—to just pay heed to the way her body wanted him.

"You're right," she said, looking down at his hand. Instead of taking it, she opened her door and got out, closing it so he was out of earshot. "We can't have it all."

THE MAYOR SAT behind his desk, reclining with his feet perched up on the edge like he was midnap. He pulled his feet down as they walked in.

"Deputy West, I heard you might be stopping by," he said, standing up and motioning for them to take a seat. His oversize belly hung low over the waistband of his pants, and his shirt was stretched tight over his paunch. He quickly tried to adjust his suit jacket to cover the stressed buttons.

His office was decorated with a collection of antiquated law books and bronzes of firemen and police officers, replicas and idols of heroes—as if he hoped that some of their traits would rub off on him.

"Thank you for seeing us, Mayor Engelman," she said, sitting down in the proffered chair as Jeremy followed suit. "This is my colleague, Jeremy Lawrence. He's helping our department with an investigation."

"Which investigation would that be?" the mayor asked, flopping down in his seat.

Jeremy leaned forward, resting his elbows on the armrests of the leather chair. "Actually, it's a homicide involving my brother, Robert Lawrence."

The mayor frowned, the action forced and out of place on the practiced features of the politician. "Robert Lawrence," the mayor said, tapping his finger on his lip like he was thinking. "Afraid I haven't heard of him."

"Huh, that's strange," Jeremy said, attacking the mayor's error. "My brother had a picture of you parked at his neighbor's house last week."

"If this guy is your brother, Mr. Lawrence, don't you think that this case is a conflict of interest for you?" the mayor asked, carefully sidestepping Jeremy's accusation.

"My professionalism is not up for debate, Mayor Engelman. However, your association with my brother is."

The mayor laughed. "This isn't some episode of *CSI*. Just because there is a picture of my car near the Whatever It's Called Mine, that doesn't mean I have any kind of association with your brother. What did you say your brother's name was again?"

Jeremy's face darkened, causing Blake to step in and divert what looked to have become a conflagration.

"His brother's name is Robert Lawrence," she said. "We were called out to his place of residence earlier this week. There, we located his remains. I was just hoping we could talk a little bit about it, in the event you could shed some light on the case."

The mayor looked down at his watch as if to say they were wasting his time and he had somewhere better to be. "I appreciate that you're trying to do your job, Deputy West—I do. However, there's nothing I can tell you about your homicide investigation. If all you have is some picture of my car in his neighbor's driveway, I'm not sure why you are standing in my office."

Jeremy's face contorted with rage. "We're standing here because you're a—"

"Vital piece of this investigation," Blake said, once again interrupting just in time to stop Jeremy from saying something that would serve neither of them. She reached down and pulled out the picture of the gun that they had found in the mine next to Robert's body. "Have you seen this gun before?"

The mayor took the photo and studied it. Jeremy looked at her, and she mouthed for him to relax. He jerked his head toward the mayor and mouthed something she couldn't quite make out, but she wasn't sure she needed to as she could still read the contempt that filled Jeremy's eyes. She shook her head, and Jeremy leaned back from the mayor's desk in resignation.

The mayor looked up. "Where did you find this gun?"

"Have you seen it before?" she asked, careful to avoid giving any information. She needed to pull him into the trap, get him to spill the secrets that only the killer would know.

The mayor gave a noncommittal shrug.

It was no wonder the man was a politician. Here he was, with his feet to the flames, and he looked calm and collected—a far cry from the reaction most people had when they thought they were a suspect in a homicide investigation. For a split second she wondered if that was what the guy was like in bed—noncommittal and dismissive.

She glanced over at Jeremy. His face was red and the vein in his neck was starting to protrude slightly. From their encounter at Robert's cabin, the mere taste of what he was capable of sexually, she had to bet he was the kind of guy who liked to revel in the glory of a woman's body—dipping his fingers down her curves, tracing the lines of her breasts.

What it would have been like to have had the chance to experience all of him…

Her body pulsed with lust. She shifted uncomfortably in her seat, then forced herself to look away and back at the pudgy face of the mayor.

"Yes or no, Mayor? Have you seen this gun before?" she reiterated, pressing her point.

"It's a Glock, isn't it?"

"Is that a 'Yes, I've seen the gun'?"

"It's possible. I just sold a gun like this a few weeks ago."

"You *sold* a gun like this? Or did you buy it?"

The mayor stared at her. "I sold one like it. I can't tell you whether or not it's the same exact gun."

"We were told that you just recently purchased a gun like this. Is that right?"

The mayor's brow furrowed, and he shook his head. "I bought my Glock five years ago from a police auction—your department's, if I recall correctly. I think it was some fundraiser."

He'd had the gun for five years? Things didn't align. The manager at the range had told them the gun had just been sold to the mayor by Todd O'Brien, but was it possible that the man had gotten it backward?

"Who did you sell the gun to?" Blake asked.

The color leeched from Engelman's face, and his skin took on the color of a dead fish.

"Something wrong, Mayor?" Jeremy asked with a little too much glee in his voice.

"N-no..." the mayor stammered. "I'm fine. I...I think I may know who your brother is after all."

"Is that right," Jeremy said, his voice almost a laugh.

"I sold his neighbor, Todd O'Brien, my gun. My Glock22 Gen 4, like the one here, but I wholeheartedly doubt they're the same weapon."

Blake's excitement bubbled up to the surface as the mayor scrambled. Finally the pieces were starting to come together.

"Why did you sell him your gun?" Blake asked.

"We both belong to the same gun club, and we got to talking about police-issued firearms. He offered me the right amount of money."

"Do you have a certificate of sale?"

Even though it didn't seem possible, the mayor's color lightened, bordering on translucent. "I...I didn't get one. It was just a spur-of-the-moment thing."

"You, of all people, should know better. Don't you think you should have gotten a receipt, Mayor?" Blake asked.

Some of the man's color returned as his face tightened. He tented his fingers in front of him on the desk. "What are you saying, Deputy West?" His voice carried an air of threat. "Are you saying that you think I had something to do with the murder of Robert Lawrence?"

"We are investigating all possible leads, Mayor." The top button of her collar suddenly felt entirely too tight, and she reached up and undid it.

"If I'm one of your leads, you are fishing in the wrong pool, Deputy." The mayor thumped his hands on the oak desk. "I am an elected official. I am expected to hold myself to a higher standard—and I do. The fact that you would question my credibility and judgment indicates a strong lack of character on your part."

"You're wrong," Jeremy rebuked. "She's doing her job. And her job has led her here. To your office. Maybe it was you who screwed up." Jeremy's face was hard, and his cheeks were red. He looked like he was struggling to keep his emotions in check.

It was strange to watch the normally stoic detective fight so hard. In a way, it made him look even more handsome than he had before, but perhaps it was simply that he was coming to her rescue. As much as she didn't buy into the heroic knight-in-shining-armor fantasy, he was doing a good impression of one.

"The only mistake I've made is letting you in my office," the mayor growled. "You have no grounds to question me."

"Oh, really?" Jeremy continued. "You are connected to the county treasurer, Roger Davy—am I correct?"

"What about him?" The mayor sat back in his chair and crossed his arms over his chest, protecting his core.

"I believe he is your brother-in-law. Yes?"

"So what? I have family. Is this going somewhere, Detective Lawrence? Or are you just grasping at straws in an effort to rid yourself of the guilt of knowing that you are virtually useless in solving your brother's murder?"

Jeremy rose to his feet as the mayor antagonized him.

"Why do you want my brother's property, Engelman?"

"It's Mayor Engelman to you, Detective," he said with a smug grin. "And I don't know what you're talking about. I barely even know who your brother is, let alone anything about his property."

"It's strange that you were photographed near my brother's property and you sold a gun to his neighbor— a neighbor no doubt you knew hated him. Then my brother is slapped with a tax lien. A tax lien that once again points back to you. You know the expression. If it looks like a duck, walks like a duck—"

"I have nothing to do with tax liens." The mayor tensed as some of his polished exterior slipped.

"Then why are you the CEO of one of the largest investment companies that specializes in acquiring tax liens, Mayor Engelman?" Jeremy spat the man's name.

"Get out of my office. Now." The mayor stood up and jabbed his finger toward the door.

Blake stood up, grabbed Jeremy and pulled him to his feet. They didn't need to kick the hornet's nest any more.

"Deputy West, it is my recommendation that you rethink your investigation," Mayor Engelman warned. "And while you are at it, you should start considering alternative job options. You and your superiors may need to think about your long-term career goals."

Chapter Twelve

Once again he'd screwed up. Jeremy leaned against Blake's patrol car, staring at the sidewalk as he waited for Blake to get off the phone. No doubt she was calling her captain and telling him about the mistake he'd made in the mayor's office. Why had he allowed the guy to get under his skin? He was better than that. Yet he had fallen into an emotional pit. Emotions had no role in an investigation—especially not when so much lay on the line. His clouded judgment might not only have affected the investigation, it may also have just cost Blake her job.

She couldn't lose her job. She had her daughter and her mother to support. It was all his fault.

He kicked the curb, sending pain up his foot.

"That's not a soccer ball," Blake said, making her way over to him.

He pushed off the car and limped as he put weight on his foot.

"That hurt?" she asked, walking to the driver's side of the car.

"I'll be fine."

"Well, if it hurts, it serves you right." She opened the

door. "I thought you learned your lesson about kicking things in the mayor's office."

"I'm sorry," he said.

She got in the car and slammed the door. Apparently she didn't want an apology now. It was funny. Earlier she had started a fight to get one, but now that he offered one up on a silver platter, she didn't want it.

He got in before she had the chance to start the car and leave him standing there.

Her face was in shadows, but even somewhat hidden, he could make out her worried expression.

"What did your captain say?" He wasn't sure he wanted to know, but he had to do what he could to stop the catastrophe that could be coming.

"You mean other than he thinks you should go back to Missoula before you start any more political wars?"

"Sure, other than that." He sank down in his seat, one motion away from ducking and covering.

"We have twenty-four hours. Then he thinks the ax is going to fall. Either I have to find the killer or we'll be out on our butts." She turned to face him. "Why did you have to go in there with guns blazing?" She motioned toward the mayor's office. "I had things under control. Instead you just had to confront him, didn't you? Is that how you investigate things—by starting a fight?"

"I'm a good detective, Blake." He felt weak saying it, but it was all he could think of in his defense. "I screwed up. We both know I screwed up. But there's no going back. From now on I'll do everything I can to make this right." *Even if it means costing me everything.*

"I'm not sure what we can do, other than find the killer. Even then, it doesn't mean that I will have this job by week's end."

"Engelman can't just fire you. There has to be a reason, besides pissing off the wrong people."

Blake laughed. "Have you been living in a hole your entire life? Sure, he can't put the real grievance on file, but if he can't find something that he can fire me for, he'll make my life miserable until he gets what he needs. He'll get his way. He always does. That's why he's the mayor."

Jeremy wanted to pull her into his arms and tell her everything would be okay. That he would fix everything. Yet he couldn't. Not after what had happened. They'd both made themselves clear on where they stood—and how each of them didn't have time or a place in their lives for a relationship. If he took her in his embrace, he wasn't sure that he could stop himself from all the feelings that seemed to flood through him when she was near. He couldn't risk losing his heart to love, especially to a woman who, right now, probably hated him—and had every right.

He thought about what Blake said. How the only way out was to solve the case. They had twenty-four hours. And he knew what they had to do. "Let's start at Todd O'Brien's. If what the mayor said was at all true, he's the man we need to see."

"He was the next one on my list."

He wasn't sure if her annoyed tone was because he had told her what he thought they should do, or if it was because he'd made another misstep in their investigation. Whatever was behind it, he had to fix it. "Did you get any results on the ballistics?"

She nodded. "They ran tests yesterday. The bullet that killed Robert was definitely from that gun, but they didn't get much on the fingerprints."

"What do you mean?"

"They found a single print from an index finger, but it wasn't one they had in the database. The only thing the tech said is that, based on the way they held the gun, the person was left-handed and they had some kind of scar on their index finger."

They could use that. "Did they pull any kind of serial number from the gun?"

"The ballistic expert tried to do an X-ray diffraction, but whoever took out the number had stippled the metal, effectively removing any trace."

There were not a lot of people who knew how or what kind of tools could create such a degree of precision in removing numbers.

He thought about the gun. A police-issued firearm. He had a feeling it was chosen especially for this murder.

Whoever did this was laughing at them.

"We need to be careful."

"Huh?" Blake asked.

"The person behind this doesn't have respect for law enforcement. They think they're above the law. They've killed once, and they won't hesitate to do it again. If we get close, our lives might be in danger."

Blake shook her head. "Just because we made a mistake in there," she said, pointing to the office, "doesn't mean that you have to be dramatic. We're fine."

Her words made goose bumps rise on his arms. Anytime he'd ever gotten complacent in his job, or thought he was safe, was when he'd found himself in trouble.

"Think about it, Blake." Her name felt like velvet on his tongue; it even tasted sweet. He paused as he just looked at her for a moment.

"What?" she asked, locking eyes with him.

"Who do you know who hates law enforcement and we've been circling?"

"Todd O'Brien."

"Exactly. If we go out there, you need to be careful. Who knows what he'll do?"

"That's crazy. I've dealt with him plenty of times. He's all bark and no bite." She shook her head.

"You're right. But this time when we go out there, it'll be different. This time he's the suspect in a murder investigation."

"He won't know that."

"If he has anything to do with Robert's death, he will. Don't underestimate this guy. We have reports that he has an active shooting range. This guy is skilled with firearms. He has had run-ins with law enforcement, and you, before. O'Brien seems to fit the bill of our suspect. He's has a need and certainly had the opportunity to kill Robert."

Blake gripped the steering wheel until her knuckles turned white.

TODD O'BRIEN'S PROPERTY looked more like a hoarder's hovel than the homestead of someone who was bragging that he was soon going to be a millionaire. The driveway was long and winding. As they drove farther and farther into the darkening forest, a pit grew in Blake's stomach. She reached down and checked her phone. The bars flicked from three to none every few feet. Hopefully they wouldn't need to call in assistance.

Her bulletproof vest pressed against her breasts, chafing her underarms as the car bounced on the cobbles and ruts that littered the road. Todd O'Brien was a miserable, angry person and likely had something to do with Robert's death, but she didn't think he would try to gun her down. They'd known each other for years. Though, admittedly, things had been growing tenser between them ever since trouble had started to brew between him and Robert.

She had never thought it would end like this—her investigating him for murder while being stuck in the car with her high school crush, who, once again, was completely unavailable.

Todd's house sat at the end of the long drive and was surrounded by overgrown brush. The weeds listed to the left like even they didn't want to be associated with the place. As Blake and Jeremy approached the front door, they were greeted by the bay of a hound dog and a rattle, as it must have jumped against the chain-link fence of its kennel in the back.

The entire place smelled like rotting vegetation and compost. In the distance, there was a small garden complete with a one-armed scarecrow that had almost completely fallen from his post. The stuffed creature looked like a drunken man, one arm sprawled over the edge of the wood, holding himself up from falling into the dirty reality that waited. Sitting on the post, above the scarecrow's head, was a large raven. It watched them, its black eye catching the little rays of sun that filtered through the forest.

Though she'd been here before, this time the place gave her the heebie-jeebies. She tried to shake off the feeling.

Jeremy walked beside her, looking confident yet cautious as he strode up the steps and knocked on Todd's door.

"Hello? Anyone home?" Blake called.

The lights were on in the living room, and she could just make out the back of Todd's balding head.

He turned and looked at them, then slowly got up from the couch and made his way to the door. The hair around his ears had grown so long that it had started to ducktail and made the bald spot on the top even more pronounced. "What are you doing here?"

"Sorry to bother you, Mr. O'Brien," she said, completely out of habit and training rather than out of genuine emotions.

Todd grumbled something unintelligible. As he moved, his face caught a shadow that filled the craters under his eyes. He mustn't have been sleeping lately, or else he had been drinking heavily.

She stepped closer. The man smelled like last night's booze and a week without a shower. That was unlike Todd. Every time she had been there in the last few years, he had been the picture of a man who had himself together. Why the sudden shift in demeanor?

"How's it going, Todd?" she asked, trying to lower his guard.

"What do you care?"

Jeremy leaned against the door frame and slid his foot into the house far enough that Todd couldn't slam the door in their faces.

"Ah, come on, Todd," he said. "Let's not be like that."

"Why are you here?"

"I was just hoping to ask you a few questions about Robert," Blake answered.

He nodded. "I figured you would be up here. It was only a matter of time. But I'm telling you, I ain't got nothing to do with his death."

"I'm glad to hear you say that," she said, but she

wasn't really sure if she meant it or not. It would be so easy if this was their man. Everything could be solved, the mayor would be appeased and Jeremy would go home. Everything would go back to the way it was. Then again, she could never live with herself if she pinned the murder on an innocent man. "I know you had your fair share of problems with Robert Lawrence."

"You're right, but that don't mean I'm stupid enough to get mixed up in somebody killing him."

Jeremy tensed. "How do you know someone killed him? We haven't released that information to the press."

Todd scowled, revealing a large crooked scar along the side of his temple. "It don't take no rocket scientist to see what's going on here. Don't you be trying to put words in my mouth. I told you. I ain't got nothing to do with his death."

"Then how did you know it was a murder, Todd?" Blake pressed.

Todd looked at her. "You know as well as I do, West. This is a small town. Word spreads faster than weeds."

"Then do you want to tell us about the gun?" Jeremy asked, taking the lead in the questioning.

"What gun?"

"The gun you bought from the mayor. The same caliber gun that was used to kill my brother."

Todd stepped back from the door until his body rested against the back of a chair. He reminded her of the scarecrow in the garden, one strong breeze away from being thrust into the dirt.

"You're right. I bought a gun from Engelman, but it got stolen."

"Is that right?" Blake asked, stepping in front of

Jeremy to preempt his questions. "Did you report it stolen?"

"I only figured it out yesterday."

Jeremy smirked as things fell apart for Todd.

"I swear I didn't have nothing to do with Robert's death. We didn't like each other, but I didn't want to kill him."

"If you don't tell us what you know, O'Brien, we're more than happy to take you in," Jeremy said, his tone low and threatening. "I'm sure forty-eight hours in the interrogation room will help you come clean."

"Wait," Todd said, raising his hands. "I'm tellin' you the truth. That gun was stolen about a week ago. I'd taken it out when—" Todd stopped and looked at them as if he hoped they hadn't heard what he'd said. "Wait… I get it. Someone who wanted me to take the fall."

"When did you take out the gun, Todd?" Jeremy pressed.

"I dunno, but that thing was taken."

"The DA is going to have a field day with you in court. You're looking at a life sentence with a defense like that."

The blood drained from Todd's sun-crisped face.

"I didn't do nothing. I'm a taxpayer. You work for me. How dare you come in my house and start threatening me?"

"We're not threatening you, Todd." Blake watched Todd's exterior crack and all his insecurities come tumbling out.

"That's BS. You came out here with the intention of intimidating me. You have no right. You have nothing. I didn't have nothing to do with Robert's death, and I ain't seen his dumb wife."

They hadn't mentioned a single word about Tiffany. Jeremy looked to her and raised his eyebrows. He had heard Todd's slip, as well.

They were standing on the wolf's tail. If they weren't careful, he would attack, but they couldn't decrease the pressure. They needed to make him lose his edge. To tell them everything he knew. Everything he was attempting to hide.

Chapter Thirteen

It was late in the afternoon, and they were still waiting.
With any luck the judge would issue the search warrant
in time for them to get back to Todd's place before it got
dark. If not, they would have to wait until the morning
when they could get enough manpower to serve the papers and pick the place apart.

"How's your burger?" Jeremy asked as Blake took
a bite of the bar fare.

She shrugged. "Fine," she said, pointing at his untouched basket of food. "You gonna eat that?"

It was the reality of being a law enforcement officer
that when he was given the chance to eat, he needed
to take it. This job could keep him on the streets well
into the night.

"I'm not hungry," he said, pushing a fry around the
basket.

She snorted as she swallowed a bite. "These burgers
are the best in town. You're missing out." She dabbed
at her mouth with a napkin.

He glanced at her phone, hoping at any moment it
would ding with the message they'd gotten their search
warrant.

"Look, it's like a pot," she said, motioning toward

her phone. "It's not going to boil if you're constantly watching it."

She was right, but he couldn't help himself. He hated the fact that they had to leave O'Brien's compound. Todd knew something about Robert's death, and leaving him standing there, when they were so close to someone with answers, was torturous. Yet there'd been little they could do, or find, without a warrant. Once they got it, they would be back. Then they would hopefully get everything they needed to pin this guy down.

"Did you get a chance to look over Robert and Tiffany's credit card reports?" he asked, still staring at the phone. "Anything that could help us get a lead on Tiffany's whereabouts?"

"I forwarded you a copy of the email from Wells Fargo." Blake had a pained expression.

What wasn't she saying?

He opened up the email on his phone and went through the list of recent purchases: mining supplies, Walmart, Home Depot...normal shopping. Nothing that stood out. The only thing irregular over the last six months of his brother's and sister-in-law's purchases was the fact that both of them had stopped using their credit cards the day of Robert's death.

"There's also an email about bank records." Blake took another bite, avoiding his gaze.

Jeremy opened the second email and clicked through their banking records. Just like their credit card there were the normal bills: electric, garbage and mortgage. He scrolled down to deposits and withdrawals. According to the records, there had been an $18,250 cash withdrawal a week before Robert went missing. The bank's statement didn't indicate who had pulled out the money.

He set his phone down on the brown Formica table, but he couldn't look away from the bank statement. There was the withdrawal request and the card used, but it didn't tell him who exactly took out the money. The longer he looked at the withdrawal, the more it seemed to pulse with life, as if the number itself was trying to tell him something.

"We need to get to the bank. See if we can get their surveillance videos and see whether it was Robert or Tiffany who pulled out the money," he said, pushing up from his seat.

"Sit down and eat," Blake said, motioning toward his food. "There's nothing we can do until tomorrow. The banks are closed."

She was right, but it didn't stop his blood pressure from creeping higher. He waved toward the bartender as he settled back into the hard wooden chair. "Can I get a Bud Light, bottle?"

He knew he shouldn't drink when they were working on an investigation, but he needed something to take the edge off. He just needed a moment, a second, to stop and think.

The bartender sat a bottle on a tiny napkin in front of him.

"Thanks," he said, taking a long drink. The bitter taste flooded his senses. He was more of a scotch man, but the beer would do.

A man who was sitting at the bar kept glancing over at them as Jeremy started to eat his burger. When they entered any public place it was as if every eye was on them and everyone wanted to hear what they were talking about.

He looked to Blake, but she didn't seem to notice the

attention they were drawing—she seemed hyperfocused on the burger in her hands.

"What are you thinking?" he asked, taking another drink and trying to ignore the man at the bar.

Blake took a long sip of her Coke, like she was avoiding having to answer him, but he waited her out.

"About Tiffany and what Todd said…" she started, but then stopped, as if she was unsure of what exactly to say.

"What about them?"

She remained silent as she spun the red plastic straw around in her pop.

"You think she's dead, don't you?" He tapped on the phone, calling her attention to the financial transactions that had suddenly stopped.

Blake looked up at him, her blue eyes were full of questions. "What do you think? You think it's possible?"

He had been a detective for too many years to be naive. There was a good chance his sister-in-law was dead. Then again, it was more than a little fishy that someone would pull out all their money, and then they find one body but not the other. For all he knew, maybe Tiffany was the one behind Robert's murder. Maybe she took the money, Robert found out and she killed him. Whoever had shot his brother had to be someone who could get close, close enough that he wouldn't stop the killer when he or she came at him with a gun.

Then again, a Glock .40 caliber had one hell of a kick. Tiffany was a small woman. If she was trying to shoot Robert, could she have done it in a single shot with such precision?

Normally, in the case of a shooting death, there was

more than one shot if there was any form of altercation. The first shot would be low, near the floor as the person tried to fend off the attack. Then there was some kind of kill shot. In the cases of homicide that he usually saw, the second and third shots were to the chest. But not in Robert's case. One shot to the head. Execution-style. There was no low shot. No evidence of defensive wounds. Nothing to indicate anything other than his brother had sat there and taken a shot to the head.

It wasn't like Robert.

His thoughts drifted to his brother's letter. *The thing I love most would be the death of me.*

Had that been Robert's final clue that his wife had been behind his death? He had hidden the note in his waistband. He must have been afraid someone would find it…someone besides law enforcement…someone who would pat down his body when he died. Who would have been capable of doing that, and why?

Maybe whoever was after him wanted his money. Maybe it was Tiffany. Maybe she wanted to take him for every last penny before she disappeared. It was possible she'd started a fight with him in the mine, shot and killed him, then imploded the entrance, thinking that he would never be found.

Yet if she was behind the murder, why hadn't she just stayed put? She could have told anyone that Robert had simply run off, gone to Mexico. His parents would have been upset. No doubt Jeremy would have looked into the disappearance, but if she had taken the time, she could have covered up any foul play long before he arrived. It would have taken some time and some planning, but it wasn't out of the question.

She could have walked away with everything. The money, the house, the mine.

She had to be dead.

If she was dead, Todd O'Brien seemed like the most logical suspect. Why else would Todd have brought her up? Why had he acted so guilty when it came to her?

The guy hated Robert. Maybe he was trying to take everything of Robert's in one fell swoop.

Normally Jeremy loved a good mystery, but not this time…not when the deceased was his brother.

He was about to ask Blake what she thought, but he stopped as the man at the bar stood up and started to walk toward them. The guy walked with a limp, like he had a problem with his hip. As he moved, Jeremy noticed the familiar line of a holstered gun concealed under the man's blue flannel shirt.

His hand tightened on the sweaty beer bottle. It seemed everyone in Montana had a gun and many had a concealed weapon permit, but it always made him twitch. There was no way of knowing what a person was capable of.

"Sorry for bothering y'all," the man said with a congenial smile. "I heard about your case out at the Foreman Mine."

"Does everyone know what happened out there?" he asked Blake, who sent him a knowing smile that reminded him exactly how small the town was.

"I live just in the ravine over from the mine," the man continued. "A few weeks back, Robert and Todd had guns out and I had to call you guys. Thought things were gonna take an ugly turn, if you know what I mean."

Jeremy's grip loosened on his beer bottle. "Is that right?"

The man nodded. "Yep, but normally I ain't got no problem with Todd. He's got land on the other side of mine. Comes through every few days to check it out, walk the fence line and make sure everything is as it should be."

"He has land on the *other* side of yours? What do you mean?" Blake asked.

"He's been buying up land left and right out near me. Been lots of foreclosures after the downturn in the economy and the uptick in taxes. Everyone's been havin' problems making ends meet. Some even been selling to him before the bank takes over."

His thoughts instantly moved to Robert. Had he been one of the ones Todd had been buying out?

Blake's phone chimed to life. She picked it up and then looked to him. "We have our warrant," she whispered after a moment.

She looked beautiful as her features lit with exuberance. Obviously she loved this chase, this bringing the wicked to their knees, as much as he did. As he watched her, he couldn't help the feeling of desire that rose in him. She wanted justice, and he wanted her that much more for it.

"You're a smart one, friend," Blake said turning back to the man at their table. "How many properties, that you know of, does Todd own?"

"The name's Court," he said. "And I dunno about how many properties Todd's bought, but I bet he's got at least a couple hundred acres of land."

"And you said he has access to some through your property?"

"He pays me an easement fee. He wouldn't have to if Robert had sold to him, but it works out great for me. It's like free money coming in every month." Court moved to sit down, carefully adjusting his hip and leg as he lowered his body.

"What do you do?" Jeremy asked.

"Now?" Court asked. "Now I'm retired, but before they downsized, I used to work for the mine adjacent to the Berkeley Pit. I fed the crusher. Malachite, pyrite and matrix on the front end, crushed ore on the other," the man said with an air of nostalgia. "I walked away with a decent retirement when the mine closed, but it didn't cover everything. Unfortunately, I had to sell off quite a bit of my land. That's how Todd got his hands on the land on the other side of my parcel. It's why I had to give him an easement."

Everything was coming back to Todd. They just needed to find the link that brought it all together and proved, without a doubt, that Todd had murdered Robert.

"At least I had it easy, and he was willing to pay me," Court continued.

"What do you mean?" Jeremy asked, trying to follow Court's train of thought.

"Your brother, he didn't want nothing to do with Todd. He hated him—along with the rest of us. From what I heard, Todd wanted to buy out your brother's place, but your brother wasn't interested. Todd was real pushy about it, something about how it was important to his investors."

And there it was. They had their motive. All they needed was probable cause, and they could bring down Robert's killer.

Chapter Fourteen

Two deputies followed them down the dirt road. They pulled to a stop well away from where Todd could see them from anywhere on his main property.

Jeremy looked positively antsy as he tapped his fingers on the base of the window. Sometimes he surprised her; for a detective, the man had a lot of tells.

Blake wasn't sure if it was because he had a young daughter or if it was something else that made him seem so different from all the other men in her life, but whatever it was it didn't help the way he made her feel. It would have been so much easier to push him away if he was the emotionless creature that most detectives seemed to be. Instead there he was, smiling while he looked out the window as the late afternoon glistened off his short dark hair.

Damn him for looking like a Hollywood star mid-pose.

She forced herself to look away as one of the deputies approached her window. No one else could think there was any type of relationship forming between them. They were nothing but friends, close, old-time friends. The kiss they'd shared could be nothing but a fading memory, an impulsive whim—no matter how badly she wanted to feel his lips again.

"Deputy West, we'll go in and take control over O'Brien while you execute the warrant. Sound good?" the deputy asked.

She glanced over to Jeremy. "That's fine," she said. "Just make sure you're ready. O'Brien may or may not have killed a man. Don't get on the wrong side of him."

The deputy nodded and returned to his car. They crept up the road and to Todd's driveway.

"You need to be careful," Jeremy said, finally looking at her. "He has to know we're coming. And if he does, he's going to be ready. This guy thinks he's above the law."

"Are you worried about me, Jeremy?" she asked, sounding impish as she tried to put him on the spot about how he felt about her.

He looked at her as if he was the one searching for answers, but she tried to keep her emotions in check.

He opened his mouth to speak, but she cut him off. "Never mind," Blake said, suddenly regretting the attempt to make him tell her what he felt. "I'll be careful in there. But you need to be focused on what you need to do. Keep yourself safe."

He closed his mouth and looked away. Instead of relief, regret filled her. She should never have hinted at her feelings. She was being ridiculous, setting herself up to take another fall. Men, she could handle. The only truly dangerous things were feelings.

They pulled to a stop in front of Todd's house, next to one of the cars that had been covered by a tarp. She stepped beside the concealed vehicle and, out of curiosity, lifted the tarp. Underneath was a maroon late 1990s model Buick. "You see this?" she asked Jeremy as she motioned to the car.

"What about it?"

"It look familiar to you?"

Jeremy shook his head, and she dropped the tarp back into place. Whatever they were looking for was inside Todd's house. His lights were on inside, illuminating the shadows that had started to fall over the place as dusk crept through the landscape.

She strode up to the porch, her hand on her Glock. Her heart hammered in her chest, but she tried to tell herself it was nothing more than Jeremy and his warning. This was nothing, just another search warrant being served. They would get the evidence they needed to tie Todd to the crime, arrest him and be back to normal before midnight. Heck, if things went really well, she could be home in time to tuck Megan into bed.

Thinking of Megan only made her heart beat louder in her ears.

She couldn't lose her edge. She couldn't let her fear beat her.

She took out her flashlight and tapped the heavy aluminum impromptu billy club against the door. "Sheriff's department!" she yelled. "Todd, answer the door!"

She stepped back, readying herself to kick, but just as her weight shifted to her left foot and she started to raise the right, Todd appeared in the large rectangular window of the door.

"What do you want? I told you I didn't do nothing!" he yelled through the window.

She pressed the search warrant against the glass, right in his face. "You can open the door or we can kick it down. Either way, we are coming in and searching your property!"

Todd stepped back, turning his back to them. Then she heard a slide and a click, the metallic sound of a round being racked into the chamber of a gun. She drew her gun and lifted it, pointing at Todd's center of mass.

"Don't do anything stupid, Todd. Just open the door and come out with your hands up!"

"I didn't kill Robert. I didn't do nothing wrong. Why can't you just leave me the hell alone?" Todd yelled.

"If you didn't do anything, then just let us in. Let us complete our investigation. If you're innocent, you have nothing to worry about. Don't create more problems by making bad decisions. Put down the gun and open the door!"

Todd was silent, and she let the seconds tick by, hoping that he would make the choice that would keep the situation from escalating. The last thing she wanted to do was get in a shoot-out and have to call down the full SWAT team. Everyone in the state would hear about the incident by the end of the day. The higher-ups would be pissed at the level of scrutiny they would have to go through. And she'd have to face the consequences.

Jeremy lowered to his knee on the other side of the door, taking a lower charge position. "Listen to Blake. Come out with your hands up, Todd."

"I wasn't even here the day your brother died. I swear," Todd argued. "I'd gone to Missoula for the day."

Jeremy sent her a questioning glance. Was such a thing possible?

"That's great, Todd. That's what we need to know. Is there anyone who can testify to your whereabouts?" Blake asked.

They were met with another long silence. If Todd was smart, he was thinking about the consequences that would befall him if he continued to play such a dangerous game. Yet she doubted he was that smart. More than likely he was thinking about a way to cut and run.

"I drove to Missoula, went to Costco and came back."

"What time did you leave?" Blake asked.

"I don't know. I don't keep a journal!" Todd spat.

His insolence didn't help his case.

"Come out, Todd. Let's talk about this like adults. Let's get this straightened out. There's no need for you to get into more trouble," Blake said.

In truth, the moment he exited that house he'd be down on the ground and arrested for felony assault on a police officer, but at least he'd come out alive.

"You've always been gunning for me, West," Todd said. "I ain't never done nothin' but pay my taxes and try to make a damned living in this forsaken town. What's so wrong with that?"

"There's nothing wrong with that, Todd. But there is something wrong when your neighbor turns up dead and you won't tell us what you know. Come on, now—make the right choice. This is your last chance. If you come out now, we don't have to get ugly. Put down your gun. Step outside."

Todd stepped from the door, and she watched through the window as he made his way to the center of the room. Then he looked at her and smiled. It was the grin of the crazed, cheeks high, a wild glaze in the eyes.

"I never wanted things to go like this," he said as he raised his gun.

The sound of the gunshot ripped through the air, the cacophony roaring in Blake's ears.

"Get down!" Jeremy yelled, reaching over and pulling at her bulletproof vest.

Todd fired again. Blake dropped to the ground. Her face pressed against the cold, jagged wood of the porch. It ripped at her skin, but all she could focus on was the *thump, thump, thump* of her heart and the burning heat rising from her chest.

She looked up. There were two holes in the wall to the side of the door—right where she had been standing.

Jeremy covered her body with his, protecting her from the gunfire. The weight of his body comforted her and made her feel safe. Jeremy wanted to protect her, to keep her away from the evils of the world. He may have said he didn't care about her, that what they felt wasn't real, but his actions said otherwise.

The heat in her chest intensified, stealing her breath. She reached down and touched the spot right near her armpit. Warm, sticky wetness coated her fingertips. Raising her fingers, she saw blood.

A third shot cut through the air. There was a thump as something hit the floor.

"I'm fine," she said, wiping her fingers off on the boards of the porch. "It's okay. I'm fine," she repeated in an effort to calm herself.

"Suspect is down!" the officer from behind them yelled.

There was the crackle of radios and hurried orders. She could hear the dispatcher talking as she spread the news of the shoot-out radio-wide.

Everyone would know. Everyone would judge her. And soon everyone would know she'd failed at keeping herself and her unit safe.

Jeremy stood up, weapon ready. The backup officer

stepped around him and kicked in the door, sending splinters of wood and glass raining down. She moved to stand up, but the pain in her chest kept her pinned to the ground.

"He's down," Jeremy said, glancing back at her.

His mouth opened in horror.

"Blake…" he said with a long, shocked exhale.

She tried to stand up again, just to prove to him that she was okay, but as she pushed herself up, her arm collapsed beneath her.

Two shots. Two hits.

Jeremy dropped to his knees beside her and rolled her over. "We have an officer down! Officer down!" he screamed, panic searing his voice.

She closed her eyes as the pain racked her body. Her chest was tight, and she struggled to breathe. The world shrank as her body went into shock and her vision tunneled.

"You're going to be okay." Jeremy reached down and ran his hand over her hair, comforting her. "Everything's going to be okay. EMTs are on their way."

"Don't go," she pleaded.

"I'm not going anywhere. As long as you need me, I'll be at your side," Jeremy said, taking her hand and giving it a gentle squeeze.

She stared into his eyes. At their centers was a veil of fear. She wrapped her fingers around his. "And I'll be at yours."

He leaned down, surprising her as he kissed her lips. Some of the pain she was feeling slipped away, replaced with the warmth she felt in his kiss—a kiss that she'd keep in her heart regardless of what life, or death, would bring.

"Suspect is down, but breathing!" the deputy in the house yelled. "Looks like he tried to off himself!"

Jeremy leaned back and looked inside. "I'll keep you safe. He won't be able to hurt you again."

Numbness started to fill her, moving from the bullet wound in the side of her chest and spreading through her body. Her thoughts went to her daughter. She had to make it out of this alive. Leaving her daughter wasn't an option.

"Megan…" Blake said, struggling to catch her breath as darkness shrouded her vision. "Tell Megan that I'll be okay. Tell her I'll be coming home."

And then all she saw was blackness.

Chapter Fifteen

Hell was sitting in a hospital waiting room. The quiet of the late night only made the agony he felt that much more palpable. No amount of magazines and monotonous television could keep Jeremy calm—not when Blake was through the doors that led to the OR. He clenched his fists as he stared at the entrance to the surgery area. No doubt the hospital staff would stop him if he rushed through those stupid doors.

He took a drink from the bitter, stale coffee that seemed to be ever present in hospitals. He prayed someone would come out and tell him what was happening. He needed to know that she was okay. That she was alive. That she would make it through this.

His whole life he had spent trying to protect his mother and father, their marriage, his brothers—constantly trying to fix the problems they created for themselves. He'd tried his damnedest to save his marriage. But no matter where he went, it seemed like he always screwed it up. His parents were fighting now more than ever, his marriage was over, his brother was dead, his sister-in-law was missing and the woman he cared about was fighting for her life.

Everything he struggled to keep safe had ended in

disaster. To solve a problem you needed to calculate the common denominator—in this case, it was him and the curse he seemed to bring onto those nearest him. The best thing he could do for those he loved was to stay out of the equation. He could love from a distance.

All the proof he needed to prove his theory could be found in his daughter, Penny. He hadn't seen her in three weeks. She was the only thing going right in his world…and he barely saw her. She was safe.

Gemma West slammed the door as she barged into the waiting room, Megan at her side. She looked around until she spotted him and then charged over to where he sat. "What in God's name happened, Jeremy?"

The guilt he'd been feeling multiplied, filling every part of his soul. "I'm sorry, Mrs. West." He couldn't bear looking into her eyes and dropped his head into his hands in shame. "I'm so sorry. I tried to keep her safe."

Mrs. West placed her hand on his shoulder, easing some of his self-hatred. "Jeremy, I have no doubt. I know how much you love her."

He jerked, looking up at her as he started to argue, but he stopped as he caught her gaze. Mrs. W gave him a soft, knowing smile.

Was she right? Did he love Blake? He couldn't argue that he felt…something.

He had never forgotten the first time he realized that he thought of her as more than a friend. She must have been about fifteen. If he closed his eyes he knew he could see her, standing out in the sunshine, her blond hair catching the rays and shining like pure gold. She had looked so happy, the light dancing through her hair and warmth radiating through her body. They'd both been so young. It wasn't long after that she'd gotten pregnant and fallen in love with another man. It had been his first, but hardly his last, lesson in rejection.

Could the pain of that rejection finally heal? Could he love her again? It didn't seem possible when you hurt that much that the whisper of love could make it all disappear.

No matter what he felt, life still stood in the way.

The door to the OR opened, and a doctor walked into the waiting room. The man looked around until he caught sight of them and then made his way over. "Are you the family of Blake West?"

Jeremy looked over at Mrs. West, who gave him a slight nod of the head.

"We are," Jeremy said. "How's she doing? Did she make it?"

The man had the dark circles under his eyes that most nightshift workers seemed to have. Jeremy looked down at his hands. His wrists were red where his latex gloves must have pressed into his skin during the surgery.

"Things are looking good. She took a round to the chest and one to the upper arm. She was extremely lucky that neither bullet hit a major blood vessel. The bullet that hit her arm only missed her brachial artery by a matter of millimeters. If it had been two millimeters to the right, she would have likely bled out on-scene." For the first time, the doctor looked down and seemed to notice Megan standing there. "I'm sorry," he said, motioning toward her. "Would you rather we talked about this somewhere else?"

Mrs. W turned to Megan. "Meg, would you please run and get us each a Coke? There's a pop machine just down the hall." She slipped her some money, and the girl edged her way toward the machine.

She looked back, her face drawn, as she made it to the door. "But, Grandma…" Megan started.

"Run along, honey. Don't worry. I'll fill you in as soon as we know what's going on. I promise."

Megan stayed glued to the spot for a moment longer, but she finally turned away.

The doctor hesitated until the waiting room door closed, and then he continued. "We removed the bullet from her chest. It was lodged in her rib, and we were afraid that, left untreated, it would cause her problems down the road."

"She was wearing a bulletproof vest," Jeremy argued.

The doctor nodded. "The bullet hit her just to the side of her vest. In fact, you'll have to take a look, but it actually nicked the Kevlar, which slowed it down and sent it off course. If she hadn't been wearing the vest, things could have been much, much worse."

"The bullet didn't hit her lung?" Jeremy asked, relief filling him.

"Thankfully it didn't enter the chest cavity," the doctor said. "She was extremely lucky that whoever did this was using a small-caliber weapon. Anything larger and she would have likely suffered significantly more catastrophic wounds."

"What is her prognosis, Doctor?" Mrs. W asked, holding on to the back of one of the blue vinyl chairs that were scattered throughout the room.

"She'll stay in the hospital overnight, but she should be going home in the morning. She will need to take it easy for the next few days and stick to her pain meds and antibiotics. If she does, she shouldn't have any residual problems. Though, again, she'll have to take care of herself."

If there was one thing Blake wasn't good at, it was standing still. This recovery would be hard on her—especially given the circumstances of their investigation.

"Mrs. West," Jeremy said, turning toward her. "Would you mind checking on Megan? I need to ask the doctor here a few more questions."

Mrs. W's face was unmoving, and Jeremy had a hard time reading her.

"Are you going to be okay, Mrs. W?" he asked, noting her pale cheeks.

"Fine, just fine," she said, forcing a smile. "Please take care of my little girl, Doctor."

The doctor answered with a nod, and she made her way from the room.

Jeremy watched as Mrs. W walked past the windows that looked out into the hallway. He turned to the doctor. "So about Todd O'Brien, did you treat him, as well?"

The doctor looked back toward the OR, as if he would rather be in the hot zone of the surgery center instead of standing in the icy chill of a detective's stare.

"Doctor?" Jeremy pushed for an answer. "Did O'Brien survive?"

The doctor wrung his hands and sat down on the chair next to him. He rubbed his hands over his face like he was tired. "I evaluated Mr. O'Brien."

"And?"

"The bullet penetrated the skull and, from the CT scans, it appears to be lodged in his frontal lobe."

"But he's alive. Will he make it?"

"He sustained a great deal of damage to his brain, so he may not. However, if there's an area of the brain that can handle an injury like this, it's the frontal lobe. It's an incredible area, Detective. Some people who have injuries to this area have little to no effects in their daily life, however others…" He trailed off.

"Others, what?"

"Maybe it's better if you talk to the neurologist handling his case."

"No. I want answers now," Jeremy urged. "What could happen to him?"

The doctor tapped his fingers together. "From where he placed the gun on his temple and the location of the lesion, he sustained the most damage to his right frontal area. Sometimes this can change a person's social behavior. They will talk excessively, have less facial control and few facial movements as they speak."

"Do you think his memory will be altered?"

The doctor gave a noncommittal shrug. "The frontal lobe controls the working memory. Damage can affect people in a variety of ways, so *if* he regains consciousness and begins speaking, it's hard to say how he'll respond. Some of these patients lose portions of their short-term and long-term memory, but others…well, there's no effect at all."

So Todd O'Brien might never give him a statement.

A traumatic brain injury that impaired cognitive function could be Todd's golden ticket. Undoubtedly, as soon as he was released from the hospital he would be tried as a felon in the shooting and likely found guilty. However, with the little information they had, and no admission of guilt, it would be hard to prove his role, if any, in Robert's death. But Jeremy had to try. He had to find more evidence. Something that proved, without a doubt, that Todd was guilty.

Or innocent.

He stopped for a second and just stared at the white fake marble squares on the floor. Could Todd be innocent? There was a tiny flicker in his core that told him it was possible. Yet if he was innocent, why had he acted out and shot Blake? He had to be guilty. No innocent man acted like Todd. He was guilty of something, something he was afraid of going to jail for, but whether or not he had pulled the trigger in Robert's death was up for debate.

He stood up. "Thanks, Doc."

"Absolutely," the doctor said, relief filling his voice. "If you have any more questions, please don't hesitate to contact me or the neurologist handling Mr. O'Brien's case."

"Can I see Blake now?"

The doctor nodded. "I had my team move her to the Med-Surg floor. She's still pretty heavily sedated, but she's awake. If you like, you and your family are welcome to go visit her."

He walked out with the doctor, making sure to thank him as they parted ways. Mrs. W and Megan were standing by the pop machine, each holding a can as he approached.

"Everything okay?" Mrs. West asked.

He wasn't sure how to answer. The key suspect in their murder investigation was now an unreliable witness. Even if he confessed, Jeremy wasn't sure that they could actually use his testimony in court.

As much as he hated to admit it, he wished that Todd would have died…that his self-inflicted gunshot wound would have done the trick. In this line of work, he wasn't supposed to feel anything. Everything was

supposed to be observed and held at arm's length in
order to save his sanity. Yet he couldn't. Not on this
case. He was too close.

This case was going to destroy him.

"The doctor said we could see Blake now." He
looked at Megan and took the girl's hands in his own.
"Meg, your mom's hurt. You heard what the doctor
said, right?"

Her blond hair hung limply in her face as she nodded. "I know."

He gave her hands a reassuring squeeze. "Don't
worry. Your mom's going to be all right. She's coming
home tomorrow."

Megan looked up at him and into his eyes. "Really?"

"Yeah, but here's the deal..." He smiled. "I need you
to help her, okay? No more messing with her handcuffs,
okay? Can you do that...just for me?"

She pushed her hair out of her face and nodded. "I'll
be good. I promise. I'll even make her food and stuff.
She loves potato soup."

"Is that right?" Jeremy said, putting his arm around
Megan. "I think that would be a great idea."

Megan hugged his arm into her chest. "I wish you
were always here."

He smiled.

Mrs. W looked at him with a shimmer in her eyes
as his heart moved with joy and an edge of sadness.
He missed Penny. He missed these moments with his
daughter. He looked at Megan. She looked so much
like her...they could almost be sisters. Penny was close
to the same age; they had the same blond hair and the
same smatter of freckles over their noses.

Against his better judgment his thoughts moved to

the future. Megan and Blake could be his life—if only he followed his heart. Penny would approve. She'd always wanted a sibling.

It was a beautiful picture he envisioned, but now was not the time for painting such thoughts.

He led Blake's mother and daughter upstairs to the Med-Surg floor and found her room. She was wrapped in a white blanket, and IVs dripped down lines that flowed into her arm. Her eyes were closed and her hair billowed out around her head on the pillow. If it hadn't been for the monotonous beep of the machines hooked to her body, it would have looked as though she was just in a restful slumber.

"You okay, Meg?" he asked.

She nodded, but she was biting her lip and there was a slight sheen of tears at the corners of her eyes. He wished he could shelter her from seeing her mother like this, but there was nothing he could do. Todd had hurt so many people he loved.

Megan walked to the end of the bed. She reached out and touched her mother's toes, so softly that it looked as though she were reaching for a porcelain doll that at any moment could crack under the weight of her fingertips.

Blake opened her eyes and smiled. "You're here." She looked to Megan and then toward him. "I'm sorry."

Her words struck him. How, in a moment like this— where she could have lived or died—could she have anything to be sorry for?

"No, Blake," he started. "I should never have put you in danger. I—" *I love you.* He stopped before he finished his thought. She needed to focus on her family and not his feelings. "I'm glad you're awake."

Blake's smile disappeared, and she grimaced. Reaching up with her uninjured arm, she touched her side where they had removed the bullet.

All his daydreams and hopes slipped from him as he watched her writhe in pain. She was hurting because of his screwup. He should have taken the bullets. He should have made her stand back. He could have saved her from getting hurt—yet he had failed. He couldn't fail her again.

"If you need me, give me a call." He stepped toward the door.

He had to take himself out of the equation. The only way he could keep her safe was by distancing himself from her life.

Chapter Sixteen

All night the monitors at the nurse's station had beeped and rung, footsteps had echoed up and down the halls and occasionally there had been the sounds of crying from other patients' rooms. Blake had barely slept; the only reprieve came when the pain meds she'd been given forced her to succumb to a fitful slumber. As morning rose, and the sounds of the day filled the ward, she was already dressed and waiting to go, her arm immobilized in a sling.

The nurses had been kind as they wheeled her to the front entrance, where her mother and daughter waited. Her mother's old Cadillac sat low, its shocks worn out from years of driving up and down the hilly landscape of Butte.

"Mom!" Megan ran up to her and gave her a gentle hug.

She tried to keep her emotions in check as she looked up at her daughter's smiling face, the freckles that adorned her cheeks and the excitement in her eyes. In a second, she could have lost everything—her daughter, her family, her life.

And for what?

Todd O'Brien had nearly succeeded in taking his

own life. He had failed, but it didn't make it fair or just. There was no justice. No rectifying the situation. One person had died and she nearly could have...and she still didn't understand exactly why.

Who, or what, was driving this madness? Was it the mayor? Was it Todd? Or was it someone else, someone who loved to manipulate and pull the strings of those around them who were stupid enough to do their bidding?

Was it all some game driven by greed and land grubbing as she and Jeremy had assumed, or was it something more?

Her mother stood beside the car door as the nurses loaded her inside like she was an invalid. Her body would heal. It would be fine. Her soul was a different story. It suddenly felt like everything she did in her work was useless. She was just stomping out fires; she wasn't changing anything for the better. She wasn't making a difference like she had assumed she would when she had joined the force. She was just another cog in the wheel of an imperfect society.

For so long she'd been trying to fight the inequity she felt at being a woman in a male-dominated profession in small-town Butte. Looking back, she couldn't say that her fight had all been worth it. Everything felt so...asinine. All that really mattered was family and those that she loved.

Loved.

Her thoughts moved to Jeremy.

More than fulfilling her duties as a deputy, she was doing this for him. He needed his questions answered. She owed him the peace of mind that came with a murder solved.

If he cared so much, though, why wasn't he here?

"Where's Jeremy?" she asked her mother as they drove out of the parking lot and down the road that led to their house.

Her mother glanced over at her. There was a look of trepidation on her face, as if she didn't want to tell her what she knew.

"What? Where is he?" Blake repeated.

"I don't know. He took this hard, you know," her mother said. "He was talking about going to Missoula, getting back to work."

"Why?"

Was he coming back? Had he given up on her? Why now, when she needed him the most, had he left her? Anger flooded her senses.

Her mother had said he'd taken the shooting hard, but if he could just leave her, that proved how little he cared.

She needed to solve this case so she never had to see his green eyes or his mischievous grin again. The doubts that she had been carrying with her about her ability to uncover the truth burned away.

The car pulled to a stop at a light. To her left was a historic building she'd passed thousands of times. This time she stared at it. Its red bricks were starting to crumble at the corners, and the white paint that marked its entrance was bubbled and peeling with age. Most days she thought the building charming, a throwback to eras and worlds past...worlds built on the needs of society and people's unbreakable spirit. She thought of the person who'd built it. It must have been incredibly hard in those days. Butte had been nothing more than a rough-and-tumble mining town, yet the person behind the creation of the building had likely risked everything to see his dreams come true.

What had it once been? On the side of the building was a faded and weathered painting that read, "Sweet Candies." It shocked her. Someone had come to this town, where miners' lives were dominated by the dark, dirty world of inner earth, and he had decided what these men and their families needed more than anything was a brightly colored treat. It was beautiful in a poetic way.

No doubt the shop owner had likely faced adversity and ridicule for his dreams. Just like her. Yet he had found the strength to follow his dreams. Could she do the same?

The car lurched forward as the light changed. She had to get through this. She had to stop worrying about Jeremy and what others thought of her. She needed to focus on the investigation and nothing else; it was the only thing she could really control.

She thought back to Robert's house and the mine. Although she had spent hours in both places, she must have missed something. But what?

"Mom," she said, breaking the silence that filled the car. "I need you to take me to the evidence unit."

"Blake," she said with an exacerbated sigh. "You can't go back to work. You just got out of the hospital. You need to go home, get some rest, and maybe you can come back in a few days."

The first forty-eight hours of an investigation were the most critical, and they had already passed that marker. If she didn't figure out everything she needed to know soon, it would become harder and harder to solve the crime.

"I need to find out who is behind all of this. It won't hurt me to look through paperwork, Mom."

"You already got Todd. What more do you need to do? You have your suspect."

Megan shifted in the backseat.

She couldn't stop now…not when she was so close, not when she could find out—without a doubt—exactly what had led up to Robert's death and what role Todd had played.

"I'll only be a couple of hours. I'll call you to come get me when I'm done."

Her mother just looked at her.

"Hey, if nothing else, you'll know that I'm not going anywhere, right?" She tried to make light of the situation, but her mother didn't seem to appreciate the humor. It struck her how, even though she was a grown woman, her mother still wanted to protect her. Though they had their issues and disagreements, Gemma West truly loved her. That love was just like what Blake felt for her daughter—it was unwavering. "Everything will be fine, Mom. I promise."

A few minutes later, her mother parked in front of the station. "I expect you to call me if you need anything."

Blake smiled. It was just like she was fifteen again and her mother was dropping her off at the school dance. But instead of resenting her as she had as a teenager, she loved her mother more for her concern. "I'll call you when I need you to pick me up."

She gave Megan a kiss on the forehead, and, as she leaned over, the stitches in her chest panged to life, reminding her of the damage her body had sustained. She pushed the pain away. "Be good. And take care of Grandma, okay?"

Megan nodded. When she looked up at Blake there was reservation in her eyes. She had seen that look before—when she had walked Megan into her first day of kindergarten, and when she had first left her baby to go back to work. Her daughter didn't want her to go. That look broke her heart.

She stepped back toward the passenger's door, but her mother put her hand up, stopping her. "You go do your job," she said, looking back at Megan like she, too, had seen the look her daughter had given her. "I have Megan. We're going to have fun today. Aren't we, honey?"

"But, Grandma—" Megan started.

"Oh, come, now. I have an idea for a new quilt. Wouldn't you like to help me pick out some fabric?"

Megan's face took on that awkward look, the one that melded the excitement of youth with the reservations of a teenager.

"Thanks, Mom."

Gemma smiled, and in her eyes there was a shimmer of pride as if she knew exactly how much this case mattered to Blake.

Blake turned and made her way into the sheriff's department without looking back. Her mother was in control; she was the rock in their lives.

The mayor was walking away from her down the hall, and she hurried so he wouldn't see her. She wasn't sure she could face him right now. She rushed through the department and toward the evidence unit. She pressed the code into the keypad, and the door opened. She walked in—and found the unexpected. Sitting at the row of desks inside the area was Jeremy.

She stopped and stared at him, unsure of what to say.

He looked up, and his eyes widened with surprise. "What are you doing here? Why aren't you at the hospital?"

"They released me on good behavior," she said with a dry, cutting edge to her voice. "My mother told me you were going to Missoula. Why are you here? And how did you get in?"

There was a breath of warm air against the back of her neck. "I let him in," a man said.

She turned and standing there was Captain Prather.

"We needed someone to work on this case in your absence. Because of his experience as a detective and his gracious offer to act as a consultant, I brought him in. We need to solve this."

"You're absolutely right, sir." She turned around and moved toward the seat at the desk near Jeremy. "It's great that we have Todd O'Brien in custody."

"Blake," Captain Prather said, shaking his head, "before you sit down, we need to talk."

A cold chill tumbled down her spine. What was happening? Why was the captain looking at her with pity and disdain? Did it have something to do with the altercation with O'Brien? Sure, she had screwed up by getting in a shoot-out, but it was hardly her fault. She hadn't wanted things to end up that way.

She moved toward the captain. She glanced toward Jeremy, but he wouldn't meet her gaze. He knew something, something he couldn't tell her.

Was the ax about to fall?

"Sir..." she started, but she stopped herself. She couldn't bring herself to beg. She couldn't allow Jeremy to see her lose her cool.

Everything would be fine.

Captain Prather led her to his office and closed the door and the blinds. Whatever was about to happen was something he wanted no one else to know about.

He turned to her as he sat down in his chair. "Deputy West, take a seat."

She did as instructed. A cold sweat started to bead on her skin. He had used her formal title. This wasn't going to go well.

"I brought you in here today to talk about the altercation that occurred on Todd O'Brien's property last night."

That was no surprise.

"I'm highly disappointed in the events that transpired between you and Todd O'Brien."

"Captain, I—"

He shut her down with a raised finger. "I was depending on you to get a handle on this case. You knew what was at stake, yet you let it slip through your fingers—and, worse, you ended up getting hurt. This is going to come back on all of us, West."

"I know, sir, but we got Todd. We got our suspect."

"Your suspect? You think he was the one responsible for Robert Lawrence's murder? The murder that, according to you and the medical examiner, took place at approximately noon on Tuesday?"

She didn't like the way he spoke. Was she being set up to take a fall?

"Yes, sir." She looked down at her hands as she waited for his blow.

"If you would have checked into Todd O'Brien a little deeper, you would have realized that he was nowhere near Robert's claim on Tuesday morning. We have record of his credit card being used at the Missoula Costco at 11:15 a.m. and then the Cenex at 11:45."

"Sir, someone else could have used his credit card." She was grasping at straws, and she knew it.

He nodded, but his body remained rigid, unwavering. "Jeremy's looking into the video footage from Costco to make sure that isn't the case. It is doubtful, however, that Todd is the person responsible for Robert's death."

The information came as a shock. What made it worse was the fact that Jeremy hadn't bothered to tell her.

"I...I did everything to the best of my abilities. Todd wasn't answering my questions. We were executing a search warrant. We would have found out the truth—"

"Mistakes in this game come at a high price, West."

"I know, sir. O'Brien made the choice to shoot. I just wanted to ask him some questions and search his property for evidence that linked him to the crime. I never wanted anyone to get hurt."

"I'm more than aware, from Jeremy Lawrence's testimony, that you may not be at fault for the events that occurred. That being said, however, there still must be a professional inquiry and investigation. Therefore, I must put you on paid administrative leave until things get figured out."

Her heart dropped. He was pulling her off the case.

She had lost what little reputation she had in the captain's eyes. She'd lost her chance to prove herself, and now it was likely she would lose her job. Everything she had fought so hard for... It was all gone.

Chapter Seventeen

Blake sat on the wooden bench outside the front of the station, waiting for her mother to come pick her up. She had been right. It was just like a high school dance—high hopes torn apart by the whips of reality that left her alone and once again calling her mother for help. This cycle was never going to end. No matter how badly she wanted to change.

Then again, maybe she was lucky to have a family like hers…a family that was always there. It may have been only her mother and her daughter, but they all had one another's backs. There was no question about loyalties or favorites. No turbulent marriage to worry about, like in Jeremy's family. Maybe that was why he couldn't trust, why he couldn't compromise. His family had to be the reason he was the way he was—for good and bad.

No matter how hard she tried to understand his actions, she couldn't come to terms with the fact that he had kept her in the dark. She had been in the hospital, but he could have come to see her and told her what he'd learned. It was her investigation. At least, it had been.

From the very beginning, he had strove to lead. The night in the mine, he had tried to tell her how to run the investigation. Was this just an extension of his need to control?

"That seat taken?" a man asked from behind her.

She turned to see Jeremy standing there. He held his hands in front of him like a repentant child. If she hadn't been so angry, so hurt, he would have looked kind of cute the way his gaze fell to the ground and an apologetic smile lingered on his lips.

Lips she had kissed. Lips she had hoped to kiss again, but now she could barely look at.

She moved toward the middle of the small bench, taking both seats. It was juvenile, but she couldn't stand the thought of him being so close. She wasn't ready to have him near her, apologizing, trying to justify why he had done what he had done.

"Whatever you have to say, you can save it." She turned back and tried to focus on the torn blue awning that adorned the restaurant across the street.

He walked around and stood beside the bench. "I know how this looks. But trust me—I didn't intend to get you in trouble."

"Then what exactly did you intend?"

She could smell the sandalwood and cloves of his cologne, but still she didn't look at him.

"I just wanted to dig up a little more information while I had the chance. I found something that I think will change everything."

"You mean the fact that Todd couldn't have been Robert's killer? Captain Prather already told me."

"I know, but I got something better."

Her head jerked up. "What?"

"I went back up to Todd's place after I knew you were okay. We found his tax records and a safe with land deeds. It looks like the guy at the bar was right. Todd was buying out the properties around him. He's the registered owner of almost all the land around the Foreman Mine. Plus, I got the license plate of the car we saw under the tarp—the one you thought looked familiar. Turns out it's registered to Tiffany Lawrence."

"What? Why would Todd have Tiffany's car? Did you get a look inside?" she asked, moving over so he could sit down next to her.

He smiled as he took the spot next to her on the bench. "It looked pretty clean, but I had it towed to the evidence yard." He motioned toward the fenced compound that sat behind the sheriff's department.

"Did you have the techs go through it?"

"They're working on it now. You wanna—" He stopped and looked down at her sling, and his face tightened with concern. "You need to go home, West."

Her anger flared as he said her name like she was just another deputy. "I don't need to do anything except finish my work on this case."

"I get it. You're trying to prove to the world that you can handle anything, but you don't have to be Superwoman, West."

"Stop calling me West like I'm some kind of stranger. We came this close," she said, pinching her fingers together, "to taking things too far. I've seen your skivvies."

He laughed, but the sound only made her more infuriated.

"What's so funny?"

"You said *skivvies*. Only my mother calls my underwear my skivvies."

"So now you're comparing me to your mother?" Her

blood pressure rose. "I'm nothing like your mother. No matter how badly you want to live out some Freudian thing."

He stopped smiling. "That's not what I meant. I didn't mean to make you mad. I just thought it was cute, that's all."

Leave it to a man to find her anger attractive, provocative even.

"If you think I'm so cute, why do you keep screwing with me? First, you want to run everything, and now you get me put on administrative leave and make me look like an idiot in front of my captain."

"It's no secret that I care about you, Blake." He said her name carefully.

"If you care about me, you have one screwed-up way of showing it." She gripped the cast-iron armrest of the antique-style bench.

"I'm trying to protect you."

She balked. "What? How are you protecting me by letting me get taken away from the job I love?"

"Do you really love your job?"

How dare he ask her a question like that? She loved her job. She went to it nearly every day and helped save the innocent. It wasn't the glorious, romantic job the television shows made it out to be, but it kept her and her family fed.

"Do you love *your* job?" She turned the question on him. "You say you're trying to help your family, but what is the truth, Jeremy? I heard about the case with the battalion chief. Was it weighing on your conscience? Was it why you needed to gain control of this investigation? Why you were happy to see me put on administrative leave?"

"I had nothing to do with your administrative leave. You know that. It's just your department's policy. I didn't write it. I don't enforce it. If I wanted to take over this case, then why in the hell would I be telling you about Tiffany's car?"

He made a point, but she wasn't mollified. "Why didn't you tell me about Robert's credit card statements and how they cleared him?"

"I didn't tell you because I only just found out. I haven't even had time to look into the video surveillance yet. Just because someone used his credit card doesn't mean that he was the one doing it."

"The captain seemed to think it was him."

"Your captain doesn't work the beat. I think it's just one hell of a convenient alibi that this guy who, according to his bank records, only shops at three places—the closest little family-run grocery store, the hardware store and the gun shop—all of a sudden branches out and goes to Costco in another town on the day of the murder. It's out of character for the guy."

"Do you think he went there just so he could be on tape?"

"It's one hell of a solid alibi if it works out that way." Jeremy nodded. "But that's not why I think he did it. I think he believes your department is lazy and stupid."

She gave a light snort. It was like Todd to think he was smarter than her and the rest of the sheriff's department. He'd never tried to hide his disdain for law enforcement. And with that level of egocentric behavior came the belief that he could get away with anything.

"I bet he thought we'd never look into the video surveillance. That we'd just take the statements at face value and go no deeper," Jeremy said. "Maybe that's why he was so jumpy when we executed the warrant. Maybe he thought he'd been caught."

She sat there in silence digesting everything that Jeremy was saying. Was he right? Was that the reason that Todd had pulled the gun? That he had been desperate enough to try to take his own life? For the first time, it started to make sense.

"If he wasn't the one to go to Costco, then who do you think it was?"

Jeremy glanced over toward the evidence lot. "I don't know for sure, but I think we need to start looking for Tiffany."

The door opened behind them, and the desk sergeant came rushing out. "West?" He hurried toward her.

"What is it?" she asked, jumping to her feet.

"There's been a report." He looked nervous, wringing his hands, and there was a line of sweat in the furrow on his brow.

"About?" she pressed, trying to help the struggling man find his words.

"There's been a fire...a fire at your house."

JEREMY'S TIRES SQUEALED as Blake took the corner entirely too fast. Safety and speed limits were for people whose families weren't in danger. She screeched to a stop behind the fire trucks that blocked the road. She slammed the door as she got out and started sprinting up the hill to her house.

"Blake, wait!" Jeremy called as he got out after her.

From the moment the desk sergeant had told her about the fire, she'd seemed to completely forget he was with her. She'd grabbed his car keys off the bench, gotten behind the wheel and screeched out, giving him no choice but to scoot into the passenger's seat or be left behind. Nothing else had mattered. Nothing but Megan and her mother. They needed her.

Jeremy ran, catching up to her. "You can't just charge in there. There will need to be an investigation."

"I don't care about any investigation. I need to know Megan's okay," she said between breaths as she ran.

As Blake crested the hill, she saw her. Megan's blond hair, her cheeks covered in a light smattering of ash and her eyes red from tears. Gemma was beside her, holding her, but she let go as Blake approached.

"It's okay. Everything's okay," her mother said, as if she could see the terror that Blake was feeling.

Blake threw her arms around Megan and, pushing back her hair, inspected her face. There was no burns, no marks other than the smudges of ash. "Are you okay?"

"I'm fine, Mom," Megan said, wiping a tear from her cheek.

"What happened?" Jeremy asked. "Are you okay, Mrs. W?"

The older woman nodded. "Oh, it wasn't anything serious. Just a little fire in the yard. Everything's fine." She motioned toward the front yard where the fire crews were dousing the stunted pine with water. The pitch-filled, stubborn tree was still smoldering, spitting and hissing as they tried to force it into submission.

Blake laughed, the sound high, maniacal. The movement made her side hurt and the stitches burn in her flesh, but the pain did nothing to subdue her hysteria.

"What's so funny?" her mother asked, sounding confused.

She tried to stop laughing so she could answer her, but fate's cruel joke was more than she could bear.

Jeremy moved closer to her, took her in his arms and, careful of her wound, hugged her. His kindness made tears well in her eyes. She tried to blink them away. It was just stress that was making her lose it like this. Just stress. She needed to pull herself together, to be strong for Megan.

She stopped laughing, swallowing the sound like it was a bitter pill. She moved to step out of Jeremy's arms, to show the world that she could keep her emotions in check, but she stopped. His warmth felt so good. His scent had changed slightly and now carried a rich scent of fear and panic. He must have felt as she did. Yet here he was, the person trying to hold her together. Why did he have to be so strong all the time?

She wanted to resent him for his strength, to hate him for the confusing mess of emotions that he made her feel, but she couldn't…not now, not when it felt so right to be in his arms. He may not love her, but he cared for her. It was foreign, to be really cared for by a man. Not even her own father had really loved her, or at least it hadn't seemed that way when he'd run away from their family when she was young.

Jeremy looked at her. Their eyes met. There was a light in his that she had seen once before—the night in Robert's cabin. She had to be wrong. He didn't want to be with her. He was only a friend—a friend she was giving entirely too much of her heart to.

She stepped out of his arms and readjusted her sling more out of nervousness than need.

"Ma'am?" one of the firefighters asked as he came up to her. "Are you the home owner?"

She looked to her mother. "We are."

He nodded. "We think we have the fire under control. However, we located a couple of things that we think you should take a look at."

"Will you guys be okay here?" she asked her mother and Megan. Her mother drew Megan back into her arms, the girl coming up almost to her shoulders.

It was shocking to see how much older her daughter seemed than only just a few days ago. It was like she had gone through a transformation in front of Blake's eyes. Or perhaps, it wasn't her daughter who had transformed but rather Blake herself. Maybe for the first time she was really seeing the world around her for the way that it was—ever changing and evolving.

She stepped over to her daughter and kissed her forehead.

"Mom, are you okay?" Megan asked, looking up at her.

"I'm fine. I'm sorry for laughing."

"Why *were* you laughing?" her mother asked. "Stress?"

"Yes, but it…" She looked to Jeremy. "I always thought that tree was just like me."

Her mother frowned with confusion as she glanced over in the direction of the tree. "I don't get it."

Blake smiled as she patted her mother's shoulder. "It's okay. Just know that I love you, Mom."

She turned and walked away, Jeremy following behind.

Her feet sloshed in the wet grass and mud of the front yard. The fire had moved down the tree and set the grass at its base ablaze, but the crew had done a good job in controlling its progression. The tree was blackened, but its bark was still twisting with serpentine orange embers that slithered into the light and then disappeared.

"What did you mean about the tree?" Jeremy asked as they stopped in front of it.

"For years, this damn thing has been struggling to survive here in this poisoned city. It tried to grow but was always held back by the chemicals that had leeched into its roots. See the way it twists there?" she asked, pointing toward a burl in the trunk. "When my father left, he was so drunk he backed the car into it. My mother wanted to cut it down, but I wouldn't let her. I loved and hated that tree, but I wanted it to survive."

Jeremy took her hand in his. "You were wrong about the tree being just like you."

She looked to him, confused.

The fireman motioned to them to follow him behind the tree. "We found this," he said, pointing at the ground.

In the unburned grass was a blackened plastic doll. Its face had melted, but the arms and legs were still discernible. A little tuft of charred red hair stuck out from the back of the doll's head. Even disfigured, Blake recognized it as one of Megan's favorite old dolls—the one from the bookshelf in her room.

Someone had been in their house long enough to find something personal and use it against them. That someone had meant to instill fear. And it worked. But more than fear rose within Blake. In addition, there was an onslaught of rage at the thought that someone had had the gall to violate their home. Not just their home, but specifically her innocent daughter's bedroom.

Who would have done such a thing? And why?

"There's something else, as well," the fireman said as he started walking toward the side of the house.

Sprayed on the siding in orange paint was a message.

DEATH AWAITS YOU

The hair on her arms rose.

"There was also a note," he said, pointing toward a white sheet of paper that was pinned to the wall.

She moved close so that she could read the words.

If you don't leave Butte, I will kill you and your family. Run, if you know what is good for you.

She slipped her hand from Jeremy's as she moved to tear down the letter, but she stopped herself. This was evidence. Evidence they could use.

"We're in luck," Jeremy said.

"How is getting a death threat lucky?" she asked, tilting her head toward the hateful note.

"Whoever wrote this doesn't know me."

"How's that?" she asked.

"You know Casper?" Jeremy smiled.

She was totally lost. "What about your brother?"

"Before he went to work for the US Border Patrol, he used to work for the FBI…as a handwriting analyst. If I call him, I bet he can have his findings back to us within a few hours. He can help us bring down this sucker. And when I get my hands on them, they'll wish they never lived."

Chapter Eighteen

Jeremy tapped his pencil on the kitchen table. He hated waiting. He hated being forced into inaction. But right now he was waiting for a lead. A lead only his brother Casper could give them, once his handwriting analysis was completed.

In the meantime, his mother kept coming in and out of the kitchen; by now she must have been on her eighth cup of tea.

"Is there anything I can help you guys with?" she asked.

Blake looked up and Jeremy saw the dark circles that had started to form under her eyes as the night descended on them. She wiggled in the wooden chair as if her injuries were bothersome.

"You need something, Blake?" he asked. "Ibuprofen or something? You look like you're getting sore."

Blake shook her head. "I'm fine—they're nothing more than flesh wounds," she said, trying to make it sound like a joke, but from the slow edge to her speech he could tell she was hurting.

"Where're her painkillers, Mom?" he asked, standing up.

She went to the cupboard next to the sink and retrieved the bottle.

"Thanks." He took out a couple of pills, then filled up a glass of water and handed them to Blake. "Take these."

"I told you...it's nothing," she argued.

"You don't have to be tough in front of me. I know how bad you have to be hurting right now." As he said it, he suddenly realized that it was likely her body wasn't hurting half as badly as her spirit was.

There was little worse than having one's home violated. Thankfully, she and her family had agreed to take his and his brother's old bedrooms. It was the least he could do to make sure that they stayed safe.

"Is Megan asleep?" he asked.

His mother nodded. "Yeah, she passed right out."

Blake looked at him. "Thanks again for letting us crash here. I'm sure we would have been fine at our place, but it's nice having—" She stopped before finishing her sentence.

Was she going to say that it was nice having him around? Or had she meant something else?

They had their ups and downs, but he couldn't help the way he felt about her. They were more than friends but less than lovers. Yet the more time they spent together, the more he was willing to give up a few things in his life. Maybe. He could never leave Missoula. He loved his job. He doubted that she would be willing to leave Butte. Her family had been born and raised here; her past was here.

His thoughts moved to the night her father had stormed out of her house. He'd been drunk and slammed his car into the tree. After that night, he'd never seen the man again...and from what he'd heard from his mother, neither had Blake.

Maybe the past could be a reason she would want to leave.

He hated to get his hopes up that she would be willing to change her life for him. The only thing she had been willing to give him lately was a piece of her mind. Not that he blamed her.

If she wanted this like he did, there would have to be compromises on both sides. And compromising had never been one of his strong suits.

He looked toward his mother. "What about Mrs. W?"

"She's watching a little television. I'll go keep her and your father company," she answered, swirling the tea bag around in her cup.

As the door to the kitchen swung shut, his phone rang. It was Casper.

"What did you find?" Jeremy asked, trying to keep his nervous excitement in check.

"It's nice to talk to you, too, snotface," his brother chided.

"Yeah, yeah. If I wanted an etiquette lesson I would ask for help from Dear Abby."

His brother laughed, reminding Jeremy just how much he missed him...and, regardless of the animosity they had held for each other, how much he would miss Robert now that he was gone.

"So you're taking on Robert's case?" Casper asked, almost as if he could tell by the silence what Jeremy was thinking about.

"Yeah. Helping out our former neighbor, Blake West."

"I remember Blake," Casper said, his voice filled

with the excitement that came with reminiscing. "She still hot?"

"Uh…" Jeremy looked over at Blake. His cheeks warmed, and he tried to staunch his blushing. For the first time that evening, she smiled. "She's as beautiful as ever."

She looked away as her features seemed to take on a reddish hue of their own.

"I'll have to check her out when I come down for Robert's services. You know when they are going to release the body?"

"Probably not until we get a handle on the murder. Speaking of…did you find anything in the handwriting analysis?" He set the phone down and put it on speaker.

"I don't know what you were expecting, but I did find some interesting things in the note." Casper paused, and there was the sound of rustling papers on the other end of the line. "If you take a look at the physical characteristics and the pattern in the note, the letters are almost at a forty-five-degree angle, and they're jagged, rushed. Whoever did this was in a hurry, but they were likely driven by passion or anger."

If they were in a hurry, they had likely written it onscene. Which meant they knew there was a chance of being seen. Yet they had thought that their mission was worth the danger.

"Looking closer, whoever wrote it was a woman."

"A woman?" he repeated, shocked by his brother's claim. "How do you know that?"

"If you look at the loops and swirls in the handwriting, it's distinctly feminine. And, based on the angle of her letters, she's left-handed."

"Left-handed, huh?" His thoughts moved to the fingerprint the tech had found on the gun.

"Did you find out anything about Tiffany yet?" Casper asked, his voice full of suspicion.

"No, but we're going to use all available resources until we do. Dead or alive, we need to know if she's involved in this."

Jeremy looked to Blake, his eyes conveying his conviction. He couldn't help noticing her eyeliner was smudged and bits of mascara had flaked onto her cheeks. Even slightly disheveled, she was still the most beautiful woman he'd ever seen.

"Thanks, Casper."

"No problem. And hey," Casper added, "if you need me, I can be there within a few hours."

"No worries. Blake and I can handle this," he said, never breaking eye contact with her. "We can handle anything."

BLAKE TWITCHED AS the brothers spoke of time, the measurement of everything in her world. Yet now the only time that really mattered was the mounting hours that had slipped by since Robert's murder. With every passing second, the chances of their solving this case were going up in smoke.

She stood up and grabbed the uniform jacket she'd hung on the coatrack by the door. "Ready?"

Jeremy looked up at her. "For what?"

"We need to get out there. Get a line on Tiffany."

He glanced at his watch. "It's almost eleven o'clock at night. Where do you think we can go that we're going to find her at this hour? First, we don't know if she's even the woman behind the fire. There's no direct evidence of her being involved. Second, we haven't heard anything about her whereabouts since the start of this investigation."

"What other woman, besides Tiffany, would care if we're investigating your brother's murder?"

"Blake, the note never mentioned the investigation. It was a death threat, nothing more. For all we know, it was just some whack-job who's been reading the paper and got it in her head that you're the devil. Who knows?"

Blake gripped her jacket so hard that her fingers on her good hand throbbed. "You wouldn't feel the same way if it was you or your family being threatened. You're minimizing this."

"I can assure you I'm not. I'm just as upset about what happened as you are, but you need to rest. When the sun comes up, you and I can go full-on guns blazing, but tonight you should take a break and let your body heal. You're no good to anyone if you end up back in the hospital because you've refused to take care of yourself."

He was right, but it didn't lessen the urgency she felt. Whoever thought they could come into her house and threaten her family needed to pay.

Jeremy stood up slipped her coat over her shoulders. "Why don't we go for a walk and get some air?"

She nodded, glad that he hadn't attempted to calm her by requesting she stay put. This was one of those times when the only thing that was going to make her better was the feel of pavement under her feet.

He opened the door and followed her outside. The night air was brisk and had started to take on the smell of fading leaves and the last blooms of the season.

They made their way down the sidewalk and started down the hill. The full moon lit their way, and far off in the distance atop a mountain was a white sculpture called *Our Lady of the Rockies.*

"Did you know that she is dedicated to mothers everywhere?" Blake asked, pointing up at the woman atop the mountain.

"You ever been up there?"

She shook her head. There were hiking tours and helicopter rides that went up to the ninety-foot statue, but she'd never been.

"You can see the Berkeley Pit and the entire city. It's hard not to think about all the people who gave their lives for this corrupt place."

"Who owns the mines around the pit?" Jeremy asked.

"The one and only Tartarus Environmental Investments—headed by our glorious mayor. They shut down the mines in the 1990s. I think they weren't making enough money per yard to keep the large-scale mines running. Ever since then they've been hurting for money."

They had cleared the mayor as a suspect, but she couldn't help the nagging feeling that he was still somehow connected.

They walked in silence, their footfalls and the occasional passing car the only sounds. Jeremy reached over and took Blake's hand, and his heat soaked into her cold fingers. It was wonderful to have a man want to touch her, to reach out and take her hand not with ownership but rather something deeper, more visceral... more caring.

She glanced down at their entwined fingers. For a moment she couldn't tell where he stopped and she began. Noticing her attention, he ran his thumb over the back of her hand, stoking her desire.

"Do you think Mayor Engelman is involved in all this?" she asked him.

He nodded. "There's something so wrong about him. It has to be more than circumstantial that all of a sudden Robert gets a tax lien. Then he ends up dead…and the mayor's company is there to scoop up the claim. I just wish we could find concrete evidence to tie him to this thing. Something he can't deny."

They walked slowly up the hill that led to Montana Tech's School of Mines and Engineering. The brick buildings in front of them acted as sentinels as they approached. On the side of one was a picture of a man wearing a hard hat and holding a pickax, and above him read Go Orediggers.

The small college campus was eerily quiet. There were a few cars parked in the lots, but there wasn't a single student hurrying across the grass or making his or her way back to the dorms. As silent and desolate as the campus seemed, it was a comfort. The last thing she wanted right now was to share the silence with anyone other than Jeremy.

There were a few lights on in the buildings, but most were black and closed down for the night. Near the edge of the campus was a gazebo nestled in bushes and covered in yellow roses. Jeremy let go of Blake's hand and made his way over to them, breaking one off. He came back to her and handed her the flower. Its heady fragrance filled her senses.

"That's sweet, thanks," she said, twirling the open bud in her fingers.

"I hope you know how bad I feel…about everything."

"The fire wasn't your fault," she said, taking another sniff of the flower.

"That's not what I mean. I mean I'm sorry for *every-thing*," he said, looking into her eyes. In the moonlight, his eyes appeared as if they were full of stars. He took the rose from her and slipped it behind her ear.

She could hold a grudge, but after everything that had happened over the past few days she didn't have the energy to deny her true feelings. He was nice to have around, and it was nice to have someone who wanted to help her, someone she could trust.

He stepped up into the gazebo and disappeared behind the roses. She followed him up the steps and sat down on the bench at the center. He walked over to her and gently put his hands on her shoulders. She reached up with her good hand and placed it on his. The concrete had started to cool in the night air. A chill moved through her, but she wasn't sure if it was the cold or Jeremy's nearness.

"I never wanted you to get hurt," he said, running his finger over the strap of her sling. "I never wanted you to feel threatened."

She looked up at him, and her lips brushed against his arm. She paused and let the sensation of his soft hairs against her skin sink into her. Ever so gently, she leaned her face against his arm and let herself just feel his touch.

"I made my choices, Jeremy. I've known ever since I chose this path that it was possible I could get hurt. What happened at Todd's wasn't your fault. I froze."

"You shouldn't have been taking point."

She didn't want to argue with him, not when he was looking at her like he was searching for forgiveness and maybe something more. He touched her face, soft at first, unsure. Taking his hands in hers, she kissed his palm. She stood up as she ran her lips down the length of his finger and took the tip of it into her mouth and sucked. His breath hitched, and his body tensed with anticipation.

Moving into him, she pressed against his body and traced his wet finger across the curve of her lip, over her chin and down her neck.

"I'm not the kind of woman who is going to stand back and let others get what I want."

He looked at her as he played with one of her loose hairs, wrapping it around his finger and unwrapping it as if he was in a daze.

"What is it that you want?"

"Right now?" she asked, her breath catching in her throat as she admitted what she had repressed for so long. "Right now, I want you."

He took her lips. His kiss was hard and hungry. He tasted of salt and the sweetness of desire. Jeremy wanted this. He wanted this as badly as she did.

Wrapping his arms around her, he led her to the concrete column behind them, pressing her body against the cold stone. It made the heat of his kiss more intense, and her body throbbed with lust.

He stopped and looked down at her sling. "Are you sure you are okay? You can do this?"

She answered with a seductive smile. There was no possible way she was going to pass up on her chance to be with Jeremy. This may be the last time they could be together. He would go back to Missoula as soon as their investigation was over, and once again she would be alone. At least this way she could be left with the memory of their time together.

One by one she undid his buttons, making her way down his shirt and exposing his chest. She felt his muscles tighten as she moved lower and ran her fingers over the ridges of his perfect body.

"I only need one good hand," she said, slipping her hand in the waistband of his pants until she found her target.

She took control of him and stroked his length. He threw his head back and pulled in a ragged breath as she moved.

After a moment, his hard, hot hand stilled hers and he withdrew it. Giving as he got, he reached down and unfastened her pants. Sliding the fabric down her thighs, he let them fall to the stone. He took off his shirt and laid it on the ground. The muscles of his chest were highlighted by the moon, making him seem mystical, like a Greek god who had come to her in the night.

Ever so gingerly, he laid her on his shirt and pulled her panties down her legs, kissing her skin as they inched lower.

She relished the feel of his moist breath and the tender movement of his kiss, but as she looked around she suddenly remembered where they were.

"Don't you think we should hurry? What if someone sees us?" she said, her voice breathless and drunken with want.

He looked up at her from between her thighs. "I've wanted this…and you…for too long to want to rush."

Reaching up, he pulled the rose from behind her ear. Ever so slowly, he traced the velvet petals over her legs, kissing each place the flower brushed. He ran the petals toward the heat at her center. As his lips moved up her thigh, she forgot her apprehension.

His tongue fluttered against her, light at first but stroke by stroke his mouth drove harder against her, making her body feel as though she would fall to pieces under the pleasure of his touch.

"No," she whispered, though her body begged her to say only yes. She ran her fingers through his hair as he looked up from between her thighs. "I want to feel you… All of you."

He leaned down and kissed her, making her tremble with lust.

"Please," she begged.

He smiled as he looked at her, his eyes mirroring her want and he moved up between her thighs.

"I'm yours…I've wanted you… This… Always." He drove himself inside of her with just the right mix of gentleness and force.

He moved inside of her, her body rising to his. She shifted her hips, pulling him deeper. Their bodies moved together until she wasn't sure exactly who was who. The world disappeared as he laced his fingers through her hair and took her lips.

Her body parted for him, taking all of him, wanting all of him…needing everything he could give.

She wanted this moment to last. Yet her breath caught in her throat as her body disobeyed her mind.

"Jeremy…" she whispered, her voice urgent and telling of what her body promised.

"Yes," he said, his mouth caressing her earlobe. "Yes, be mine."

She let herself go as he drove hard and fast inside of her.

Stars flecked her vision and, as Jeremy's body mimicked hers, for a moment she wasn't sure if something that felt so glorious and right could be real.

Jeremy lowered his body, letting his head fall to her chest as if he wanted to listen to the sounds of her heart. She held him, running her fingers dazedly over the muscles of his shoulders and through his hair.

She had waited for so long for this moment, if only it could last forever.

Chapter Nineteen

Jeremy wasn't the type to smile like an idiot, but he couldn't help the contented grin that had taken over his face and made his cheeks grow sore. He couldn't believe how lucky he was, at least for one night.

He held Blake's hand as they crested the hill that led back to his parents' place. As they approached, the front porch light was on, but inside the house was dark. He was a bit relieved. There was no way he could have hidden what had happened and the giddiness he felt.

Making love with Blake was everything he'd hoped it would be. And he never wanted it to end. But he knew it must. She needed to rest, and they had a case they needed to get back to in the morning. A case riddled with questions.

As if she read his mind, she asked him one. "When you guys went back to Todd's place, did you find any evidence of a woman living at his property?"

"Why?"

"What if Tiffany had been living with Todd? Maybe she had been there, hiding out. Maybe that was what Todd was hiding."

It made sense. If Blake was right, it was no wonder

that Todd wanted nothing to do with them or their investigation.

"Was Todd's truck still there?"

He frowned. "I don't think so."

"Then I think we need to put an APB out on his truck. If we find it, we may find Tiffany."

OVERNIGHT A LATE-SUMMER storm had rolled in. The gray, ominous clouds that had dampened the earth still loomed overhead, threatening more rain. They had been making phone calls all day, tracking down Tiffany's friends, and they had gotten their first solid lead when they had called a woman named Judith. She had sounded concerned about her friend's disappearance, but there had also been an edge of panic in her voice that made Blake want to reach out and talk in person with the woman.

The truck sloshed through the mud puddles, kicking up fat droplets of muck onto the windshield as Jeremy bumped down the road that led to Tiffany's best friend's house.

Despite her administrative leave, Blake had refused to be left out of this investigation. It felt strange to not have her badge on her chest. Yet with or without her badge, she had to protect her family, and the only way she knew how was by stopping whomever had threatened them. It had been painful to watch as Megan had spent the morning cautiously lurching around the house, looking out the windows toward their home and talking about the threat. Megan had wanted to go home, but the idea hadn't been discussed. They needed the relative safety of Jeremy's parents' place.

Jeremy's mother had seemed almost excited at the

prospect of others helping to keep her from her routine with her husband, though she still gave the man the side-eye every time they were in the same room together.

As long as she could remember, the Lawrences had always had a turbulent relationship, but with Robert's death it was doubtful that their marriage would survive. The resentment that surfaced after a child died, even an adult child, rarely brought a couple together. In all honesty, it was a wonder they were still married, but it made sense as to why Jeremy seemed to steer away from anything approaching a relationship—with the exception of last night.

She licked her lips. She could almost still taste his kiss.

Looking over at him as he talked on the phone, she watched as his mouth moved. The simple action made her warm with lust as she thought of all the places his lips had traveled in the moonlight.

Jeremy hung up and turned his attention back to the road. "I told Judith we'd be there in less than five minutes. You get an update on the APB on Todd's truck?"

She shook her head. No one had seen the truck or the woman they were looking for. It was like they were chasing a phantom—and maybe they were. If Tiffany Lawrence was dead, their investigation was, as well. Even though they could prove Todd was land grubbing, there was no proof that he had killed Robert. They had only a few leads, and even fewer people who seemed to have any usable information.

This was her last hope to save her career. If they didn't solve this case, she had no doubt that not only would she be fired from the department; it was unlikely that she would ever be hired in law enforcement again. She would end up right where she had started, a single mother without a dependable income, left to find a path in life that would keep her and her family above water.

"You okay?" Jeremy reached over and touched her neck, gently stroking his strong, callused thumb over her skin.

She melted at his touch. "Absolutely."

Her mother would have called out her lie in an instant, but Jeremy just looked at her. Perhaps he didn't know she was lying, or else he had decided to delve no further. Either way he remained silent as they slogged down the road.

They pulled to a stop in front of a big, beautiful log cabin and walked up the slate path. The impressive structure had a green metal roof and a hand-carved alder front door complete with a horse's head door knocker. The place oozed wealth.

She pressed the doorbell, and chimes sounded. A woman in a black maid's uniform answered the door. In all of her life, this was the last kind of place she would have expected to find a friend of Tiffany's. The last time Blake had seen Tiffany, she had been strung out on liquor and taking wide, drunken swings at her husband. To say she was an alcoholic was an understatement. But was it possible that Blake had gotten her all wrong? Had she just seen the woman at her low point, the recipient of a ticket for disturbing the peace?

"May I help you?" the maid asked, looking them up and down.

"We're here to ask the lady of the house a few questions about Tiffany Lawrence. Is she around?" Jeremy asked. He looked as taken aback as she was at the juxtaposition between Tiffany's lifestyle and her best friend's, but he kept quiet.

The maid looked back over her shoulder. "I can see if she's available, sir." The door clicked shut behind her as she left them standing there to wait.

"Are you sure we have the right place?" Blake asked.

Jeremy shrugged. "I got this woman's name from my mother. She said she had seen Tiffany and this Judith woman running around as thick as thieves."

"But your mother didn't tell you she was loaded?"

He shook his head as the front door opened and a slim blonde stood before them. Her perfectly coifed hair reminded Blake of one of the cover models that adorned *Vogue.*

"How do you do, ma'am," Jeremy said, acting the gentleman. "Do you mind if we come in?"

The woman nodded and motioned for them to follow her inside. Her stilettos tapped on the marble floors, echoing in the cavernous entrance. "I'm so glad you called. I've been so worried about Tiffany," she said, her voice carrying the lilt of the well educated. "Is it true that she may have been murdered?" She stopped walking as they entered the living room and turned to face them.

"We aren't at liberty to discuss that, ma'am," Jeremy answered.

For some reason, Blake couldn't help the feeling of jealousy that crept through her. Just because the woman was well kept, skinny and beautiful didn't mean that Jeremy wanted her. Though, admittedly, he was being more formal than she had ever seen him. Her jealousy grew, making an angry knot form in her stomach.

"Are you friends with Mrs. Lawrence, Mrs...." Blake waited for a moment as the woman looked her over.

"It's Ms. Judith Davy," the woman said, thumbing the heavy-looking diamond and matching wedding band on her left hand.

Of course she was a Davy. Marcus Davy had been one of the founders of the mines in their city. It made perfect sense that the woman before them would be related.

She glanced over at Jeremy, but he seemed focused on the massive river rock fireplace that ran from the ceiling to the floor of the living room.

"Nice painting," he said, motioning above the mantel at an oil painting of an elk bugling as it stood in a running brook. Snowy mountain peaks dotted the background.

"Thanks, it's my husband's. He's more of an outdoorsman than I am. Tiffany and I bonded over that," she said, perching on the edge of the leather sofa. She motioned for them to take a seat across from her.

"What do you mean you bonded over that?" Blake sat down. The pedestal of the coffee table between them was a bronze statue that looked like fish swimming through a stream.

Ms. Davy adjusted the cuffs of her sweater. "Well, Miss—"

"It's Deputy West," Blake said, once again wishing she was wearing her uniform.

"Excuse me, *Deputy* West," Judith said with the raise of an eyebrow as she looked at Blake's department-store button-down white blouse.

Jeremy looked over at her and frowned. "Anyway,"

he said, turning back to Ms. Davy, "how would you classify your friendship with Tiffany?"

The woman relaxed a bit, easing back into the safety of her sofa. "Tiffany and I have been friends for a long time now. She loves to come over. We often shop for antiques together."

The tale screamed foul. Tiffany had always seemed more likely to take methamphetamines than to spend a day shopping, but Blake remained quiet. Maybe Tiffany had been a social chimera—able to spend the days in the mine alongside her husband, and in her off time climb the ladder of high society.

"Have you been in contact with Tiffany lately?" Jeremy asked.

"I heard about what happened to her husband. I tried to call her the other day, after I heard, but she didn't answer." The woman's face contorted as if she was angry with herself for talking to them.

Everything about this place and this woman felt wrong.

"Had you talked to her in the days before you heard about Robert's death?" Blake pressed.

The woman glanced to her left. "Absolutely not."

The woman was lying. Blake could hear it in her inflection. It was the same sound she had made when she had lied to Jeremy. The sound was too high, the air too flippant. She was certain Ms. Davy was a fraud.

"When was the last time you talked to her?" Jeremy continued.

Blake moved toward him and was going to signal him that it was time to go, but she held back.

"I talked to Tiffany about a week ago. My husband

and I had invited her and Robert over for supper. Unfortunately, at the last minute, Todd couldn't make it."

"Who did you say your husband was, Ms. Davy?" Blake asked.

The woman looked over at her and smiled. Her teeth were long and sharp, and she reminded Blake of a tiger. "My husband? Oh, his name's John."

"John Davy? Like the golfer?" Blake asked.

The woman laughed, the high sound stinging her ears. "Close, that's John Daly. No, I didn't take my husband's name when we got married. My husband is the mayor... Mayor John Engelman."

"He's your *husband*?" Blake tried to sound assertive, but her voice came out as a breathless squeak.

Judith smiled, her tigerlike fangs reappearing. "Are you friends of his?"

Blake bit her tongue so hard she could taste the iron-rich flavor of blood.

"We're acquainted. He was at the shooting competition the other day—is that correct?" Jeremy asked.

The woman gave a shrill laugh. "Oh, yes. We hired him to make a speech at the finals."

"*You* hired him?"

"Not me, but I'm on the board for the Montana Handgun Association."

"You're a sharpshooter?" Jeremy leaned forward, tenting his fingers in front of him like he was calling forth the beast.

She laughed. "I'm decent with a gun, but it's just a hobby—you know, something to give me a break from work."

"What kind of work is it that you do, Ms. Davy?"

"I'm the CFO for my husband's company, Tartarus

Environmental Investments." Her phone rang and she hurried across the room to pick it up. She answered it, saying something in what Blake assumed was Japanese.

She must have asked the caller to hold, because she lowered the phone and turned to them. "Detective, Deputy, I'm afraid I can't be any more help in your attempt to find Tiffany. I need to get back to my work. I'm sure you know how it is." She forced a smile as she lifted her phone like it was evidence of her business, but there was a new strain in the way she moved, as if it was crucial they leave.

"We understand," Jeremy said, holding out his hand to help Blake stand. He gave it a light squeeze, reassuring her that she wasn't alone in her suspicion.

Every cell in her body screamed for her to slap her cuffs on the woman and take her straight to jail, but there wasn't room for any more mistakes. Judith was a powerful and dangerous woman.

Chapter Twenty

Blake reached over and turned on the heat in the truck, but no amount of warmth would dispel Jeremy's numbness. How could they have missed this earlier? There had been so many lines running to the mayor, so many motivations to get Robert's land and mineral rights. Yet they had written him off. They'd never thought to check out his wife. Was she the killer they had been looking for all along?

Judith hardly seemed like the type who could walk up to his brother and put a round in his head, but if he'd learned one thing in his years as a detective, it was that killers looked like everyone else. If anything, a killer was more likely to be the innocent-looking neighbor rather than the schizophrenic transient. It was always the ones that people didn't see coming that ended up being the most dangerous—and the hardest to pin down.

Blake looked over at him and shook her head. "What are we going to do?"

He swallowed back the lump in his throat. "It's more important than ever that we find Tiffany. We need someone...anyone...who can help us figure out what in the hell is going on."

Blake nodded, but her lips were pursed like she knew

exactly how unlikely it was that Tiffany would hold the answers they needed. "Ms. Davy was definitely in a rush to get us out of her house. Who do you think she was talking to?"

"No idea, but something was up."

His phone rang, the sound making him jump. "This is Lawrence," he answered.

"This is Sergeant McDonald with the Montana Highway Patrol. I'm just outside of Butte and I believe I have a truck pulled over that matches your description. I have taken the driver into custody. How would you like me to proceed?"

He pulled over, the truck's tires sliding in the muddy grit on the side of the road.

"Do you have an ID on the driver?"

"The woman doesn't have any form of identification, but she says her name is Sophia Lawrence."

Lawrence? It had to be Tiffany. "What does the woman look like?"

"Dark hair, about one hundred sixty-five pounds, and a tattoo of a peacock on the inside of her right forearm."

Tiffany had gotten the peacock tattoo with his brother when they had eloped in Vegas. The sergeant had their woman.

"She's the one we're looking for. Bring her into county lockup."

"No problem," the sergeant answered.

"And hey, thanks for tracking her down."

"Wasn't hard to find her. She was pulled over with a flat tire," the sergeant said. "Is it true that she's being investigated for her role in that homicide I heard about? The one in the mine?"

"News travels fast."

The sergeant laughed. "There are no secrets in our line of work, brother." The man hung up.

Blake shifted in her seat like she could hear their conversation. Jeremy reached out and put his hand on her thigh.

She looked down at his hand. He'd wanted to be able to touch her like this for so long that it almost seemed too good to be true—like the world was just waiting for the opportunity to strike them down.

Maybe fate's weapon of choice was going to be Tiffany. It was impossible to know what she would tell them, but if everything went right, she would give them the last pieces of the puzzle.

With the closure of their investigation, it would likely be the end of his time with Blake. Their stolen moments would be the only things left to remember her by when he went back to his life in Missoula. Yet with only memories to keep him, he couldn't help the feeling that he would go back to a life that would be incomplete.

WHEN THEY ARRIVED at the station, Sergeant McDonald led them to the multimedia area where the soft interrogation room was being broadcast across the monitors. The room on the screens had pictures of trees and birds, magazines were strewn across the coffee table and there was an overstuffed couch. The place had more in common with a doctor's waiting room than a regular interrogation room, which usually held nothing more than a table and a plastic chair that got hard on the perpetrator's behind after a few hours of sitting around and waiting.

"How long has she been in there?" Jeremy asked.

"About an hour. Maybe a little longer," the sergeant

said. "She was a spitfire when she came in. Apparently this isn't how she wanted to spend her afternoon."

"Did you find out where she was going?"

The sergeant reached up and gripped the top of his bulletproof vest in his resting position. "I caught her at the northern edge of the county, heading toward Canada. There was a gas station map on the passenger's seat. I bet you money she was trying to figure out a back road that could get her out of the country—that was, until she got the flat. You're damn lucky we caught up to her."

They were lucky, but why had Tiffany been running? Only the guilty ran; the innocent stayed put.

"You got her from here?" Sergeant McDonald asked.

Jeremy nodded. "Thanks again."

The sergeant gave them a quick two-finger wave and left the room, looking happier than hell that this wasn't his problem anymore.

Jeremy gave a light laugh.

"Something funny?" Blake asked, crossing her good arm over her chest as she leaned against the wall.

"Nope," he said, pulling himself together. "You want to go in there with me?"

"I'm supposed to be on leave. If I go in there, our entire investigation will be compromised. Anything she says might not be admissible in court. We have to make sure to follow protocol."

He stepped closer to her and moved in to kiss her, but stopped as he remembered they were in the station. No one was around, but they still needed to keep it as private as they could.

Blake moved away, almost as if she was thinking the

same thing—or was she thinking something else? Was it possible she regretted sleeping with him?

"You need to get in there," Blake said, motioning toward the interrogation room. "If Ms. Davy is involved, then it's only a matter of time before she runs. She has the money to go anywhere, anytime. If she gets loose, there's little to no chance that we'll get her back."

Blake was right, but he wasn't ready to let things go between them. He wanted answers. Leaving his heart open and exposed wasn't something he was used to.

He tipped his head as he forced himself to stay quiet about what was going on inside. Whether he wanted them to or not, his feelings could wait.

Jeremy turned to go out of the media room.

"Wait," Blake called after him. He turned back. "Good luck in there. I hope you get the answers you need."

"You mean the answers *we* need." He closed the door as he made his way out and across the hall. At the door to the interrogation room, he took a long breath and forced himself to focus on the task at hand. He pushed opened the door, seeing Tiffany seated in a corner of the sofa, her arms crossed over her chest like she was protecting herself from attack.

"Well, well, Tiffany," he said as he took a seat across the room. "Long time, no see."

In truth, he'd been in the woman's presence only a handful of times, and the last time he'd seen her had been a little over three years ago. She had changed. Her dark hair had more gray and her face was now so thin that her tan skin hung loose on her cheeks. She looked haggard. In a way, he found comfort in the fact she was stressed. It proved that she was feeling something about Robert's death. Whether it was guilt or sadness he had yet to find out.

Tiffany glared at him. "What in the hell are you doing here?"

"Thought I'd come for a visit. Catch up. A lot's changed in the last few days with Robert's death and all."

Anger sparked in her eyes, and she opened her mouth to speak but held back.

He was getting a reaction. *Good.* Truth could be found in moments when emotions reigned.

"Did you really think you would get away with it?"

Her face contorted with rage. "I didn't shoot Robert."

"If you didn't do it, why haven't you come forward? You had to have known we were looking for you. Instead you ran. I'm sure you can understand why we have you sitting in cuffs right now."

"I didn't want to get caught up in all of Robert's crap. I'm so tired of it."

"Well, lucky for you, Robert's affairs are now yours."

Tiffany cringed. "I don't want nothing of his."

"Other than the money you took out of the bank last week, you mean?"

"I took the money because I was leaving his sorry behind. What does that have to do with anything?" Tiffany raised her chin in indignation.

"Nothing, but it sure is strange that you wipe out the bank accounts, then disappear just around the time your husband was murdered. Don't you think?"

"Look, I took the money, but I didn't kill your brother. We had our problems, but I never wanted him dead."

"Did you want to threaten my partner, Deputy West, and her family?"

"Deputy West? You mean Blake?"

"You on a first-name basis?"

Tiffany rolled her eyes, the movement almost adolescent and in direct contrast to the wrinkles that surrounded her lips. "I've met her a few times."

"And?" He motioned for her to continue.

"She's been up to Robert's and my place, breaking up fights. I ain't got no problem with her. If anything, she's saved me from spending a few nights in jail over the years. I wouldn't want nothing bad to happen to her. Don't she have a kid?"

Jeremy nodded.

He wasn't positive, but from the way she spoke and the way her body seemed to relax, he guessed she was telling the truth. But just because she didn't have something to do with the threat on Blake didn't mean she didn't have a hand in Robert's murder.

"You guys like to fight? You and Robert?"

"You know how it has been between him and I. Nothing ever changed."

"So you killed him?"

"I told you, Jeremy, I didn't kill your stupid brother," she said, looking him square in the eye. "There were days where I hated his guts, but I ain't stupid."

"What do you mean by that, Tiffany?"

She snorted. "Everybody in this whole damn county knows about me and your brother. We had some good fights over the years." She paused and looked away. She gave a reminiscent chuckle. "It's what made us *us*, you know?"

One thing he knew well was couples fighting. His

parents had done it for so long that he still had nightmares of some of their fights from his childhood. It must have been the same for Robert, but unlike him, Robert had chosen to perpetuate the unhealthy cycle their parents had taught them.

If things worked out with Blake, they couldn't be like the rest of his family. It would be hard, but he couldn't let their relationship fall down the path his brother had taken.

"Do you know if Todd bought a gun in the weeks before Robert's death?"

Tiffany's face darkened as she nodded. "He bought it off the mayor, and then he got the dang thing stolen. I kept telling him to shut up about that gun, but he never listened... But I'm telling you, I don't have nothing to do with what's going on."

He nodded. "Why did Todd O'Brien have your car?"

Her cheeks turned ruddy, and a thin sheen of sweat developed on her forehead as she bit her lip. She ran her hands down the legs of her pants, drying them.

"Tell me the truth, Tiffany. That's the only way you are going to get anywhere here."

"Todd and I are friends." The redness in her cheeks darkened.

"How *good* of friends?" He knew the answer, but he had to have her admission.

She looked away. "We been dating on and off for a while now. 'Bout six months maybe."

"Did Todd have something to do with Robert's death? Had Robert found out about you two?"

"Robert knew. I moved out of our house about a month ago. The last time Blake was up I said, 'Enough is enough,' and got the hell out of there. Todd ain't no peach, but he's better than that brother of yours. All Robert ever cared about was that stinking mine."

"Would you say you *hated* Robert?"

She didn't look at him. "If you knew your brother like I did, you woulda hated him, too."

In their adult lives, he and his brother hadn't been close, but he hadn't hated Robert. Yet it wasn't hard to imagine how Tiffany could have gotten there.

"Did you want to get back at him for the way he treated you by having Todd force him off his land?"

Her eyes flew to his. "How in the hell do you know that?"

It was as good as an admission. She'd been in on Robert's buyout. "What about the tax lien? Was that part of your or Todd's doing?"

"I didn't have nothing to do with that. That was all Todd's idea. If he wouldn't have been such an idiot, we could have found another way, but he was cash poor. Stupid man got mixed up in something he shoulda never been messing with."

"How's that?"

Tiffany rubbed her hands on her legs again, leaving behind a line of sweat. "He shoulda never got wrapped up with the mayor and his wife. Those two are nothing more than money-hungry vipers. I told him. And look where it got him—a one-room suite in the ICU."

Todd would be lucky if he ever left that hospital, but Jeremy said nothing.

"If you want to know who murdered my husband, look to them. Those two will stop at nothing to get what they want."

"What do you mean by that?"

"Those two have been using Todd as the front man

to scoop up land around the Foreman Mine for years. If you look at the map, Todd's name is on most of the land that makes up the ravine that the Foreman Mine sits on."

"Why do they have him buying up the land?"

Tiffany gave him an are-you-really-that-ignorant kind of look. "They have a lot of irons in the fire. Because of their company and the fact that John holds an office, it would blow back on them if they were ever caught buying up county foreclosures. So they set it up, and Todd signs his name on the dotted lines. He gets one hell of a kickback."

"Why do they want all this land?"

Tiffany sighed like he was a pain in her butt. "Robert's mine has been doing good. His claim sits right in the middle of a major source of copper ore. It could be worth millions, or more, depending on their buyer."

"What do you mean, depending on their buyer? Aren't they trying to get a mine in there?"

Tiffany shook her head. "Their company is going through hard times. Tartarus Environmental Investments has been putting out money hand over fist to get the mineral rights to the area along the vein. Right now they couldn't afford to get a bulldozer, let alone the money it would take to put in a full-scale mine."

"So they're putting the land together to sell?"

Tiffany nodded. "And it hinges on Robert's claim. The Japanese buyers won't make a move until the parcel is complete and they have open mineral rights. Judith was desperate. She was afraid that if they didn't act quick, the buyers would walk. She couldn't wait for the tax lien to go to auction. Normally that would have worked, but Robert had started to look for a lawyer. He wanted to take them down. He was threatening them. Hell, he even threatened Todd."

"So Robert knew that your friends were all working together to take his land?"

Tiffany looked down at her hands, like all of a sudden she felt bad for her role in stripping his brother of his land, but it didn't lessen the fact that, in a way, she'd had a hand in Robert's death. Everyone who had been involved with the mayor and his wife had had a hand in his brother's murder, but the only one he could arrest was the one who had pulled the trigger.

"I didn't want things to go down like this. I hated Robert, but I never wanted him dead. It was all Judith's idea. They had to save their business. They couldn't risk a lawsuit or the political ramifications that would happen if their dealings came to light. If Robert had acted, the buyers would have certainly backed out of the deal."

He thought about the phone call they had overheard at Ms. Davy's house. No wonder she had been in a rush for them to leave. She'd been trying to save a deal years in the making...a deal that, if it had fallen through, would have ruined her and her husband's company.

It all made sense, but there was only one sure way to know if Tiffany was telling the truth about the mayor and his wife. "Can I see your hands?"

Tiffany frowned. "Why?"

He thought back to the fingerprint the techs had pulled from the murder weapon. The techs had determined the person who'd fired the gun that killed Robert had a scar on his or her index finger. Now he needed to see Tiffany's.

"Just let me see them."

Tiffany stuck out her hands. Her fingernails were

short and had dirt stuck underneath. He turned her hands over. Her index fingers were unmarred. She wasn't their killer.

"Can you sign your name for me?" he asked, pulling a pen from his pocket and handing it to her.

She took the pen.

"Right there on the magazine is fine," he said, pointing toward *Good Housekeeping*.

She signed with her right hand. This meant she hadn't left the note at Blake's house, because whoever had written it was left-handed, according to Casper.

He didn't have the killer...but he had the one who would help him break the case.

"Thanks," he said, taking his pen back and slipping it in his pocket. "How well do you know Ms. Davy?"

Tiffany shrugged. "We used to be friends. Real good friends, up until lately. We never should have mixed business and friendship."

"Do you know if Judith has a scar?"

"A scar?"

"On her hand or fingers possibly?"

Tiffany sat back against the couch as she thought for a moment. "She's a smart woman, likes to get involved and to know how their money is being spent. A few years ago she was up at the mines. There was an accident with some of the explosives, nothing major, but she had to have stitches."

Jeremy's skin tingled as it always did when he was close to catching his suspect. Judith Davy knew explosives...and probably just the right amount to collapse the mouth of a mine.

"If what you're saying is true, then you are going to need protective custody. Your life may be in danger."

"Why do you think I had to leave?" Tiffany scoffed. "You can't mess with people like the mayor and his wife and not expect to get hurt."

Jeremy had everything he needed. He had his probable cause. All they needed now was to take Judith Davy into custody and get her prints. Once they matched, they had their killer.

Chapter Twenty-One

The evening air had taken on a cold edge, the kind that promised snow was just over the horizon. Blake had always loved this time of year, the end of an era, the start of a world masked with white and waiting for the rebirth that would come in the spring. More than anything it promised a refreshing change.

The lights were on in the shop that sat just at the end of Judith Davy's driveway. As they neared she could make out a brand-new Mercedes and Mayor Engelman's Land Rover, complete with vanity plates that read *NMBR1*. She snickered. His reign as number one was about to be over. In a matter of minutes, he would be married to a woman cuffed and stuffed in the back of a squad car.

Hopefully if the district attorney dug deep into this case, they would be able to finish pulling the legal threads that would also put John Engelman in the hot seat, but knowing him, he probably had his lawyer on speed dial. Then again, even people like Engelman screwed up. If they didn't, she and Jeremy wouldn't have been rolling up their driveway with an arrest warrant.

Jeremy stepped out of the car carrying the warrant the judge had given him before she even had it in Park.

"Hey, wait up," she called after him. "We don't know how she's going to respond here, so you need to be careful."

He stopped and waited for her to catch up. "I doubt she's going to do anything stupid. She has her posse here. The only thing we need to worry about is doing things right."

"What do you mean?"

"Look," he said, pointing to the Mercedes. "Who drives a Mercedes AMG S65 in this state? That car right there costs more than two hundred thousand dollars brand-new."

She stared at the car. It was pretty, but who needed a car that cost more than some houses?

"That has to be their lawyer," Jeremy said. "No doubt the judge who signed off on the arrest warrant was the same man who gave the mayor and his wife a call to let them know we were on our way. The call to their lawyer was probably the first one they made as soon as they found out."

The made their way up to the house and its hand-carved door. They didn't have to knock.

The door swung open, and Mayor Engelman stood waiting, his arms crossed over his chest and an angry look on his face. "As soon as this is over, your asses won't be able to get a job at Dairy Queen."

Jeremy smiled at the threat. "It's okay, Mr. Mayor. I never liked ice cream anyway."

The mayor's cheeks reddened, and his lips tightened with rage. "You stupid son of a—"

"Stop." Judith Davy stepped to the mayor's side and put her hand on his arm. "Everything will be fine. Won't it, Mr. Deschamps?" She turned to the gray-haired man who walked beside her.

Mr. Deschamps made his way over to them and looked them up and down. "If the investigation is anything like these two Barney Fifes, I think we'll have you out of jail and free and clear of all charges in a matter of days, Ms. Davy."

"Being charged with murder isn't quite like getting a speeding ticket," Blake said, unable to keep quiet any longer. "The press and the DA are going to have a field day with this. There's nothing the public likes better than the guilty—especially the indulgent overentitled snobs of the world—getting what they deserve."

"And what exactly is it that you think I deserve, little pig?" Ms. Davy sneered.

"Not only did you murder my friend's brother— you threatened my family." Blake stepped closer so she could look straight into the woman's eyes. "*No one* will ever get away with hurting the people I love. Not you. Not your husband."

"Oh, honey, did you hear that?" Ms. Davy said with a patronizing smirk. "Isn't her little threat cute?"

"May I please see your hands, Ms. Davy?" Jeremy asked.

She looked to her lawyer, who gave an acknowledging tip of the head. She stuck out her hands. On the index finger of her left hand was a long, jagged scar.

"Would you please step outside, Ms. Davy, and put your hands on the wall?" Jeremy asked, but the tone in his voice made it clear it was an order.

She followed his orders. "Frisk away. This will be the one and only time you'll ever get to touch me."

Jeremy ran his hands over the woman's body, looking for hidden weapons, but she was clear. He slipped the cuffs on her.

As they made their way back to the car, Judith turned back to her husband and the lawyer. "I'll see you in a few days. There's bail money in the safe."

Mr. Engelman nodded, but he turned away from his wife like he knew that this was something they would fight, but it was one thing his wife would never walk away from.

This time, their greed had gone too far.

Chapter Twenty-Two

Things with the mayor would only get worse, but at least they had the person responsible for Robert's death behind bars. Even so, Blake's heart was heavy. Everything was over...including her time with Jeremy. The back door leading to his parents' patio opened and Jeremy walked out carrying two pints.

"Want a beer?" he asked, lifting one of the cups.

"Sure, thanks," she said, forcing a small smile as he handed it to her.

Her mother and Megan were out in the backyard with Jeremy's parents. They were all sitting around a fire pit, laughing and joking as they roasted marshmallows. She should have felt happy, surrounded by the people she cared about, but she couldn't let go of her uneasy sadness.

"I bet you're relieved. Sounds like Captain Prather's going to reinstate you once the investigation clears."

She nodded, thumbing the edge of the cold glass. "Yeah, but I'm still going to have to deal with the mayor."

"Until the next election."

"A lot can happen between now and then," she said, then took a long pull from the hops-flavored beer.

"He can't fire you. Not without the threat of a lawsuit anyway."

Jeremy was right, but it didn't make her feel any better. The weight of politics and the repercussions of this investigation would hang over her until the end of her career, at least if she continued working in Butte.

She turned to him as he sat down next to her. The late-evening sun caught the bits of red and amber in his hair and made him look even more handsome, but his eyes were filled with concern and a heaviness she hadn't seen in them before.

"Have you ever thought about leaving?" he asked, looking down at the beer in his hands.

She considered it for a moment. "If I left, everything would change, Jeremy. We'd have to move. Start over. Megan would have to change schools. My mother would never want to leave her home. She's lived here forever." She looked over at her mother and her daughter.

She was struck by how much her daughter looked like her. The same unruly blond hair, the same blue eyes, even the way she looked around at the world, like she was just waiting for the next thing to happen. Would she grow up and make the same mistakes?

Blake shook her head at the thought. Something had to change. Somehow she needed to save her daughter from this world of fires and death while at the same time teach her how strong they could be. Perhaps she could even show her that there were good men out there, men who had hearts of gold and could look past the imperfections in a person and just love them for who and what they were.

She could teach her how to live a healthy life, one centered on family, hope and trust.

"I talked to the captain in Missoula today." Jeremy took a draw from his beer.

She tensed. "When do you have to go back to work?"

"In a couple of days. But that's not why I called him." Jeremy reached over and took her hand. "He said that there is a job there for you in the city if you want it. It would be a little different, definitely busier than the sheriff's department, but the pay would be higher. I could help you get your mother set up, and there are fantastic schools for Megan. She'd have her choice. She could even go to the same school as Penny if she wanted to."

Blake's body tingled with excitement. Was this something she really wanted? She looked at Jeremy, searching his eyes. He had to love her if he was helping her to build a new future. Didn't he?

"If you don't want to move, I can come to Butte. My parents' lawyer has read Robert's will. According to the terms, Tiffany gets nothing. Everything goes to my parents."

"Tiffany gets nothing?"

Jeremy shook his head. "I think that may have been part of the reason she had wanted him to lose everything...why she had been behind Todd's buyout."

"Can your parents afford to pay off the tax lien?"

Jeremy shrugged. "I think so, but if you wanted, we could pay it. We could become miners...if you wanted to stay in Butte. I would do whatever it takes to make you happy."

It was noble that Jeremy was taking steps to stop Tartarus Environmental Investments from getting their hands on his brother's land, but he had told her he never wanted to mine. He was willing to compromise who he was for her, but she didn't want him to. Not like this.

"We can't stay here, Jeremy."

"Are you saying you want to move to Missoula with me?"

She couldn't help the feeling of love that filled her, but was love enough of a reason to leave her home? To build a new life? Falling in love was a risk…

But there was nothing that she wanted more than to follow her heart.

"I…I think I'll take the job." Her body tensed. "And, if it's okay, I want my mom to go with us. She drives me crazy sometimes, but she's my best friend. I don't know what I'd do without her."

"I thought you might say that. If you want, we can look for a house—one with plenty of space." Jeremy smiled as he set down his glass. "But first, I have something for you."

He reached in his pocket. "I know this is fast, and I have no idea what you are going to say, but I've been thinking…I want to do this right. I've loved you since we were kids. I know things haven't always gone as we've wanted them to, but I love you and I always will." He got down on his knee in front of her. "The other night, after the fire, I went back and took a branch of the tree. It took me a few hours, but I carved this for you." He opened his hand. In his palm was a ring made of wood.

Her heartbeat thundered in her ears, making it almost impossible to hear him as he spoke.

"You told me that you always thought of that tree as a metaphor for you and your life. I don't know if you meant it as a good thing or a bad thing, or both, but as I thought about it, all I could think about was how beautiful it was. A tree lives its entire life supporting the lives around it, the grass at its feet and the leaves on its branches. You are just like the tree, loving and supporting those around you. I love that about you. And when you look at this ring, I want you to see that even when we get burnt by life, you can always have a new beginning."

He took her trembling hand and slipped it on her ring finger. It fit perfectly. "If you want, this ring can be a symbol of our promise to create a new future...a life with each other."

"I...I..." she whispered, moving her hand right and left as she looked at the ring's swirling pattern.

He reached up and cupped her face. "I love you."

Tears filled her eyes, but she tried to blink them back. "I love you, too." She got down on her knees and buried her face into his neck. She let her tears fall.

For once it felt good to be measured by time. Their love wouldn't last seconds or minutes or hours. No. Their love would last a lifetime.

* * * * *

Every cowboy has a wild side—
all it takes is the right woman to unleash it...

Turn the page for a sneak peek of
BLAME IT ON THE COWBOY,
part of USA TODAY *bestselling author*
Delores Fossen's series
THE McCORD BROTHERS.

Available in October 2016
in ebook!

LIARS AND CLOWNS. Logan had seen both tonight. The liar was a woman who he thought loved him. Helene. And the clown, well… Logan wasn't sure he could process that image just yet.

Maybe after lots of booze though.

He hadn't been drunk since his twenty-first birthday, nearly thirteen years ago. But he was about to remedy that now. He motioned for the bartender to set him up another pair of Glenlivet shots.

His phone buzzed again, indicating another call had just gone to voice mail. One of his siblings no doubt wanting to make sure he was all right. He wasn't. But talking to them about it wouldn't help, and Logan didn't want anyone he knew to see or hear him like this.

It was possible there'd be some slurring involved. Puking, too.

He'd never been sure what to call Helene. His longtime girlfriend? *Girlfriend* seemed too high school. So, he'd toyed with thinking of her as his future fiancée. Or in social situations she was his business associate who often ran his marketing campaigns. But tonight Logan wasn't calling her any of those things. As far as he was concerned, he never wanted to think of her, her name or what to call her again.

Too bad that image of her was stuck in his head, but that was where he was hoping generous amounts of single-malt scotch would help.

Even though Riley, Claire, Lucky and Cassie wouldn't breathe a word about this, it would still get around town. Lucky wasn't sure how, but gossip seemed to defy the time-space continuum in Spring Hill. People would soon know, if they didn't already, and those same people wouldn't look at him the same again. It would hurt business.

Hell. It hurt *him*.

That was why he was here in this hotel bar in San Antonio. It was only thirty miles from Spring Hill, but tonight he hoped it'd be far enough away that no one he knew would see him get drunk. Then he could stagger to his room and then puke in peace. Not that he was looking forward to the puking part, but it would give him something else to think about other than *her*.

It was his first time in this hotel, though he stayed in San Antonio often on business. Logan hadn't wanted to risk running into anyone he knew, and he certainly wouldn't at this trendy "boutique" place. Not with a name like the Purple Cactus and its vegan restaurant.

If the staff found out he was a cattle broker, he might be booted out. Or forced to eat tofu. That was the reason Logan had used cash when he checked in. No sense risking someone recognizing his name from his credit card.

The clerk had seemed to doubt him when Logan had told him that his ID and credit cards had been stolen and that was why he couldn't produce anything with his name on it. Of course, when Logan had slipped the guy an extra hundred-dollar bill, it had caused that doubt to disappear.

"Drinking your troubles away?" a woman asked.

"Trying."

Though he wasn't drunk enough that he couldn't see what was waiting for him at the end of this. A hangover, a missed 8:00 a.m. meeting, his family worried about him—the puking—and it wouldn't fix anything other than to give him a couple hours of mind-numbing solace.

At the moment though, mind-numbing solace, even if it was temporary, seemed like a good trade-off.

"Me, too," she said. "Drinking my troubles away."

Judging from the sultry tone in her voice, Logan first thought she might be a prostitute, but then he got a look at her.

Nope. Not a pro.

Or if she was, she'd done nothing to market herself as such. No low-cut dress to show her cleavage. She had on a T-shirt with cartoon turtles on the front, a baggy white skirt and flip-flops. It looked as if she'd grabbed the first items of clothing she could find off a very cluttered floor of her very cluttered apartment.

Logan wasn't into clutter.

And he'd thought Helene wasn't, either. He'd been wrong about that, too. That antique desk of hers had been plenty cluttered with a clown's bare ass.

"Mind if I join you?" Miss Turtle-Shirt said. "I'm having sort of a private going-away party."

She waited until Logan mumbled "suit yourself," and she slid onto the purple barstool next to him.

She smelled like limes.

Her hair was varying shades of pink and looked as if it'd been cut with a weed whacker. It was already messy, but apparently it wasn't messy enough for her because she dragged her hand through it, pushing it away from her face.

"Tequila, top-shelf. Four shots and a bowl of lime slices," she told the bartender.

Apparently, he wasn't the only person in San Antonio with plans to get drunk tonight. And it explained the lime scent. These clearly weren't her first shots of the night.

"Do me a favor though," she said to Logan after he downed his next drink. "Don't ask my name, or anything personal about me, and I'll do the same for you."

Logan had probably never agreed to anything so fast in all his life. For one thing, he really didn't want to spend time talking with this woman, and he especially didn't want to talk about what'd happened.

"If you feel the need to call me something, go with Julia," she added.

The name definitely wasn't a fit. He was expecting something more like Apple or Sunshine. Still, he didn't care what she called herself. Didn't care what her real name was, either, and he cared even less after his next shot of Glenlivet.

"So, you're a cowboy, huh?" she asked.

The mind-numbing hadn't kicked in yet, but the orneriness had. "That's personal."

She shrugged. "Not really. You're wearing a cowboy hat, cowboy boots and jeans. It was more of an observation than a question."

"The clothes could be fashion statements," he pointed out.

Julia shook her head, downed the first shot of tequila, sucked on a lime slice. Made a face and shuddered. "You're not the kind of man to make fashion statements."

If he hadn't had a little buzz going on, he might have been insulted by that. "Unlike you?"

She glanced down at her clothes as if seeing them for the first time. Or maybe she was just trying to focus because the tequila had already gone to her head. "This was the first thing I grabbed off my floor."

Bingo. If that was her first grab, there was no telling how bad things were beneath it.

Julia tossed back her second shot. "Have you ever found out something that changed your whole life?" she asked.

"Yeah." About four hours ago.

"Me, too. Without giving specifics, because that would be personal, did it make you feel as if fate were taking a leak on your head?"

"Five leaks," he grumbled. Logan finished off his next shot.

Julia made a sound of agreement. "I would compare yours with mine, and I'd win, but I don't want to go there. Instead, let's play a drinking game."

"Let's not," he argued. "And in a fate-pissing comparison, I don't think you'd win."

Julia made a sound of disagreement. Had another shot. Grimaced and shuddered again. "So, the game is a word association," she continued as if he'd agreed. "I say a word, you say the first thing that comes to mind. We take turns until we're too drunk to understand what the other one is saying."

Until she'd added that last part, Logan had been

about to get up and move to a different spot. But hell, he was getting drunk anyway, and at least this way he'd have some company. Company he'd never see again. Company he might not even be able to speak to if the slurring went up a notch.

"Dream?" she threw out there.

"Family." That earned him a sound of approval from her, and she motioned for him to take his turn. "Surprise?"

"Crappy," Julia said without hesitation.

Now it was Logan who made a grunt of approval. Surprises could indeed be crap-related. The one he'd gotten tonight certainly had been.

Her: "Tattoos?"

Him: "None." Then, "You?"

Her: "Two." Then, "Bucket list?"

Him: "That's two words." The orneriness was still there despite the buzz.

Her: "Just bucket, then?"

Too late. Logan's fuzzy mind was already fixed on the bucket list. He had one all right. Or rather he'd had one. A life with Helene that included all the trimmings, and this stupid game was a reminder that the Glenlivet wasn't working nearly fast enough. So, he had another shot.

Julia had one as well. "Sex?" she said.

Logan shook his head. "I don't want to play this game anymore."

When she didn't respond, Logan looked at her. Their eyes met. Eyes that were already slightly unfocused.

Julia took the paper sleeve with her room key from her pocket. Except there were two keys, and she slid one Logan's way.

"It's not the game," she explained. "I'm offering you sex with me. No names. No strings attached. Just one night, and we'll never tell another soul about it."

She finished off her last tequila shot, shuddered and stood. "Are you game?"

No way, and Logan would have probably said that to her if she hadn't leaned in and kissed him.

Maybe it was the weird combination of her tequila and his scotch, or maybe it was because he was already drunker than he thought, but Logan felt himself moving right into that kiss.

LOGAN DREAMED, AND it wasn't about the great sex he'd just had. It was another dream that wasn't so pleasant. The night of his parents' car accident. Some dreams were a mishmash of reality and stuff that didn't make sense. But this dream always got it right.

Not a good thing.

It was like being trapped on a well-oiled hamster wheel, seeing the same thing come up over and over again and not being able to do a thing to stop it.

The dream rain felt and sounded so real. Just like that night. It was coming down so hard that the moment his truck wipers swished it away, the drops covered the windshield again. That was why it'd taken him so long to see the lights, and Logan was practically right on the scene of the wreck before he could fully brake. He went into a skid, costing him precious seconds. If he'd had those seconds, he could have called the ambulance sooner.

He could have saved them.

But he hadn't then. And he didn't now in the dream.

Logan chased away the images, and with his head

still groggy, he did what he always did after the nightmare. He rewrote it. He got to his parents and stopped them from dying.

Every time except when it really mattered, Logan saved them.

LOGAN WISHED HE could shoot out the sun. It was creating lines of light on each side of the curtains, and those lines were somehow managing to stab through his closed eyelids. That was probably because every nerve in his head and especially his eyelids were screaming at him, and anything—including the earth's rotation—added to his pain.

He wanted to ask himself: *What the hell have you done?*

But he knew. He'd had sex with a woman he didn't know. A woman who wore turtle T-shirts and had tattoos. He'd learned one of the tattoos, a rose, was on Julia's right breast. The other was on her lower stomach. Those were the things Logan could actually remember.

That, and the sex.

Not mind-numbing but rather more mind-blowing. Julia clearly didn't have any trouble being wild and spontaneous in bed. It was as if she'd just studied a sex manual and wanted to try every position. Thankfully, despite the scotch, Logan had been able to keep up—literally.

Not so much now though.

If the fire alarm had gone off and the flames had been burning his ass, he wasn't sure he would be able to move. Julia didn't have that problem though. He felt the mattress shift when she got up. Since it was possible she was about to rob him, Logan figured he should at least see if she was going after his wallet, wherever the heck it was. But if she robbed him, he deserved it. His life was on the fast track to hell, and he'd been the one to put it in the handbasket.

At least he hadn't been so drunk that he'd forgotten to use condoms. Condoms that Julia had provided, so obviously she'd been ready for this sort of thing.

Logan heard some more stirring around, and this time the movement was very close to him. Just in case Julia turned out to be a serial killer, he decided to risk opening one eye. And he nearly jolted at the big green eyeball staring back at him. Except it wasn't a human eye. It was on her turtle shirt.

If Julia felt the jolt or saw his one eye opening, she didn't say anything about it. She gave him a chaste kiss on the cheek, moved away, turning her back to him, and Logan watched as she stooped down and picked up his jacket. So, not a serial killer but rather just a thief after all. But she didn't take anything out.

She put something *in* the pocket.

Logan couldn't tell what it was exactly. Maybe her number. Which he would toss first chance he got. But if so, he couldn't figure out why she just hadn't left it on the bed.

Julia picked up her purse, hooking it over her shoulder, and without even glancing back at him, she walked out the door. Strange, since this was her room. Maybe she was headed out to get them some coffee. If so, that was his cue to dress and get the devil out of there before she came back.

Easier said than done.

His hair hurt.

He could feel every strand of it on his head. His eyelashes, too. Still, Logan forced himself from the bed, only to realize the soles of his feet hurt, as well. It was hard to identify something on him that didn't hurt, so he quit naming parts and put on his boxers and jeans. Then he had a look at what Julia had put in his pocket next to the box with the engagement ring.

A gold watch.

Not a modern one. It was old with a snap-up top that had a crest design on it. The initials BWS had been engraved in the center of the crest.

The inside looked just as expensive as the gold case except for the fact that the watch face crystal inside was shattered. Even though he knew little about antiques, Logan figured it was worth at least a couple hundred dollars.

So, why had Julia put it in his pocket?

Since he was a skeptic, his first thought was that she might be trying to set him up, to make it look as if he'd robbed her. But Logan couldn't imagine why anyone would do that unless she was planning to try to blackmail him with it.

He dropped the watch on the bed and finished dressing, all the while staring at it. He cleared out some of the cotton in his brain and grabbed the hotel phone to call the front desk. Someone answered on the first ring.

"I'm in room—" Logan had to check the phone "—two-sixteen, and I need to know…" He had to stop again and think. "I need to know if Julia is there in the lobby. She left something in the room."

"No, sir. I'm afraid you just missed her. But checkout isn't until noon, and she said her guest might be staying past then, so she paid for an extra day."

"Uh, could you tell me how to spell Julia's last name? I need to leave her a note in case she comes back."

"Oh, she said she wouldn't be coming back, that this was her goodbye party. And as for how to spell her name, well, it's Child, just like it sounds."

Julia Child?

Right. Obviously, the clerk wasn't old enough or enough of a foodie to recognize the name of the famous chef.

"I don't suppose she paid with a credit card?" Logan asked.

"No. She paid in cash and then left a prepaid credit card for the second night."

Of course. "What about an address?" Logan kept trying.

"I'm really not supposed to give that out—"

"She left something very expensive in the room, and I know she'll want it back."

The guy hemmed and hawed a little, but he finally rattled off, "221B Baker Street, London, England."

That was Sherlock Holmes's address.

Logan groaned, cursed. He didn't bother asking for a phone number because the one she left was probably for Hogwarts. He hung up and hurried to the window, hoping he could get a glimpse of her getting into a car. Not that he intended to follow her or anything, but if she was going to blackmail him, he wanted to know as much about her as possible.

No sign of her, but Logan got a flash of something else. A memory.

Damn.

They'd taken pictures.

Or at least Julia had with the camera on her phone.

He remembered nude selfies of them from the waist up. At least he hoped it was from the waist up.

Yeah, that trip to hell in a handbasket was moving even faster right now.

Logan threw on the rest of his clothes, already trying to figure out how to do damage control. He was the CEO of a multimillion-dollar company. He was the face that people put with the family business, and before last night he'd never done a thing to tarnish the image of McCord Cattle Brokers.

He couldn't say that any longer.

He was in such a hurry to rush out the door that he nearly missed the note on the desk. Maybe it was the start of the blackmail. He snatched it up, steeling himself up for the worst. But if this was blackmail, then Julia sure had a funny sense of humor.

"Goodbye, hot cowboy," she'd written. "Thanks for the sweet send-off. Don't worry. What happens in San Antonio stays in San Antonio. I'll take this to the grave."

* * * * *

Don't miss
BLAME IT ON THE COWBOY
by Delores Fossen,
available October 2016 wherever ebooks
are sold.

MILLS & BOON®

INTRIGUE
Romantic Suspense

A SEDUCTIVE COMBINATION OF DANGER AND DESIRE

A sneak peek at next month's titles...

In stores from 20th October 2016:

- **Landon** – Delores Fossen *and*
  Navy SEAL Six Pack – Elle James
- **The Girl Who Cried Murder** – Paula Graves *and*
  In the Arms of the Enemy – Carol Ericson
- **Scene of the Crime: Means and Motive** –
  Carla Cassidy *and* **Christmas Kidnapping** –
  Cindi Myers

Romantic Suspense

- **Runaway Colton** – Karen Whiddon
- **Operation Soldier Next Door** – Justine Davis

Just can't wait?
Buy our books online a month before they hit the shops!
www.millsandboon.co.uk

Also available as eBooks.

1016/46

Reese Ryan writes sexy, deeply emotional romances full of family drama, surprising secrets and unexpected twists.

Born and raised in the Midwest, Reese has deep Tennessee roots. Every summer, she endured long, hot car trips to family reunions in Memphis via a tiny clown car loaded with cousins.

Connect with Reese at ReeseRyanWrites on Instagram, Twitter and Facebook or at reeseryan.com/desirereaders.

Joss Wood loves books and traveling—especially to the wild places of Southern Africa and, well, anywhere. She's a wife, a mum to two teenagers and slave to two cats. After a career in local economic development, she now writes full-time. Joss is a member of Romance Writers of America and Romance Writers of South Africa.

Also by Reese Ryan

Savannah's Secret
The Billionaire's Legacy
Playing with Desire
Playing with Temptation
Playing with Seduction

Also by Joss Wood

His Ex's Well-Kept Secret
One Night to Forever
The CEO's Nanny Affair
Little Secrets: Unexpectedly Pregnant
Friendship on Fire
Hot Christmas Kisses

Discover more at millsandboon.co.uk